IDY

The Bride Hunter

The Bride Hunter

AMY APPLETON

ISIS
LARGE PRINT
Oxford

First published in Great Britain 2008
by
Orion, an imprint of
The Orion Publishing Group Ltd.

Published in Large Print 2008 by ISIS Publishing Ltd.,
7 Centremead, Osney Mead, Oxford OX2 0ES
by arrangement with
The Orion Publishing Group Ltd.

British Library Cataloguing in Publication Data
Appleton, Amy
    The bride hunter. – Large print ed.
    1. Marriage brokerage – Fiction
    2. Love stories
    3. Large type books
    I. Title
    823.9'2 [F]

ISBN 978–0–7531–8134–8 (hb)
ISBN 978–0–7531–8135–5 (pb)

Printed and bound in Great Britain by
T. J. International Ltd., Padstow, Cornwall

To my parents, for showing me London,
and to Rich, for keeping me here

CHAPTER
ONE

First things first. I am *not* a pimp (whatever my mother says).

I know I'm not alone in having parents who don't understand me. Half of my uni friends get lectures from their fathers about "finding a proper job" every time they go home for Christmas. And these are people who *have* proper jobs: web designers, lifestyle managers, recruitment consultants.

OK, I admit my work is harder to define. Let's just say it was a mistake even attempting to describe what it involved to Mum. The more I tried to justify myself, the seedier it sounded.

So, just for the record. Pimps generally don't live with their maiden aunts in the loft of a Richmond-upon-Thames town-house while they pay off horrible debts and attempt to save for a deposit on a shoebox-sized London flat. Pimps don't watch old Hollywood weepies or read psychology tomes to increase their understanding of the mysteries of attraction. And pimps never, ever . . .

"So will you be watching from the sidelines all night? You'll no find yourself a man, if you act like a wallflower."

"Um, then I'd better join in, I suppose." I allow myself to be dragged into the melee by an assertive Glaswegian grandmother.

Where was I? Oh yes. Pimps never, ever attend Scottish country-dancing classes in East London community halls on behalf of an American millionaire who insists that only a Caledonian girl will make his heart sing.

Dwight MacKenzie owes me. Actually, he's already paid me a £3,000 retainer, with even more to be delivered on *completion* of my mission: loose change to my average client, and to be fair, that kind of money is compensation enough for the humiliation about to be inflicted on me by octogenarians in kilts. Money can't buy you love, but if you're a multi-millionaire, it'll definitely buy you a helping hand.

The hall is as cold as a Scottish castle, though considerably less picturesque, and my fellow dancers fall into three categories: gnarled old men with bony knees and threadbare socks; stout matriarchs with polyester cable-knit cardigans and determined expressions; and younger girls who keep peering at the door, perhaps expecting Bonnie Prince Charlie to come bounding in to rescue them. The only man under fifty in the whole place is *terribly* light on his feet and looks to me like the guy who put the gay into the Gay Gordons.

My new dance partner is one of the matriarchs. Her complexion matches her crimson jumper and she's very round and very short, like Mrs Pepperpot. As she takes

my hands, her wiry grey bun only reaches my nose —
and I'm five foot five.

"Normally you'd be the man, eh, hen?" she says,
then smiles. "But I think I'd better lead because you're
new."

"OK," I say, as the music starts and she begins to
propel me forwards. Did I mention that I have two left
feet? Still, I can't stand in the way of true love.

"Don't tell me," she says, "you're after your very own
Braveheart?"

"Um. Well, not quite."

"Or maybe your own Renton?"

"Renton?"

"From *Trainspotting?* Now, maybe all the drugs and
vomit were a wee bit strong, but Ewan McGregor has
plenty going on under his sporran."

"No, I'm not after him either."

She pushes me away, gives me a hard stare, and then
pulls me back towards her, in time to the music. "All
I'm saying is, English girls never come here unless
they're searching for their very own Scotsman."

I wonder what she'd say if I told her I was after a
Scots*woman?* I decide on a little white lie. "OK. I
admit it. Though I'm really after my very own Sean
Connery."

She grins. "Huh. If you find one, hands off. Been
waiting for one of those all my life."

I'm beginning to warm up nicely now, what with all
this jigging and reeling. Well, more jiggling than
anything, if I'm honest. Country dancing and C-cup
boobs aren't a match made in heaven. "So, I wouldn't

be the first to come here looking for a male piece of skirt, then?"

"Oh no. But the English lassies rarely stay the course once they realise most of the men are older than Edinburgh Castle. The Scottish girls are made of stronger stuff." She indicates the three youngest women in the room, each one in the grip of a knobbly partner. "Came for the men first of all, but stayed because the dancing's in the blood."

I crane my neck to assess the women's Dwight-potential. Number one is pretty and willowy, with letter-box red Celtic curls, a fantastic smile, and good teeth. I'd guess — speculating wildly here, but what do you expect of a girl whose dream career would have been writing the quizzes in *Cosmopolitan*? — that she has a good heart to go with them. However, she fails to meet Dwight's needs in one crucial respect: he's definitely not the tallest American in London, so she'd tower over him.

Number two is shorter, but has porridgy caber-tosser's arms. Dwight might be a born romantic, but he's also a body fascist, buffed to perfection. He's already rejected two charming actresses I spotted in *Macbeth*, simply on account of their dimpling. I think it's part of my job to encourage my clients to broaden their horizons a little, see the potential for love in unexpected places, but these men are used to getting what they want, whether it's an Aston Martin Vantage in just the right shade of red, or a sirloin steak in just the right shade of blue (it's no coincidence that most of my go-getters like their meat borderline raw). And ultimately I do agree that true love should never involve compromise.

The third girl has the perfect body, but it's enclosed in a skin-tight yellow leotard, accompanied by matching kids-from-*Fame* legwarmers. Even her hair is a frightening shade of bottle-blonde. The overall effect is all the more alarming as everyone else is wrapped up warm, and though I admire her stoicism, I don't think Dwight would appreciate her rigid nipples. He is very keen on *modesty* in a woman, not least because his Californian ex-wife left him for the aerobics teacher who taught the advanced pole-dancing class on Sunset Boulevard.

"Ouch!"

My dance partner yanks my arm so hard it nearly pops out of its socket, and I attempt to copy the others as they half-trot, half-skip towards the centre of the hall in time to the frantically cheerful music.

"Your mind seems to be wandering, hen," she says. "Very high-risk when you're new to this."

And with that she flings me away, towards an old man in a purple kilt. As his rheumy eyes focus on me (specifically, on my cleavage), I sneak a look back and see Mrs Pepperpot winking mischievously.

"Well, hello, my dear," he pants as he clamps long, wizened fingers around my waist. "I'm always so pleased when we have new blood. My name's Sean, by the way. As in *Connery*."

"I'm Rebecca," I mumble, as his moist breath condenses on my neck, "Or Becca to my friends."

"Oh, I definitely want to be your friend," he says, tightening his grip.

I have no qualms about fending off men my own age, but there's something unseemly about slapping down an octogenarian with octopus hands. And I'm convinced he knows it *and* plans to take full advantage.

The things I do for love . . .

After ten long minutes of poking, groping and general harassment by sleazy Sean, I am deeply relieved when the dance teacher announces a short comfort break. I have to make a split-second decision: take tea and shortbread petticoat tails with the grannies, and pick their brains about eligible granddaughters, or follow the three girls into the ladies' loos.

I choose the latter. The toilets are freezing, but at least Sean can't follow me inside.

Caber-Tosser and Letterbox Hair are primping in front of the mirror, so Chickpea Nipples must be inside a cubicle. They look up as I enter the room.

"Hi." I give a little wave.

They smile back. Caber-Tosser speaks first. "I see you've survived trial by our very own Loch Ness Monster."

I nod. "Shouldn't that be a Lech-ness Monster?" Rule One of Matchmaking: use humour to create rapport with potential matches.

Letterbox frowns. "Oi, that's my granddad you're talking about."

Shit. So much for Rule One. "I'm sorry, I didn't mean . . ."

6

Chickpea emerges from her cubicle, dazzlingly yellow like a cartoon superhero. *Killer Nipple Girl*, maybe, or *Wonderbra Woman*. I begin to sweat slightly. These three are quite intimidating in a confined space.

But then she grins. "Take no notice of Lorna. She's winding you up. We've all passed through the wandering hands of that old bastard. It's like an initiation test. You passed. So welcome to the club." She holds out her own, impeccably manicured hand. "I'm Carole, by the way."

Caber-Tosser takes her cue. "And I'm Tina."

"Becca," I say, as I mentally match their real names with the nicknames I have given them. When you meet thousands of potential date candidates every year, you need tricks to ensure total recall. "So have you all been coming for ages?"

Chickpea Carole nods. She's clearly the leader of the pack. "Uh-huh. Couple of years. I came because I loved dancing back home in Scotland. And these two came for the men."

Letterbox . . . no, what's her name again? Lorna, pulls a face. "Yeah, and what a disappointment that was. But we keep coming because it's a laugh."

Tina with the fat arms finishes applying her lip gloss. "Did you know that Scottish country dancing is one of the best activities for promoting a sense of well-being?"

"No, really?" Actually, I'm lying. It was one of the main reasons for coming. After exhausting Scottish theme pubs and London branches of the Tartan Army in search of likely females, not to mention my disastrous encounters with the dimpled ladies of

Macbeth, I read a piece in a psychology magazine about how country dancing is better than Prozac for positive mental attitudes. And Dwight is intimidatingly positive himself.

"Oh yes," says Lorna. "It's the concentration, you see. And the rhythm. You can forget yourself while you're doing it. We're addicted."

"Mind you," Carole says, as she straightens her bra so her chickpeas are perfectly aligned under her leotard, "it may also have something to do with the fact that we end every dancing session with a few drinks in the pub. You can come along, if you like . . ."

Thank you, St Valentine! See, matchmaking is all about networks. "You're on. So long as the Lecherous Monster isn't invited?"

Carole shudders. "Now that is not funny. Not funny at all."

By the time we get to the Ring o' Roses, a neighbourhood boozer about ten minutes' walk from the hall, the happiness effect is definitely rubbing off on me. I love this about my job: meeting new people, entering weird new worlds.

The only cloud in my jig-induced blue sky is the lack of bridal candidates. Dwight is not the most patient of men, and his response to my standard "you can't hurry love" line was "why the hell not?" Dwight is the ultimate in what I call a Marriage-Ready Man: solvent, motivated and horny. The moment I find a woman who ticks all his boxes, he'll be up the aisle in a flash.

Then I see her. She's sitting in the corner, waving over my three companions, and I follow them, my fingers crossed behind my back. As we approach, I think myself into character as Dwight, working my way through his checklist of essential requirements . . .

Petite — check. She's as tiny as Clare Grogan. I'd hazard a guess that her waist — hip ratio is spot on the 0.67 blueprint that's appealed to men since the Stone Age.

Cute — check. She has elfin features, and light brown hair curled into a sweet bob that frames her pointy face.

Young, but not too young — check. Couple of years younger than me, maybe. If I had to guess, I'd say twenty-five.

But then I panic. The fatal flaw in my assumptions here is a pretty fundamental one: why on earth would my three country dancers restrict themselves to Scottish friends? The chances are she's English or Polish or . . .

"And this is our new recruit." Carole pushes me forward as she explains that I've come along for a restorative drink after my ordeal by groping. Pixie smiles — oh, Dwight would melt in the warmth of that smile — and holds out her childlike hand.

I shake it. "I'm Becca Orchard."

"Welcome to the gang, Becca. I'm Heather Campbell."

Bingo! Love — thirty to the Bride Hunter.

CHAPTER
TWO

"... So her name is Heather, her accent is an American's fantasy of a girl from the lochs, she grew up surrounded by horses and dogs and, get this, she even works for an animal charity. She couldn't be more perfect!"

My aunt Georgia passes a cup of espresso through the sash window, and then limbos through the narrow gap on to the tiny balcony. It's twenty years since she wowed ballet critics with her debut as the Dying Swan, but she still has enviable poise. "A completely flawless creature, eh? I wonder where she's hidden all the dead bodies?"

"Oh, come on. I might just have hit the jackpot this time, Georgie."

She closes her eyes to savour the spring sunshine, before moving her chair into the warmest spot. "True. It might be perverse of me but I can't help hoping she has at least one terrible habit or skeleton in the cupboard. Otherwise she'd be dull, dull, *dull*."

"Your trouble is you've lived in London too long."

"And yours," she says, sprinkling precisely three *grains* of sugar into her coffee, "is that you still have the innocence of a country bumpkin. And that will be your

10

undoing, like Little Red Riding Hood in the wicked forest."

"But my innocence is precisely what my gentlemen clients want, Georgie. They're so cynical themselves that they've lost all hope of finding a girl who doesn't want them for their money. If I got hard-nosed too, stopped believing I can find the ruby in the dust . . . well, I'd be no use to them. They'd be better off taking their chances among the she-devils and gold-diggers in nightclubs or on the Internet."

She smiles indulgently. "Oh, OK. Stay a born romantic if you like. See if I care. What does your silly old auntie know, after all?"

My silly old auntie knows: how to score a table at The Ivy (or Hakkasan or Claridges or whichever is the hottest hangout this week); how to get to the head of the waiting list for the new season's Balenciaga bag (though she finds being on any waiting list "distinctly degrading, Becky, like those women who had to queue for stale bread in Moscow in the days before the Russians came and bought up half of Chelsea"); how to tell if a man is a mere Platinum card-holder or an Amex Centurion owner *just from his socks*; how to buy contemporary art; how to get upgrades *everywhere*; how to dance *en pointe* and how to shift a stone in a single week.

Not that she ever carries so much as an excess ounce of weight. At forty-five, she still fits into the clothes she wore at seventeen. What's more, she can get away with them, because she has always dressed with what magazines call *timeless elegance*: fluid fabrics in cream

11

and white and black, cut to accentuate her slender body, but still draping to suggest sensuality, despite her boyish physique. She saves the drama for her make-up: indelible scarlet lipstick bought from a Parisian pharmacy, and cat's-eye kohl in whichever colour is most fashionable this year (currently turquoise). She made me up once, but I looked like a circus clown. I inherited her thick chestnut hair and her good ankles, but everything in between takes after my mum: the practical, slightly curvy shape of a farmer's wife. If I didn't love Georgie to pieces, I'd be insanely jealous.

I could never have started my business without her. In fact, without her, I'd probably still be in Gloucestershire, married off to the monosyllabic son of a travelling animal-feed salesman, breeding merrily like my big brother. Not that there's anything wrong with that life, but I'd rather be sitting on a balcony overlooking the Thames and the beautiful people, than sitting in a barn overlooking dozens of moody cows tethered to shiny metal machines by their horrid grey-pink udders.

When I was a little girl, Georgie was a messenger from another world, opening my eyes to a life beyond the milking parlour. On her rare visits to the farm, it was as if a giraffe had suddenly popped up in the barn, a creature with the same number of limbs and eyes and ears as the rest of us, but one thousand times more exotic. She moved like leaves in the breeze and smelled of Chanel 19. At the age of eleven, my mum's baby sister had been transplanted from an unheated cottage in the grounds of the smelliest pig farm in the county, to the eighteenth-century splendour of the Royal Ballet School's White Lodge in the heart of Richmond Park. The first time she saw it, she says, she felt like a character from a Jane Austen novel. Funnily enough, there was no going back.

"You've taught me all I know, auntie, that's for sure."

"Ah, dear Becky, if only if were true. But thank you for saying so." She pokes her walnut-brown legs through the ornate bars of the balcony, her feet shrouded in lilac Chinese slippers, as always.

For years, she refused to let me see her below the ankles: "Precious niece, there is nothing, but nothing, as ugly and disenchanting as a dancer's feet." She only agreed when I threatened to take up ballet myself, unveiling the damage as a warning. They weren't *ugly* as such — nothing about Georgie could be described as ugly — but they were shocking all the same; misshapen and mangled as a labourer's hands, and so incongruous on the extremities of the nearest person to a goddess I'd ever known.

I drain my coffee, then stand up. "I have to go and get monochrome."

"Oh Lord, the City is so tiresome at this time of year. It's as if they're terrified of being sacked if they so much as don a pastel tie. So who are you fixing up today?"

"It's my *secret* one, remember? First face-to-face meeting."

"Ah. Hence the dullsville clothes, eh? Well, *bonne chance*, Agent Cupid. Don't blow your cover."

★　★　★

As the Tube train begins its descent, I feel my identity disappear, along with the daylight. I used to make this journey twice a day, and I don't quite know how I managed it without going crazy. To live in London had been my greatest ambition, but when I first got here, the thing that shocked me most about the place was how little sunshine I saw, and how soon I became ghostly, and indistinguishable from the rest of the commuters.

Today at least my anonymity is tactical: the more I look like everyone else, the more likely I am to pull off this undercover mission. With most of my clients, I allow myself a little leeway in my dress and behaviour. I wouldn't dare do full-on Barbara Cartland, but a pink blouse (it makes my eyes look greener) and maybe my favourite Victorian butterfly brooch (never, ever a sickly heart) are enough to suggest my softer side. My clients are the kind of men who surround themselves with the sharp-edged, platinum-and-mahogany trappings of mega-wealth, so a little frill goes a long way.

But in the case of Edward Lincoln, head honcho of the Overseas Opportunities Fund of Anemone International, I must be as colourless as every other city wannabe. Because Edward has no idea that he's being matchmade. And I still have no idea whether I'm even willing to take the assignment on.

I get off at Temple, the business end of the Thames, a world away from the beer-and-rowing stretch at Richmond. I walk up Fleet Street, into the heart of the City. The pavements are deserted: at eleven o'clock, anyone who matters has been at their desk for at least

14

three hours, probably four. I don't miss the presenteeism any more than I miss the commuting.

OK, so maybe I'll admit to missing the adrenalin, the borderline psychotic sense of purpose that fizzed around the offices of Benson Associates. Any sense of *common* purpose was an illusion: we'd have fought each other for the last biscuit in the communal kitchen, never mind a lead that could have helped us increase our commission. But we *felt* like we were in it together, doomed soldiers in a fox-hole, and that's one feeling I can't reproduce on my own in my office-cum-bedroom in Georgie's loft.

Get a grip, Becca. You hated it! I shake my head at my own weakness, and a street cleaner gives me a strange look. No use indulging in misplaced nostalgia. It's not as though I had a choice about leaving my job, and there's no way I'd go back to it. Not even if Marcus Benson got down on his knees and begged me . . .

The image is so implausible — Marcus, begging anyone for *anything*. Marcus, risking damage to his Armani trousers — that it makes me giggle. I have to count to a hundred before I'm calm enough to enter the icy reception of Anemone International.

I take the lift to the fourth floor: Edward's floor. My latest husband-to-be is one of the smartest guys in his field, with a Tomahawk missile's ability to hone in on an undervalued company, but apparently no track record whatsoever with the female of the species.

"Hi, I'm Rebecca Orchard, from Orchard Occupational Psychology. To see Edward Lincoln?" I always use my full name for work, to seem a bit more heavyweight. I hand my card — cobbled together over the weekend on my laptop — to the receptionist. Nine times out of ten, the girl on the front desk tells you all you need to know about a potential client's taste in women . . . but if this one's anything to go by, he likes middle-aged matriarchs with Peter Pan collars and hairy moles. Makes a pleasant change.

I think I might quite like Edward Lincoln.

But his situation does present me with something of a moral dilemma. After two years as a head-hunter, when my morals were tested on a daily basis, I swore when I started up on my own that only the whitest of white lies were permissible to assist the course of true love. That's why I don't mind fibbing to the country dancing brigade. It's harmless and plausible: after all, if I hadn't taken a lifelong vow of singledom after the Benson affair, there's no reason why I wouldn't have been looking for Mr Right in a Skirt.

And compared to the whoppers we told in my head-hunting days, it's nothing. My colleagues would happily pretend to be an A&E doctor calling about a target's child, or a clap-clinic nurse calling with test results, all to evade overzealous secretaries. Another reason why I wasn't sorry to leave that behind . . .

Edward's case, however, is borderline in the morality stakes. I wouldn't have considered it at all if I hadn't already matchmade Perry Todd, his posh, plump and follicly challenged boss, with Idoia, an adorable Spanish mosaic artist, in one of my first bride-hunting expeditions. Last week he asked me for a "fun, informal coffee" (as if there's any such thing in the City) and revealed his dastardly plan.

"Thing is, Rebecca," Perry told me, punctuating each sentence with a bite of Danish pastry, "Got this chap. Good chap. Going places. Brainy as fuck. One problem. No woman. No sign of a woman. No sign even of interest in a woman."

"Might he not be gay, Perry?"

Perry shook his head. "Considered that. No. Comes along to lap-dancing at Christmas and special occasions. Responds in the — ahem — appropriate manner. Sorry. Truth is, he's a numbers chap. Not much conversation."

I decided not to press the gay point. "Well, I'd be happy enough to meet him, discuss whether he's interested."

Now Perry looked shifty. He even put down what remained of his Danish for a second. "No. No, you see — how do I put this . . .? Delicate one. Not sure he quite realises the importance of a wife. To his career. Done OK so far but a man can only go so far with odd socks and egg down his tie."

I nodded. I'd seen Perry's attitude a million times before: senior partners who were happy to conduct one-night stands with half the girls in the office, but would block the promotion of anyone who hadn't got hitched, on the grounds that only a wife could guarantee *stability* and *family values*. "So?"

"So. My suggestion. Um. Look, Rebecca. I really want this chap as my number two. But the board won't even consider a bachelor. So I wanted to hire you. For him."

"Very generous, I'm sure, Perry. But he does need to agree."

Sulky frown lines appeared in the florid skin of his forehead. "Oh, does he *have* to? I mean, straight away? Sure, it's the tiniest bit unorthodox. But it's for his own good." His face took on a moony look. "Idoia's transformed my life, you know that. Is it really so wrong? To want to do the same for Eddy the Plank?"

I stifled a smile at the nickname. "Poor bloke. But I don't think . . ."

"Go on. For me? Only talking about leading the horse to water. Up to him whether he decides to take a sip at the fountain of womanhood. Oops. Sounds a bit rude!"

"He may just be happy single, Perry. Have you thought of that?"

Now he looked baffled. "No one's happy single, Rebecca. All a pretence. Meant to go two-by-two, like the ark. Speaking of which, how's *your* love life?"

I shouldn't have said yes. In fact, I'm not actually sure I did *say* yes, but once he hit my Achilles heel, I had to change the subject somehow and before I knew it . . .

"Miss Orchard? I'm Edward Lincoln."

Eddy the Plank stands before me in full, awkward glory. I'd rather assumed he'd be a stout toff like Perry, but instead he's tall and slim. Forty-ish. Fair hair, pouty lips, flushed cheeks. You wouldn't look

18

twice at him in the street (unlike his boss, who bears an uncanny resemblance to Toad from *Wind in the Willows*).

But it's immediately obvious that Edward Lincoln lacks the love and attention of a good woman. The hair's too long, an undisciplined fringe hiding his eyes: from the few glimpses I get, they're a striking blue. His trousers are too short (though at least his Betty Boop socks do match), and his shirt has that "fresh from the packet" look.

Despite standing at least six foot, he reminds me of a labelled-up WW2 evacuee still waiting to be billeted, after all the cuter, rosy-cheeked children have been snapped up.

"Call me Rebecca. Thank you for making the time to see me," I say, smiling briskly and offering my hand. He shakes it, hard, and leads the way to a characterless office overlooking a grimy yard.

"Not as though I had much of a choice, is it? Perry never takes no for an answer," he says. He has a soft Northern accent. Yorkshire, I think: I recognise it from the trips to the County Shows I used to go on with Dad when he was trying to make a name for our Double Orchard Farmhouse cheese.

"Well, I'll try to be as brief as I can."

He scowls, but it doesn't seem to be directed at me. "No. Sorry. That was rude. You're only earning your living. Not your fault that bloody Perry's got this daft idea in his head about workplace culture. He reads too many management magazines."

I cough. "It's only an initial report. To see what we could do for you . . . all of you, that is. Not you in particular."

He makes an effort to smile. "So what do you want to know?"

"Um . . ." This shouldn't be too difficult. In a previous life, before I met Marcus Benson at a student party and allowed myself to be whisked away to a life of head-hunting and corporate expense accounts, I was planning on becoming an occupational psychologist. Unlike the rest of my family, I had no interest in livestock but the human animal has always fascinated me. "Well, my role is to find out how Anemone works, really. Not how the systems work — your profits suggest the systems are working pretty well. So I'll be taking the temperature of the place, if you like."

"And where are you sticking your thermometer?" he says, dead-pan.

"Well, down on the farm, where I come from, we use the business end," I say, taking a risk that he has a sense of humour, beneath all that hair. "But here in the City, you know, people tend to be more genteel."

He chuckles, and it transforms his shy, stern face, just for a second, before the defences come back up and the crosspatch expression returns. "Put it this way, Miss Orchard, um . . . Rebecca, I'm happy with the business end if it gets the job done more quickly."

In that second, I decide I *do* like Edward Lincoln. What's more, I know I can help him. With a bit less scowling and a bit more chuckling (and a fringe-trim), I could find him a hockey team of gorgeous girls who'd love the chance to choose his socks. But I have to believe that he wants that as much as his boss does. "Righto, Mr Lincoln. To the point then. As a senior manager here, you must realise that your own attitudes and interests set the tone, the *culture* of the workplace. So I'd like to ask you a series of questions. Try to respond without thinking too much, there are no wrong answers. First of all, what do the words 'work — life balance' mean to you?"

CHAPTER
THREE

In the bride-hunting business, you need ground rules. Mine are simple. Never do anything morally dubious (OK, let's gloss over the case of Edward Lincoln, just for a second). Never date your clients (easy, because I never date anyone). Never work with a man you actively dislike or believe is undeserving of love, however much money he's offering. And never bring a client home.

You know, sometimes I have to admit that I can understand why my mum thinks I'm a high-class madam.

I don't bring clients home a) because it doesn't belong to me and b) home is my sanctuary. Number 16 Eve Terrace is the prettiest house in London, or maybe I'm biased. It certainly seemed like heaven when I reached the ripe old age of eight and was finally allowed to visit the big bad city and stay overnight under the decidedly casual care of my Aunt Georgie.

Those trips opened my eyes to the world beyond the farm. She offered precious little parental guidance, and laughed at adults who constantly instructed their children to "keep still so you don't trip on the escalator" and to "get away from the water, you'll fall in". Instead, she was focused on fun. Once I'd got over my shock at the vastness of London, I was entranced, and everything revolved around that narrow Victorian townhouse. She did occasionally take me to the *proper* things an aunt should (she was never my godmother, too irresponsible for that): the V&A, the Science Museum, the Changing of the Guard. But it was the crazy stuff, the stuff I couldn't tell my parents, that I remember most vividly. Feeding huge clouds of pigeons in the days before birdseed-sellers were banned from Trafalgar Square. Being sneaked into the snugs of riverside pubs to drink warm Britvic orange while my aunt entertained her coterie of chain-smoking rakes and mournful ex-ballerinas with tragically fallen arches. Eating crimson-coloured roast chicken plucked straight from medieval-style rotisseries by grumpy Chinese waiters in Bayswater.

The house itself was a taboo subject, as if it were an embarrassing affliction my aunt suffered from, and even today I don't know the full story. Georgie's dance career was short-lived, despite early promise. At twenty, she was the bright young thing of the London ballet scene. At twenty-two she vanished, apart from the occasional airmailed note with a smudged Cyrillic postmark reassuring my grandparents that she was well, and happy. During that time, I sometimes thought I'd imagined her visits to the farm: she seemed as ethereal and improbable as a princess from a storybook.

She returned to London aged twenty-five, without a word to explain either her absence or the acquisition of the red-brick townhouse. I suspect the story behind it would be worthy of a ballet in itself, but my aunt refuses to discuss it.

I moved here when I was twenty-one, just a month after I met Marcus at a fateful student party. Four weeks was all it took him to sweet-talk me out of a psychology career, into his business and — inevitably — into his bed. I stayed with Georgie in my first weeks at Benson's, while I looked for a flat-share. Every night I'd come home, climb the Parisian-style spiral staircase to the loft room, and stick my head through the window to peep down at the cobbled streets packed with exclusive boutiques, the railway and Tube lines that took me and a million others into work (usually it felt like we were all crammed into a single, sweaty carriage), and — if I stood on tiptoes — even the river beyond. All that life — and at last I was part of it. Eve Terrace is where I first felt like a Londoner.

After a month, I found somewhere I could afford, over the bridge in Twickenham: a damp room with no river view, so small that my wardrobe was in the corridor. But I knew I couldn't stay at Eve Terrace for ever, and that gloomy little house by the railway line was my gateway into *young* London. As house-mates we explored the city together. On the top floor lived a wild Italian art student who took us to galleries and Soho coffee shops. Next was a probationer policeman with designs on Scotland Yard, who took us all on tours of low-life London. I was next and then, in the basement, was Helga, a half-Swedish, half-Liverpudlian sports physio, who dragged us out drinking with the local rugby mob, from the director's box to their

24

favourite night spots. She's still my best friend, though neither of us can quite believe what we used to get up to.

Of course, eventually I moved in with Marcus, and though I planned to save for my own place — I worked out that I could just afford a studio flat in Battersea or the dodgy end of Clapham — he persuaded me that was daft, when I could live in luxury with him for as long as I liked, so long as I paid my share of the bills.

And when the job and Marcus and my home all disappeared in the space of a single, relentlessly bleak March afternoon, I came back to Georgie's lovely loft. Jobless, penniless, hopeless.

Helga tried to help, but she was more used to mending broken legs than broken hearts. It was Georgie who gave me the kiss of life. She took me to the old haunts, and though I've dined at the Chef's Table at most of Gordon Ramsay's restaurants, that rotisserie chicken in Bayswater tasted like the best thing I'd ever eaten. As I had my first proper meal in weeks, my aunt shared her hard-won philosophy on love.

"Some of us are born single, precious niece, and some of us have singledom thrust upon us."

Most importantly of all, it was Georgie who pointed out that the odd bit of (highly successful) matchmaking I'd been doing informally for time-poor high-fliers, could be the basis of a new career. I certainly wasn't going back to the old one.

She even came up with the name Bride Hunter. "Matchmaking sounds far too passive. The average City boy likes to think of himself as an urban warrior, with London as his battleground. So why not play along?"

Two years on, I earn half what I earned at Benson's, but my contribution to the sum of human happiness is a hundred times greater. OK, so my clients are filthy rich, but does that mean they're not entitled to fall in love? I truly believe it's harder for a rich man to find The One in a city of she-devils, so I see my job as a public service.

Not that I'm trying to justify myself, or anything.

I carry my second coffee of the morning up the spiral staircase to my office, and open my diary. Today, with any luck, I should be adding to my happiness creation quotient when Dwight and Heather have their first date. It's taken me six days to set it up. That's about average for one of my dates. Though of course I'd insist that there's no such thing as *average* when it comes to Rebecca Orchard Associates.

First I called Chickpea Carole and asked if Heather was single, explaining that I knew a guy who'd be perfect for her if she was. Then, armed with Heather's details, I cross-checked her name on the electoral register to make sure she is who she says she is. I even — in view of Georgie's conviction that anyone so textbook is bound to have a few skeletons in her closet — followed her from home to work at the Action for Animal Welfare (AAW for short) HQ in Victoria, snatching a quick photo on my camera phone to run past Dwight for his approval. A little light Date-Vetting is all part of the service, though whenever my chaps get serious, I usually suggest they hire private detectives, just to be on the safe side.

Once I'd ruled out serial killing and gold-digging tendencies, I emailed Dwight the photo, then talked him through Heather's good points, and he sounded thrilled. I do think she's a good match, on paper at least. Only then did I call Heather. It's often a slightly awkward initial conversation, as I never know in advance whether to be up-front about my *service*, but most girls respond well to flattery and the prospect of lunch with a Marriage-Ready bachelor.

In Heather's case, I had a sense from that one meeting in the Ring o' Roses that she was a livewire who'd try anything once. And I was right: I didn't need to explain quite *how* I'd got to know this perfect man, because she responded exactly as I'd predicted, with a delighted laugh and an immediate *yes*. It might be instinct, or it might be my psychology training, but I'm a good judge of character. With one terrible exception.

So now, with everything in place for the perfect date, I call Dwight to go through the arrangements.

"Hey, Cupid! Just now I thought I was hearing wedding bells, but then I realised it was my cellphone."

"Not that your expectations are high or anything, eh, Dwight?"

"Rebecca, you think she's the one, I hired you, I believe you. I trust the people I hire because I have confidence in myself."

I'm beginning to wish I hadn't been quite so gushing when I first told him about Heather. "Well, that is really

27

great, but do remember what I said about not being *too* full on when you meet her."

"You're worried I might scare her off?"

"Not at all . . ." Yes, I bloody am. Dwight is what you'd call *direct*. The first date I sent him on, at Zuma in Knightsbridge, he launched into an earnest and detailed account of the way he intended to "run" his next marriage (based on the lessons of his first), what he expected from his partner and what he would do for her, right down to number of orgasms per calendar month. All before the poor girl (a very sweet children's nurse from the Orkneys) had finished her miso-marinated foie gras. "It's just I know my clients sometimes find it hard to switch from business mode into fun mode in the middle of the day."

"No, I'm cool. I've been reading *Heat*, like you suggested, so I can talk about Jordan the woman just as well as Jordan the country. I even know who Lily Allen and the Arctic Monkeys are."

I smile to myself, knowing that Dwight will feel the need to demonstrate his newly honed street cred within seconds of meeting Heather. Though quite how he's going to work all that into the conversation while they take the Animal Lovers' route around the Tate Britain gallery, I dread to think.

"So, you know what you're doing, then? Meet her at the entrance to the gallery, pick up the leaflet *spontaneously*, as if you've never heard of it before, and then follow the little map taking you to different animal paintings."

28

"Sure. I read up on the paintings already. Nothing so bad on a first date as nothing to say."

That's the least of my worries. "Great. Then you produce the tickets for the Damien Hirst spotty boat which I'll give you when we rendezvous beforehand. Take the boat to the London Eye. I've pre-booked you a champagne flight, but I decided against a private capsule, as that seemed a bit intense for a first date." And a bit flash: the last thing a multi-millionaire wants to do early on is reveal his net worth. Which in Dwight's case would be enough to turn any girl's head.

"We can have that private capsule when I propose, huh?"

"Dwight . . ."

"I know, I know. Don't think too far ahead. It sounds great, Rebecca, just great. Except . . ."

Oh no. This is the bit where he tells me he likes everything about it except the gallery visit, the boat and the London Eye and the . . . "What?"

"It's cool. I just wondered, there doesn't seem to be any kind of Scottish theme to the date. And you know how important my heritage is to me."

Shit. *Shit.* "Well, with you both having such strong Scottish connections already, Dwight, I thought it wasn't strictly necess —"

He tuts. "I really would like there to be something about the day that connects with our shared origins."

I rack my brains. Kilts. Castles. Haggis. Bingo! "Ah, yes, of course. But then that's what the picnic's for. I'll be handing you a culturally appropriate picnic when we meet, to tuck into on the Eye." I hesitate. Haggis isn't exactly picnic fare. "Just a few tasty things. Shortbread. Finest Scotch whisky. Um . . . Highland raspberries with cream. All in a MacKenzie tartan rucksack."

"Hey. I like that." He sounds happier now. "Can't believe I doubted ya, Rebecca. You're the best. See you in ninety, huh?"

"Yes, Dwight. See you in ninety."

I put the phone down, allowing myself five precious seconds of striking my forehead — gently — against my desk. Then I race down the spiral staircase faster than a member of a SWAT team responding to an emergency.

Which, in bride-hunting terms, this is.

"Georgie. AUNTIE GEORGIE! Help! Where in London can I buy fresh Scottish raspberries in April?"

CHAPTER
FOUR

Georgie and I collapse on to a metal bench on the Embankment as the London Eye makes its imperceptible revolution through a brilliant blue spring sky.

"We did it?" I ask, as the pain in my feet begins to subside.

"We definitely did it, precious niece," she says. "Game, set and match to the bride hunter."

Actually, we failed with the Highland raspberries, substituting an Israeli punnet. I was uncomfortable about kicking off a relationship with even the most harmless of deceptions but Georgie told me not to be so daft. And then she distracted me with her genius idea of hot toddy with heather honey, decanted into individual turquoise and jade Chinese lacquer flasks which she'd spotted during her black-cab mercy dash to Liberty.

"Heather honey? For my new honey, Heather?" Dwight exclaimed when I talked him through the hamper's contents. "You are a Grade A genius, Rebecca."

I must admit things do seem to be going well. I'm always on hand for my clients' first dates — sometimes I even rig up a Bluetooth headset-enabled surveillance operation, so I can offer step-by-step instructions. I don't mention the second reason to my clients, but I also like to keep an eye on the women, just in case my impeccable judgement has failed me and I've inadvertently set a man up with a stalking gold-digger.

I'm going for the low-tech approach today, following Dwight and Heather at a discreet distance, and so far Heather is less gold-digger and more dating gold. She laughs at Dwight's jokes, smiles admiringly as he regales her with comparisons between the Rake's Progress painting, and a Posh and Becks house party, and responds with girlish delight to Damien Hirst's spotty boat, which takes them (and us, in very wide-brimmed, maiden-aunt straw hats) along the busy river from the Tate Britain to the Eye. Even Georgie was impressed.

They've been easy to track: bizarrely they both turned up wearing sage green suits, Heather's with a fantastically short skirt to show off a great pair of legs. They looked like a couple of forest elves let loose in the big city. I've only lost sight of them now their Pod has taken off, but I imagine her gasping in response to the champagne and the view. The Eye is an old favourite of mine: the height adds the tiniest frisson of danger, which psychological studies prove can increase the chances of sexual attraction. The body misinterprets an increased heart-rate as the first signs of arousal. I don't see it as cheating: just giving Cupid a helping hand . . . I call it Romantic Conditioning — manipulating the dating environment just a touch, to enhance the chances of love developing.

When Marcus took *me* on the Eye — in a private pod, where he seriously expected me to join the Mile-High Club, in recognition of his generosity — I couldn't get over how unexpectedly *lush* the city was; a billion trees eclipsing the tarmac and the smog.

"She's got her technique off pat," Georgie says.

"You make it sound like she's only pretending. Don't you think she might genuinely be nice?"

My aunt sniffs, still irritated that I made her wear the terrible hat. "Possible. But not terribly likely."

"Come on, Georgie. She doesn't even know he's loaded."

"Oh, she'll know, Becky. A man like Dwight has money seeping from his pores, and in the stitching of his hand-made shoes."

I shake my head in mock horror. "You're such a cynic. Incapable of believing in the potential of love."

"Well, what about Dwight, then? He'd convinced himself Heather was his true love before he'd even met her. He deserves all he gets."

Here she has a point, and I must admit I am nervous about Dwight convincing himself he's in love before he has time to know for sure.

That doesn't mean I lack confidence in my matches. On the contrary.

Matchmaking works because we don't know ourselves nearly as well as we think. It takes an interested outsider — your mum, your best friend or, if you pay for the privilege, me — to work out what you *really* need in a mate. The right matchmaker takes into account all your strengths, your weaknesses and what I call your Marmite Factors, those non-negotiable ultra-trivial quirks and foibles we all have. Do you love Marmite, or loathe it to the extent that you wouldn't actually date someone who ate the stuff in case you tasted it on their lips after breakfast? Is *Pop Idol* the work of the devil, or a work of postmodern genius?

But I can only take care of 95 per cent of the equation. I can line up girls or boys who tick all the boxes, on-paper-perfect specimens who look like your exes enough to fall into the "your type" category without giving you déjà vu, and who, crucially, are available.

That last five per cent is down to chemistry, pure and simple. It's something no matchmaker, online dating service or psychological test can ever calculate. It's the only factor where the getting-drunk-at-a-party method of meeting a life partner has the edge. But love is far too important — and dangerous — to be entrusted to pissed people. I should know.

"Georgie, he's just a man who knows what he wants and Heather fits the bill. But I don't believe even he would be able to talk himself into being attracted to her unless there genuinely was a spark between them."

"Yes, but it's spring, Becky. Look around you. Everyone wants to be in love in spring. Even *I* can almost kid myself it would be fun."

She's right. The Embankment is like a Discovery Channel programme, featuring thousands of human animals exhibiting ritual courtship behaviour, from the look-at-me-look-away-look-at-me eye contact stage, to the limbs-so-dangerously-entwined it's a wonder they

34

can walk stage, all the way through to the heavily-pregnant-I-couldn't-run-away-now even if I tried stage. "Well, it *is* fun, Georgie. That's nature's devious little trick to make us fall in love."

She gives me a curious look. "You know, just because I am an old maid, doesn't mean you have to give up on the whole idea for ever."

"Old maid? You're forty-five, Georgie, not eighty-five. Anyway, I seem to remember you telling me love was overrated when I split up with Marcus."

"Ye-es. I lied. It was two years ago and I was only saying what you wanted to hear at the time. Of course, a few of us are destined to stay single, but I don't think you're one of those. You believe in love, for God's sake. You make a living out of it. You're good at it. Wouldn't it be an awful shame if all you ever did was make it happen for other people?"

I feel my bottom lip begin to pop out like a sulky child's, so I bite it back. "Georgie, I know you mean well, but I think as a psychology graduate, my self-knowledge is more advanced than most people's. Yes, I believe in love. I also believe that Yogic flying and Scottish country dancing are valid lifestyle choices, but I've tried them too and they're not for me, either, thank you very much. The same applies to romance."

"That sounds awfully well-rehearsed, but I don't believe a single bloody word of it. Love is not a spectator sport."

I sigh. In the far distance I spot two green figures. Dwight and Heather step off the Eye, leaning into each other for support as their feet make contact with Planet

Earth for the first time in thirty minutes. Would I want that wobbly feeling again? Endless uncertainties. Bungee-jumping in your stomach whenever the phone rings — or doesn't. Opening your heart up so wide that you can never quite close the gap again, so that two years on, even the mention of your ex's name stings savagely, just for a moment, like a beauty therapist sneaking up and waxing your bikini line when you weren't expecting it.

"Believe what you like, Georgie, but remember the saying: a woman needs a man like a fish needs a bicycle. Which is, of course, why I am only in the business of bride-hunting. And I'd never hunt for husbands."

She shrugs: my aunt even makes a shrug look elegant. "Whatever you say, Becky. Is it too early for a vodka martini?"

I leave Aunt Georgia at Mo*vida, arguing with a cross-eyed Russian oligarch about which nation distils the best vodka, and make my way into the City for a meeting with a potential new client. I aim for three clients on my books at any one time — any more is chaos, any less and my studio flat deposit fund has no chance at all of keeping up with crazy London house-price inflation — and as I only have Dwight at the moment, I need more work. Edward is still a maybe . . . I need to be convinced the ends — the potential for a happy pairing — would justify the devious means.

So, Sam Ottoway, Barrister-at-Law, could be the next in line for the Orchard treatment. His PA emailed me first of all, brisk and to the point, explaining that I'd been recommended by an anonymous friend, suggesting two appointment times, and then sending over Sam's deeply impressive CV. He's a criminal defence lawyer, a modern-day Rumpole of the Bailey, and I found a few of his cases on the internet: clever, hard-nosed defences of hard nuts. You don't make QC at thirty-seven unless you're hot, and Sam seems to be cooking. I can see it now: the stunning house in Wimbledon or penthouse in Clerkenwell, the impressive golf handicap, the small collection of investment pieces from Young British Artists, the Davidoff humidor stocked with Cuban cigars. And the speed-dial to the late-night gourmet delivery service, the personal trainer he pays £100 a session to in cancellation fees, and the *mountain* of work between him and ever finding someone to love.

His baby-faced PA (note for file: he likes his women young, if this child is anything to go by) shows me into a windowless oak-panelled meeting room, which smells of tobacco and sweat. Portraits of haughty lawyers hang from the walls, and the wood deadens sounds from outside. I feel a childish urge to sing at the top of my voice, and I distract myself by doodling a picture of Dwight and Heather in matching kilts, with a Scottish kirk behind them.

I've just begun drawing the bridesmaids — I can't *think* why Georgie is so convinced I'm a born romantic — when the door creaks open and a tall, drawn, blonde woman in a fitted black suit marches in, carrying an enormous file. Bloody hell. Sam Ottoway must be even more of a go-getter than I thought if he needs two PAs. I wonder if this one is more his type: she looks like she sleeps in a coffin and has an allergy to garlic.

She sits down and I cover my doodle with my hands.

"So, you're the infamous Bride Hunter, then?" Her voice is tight and sarcastic: all the better for terrifying pupil barristers, I suppose.

But she doesn't scare me. Furthermore, I have no intention of being pre-screened by some over-protective matriarch to assess my suitability for Mr Ottoway. "That's my nickname, but I offer an entirely bespoke service for the professional who's serious about finding a partner. I only take on a handful of clients — no more than three at any one time — to ensure personal attention. And without wishing to be rude, I always have to meet the client before taking them on, to ensure we have shared objectives." There! That's telling Ms Hoity-Toity. I lean back in my chair.

"That won't be a problem," she says. "But before we go any further, can I ask what methods you use when finding these *partners*?"

My hackles rise, but clearly there's a ritual here: I have to negotiate with the troll guarding the cave to gain access to the emperor. "Well, I have a background in psychology and in executive search," I say, struggling to remember the spiel I had scripted so carefully when I was starting out. These days, my track record tends to speak for itself. "And yet time and time again, I was encountering talented, brilliant people who didn't have the time to trawl the bars or the Internet for the right person. There are, as I'm sure you realise, many women out there with . . . shall we say, a predatory interest in the size of a man's bank account, rather than the size of a man's heart?"

I think I've pitched that just right: she looks like the type to be protective of *her* boss, and the lack of a ring on her finger suggests she's failed so far to land her own City boy. Hardly surprising when she seems to have had her smile muscles frozen in a tragic Botox accident.

"Interesting," she says, apparently in no hurry to fetch the man of the moment. "So how do you find these rare creatures who are unmotivated by mammon?"

"First of all, I discuss the needs and requirements extensively with the client: not just hobbies or interests, but lifestyle, values, expectations of marriage. All the things no one really likes to talk about, but are proven to dramatically affect the long-term future of a relationship. I build up a DCV — a CV of a client's dating history, and also create a Cupid Collage, which acts as a visual aide-memoire to ensure any candidates match the physical requirements of my client. In addition, I use psychological profiling and other techniques to identify the right kind of woman, and I have extensive networks across the UK and overseas, to ensure that geography is no limit to finding her."

"Sounds expensive."

I outline my rates. "It's less than many of my clients spend on a weekend break. And of course, on a very practical level, the financial benefits of a happy, successful marriage have been exhaustively recorded in research."

"And your success rate?"

"I'm one client short of one hundred per cent in terms of marriage," I say, "but that's only because that particular client has taken his fiancée around the world on his yacht. He plans to pop the question on Midsummer's night, in Monte Carlo."

"How remarkably romantic for a man," says the sourpuss.

"I must admit that I do sometimes offer a little advice to my clients on wooing. Only because they're too pressed for time to give thought to the tiny extras that make a difference, of course."

Sourpuss bares her teeth — they're disappointingly un-vampiric — and for a moment I wonder what I've said to deserve the snarl. Then I realise she's *smiling*. "You're hired."

I shake my head. This woman is really winding me up now. "Er. No. You haven't been listening. I don't take on clients without meeting them, and if Mr Ottoway is too busy even to meet his matchmaker, then frankly I think his chances of finding time for a soul-mate are awfully low and we're all wasting our time."

"Oh, I do hope not." She holds out her hand. "Because *I'm* Sam Ottoway. And I am really hoping you can find me a husband."

I almost ended the meeting there and then, but Samantha Harriet Ophelia Ottoway threatened me with sexual discrimination legislation, and I decided there was nothing for it but to hear her out, and then, very carefully, explain that I didn't feel we had a *mental* connection and therefore I'd be unable to proceed. It's not as if I haven't turned people down before: there was the banker who thought paying my fee would entitle him to a few sessions in bed with me to sort out his sexual technique. Not to mention the Italian CEO who brought his mother along to the first interview.

We've now been squeezed into the corner of a tiny French wine bar for two hours, and Sam is still going strong. She's taken ninety minutes to outline the great cases of her career (a rogues' gallery of thugs, rapists and robbers — or, according to Sam, injured innocents who needed saving from outrageous miscarriages of justice). She's now moved on to the even greater injustices suffered by successful women.

"... and when I see the bloody newspapers going on about how career women are obsessed with *having it all*, it makes my blood boil. I don't want it all. Just a career and a man who won't be rendered impotent by the fact that I have a brain as well as a cleavage," she rails, her voice slurring. Actually, I am amazed I can still decipher what she's saying at all, given that we're on our third bottle of Sancerre, with only a plate of cheese to soak up the booze. At most I've had two glasses, just enough to make me slightly less terrified of her. She's had the rest, just enough to give the tiniest glimpse of the human being behind the black-designer suit of armour.

I can't imagine working with this woman, but I'm beginning to understand why she is the way she is. Being a barrister is all about acting, and Sam has developed a fierce, impregnable persona which has taken her over. But in yellowy candlelight, the vampire angles of her face are softened: her eyes are perfect almond shapes, and they widen as she talks. Despite her height, her hands are delicate, like a little girl's, and they flap and circle the air as she talks.

"So when was the last time you went out with someone?"

"Oh Christ almighty. Even that dating language drives me mad. Go *out* with. It's so imprecise. I last fucked a man two months ago. I last went on a date with a man . . . oooh . . . it must be three years." She stabs her fork into a piece of goat's cheese and chews it defiantly. "Does that shock you?"

I hesitate, not knowing what the *right* answer is. I suspect Sam likes to shock: why else would she have pulled that trick on me in her office? But I'm not playing her game any more. "Why would it?"

"I don't know . . . a professional woman like me indulging in casual, risky sex. Don't you find it somewhat *desperate*?"

No, I think, but you clearly do. "If I'm honest, I think 'good for you'. If you're confident enough to know what you want at work, why not in your private life, too? Though perhaps the fact you called me suggests that casual sex isn't enough for you."

Her eyes narrow. "How old are you, Rebecca?"

"Twenty-seven." I don't know what made me answer her, I'd never normally reveal anything personal to a potential client (even one I have no intention of

42

working for). I guess she must have used some secret barrister interrogation technique.

"Well, you couldn't possibly understand."

I think back to her CV: she's thirty-seven. "There's only ten years between us."

"Ha!" Her mood changes in an instant, and this time the candlelight isn't forgiving enough to hide her contempt. "Ten years when everything will change, let me tell you. Ten years when the first greys appear, ten years where you begin to catch sight of your mother in shop windows everywhere, and you wonder why she's following you around, before you realise it's *you*, looking unarguably middle-aged. Ten years when men will stop noticing you, and women start giving you sympathetic looks when you answer no to the inevitable *And do you have kids?* question."

"Right. Doesn't sound much fun, I must admit." I sneak a quick look at my watch. Ten to nine. How much more can she drink before she falls over? "So . . . do you want kids, then?"

"How can anyone know for sure, Rebecca?" Her voice has got louder suddenly, and I think the booze has really kicked in now. "But on balance, I think I'd rather not miss out on that particular experience."

I want to tell her that motherhood isn't like the new ride at Alton Towers, or a spectacular Madonna concert, but then what do I know? My biological clock has been on snooze since the fateful day I dreamily asked Marcus what our children might look like, and he said he hoped they'd be white, sleek and twenty-seven feet long, because the only berths he was interested in were inside a speedboat.

My pause for thought grows into an awkward chasm. We sit in silence for two long minutes, punctuated only by guffawing and back-slapping from a neighbouring tableful of self-satisfied young men. Eventually I take a very obvious look at my watch, and let out a sigh of mock-surprise. "Bloody hell! Nearly nine o'clock already. The evening's just flown by, Sam, but I really am going to have to shift."

She moves her head, slowly, to face me directly. "So. Are you going to help me, Rebecca?"

"I . . ." When it comes to it, I do find it bloody difficult to say no. I try to imagine how Georgie would handle it. "The fact is, Sam, I don't feel entirely qualified in your area. Men, that is. My work has been so focussed on finding the right women for my clients. That's where all my networks are, where my expertise is: I just don't think it's transferable."

"Forgive me, but that sounds like utter bollocks." Her forehead creases in irritation, and she shakes her head crossly. No, I definitely couldn't work with this woman, Sancerre or no bloody Sancerre. "Ignoring your blatant sexism for a moment, Rebecca, you must realise there's bound to be crossover. Apart from anything else, you come into contact all the time with single, eligible men who could be looking for a woman exactly like me . . ."

What Georgie would do at this point is to tell her the truth: that Sam is the complete opposite of what they're looking for. Not only is she too old, but she's also too sour, brusque and self-contained. She's not feminine enough, and worst of all, there's a distinct *edginess* to her, a hint of a dark side that I don't think would take much to unleash. My clients might possibly employ her, but they'd never date her in a million years.

Can I help her? She definitely needs help, as I can't imagine she'll change on her own. And I've taken on some pretty hopeless cases in my time: the manic-depressive oil baron who wrote terrible poetry, the sweet banker with a mild case of Tourette's, both now happily married.

But I know where I am with men, whereas Sam makes me nervous. I can't let a misplaced sense of sisterhood cloud my judgement. "It's a business decision, I'm afraid. It'd be unethical to match two clients, anyway, and as a woman working for herself, I can't allow my strategy to be led by a one-off request. I'm sure you understand the pressure I'm under."

"But . . ." She reaches drunkenly for her glass of wine and for a horrible moment I think she's going to throw it at me. Instead, she takes a huge swig and then does something far, far worse.

She bursts into tears.

I finally arrive home at ten-thirty, after making sure my broken-down barrister got back to her grand Clapham house in one piece. In the course of the journey, she went on a round trip from tearful, to angry, to bitter, and back to tearful again. Then she gave me a fistful of £20 notes to take the cab all the way to Richmond, and made me promise not to mention the incident to anyone. At least in the bar her curtain of perfect blond hair flopped in front of her flushed face, so no one but me knew she was falling to pieces.

"It's the bit they left out of the school careers lessons," she said, as she stumbled out of the taxi. "The bit that says that if you're a successful woman, you reduce your chances of finding anyone to share your success with. Remember that, Rebecca. Build up your business, sure, but don't forget to find a man along the way, or you'll end up like me."

I wish Georgie was home — after Sam's dire warnings, I could really do with my aunt's no-nonsense declarations on the pleasures of staying single — but the windows are dark when the taxi drops me off, and she's texted me to say she's gone to Chelsea to play poker with her Russian vodka enthusiast. I should really have called Dwight for a progress check, but when I get back to my loft, tripping a little on the spiral staircase, I find he's already sent me an email:

Call off the search, Cupid! You've hit the jackpot with Heather, she's the Flora Macdonald to my Bonnie Prince Charlie, rescuing me from my island of lonely single life. Get shopping for a wedding outfit, bride hunter!
Grateful thanks,
Dwight

Maybe it's my evening with laugh-a-minute Sam, but for some reason the message just makes me feel even edgier: what if Dwight's got so tired of looking and being alone, that he's convinced himself Heather's the one, before he could possibly know for sure?

Behave, Becca. You're good at this, remember.

I make my way back downstairs, help myself to some of Georgie's latest number-one favourite vodka (Jewel of Vodka Classic replaced Stoli in her affections after a raucous tasting at Fortnum's last year), and squeeze out on to the balcony, to watch the drunks and the workaholics making their way home across Richmond Green. I do love London, and I do believe that the city I've made my home is the cure for everything, from boredom to insomnia.

But just occasionally it feels cold and pitiless and populated by eight million lost souls. Just occasionally London feels like the loneliest place in the world . . .

CHAPTER
FIVE

Edward Lincoln is wearing a dressing gown in the sauna, and refuses to take it off, despite temperatures high enough to roast a turkey.

Shame, because from what I can see, the body beneath the towelling is in decent shape. A bit pale, maybe, but when I asked him about leisure time during our first meeting, he admitted he hasn't had a holiday in two years (and to be fair, neither have I). At least he's not one of those men who spends hours every week sandwiched between the sweaty tubes of a sunbed to maintain a golden glow.

Edward's work-life balance doesn't exist. He works from seven in the morning till nine or ten at night, spends weekends reading work documents or recovering, and his only luxury is gym membership, though judging from the quizzical look the receptionist gave him when he presented his card, he's not exactly a regular. "I'll just update this, if that's OK," she said, tapping away at her keyboard, "because we switched to biometric cards over a year ago now. *Someone* hasn't been making the gym a priority."

Poor Edward. This is Phase Two of my entirely invented occupational psychology assessment, which happens to bear a very close resemblance to the early stages of my bride-hunting methodology. I never bother to ask my clients what they find attractive in a woman, because most of them fib and talk about a kind personality or sense of humour, and completely neglect to mention the more immediate appeal of enormous knockers. Instead, I always take them to a location where I can see for myself what catches their eye. Gyms and spas are usually the best option. However hard they try, men can't help themselves when they're sur-rounded by near-naked females.

After getting lost in the changing rooms, Edward finally emerges wearing the robe and a look of grim determination. I wasn't even sure he'd swallow my reasons for coming here, but he's too cross with Perry to think too much about me.

This is the flashest place in the area, £300 a month *minimum*, so given his rate of attendance, he's paying around £3,000 per visit (though that's still considerably less than a jeroboam of Cristal at Chinawhite, after all). The club is a pristine glass-and-steel affair, like a Bond villain's greenhouse, with stunning views of London from every angle. I can't imagine it would be very relaxing if you're a big name in the big city. You can probably see your own office — and the offices of your deadliest rivals — from the discomfort of your running machine.

That might explain why there are no city folk on the running machines today: I've timed our visit so that we're firmly in Ladies who Lunge territory, a mixture of yummy mummies tackling their errant tummies, and glamorous wives from the shires who've treated themselves to a spa day. None of these women are in any way suitable for Edward, but they represent a good cross-section of the female form: from surgically smoothed specimens with not a centimetre of spare flab, to more generously proportioned creatures. Now all I have to do is follow his gaze and I'll get a good idea of his taste. Except he keeps his eyes firmly fixed on the limestone floor as we head for the enormous sauna, and now we're alone in its sweltering interior.

"Now, Edward, are you more into cardio or weights?"

He half looks at me, studiously avoiding glancing towards my swimsuited body (it's not *that* bad, is it?). "Neither. I'm into lying in the sauna until my internal organs are medium-rare, and then picking up a curry on the way home to reward myself for my hard work."

"Is that why you only come here once a year?"

He smiles sheepishly. "Don't know why I joined in the first place. I think it was the New Year before last. Some girl approached me with a leaflet on the street. Special offer, good intentions, new you, resolutions. The more you pay, the more likely you are to keep it up, that was my logic."

"Hasn't worked, then?"

"Does it look like it?" He looks down at his body, ruefully.

"Well, I don't know, do I? You might have the physique of Charles Atlas under that dressing gown."

His face — already pink from the heat — flushes cherry-red. "Funnily enough, I don't. At best, I might have the body of Prince Charles. I should resign my membership. I bet they're embarrassed to have me making the place look messy."

"God, you're so hard on yourself, Edward. You've got a lot going for you. One of the leading lights in your field, according to Perry. Brain the size of a large planet, which most women find as attractive as a Mr Universe torso." I really want to go further, tell him it's no wonder he's single, that self-deprecation is acceptable, but self-loathing will never get him laid. I have to bite my lip to stop myself going all *Supernanny*.

Edward laughs. "Perry only says that because his own brain is the size of a ping-pong ball. Surprisingly decent bloke at heart, but not the brightest."

I nod. "Yes, but he has a certain raw cunning, doesn't he? And very savvy when it comes to spotting people like you, who can help him to the top."

"You've got him sussed. Did you know him before he hired you to do this shrink bit, then?"

I hesitate. "We'd met . . . socially. And I'm not a shrink. I'm just professionally nosy. It's my job to understand what motivates people, how to make them happier, so they work better."

He reaches forward to ladle water on to the hot coals, then waits for the sizzle and steam to subside before speaking. "But do happier people really work harder? I'm a miserable old bugger, but I work harder than anyone in my office. So I should, mind you. I lead the team, I get the highest salary, fair enough that I should be the one who puts the most hours in. But if I had a life, well, I might not be so bothered any more."

I'm stumped for a moment. What if he's right? A real occupational psychologist would have reams of statistics to quote back, but somehow I doubt my research on the psychology of love will satisfy him. "Ye-es, I take your point, but I think you'll find happy people work smarter, not harder." There. That sounds convincing. *Doesn't it?*

"Like Perry, you mean? I suppose I can see that. Tell you what, he's a changed man since he got married."

"Really? In what way?"

"Well, he was never sober before, for a start. Used to turn up pie-eyed every morning, and none of us could believe any sane woman would get involved with him, but we met her at the Christmas party and she seemed sane. More than sane. Normal. Not to mention stunningly pretty. Though she obviously rules the roost!"

I allow myself the tiniest smile of satisfaction. I always knew Idoia was more than a match for Perry. "There you are, then. And I bet he works more effectively now he's not pissed all the time. The love of a good woman, you see. What about you, Edward? Are you in the market for a wife?"

His shoulders slump, and he shows a sudden fascination with the knot in his dressing-gown belt. "Ah, well . . . I don't have a lot in common with women, it seems."

Inside our wooden box, the temperature seems to rise and I fight the urge to break the silence, to change the subject and let him off the hook. This could be my best chance of finding out whether Edward really wants my specialist help, or whether he'd prefer to be left alone.

Eventually he sighs. "I suppose this is part of the bloody assessment, too, is it?"

"Only tell me what you want to tell me, Edward. It's up to you how much you want to share. Though nothing goes any further than these four super-heated walls."

"I'm not gay, if that's what you're thinking," he mumbles. "Not that there's anything wrong with being gay. Oh, shit. I hate talking about this stuff."

I really should put him out of his misery. "You don't have to, then."

He huffs, and I reckon he's losing patience with himself, rather than me. "No, it's OK. I suppose it's all relevant, up to a point. I went to a boys' boarding school, on a scholarship. You wouldn't believe how hard my parents fought to get me in. For two years I worked harder at weekends than I did at primary school. IQ tests, logic puzzles, practice tests from WH Smith."

"Right . . ." I remembered his CV, the long list of A grades, followed by the degree from Cambridge. "Well, it worked, didn't it?"

"Oh, yeah. I got the scholarship and then all the right results, that's for sure. But after seven years in the company of dysfunctional rich boys, I was an utter failure on the subject of girls. Bloody good at algebra, though."

"Most men would say they never understand women, so you're hardly unique, Edward."

"Yeah, but most men manage to bluff their way through it." He picks at a splinter in the pine slat.

"So . . ." I try to put it as delicately as possible, "have you never had any experience with women at all?"

"Am I a virgin, do you mean?" he says, trying to hide his embarrassment behind snappiness. "No, not quite. There was a girl at university who shared my weird love of economic data and we . . . well. You know. Helen. Very bright. She went to America in the end. And though it was fun while it lasted, I can't claim it gave me any useful tips for dealing with the rest of the gender. Helen wasn't really your typical woman. I mean, how many girls would get turned on debating Keynesian theories on the mixed economy?"

I smile. "Not many, it's true. But you would like to find someone, if you knew how?"

"Yes. Of course I would. Do you think I want to be the sad old bastard in the office who's married to his job? But unless someone invents a personality transplant, I'll be leaving the vast inheritance I'm working so hard to accrue to Battersea Dogs' Home and the taxman." He stands up, clutching the edges of his dressing gown together in case I get a sneaky glimpse of his torso. "Which surely has to be good news for Anemone International, doesn't it? Now, if you'll excuse me, I think I need to cool off."

I catch up with Edward again by the smoothie bar, where robed women are giggling like schoolgirls. He doesn't look at any of them. Instead, he orders an In the Pink SuperFruit Burst, and hands it to me. "Peace

54

offering," he says. "And an apology. That was rude of me, before. I hate talking about personal stuff, but I know you're only doing your job."

It's my turn to blush now. "No, I should apologise. I went too far, Edward. None of that was any of my business."

He takes a sip of a bright green drink through a straw. "Look, Rebecca, I'm a loser. When the going gets tough, Eddy the Plank buggers off rather than having to make conversation."

"You don't seem to have any trouble talking to me."

"Yes, but I don't see you as a woman."

I raise my eyebrows. "Gee, thanks."

"You know what I mean. This is work-related. Safe."

I take a deep breath "You know, Edward, it's all in the mind. You just need to learn to show off your good points. You've got a great, dry sense of humour, women like that. If you could stop panicking, you'd be fine."

"Ah, thanks for trying, Rebecca. But I'm not actively *unhappy* like this, and I hope I don't make my team unhappy either. That's all I want to take away from this exercise you're doing, the reassurance that I'm getting it right, most of the time."

"I don't think you've any worries on that score. You're a good boss, nothing to teach you there. But . . . well, I shouldn't even really be suggesting this, but I'd love to help you with the other stuff."

"Suggesting what?"

"It might sound daft, but what the hell. I think I've got the solution to your problem, Edward, or part of it. My aunt Georgia. She's possibly the most glamorous woman I've ever met. I mean, if I wasn't related to her, I'd be terrified to talk to her."

"Ri-ight."

"I will get to the point, I promise. The thing is, Georgie isn't actually scary at all. She's lovely. And a bit lonely . . ." I cross my fingers in my dressing-gown pocket. My aunt is the least lonely person I know: and anyway, according to her, it's impossible to be lonely in London. "I had this other friend, like you, really, a bit shy around women, but I knew he just needed some guidance. Anyway, to cut a long story very short indeed, he took my aunt out to dinner. She got a night out with a younger man, he got some brilliant dating tips." I pause for a sip of smoothie before delivering the killer line. "He's now married, lovely girl, and expecting his first baby any day."

Edward stares at me. "All down to your aunt?"

"No! All down to him. He had the potential all along, but he just needed someone to tease it out of him, show him what's what. You wouldn't, I don't know, perform heart surgery without someone showing you how, yet men are expected to chat women up without any guidance. All my aunt did was point him in the right direction . . ."

He frowns. "Hmmm. I don't want to look a gift-aunt in the mouth, Rebecca, but I don't think I could do that. It wouldn't feel real."

Oh go on, I want to shout, *shake yourself up a bit, we can change your life, just give me the word.* But I don't. " Edward, it's your decision, of course it is. But in my capacity as Anemone's occupational psychologist," I hesitate, waiting to be struck down for my fibbing. Nothing happens. "I can't help thinking that overcoming this *block* could release you from other self-limiting beliefs, thereby improving your performance in all areas."

He shrugs. "You're not going to let up on the psychobabble, are you?"

"Nope."

He sucks the last of his smoothie up through the straw, and the gurgling reverberates noisily around the glass atrium. "I'll think it over," he says, finally. "That good enough for you? Now I need to stop lazing around on company time, and get back to the office. If I'm excused, that is, Miss Orchard?"

"You're excused. For now."

After nicking as many Occitane Verbena shower gel miniatures as I can fit in my sports bag, I wait for Edward in reception. I thought he'd be the type to make a very speedy exit, so I haven't bothered to dry my hair or put make-up on. I look a sight but then I'm heading straight back to Richmond on the Tube. I really need to talk this through with Georgie. Maybe I am being way too pushy with the poor man. After all, Georgie and I are proof positive that you can be happy *and* single.

"Well, well, well."

I recognise his voice at the first "well". During the second, I weigh up my options and work out that I have no chance of escape. And by the end of the third, my insides feel as though someone's whizzed them up inside Mum's ancient Kenwood Chef.

"Marcus," I say, before I trust myself to look up. Yep. He's still got it. The bastard. Every jet-black hair in place, every tiny line round his moss-green eyes drawing attention to their cheeky sparkle. Even the artful five-o'clock shadow (it's still only lunchtime) frames his jaw to perfection. "Long time, no see."

He's in an Armani suit, of course, and hand-made Olga Berluti shoes (£2,500 a pop). If he thought he could get away with keeping the suit on during his workout, he probably would. He didn't come to this gym before, he went to the Third Space, but then he'd change sides faster than a daytime TV presenter if it raised his profile. Loyalty isn't in my ex-boyfriend's vocabulary.

He smiles at me. "Two years, in fact. Haven't spotted you here before." Everything Marcus says seems to have a minimum of two meanings: a straightforward interpretation of what he's just said, plus a whole array of extra layers. *Two years* is roughly the amount of time we've been apart, yes, but it's also a challenge (he wants me to say two years two months, because I bet he knows I'm still counting) and a boast (because he looks younger and better than he did then, while I . . . oh God, right now I couldn't look worse if I tried). And as for what he's insinuating with *haven't seen you here before*, well, I wouldn't know where to begin.

"Rebecca?"

Edward has emerged from the changing rooms, his hair slightly tousled, and his tie skew-whiff.

"A friend?" Marcus asks. "Or a client?"

Oh *shit*. Double-shit. Even though I haven't seen him since that fateful day, Marcus has managed to put the word out via my old colleagues that he sees my new business as laughable and unsustainable and cringeworthy (it's one of the few things he and my mum would agree on). Knowing Marcus, he'll have no problem saying so to my face. Now, if this was any other time, I wouldn't care — well, not all that much — I'm a big girl now.

But if Marcus says anything out of turn, then it's game over with poor Eddy. And given what he's told me today, I don't think his fragile ego would ever recover from the humiliation of having been set up by Perry.

"A friend," I say firmly, grabbing Edward's arm and linking it through mine. "A good friend."

Marcus winks. "Oh, like *that* is it?"

I stare at Edward, willing him to understand what's going on. He gawps back, stunned into silence by close proximity to my elbow. "Edward, this is Marcus. We used to know each other. Two years ago."

Edward nods, though he clearly doesn't have a clue what's happening.

"Yes," says Marcus, "we knew each other *very* well, didn't we, Bex?"

The familiarity of the nickname sends a shudder down my spine, followed immediately by an intense longing, accompanied by a fragment of memory. The moment when Marcus first kissed me. It takes my mind less than a second to restore control of my treacherous body, reminding me of all the cruel things Marcus did. But I still have to concentrate hard on staying upright.

At least the penny seems to have dropped with Edward, because he squeezes me closer to him. "Really, darling?" he says, sounding like a rather bad amateur actor in the first read-through of a bedroom farce. "You've never mentioned him before. Naughty girl."

But his act seems to fool Marcus, who looks as though he's been slapped. *Wonderful.* I could kiss Edward. In fact, to his surprise — and mine, I do. Only on the cheek, mind you, but he smells surprisingly good. Must be the Occitane shower gel.

"Have to go, Marcus," I say, making an exit before Edward's rather gormless expression gives it away. "Enjoy your workout."

And I stride out of the door with my stealth client/pretend boyfriend, feeling invincible.

"Thank you, Edward," I say, when we finally get out on to the street.

"That was the right thing to do, was it?" He sounds terribly anxious.

"Definitely the right thing to do. Brilliant. Only thing is, it might be a good idea to let go of my arm now, if you don't mind . . ."

CHAPTER
SIX

I decide not to mention Marcus to Georgie, even though two hours later, I'm still feeling shaky. Luckily my other exploits provide more than enough for her to chew over.

"One hour with this Eddy the Plank chap and I'll have him sorted," she tells me, as she mixes two perfect Brandy Alexanders. Somehow she maintains that perfect figure on a diet of croissants, cocktails and coffee.

"Oh, I know that, Georgie. The problem will be getting him to meet you in the first place. I have to respect his right to say no."

She sieves cocoa powder on top of both cocktails, then passes one to me. "Rubbish, Becky. He doesn't know what he's missing, and it's my moral duty to help him realise. Cupid will find a way. I favour the old 'accidentally bumping into him' routine next time you meet him. But what about barrister girl?"

Sam's phoned me six times since I delivered her home the night before last, and I haven't picked up once. The calls veer from shameful apology, through to wheedling requests to reconsider, and even overt flattery. She hasn't resorted to threats yet but I'm sure it's only a matter of time. "It's not that I don't feel sorry for her, Georgie. I just think she's going to be terribly hard work."

"Mmmm." She clinks her glass against mine. "Let's drink to the infinite variety of love, precious niece. The thing is, you've had male clients who were bloody hard work. Are you *sure* you're not discriminating against her?"

"Georgie! How could you? I know what it's like to be discriminated against." Five years as a head-hunter left me in no doubt that the corporate world is still firmly weighted in favour of the male of the species. Most of the women who came to work for Marcus disappeared in a blizzard of sodden tissues: even Kelly, one of the most successful female head-hunters in the City, jacked it in around the same time as me to become a lap-dancer, "because the men I pole-dance for are a damned sight more polite and appreciative than the blokes we worked at Benson's." She had a point.

"Actions speak louder than words, Becky, and I think you are being sexist. Personally, I reckon it'd be fun to go husband-hunting for a change."

"It's not really my core business, though, is it?" I lie back on the lilac chaise longue and close my eyes. Georgie and her house are so bloody tasteful, like a Graham and Green catalogue, that I find it almost impossible to disagree with her without seeming crashingly *loud*. "And you're always telling me not to lose sight of the main objective, which in my case is saving enough to buy my own place."

"Ungrateful wretch!" Then she laughs. "I think there's a deeper psychological hang-up here, though."

"Which I'm sure you're going to share with me."

"It'd be a shame not to. I think you're refusing to take Sam on because if you did, you'd be forced to start looking at men as human beings and *potential dates* again, instead of just as clients."

"That's like saying that I see my clients as meal tickets? You might as well accuse me of being . . . I don't know . . . a harlot? You're worse than Mum."

She dips her little finger into her glass, and then licks off the last drops of brandy-flavoured cream. "You know, I've always thought harlot is rather a glamorous word. Anyway. Don't change the subject. Of course I'm not suggesting that you don't devote tender loving care to finding each chap the perfect wifey. But all your assessments and psychological mumbo-jumbo are also a very effective way of distancing yourself from the fact that men are a potential source of happiness as well as job satisfaction."

"Happiness! After all that happened with . . ." And I stop myself saying Marcus. Oh God, I do hope that meeting at the gym isn't going to make me lovesick all over again.

"Yes, yes," Georgie says impatiently. "After all that happened with Marcus Benson, founder member of the Society of Total Bastards. I know what you went through, Becky. I could have killed him with my bare hands for the way he behaved towards my baby niece. Except throttling would have been too good for him. But now, quite frankly, it's time to see him for what he was, put him back in his box, and move on. He's too boring for words."

Sometimes Georgie has a bluntness that I'd find unforgivable in anyone else. But she's right. It was pretty wonderful to see his handsome face fall when Edward implied that he wasn't even important enough to warrant a mention. Maybe I've crossed the line from pain to boredom at long last.

"Well?" she says.

"I suppose two years is long enough. But I swear that what happened with Marcus has nothing to do with my decision about Sam."

"Prove it."

"Oh, God, Georgie, I don't want to turn this into some kind of playground dare. Sam's a nightmare. She really is."

"Ah, but surely even nightmares deserve a crack at the transformative power of true love?"

"I need another drink."

Georgie measures out the ingredients thoughtfully: Remy Martin, Crème de Cacao, cream. Then she shakes and the drink turns a flawless beige colour, like one of her linen suits. "Here's my suggestion. You don't say yes, you say maybe. You tell her you need to do some market research to work out whether there's a demand for a female-friendly service *and* whether the kind of man she wants is out there."

"And the advantage of all this is what exactly?"

"I'd have thought it's obvious. You shut me up for a while. We get to go to some marvellous man-hunting locations, *and* it's all a legitimate business expense as you're exploring expansion potential. Nights out on the tax man. My favourite kind."

Sometimes with Aunt Georgie, it's best to admit when you're beaten.

We begin in Cupid HQ, i.e. the loft. It's a bit of a squeeze up here for two people, but Georgie lies down on my bed, while I sit in the second-hand Eames chair she bought me when I first set up the business. I switch on my pink i-Mac, and open a computer file on Sam Ottoway.

"So, remind me what we do first?" Georgie asks. She's always treated my methods with the contempt of one who has never had any trouble attracting Mr Rights, Mr Wrongs and everyone in between. Maybe that's why she's never fallen in love in all the years I've known her: like a chocoholic in a sweet factory, she's lost the taste for it.

"I start with five words to describe the client, for the Partner Person Specification. In Sam's case those would be . . ." I hesitate. "Well, if I am honest, the words would be shrewish, crotchety, ambitious, demanding, unbalanced."

"Aha, Becky, but you're cheating. You always spend ages with your male clients bigging up the positive. That pig Perry came out sounding like Mr Personality."

"Perry isn't a pig! He's . . ." I try to remember my five words, ". . . gregarious, generous . . ."

"Gullible, gluttonous and gormless. And that's just the Gs."

"No, the other words were playful, charming and smart."

"Cunning, you mean. And less of the playful, more infantile. Anyway, you've just proved my point. You can put a positive spin on anything if you try hard enough. So yet again you're discriminating against poor Sam."

I sigh. "Right. Well, what's the positive way of saying crotchety, then?"

"Fiery?"

"Still not really a plus point."

"Passionate, then."

I type in the word. "OK. What about demanding? Now, I know that in itself demanding isn't a bad quality, but it's not something your average man would seek out."

"You seem to be forgetting that you're not assessing Sam for one of your clients, you're building up a profile to find a man who can match her requirements. What about discerning?"

I nod. "I'll accept that. I suppose ambitious is allowed, too. Which leaves shrewish and unbalanced."

"How about mercurial instead of unbalanced? And I think we ditch shrewish altogether in favour of something nicer. She's bright, isn't she?"

"Scarily bright. So I'll put down intelligent. Intelligent, mercurial, discerning, ambitious, passionate."

"There we are then," Georgie says. "I'd go on a date with her."

"Yes, but you date *men*. I could find her any number of willing girls if she was a male barrister. Classic Alpha

Male romantic hero, but the qualities you've just described have never come up in conversation when I've asked men what they're looking for in a wife."

"It's a *challenge*, precious niece. But you thrive on a challenge and I really can't believe she's harder work than Perry. What next?"

The rest of the form is tricky, because I didn't get any of the information I usually note down at the first meeting: family background, sibling birth order, spiritual or religious beliefs, star sign, and all the rest. Maybe I have been unfair to Sam: I don't judge my male clients because their bank balance is getting in the way of finding true love, so why did I dismiss her so quickly?

"Right, so we think she needs a man who can stand up to her . . . who is successful in his own field, earning at least as much as she does . . . probably not a lawyer, because the competition between them would be too much. Oh, and he needs to be ready for children like *yesterday* if she's in a hurry to have kids. I wonder whether we can get candidates to give a sperm sample, just to check the swimmers are up to scratch."

"I think you're getting carried away."

"Maybe," she says, getting up from my bed. "Tell you what, I'm in party mood after those Brandy Alexanders. Shall we go manhunting?"

"Georgie, I haven't worked out her Marmite Factors. We don't know what her type is. I haven't even started making a Cupid Collage . . ." I wave towards the mood boards I create for each of my clients: a collection of postcards and images and ideas torn out of magazines, all glued to a piece of heavy black card. It's my road-map for finding them the right person, complete with stills from their favourite films, lines from their best-loved books, plus ideas about how their ideal partner might look, and where they might go on a dream first date.

"This isn't a kindergarten art class, Becky. And remember that if men are visual creatures, we women are led by our minds. Sam will fall for a man who talks the talk, who appeals to her mind. And we're going to find him."

Like I said, there's no point in arguing with my aunt once she's made her mind up about something.

If I was an insecure person, I'd never go out on the town with Georgie. She might be nearly two decades older than me, but when we're together, she's always the one who turns heads. Even tonight, in caramel cotton trousers, and a plain white shirt, she has that luminous, other-world quality about her.

In an attempt not to be totally eclipsed, I've applied enough Clarins Beauty Flash Balm to perk up a catwalk's worth of under-nourished models. I look nice enough — I have a new dress that ticks all the boxes: pink, to make my eyes look green as emeralds, v-neck, to emphasise my bust without looking like a *Carry On* star, and a petite fitting that doesn't swamp me.

Georgie and Marcus have both had an influence on how I dress. My aunt was my very first fashion icon, a living primer in unbearable elegance. Alas, her uncompromising neutral-colour palette and classic cuts never *quite* worked on my curves: on a bad day, I looked as dowdy as the blue-stocking daughter of a Tory MP.

Then Marcus came along and introduced raw sex into my wardrobe, as well as my life. Or, at least, he did in the early days. Our relationship resembled a movie plot. He took me round his favourite stores — imagine Richard Gere in *Pretty Woman*, without the prostitution storyline — and encouraged me to take risks with hemlines and necklines. "Higher . . . Lower . . ." he instructed, like a contestant in *Play Your Cards Right*. At work, my clothes were tasteful yet closely tailored, but after work, I was the Jessica Rabbit of the head-hunting world, paraded by Marcus. "Brains and beauty, tits and ass," he used to whisper to his friends, and then later he'd insist he was being ironic.

Then, six months before we split up, everything changed. He began to criticise the very aspects of my wardrobe that he'd chosen so carefully. "You look *tarty*," he'd say, when I wore his favourite dress, the one that was previously guaranteed to make us late for a party. The number of outfits which met his approval dwindled until I found myself leaving the house looking less like Jessica Rabbit, and more like Dustin Hoffman in *Tootsie*.

His behaviour made me edgy and confused. I devoted half my time to second-guessing his unpredictable reactions, and the other half to trying to understand where I'd gone wrong. Now, I think the insults were his way of justifying to himself the betrayals he was planning to commit. Or, perhaps, had already started committing. I'll give him the benefit of the doubt and imagine he did it unconsciously. The alternative seems too unpleasant, even for someone with Marcus Benson's track record.

My *personal style* now is pitched somewhere between Georgie's sophistication, and Marcus's sassiness. This evening's pink frock combines the two perfectly, yet I'm happy to admit it isn't me who has rendered the entire bar of the Pitcher and Piano speechless.

"So what does a girl have to do to get a drink round here?" she says, with a provocative raise of the eyebrow. The taxman doesn't have to worry too much about stumping up for our night out because, seconds later, she has men queuing up to buy her a bottle of wine. We take our glasses outside, and she's followed by a small group of blokes, Pied-Piper style.

The pub has a huge raised terrace overlooking the Thames, and it's packed with stoical drinkers, determined to pretend it's summer despite the biting April wind. The less hardy huddle around tall patio heaters, ignoring the smell of gas, but Georgie heads for the edge of the terrace. She peers down at the wide river, her back arched and her eyes closed, leaning against the railing like Kate Winslet in *Titanic*. She knows she's being watched, but then again she'd miss it if she wasn't. She turns slowly and scans the other customers before speaking.

"So. Potential husbands at three o'clock, five o'clock and eleven o'clock. The rest are too young or too ugly. Would you agree?"

I've been appreciating the view of the water, but as I follow her gaze, I know she's spot on. Three o'clock, to our right, is mid-forties, salt-and-pepper hair, and has abandoned his jacket to show he's too tough to feel the cold. A partner in a firm of estate agents, maybe, with a tennis club membership, a sports car and a couple of teenaged kids to pay for from his first marriage. But he has a certain presence. Worth a chat. Five o'clock is a little younger and very good-looking, with the tanned skin of a man who spends his spare time on his private yacht. And eleven o'clock is the youngest of all, friendlier looking, wearing expensive skinny jeans and a wicked smile. If I was in the market for a man, I'd probably go for him, but for Sam, I think number two would work best. That's what makes me good at my job — my ability to stay detached at all times.

"Agreed. So I suppose the next stage is . . ."

"Reconnaissance. Yep. Five minutes maximum with each one, then we're moving pubs. This is just the start! We'll find you a husband before you can say *just married*."

"Um, Georgie. Just don't forget. We're not looking for me. We're looking for Sam."

She gives me a withering look. "Yes, that's what I meant, you dolt. Find you a husband for your client, obviously. All in aid of the Rebecca Orchard Studio Flat Fund. Right, let's begin at three o'clock . . ."

CHAPTER
SEVEN

Monday morning, and my first job will be calling Sam to let her know that not only am I prepared to take her on as a client, but I already have some potential dates lined up. But before I get a chance, Dwight calls.

"I have just had the most *incredible* weekend of my life."

Bingo! "Ooh. What a lovely thing to hear to start the week." I settle down into my chair to hear the full story of Dwight's first weekend away with Heather. Whatever my niggling doubts about the speed of this particular relationship, I am a sucker for moments like these.

"Rebecca, she is perfection. My lucky Heather. She's so . . . natural. And funny. And sweet. And utterly beautiful. I feel twenty years younger. I'm in love."

Bless him. Dwight's brain is so flooded with dopamine and vasopressin that he can't think straight. And isn't that the best high money can't buy, the buzz we're all seeking?

Except me, of course. I prefer *my* buzz second-hand.

"I'm thrilled, Dwight. So where did you go?" I keep my fingers crossed that he hasn't misjudged it horribly, taken her to some flamboyant Southfork-style hotel and ordered caviar and Cristal by the crate. I think it's still way too early to go flashing his cash: even the sweetest, loveliest girl can have her head turned by unimaginable wealth.

"We went to this low-key little place in Hampshire, so cute. We went riding and fishing, just like we will in Scotland when we have time."

"Low-key? I thought you said it had a helipad."

"Sure. I think all Four Seasons hotels have a helipad nearby."

Gulp. "As in the low-key Four Seasons hotel that charges three hundred a night excluding breakfast?"

"The suites are four-fifty, but they're very tasteful. I know you think I'm some kind of dumb, brash Yank, Rebecca, but credit me with a little style . . ."

"I'm sure she had a wonderful weekend. I can't think of anywhere nicer." And actually, I can't. I visited it once when I was suggesting wedding venues for one of my clients: it was the ultimate in English country living, without the draughts and the haughty aristocrats. "It obviously lived up to expectations."

"So, don't you want to know just *how* well we got on, Rebecca?"

"Dwight! Don't be daft. The bedroom door stays firmly shut as far as I'm concerned." Not that I don't keep my fingers crossed that a good match on paper will prove equally satisfying between the sheets.

"Oh." He sounds disappointed, as if he's dying to give me the full, X-rated account. It's difficult for men, isn't it? Girls will sneak their mobiles into the bathroom to update their best friends within minutes of the first time if they can get away with it. But boys have to content themselves with nudges and hand gestures.

I take pity on him. "All right, Dwight. I suppose you can tell me if you really want to. Though it's not very gentlemanly, is it?"

He laughs. "That's the weirdest thing of all. I only want to tell you because there's not much to tell. Sure, she kisses like a dream, and we certainly . . . snuggled up. No more, though, Rebecca. We decided it'd be so much more fun to take it slow."

Clever Heather. "And this was your idea, was it, Dwight?"

"OK. Maybe not *entirely*. I can't say it wasn't . . . well, kinda challenging, at times, but Heather was right. We're both ambitious, driven people. We go after what we want and at our age, we know all about instant gratification. But we could do with a few lessons in anticipation, and I tell you, it's beating lust hands down. Now I know why teens are so horny all the time."

"Um. Great. I'm really pleased for you." I was about to do my *take it slow* speech, but I realise that taking it slow is precisely what's making this once-bitten, twice-shy divorce fall so deep and so fast. "Though, you know, Dwight, remember that you've only known her a couple of weeks."

"Sure, Rebecca. I know what you're saying. You're the voice of reason. All I'm saying is, I've never felt this way before, and it's thanks to you. You're the best."

He asks me to investigate the cost of weddings in Scottish castles ("just hypothetically . . ."), then rings

75

off. I turn to his Cupid Collage, with its pictures of remote beaches and lochs and the Dagenham Girl Pipers, and move Heather's photograph a little closer to the photo of Dwight. Soon I'll be moving the whole lot into a wedding album to go with the others in my collection.

Either Heather's never felt this way either, or she's as canny as she is cute. Whichever it is, Dwight seems to have met his match.

I manage to get hold of Sam during the lunchtime court recess — she's midway through what she calls "a little light relief", defending the Notting Hill Hustler, a seventysomething widower who specialises in flogging houses that don't actually belong to him.

When I tell her I've decided to try to find her a husband, she sounds completely unsurprised, as though she's known all along that I'd give in.

"So when can I meet the first candidates?"

"Well, to be honest, Sam, I think it's better if we meet face to face again. I'd like to go through my normal process of research and evaluation, so that I can be sure I'm not wasting your time with men who are entirely unsuitable."

"Oh, bollocks to that. We all know it's about chemistry, anyway, so I might as well get stuck in, work my way through the list. I'm free tonight."

"That's a bit soon, Sam, wouldn't you rather —"

"Yes, tonight would be perfect because the jury are going out straight after lunch and I don't think they'll take long to acquit Bernie. So I'll be in the mood for celebrating, letting my hair down a bit."

I think back to her drunken rant in the wine bar, and shudder. But maybe it's better to get this over and done with. I'm pretty sure no one will be good enough for Sam Ottoway, so that'll be the end of that. "I'll see what I can do, though I can't promise anything at such short notice."

"Come on, Rebecca, don't be so defeatist. I'm sure you can rustle me up a man for one dull Monday night. And don't worry about the venue. I'll meet them on a park bench if needs be."

I decide not to remind her that, by her own admission, she has no problem finding men for a single night. It's finding a keeper that's proving more of a challenge. Instead, I tell her I'll be in touch, and wearily open the computer file containing the dozen phone numbers Georgie picked up the other night.

Now . . . how exactly am I going to sell the idea of a blind date to those magnificently eligible bachelors?

Seven hours later, I'm skulking in the back of All Bar One at Waterloo with my Diet Coke, feeling as nervous as if I was going on the date myself. I always feel that frisson, even though my client's first dates are planned to perfection. Transport arrangements confirmed in triplicate, the best tables and views staked out, conversational strategies planned to avoid awkward silences.

But Sam was having none of that. "I don't care about the venue, so long as I'm close enough to the station to make a quick getaway the moment we run out of steam. And don't worry about telling me about him. I'll find out soon enough."

So, armed with only her date's mobile number and the sketchiest description ("six two, naturally blond hair, cheekbones you could grate cheese on, and he says he'll be wearing a white leather coat and carrying a copy of *GQ*"), Sam is embarking on her quest for love.

Actually, Lee Laker is rather a catch. Georgie found him outside the White Cross pub, the very last stop on our manhunting expedition. Lee is the ultimate in self-made men, thirteen stone of raw ambition and testosterone poured into this season's designer casualwear. After ducking and diving his way through school, he set up a market stall selling kettles and electric blankets. He switched to the mobile phone industry in its infancy, when each handset was still the size of a terraced house. By thirty, he'd earned enough to retire, but of course he hasn't. According to my notes, he has "big plans for China" and believes the secret of happiness is "setting crazy goals and giving myself a massive bonus when I exceed them".

Of all the go-getters in our hunting session, I thought Lee was the least likely to judge Sam for using a matchmaker, and I was right. When I explained what I was doing, there was a pause before he burst out laughing. "Good on her! If you can't find what you want, get in the people who can. Sound business decision. Like her already. Not one of these women who only want men for sperm and sex, though, is she?"

"Oh, no. She's specifically told me that even though she's had to take the initiative by hiring me, she definitely wants her dates to take the lead."

"You can always rely on Lee Laker for a good time," he said. "If there's one thing I can't resist, it's the thrill of the chase . . ."

I can see him now, checking his reflection in the long mirrors behind the bar. Rough around the edges, sure, but he's the only man here who could carry off that coat, and, anyway, I wouldn't be surprised if wide boys are precisely Ms Ottoway's type. Why else spend your life hanging around court rooms, where wideboys rule the Underworld?

I open my book and reread the first line for the hundredth time: *On an exceptionally hot evening early in July, a young man came out of the garret in which he lodged . . .*

It's *Crime and Punishment*, chosen specially from Georgie's bookshelves in Sam's honour. A heavyweight classic is just the job for lone surveillance, accompanied by my dowdiest clothes and a well-rehearsed scowl: together they make me look utterly unapproachable. I never bring books I actually want to read, in case I get lost in the story and forget to keep tabs on my clients.

As I stare at the page, I can feel someone's eyes on me, and I try my hardest to look intimidatingly clever.

"Nothing like a Dostoevsky and a Diet Coke to make the evening go with a swing, eh?"

Oh shit. Clearly I need to invest in an even nastier set of clothes. I ignore the speaker.

"You a fan of the Russian greats, then?" the voice continues. "I'm more into Pasternak myself."

"No. I'm reading it for a bet." I look up, now, as this guy is clearly not going to take the hint. He smiles at me, but it's a slightly defensive smile, less confident than the amused voice would suggest. He's not bad-looking — I'm sure Georgie or I would have considered him for Sam. He's tall and broad, but not at all fat, and dressed not in standard Waterloo City-boy uniform, but jeans and a T-shirt the colour of Demerara sugar. His eyes are the same shade.

Not that he's my type, of course. What kind of man approaches a girl in a bar? It's such a cliché. And he's too well built and too smiley and too . . . well, the truth is, no one's my type any more.

"If you want," he says, "I could tell you the ending and then you won't have to bother to read it for your bet. I'm happy to take a drink as fair exchange." He's not giving up, though his voice wavers a little.

I sigh. I could do without this while I'm trying to work. "I've nearly finished it anyway."

He looks down at the book, the corner turned over on the page marked Chapter One, and raises an eyebrow. "Oh, go on. Or at least let me buy you another drink. Only I spent ages practising my chat-up line, and my mate Tommy over there, won't let me forget it if you send me packing straight away."

He points towards a bloke sitting four tables away. The mate is easy to spot, plump and casually dressed, in a sea of city-slicker suits. He raises his beer bottle to me.

I feel my resolve softening: a single girl sitting in a bar is probably fair game. It's not Demerara Eyes' fault that he's picked the one customer who's taken a vow of chastity. "The thing is, I'm waiting for someone . . ."

"And it's definitely not me you're waiting for?" he says, and though it's a corny line, he knows it. There's a note of wry amusement in his eyes which stops me cutting him dead.

"I'm accounted for, I'm afraid," I lie, and at that moment, I spot Sam sweeping in through the door in her black coat, like an oversized bottle-blonde bat. She strides up to Lee, plonks her huge briefcase on the bar counter, and just as he's about to launch into an air kiss, she grabs his hand and shakes it vigorously. His jaw drops so far I'm sure I can see his tonsils from here.

There is no way on this earth that it's going to work between them.

"Your friend's arrived, then?" Demerara Eyes nods towards Sam.

"No, no, not yet," I say, and as I turn back towards him, something occurs to me. Now I'm husband-hunting, perhaps I shouldn't be so hasty in rebuffing all male attention. This guy could be date material for my client; at least he's got balls. Though whether any man will have the balls to match Sam is debatable. "So maybe I will have that drink after all. Diet Coke, please."

"Coming up. I'm Adam, by the way," he says.

"Nice to meet you, Adam By-the-Way. I'm Becca. Incidentally, have you *really* read this entire book?"

He shrugs. "Maybe not *Crime and Punishment*. But I've got three series of *Law and Order* on DVD."

"Perfect." I glance over at Sam, who isn't letting poor Lee get a word in edgeways. I give it five minutes. "I know a girl who'd absolutely love to swap them for her *Rumpole of the Baileys*."

CHAPTER
EIGHT

At 6a.m. my phone rings, the illuminated display turning my bedroom gloomy blue: it reads SAM OTTOWAY CALLING.

Shit. I don't think I can cope with a savaging before dawn. I press IGNORE.

When she calls back twice in two minutes, I realise she's not giving up. I stayed for one more drink last night, long enough to acquire Adam's phone number (for Sam's sake, of course) and to ask him, *hypothetically*, to rate the different women in the bar. She came out as "scary but sexy", which was enough to reassure me that he could be a future date. I think he might appeal to her: he's no banker — in fact, we didn't get round to discussing what he does for a living, which is bloody unusual in the City, as usually a man is crowing about his salary within seconds — but he has that all-important sense of humour. And I think any man who dates Sam is going to need one of those.

As I left the bar, I saw that Sam had trapped Lee in the corner, her arm against the wall, and her briefcase blocking his other escape route. She was monologuing away like a Shakespearian hero.

I press ANSWER and brace myself.

"Not a bad start at all, bride hunter," she barks.

Now I'm awake. "Really?"

"Yep. In fact, I'd give him six."

"Out of six?"

"You've been watching too many episodes of Strictly Come Dancing. No, six out of ten. That's for technical excellence. And four for artistic impression."

"You went dancing?" I slap my cheek, wondering whether I'm actually still asleep and this is a bizarre stress dream.

Sam tuts. "Doh! No, I mean in the sack. He wasn't a bad fuck at all. Bit of a show-off, perhaps — I bet he's unbearable on a ski slope, look at me, look at me, all black runs and slaloms."

I lie back on the pillow. Oh God. What have I done?

"Rebecca? Are you still there?"

"Um . . . yes. So . . . well, obviously you hit it off. Did you swap numbers?"

"I already had his, didn't I, because *you* gave *it to me*? Have I woken you up or something? You're being particularly dense today."

"Well, it is early . . ." I'm about to object to her dawn call when I stop. I look up through the skylight at the charcoal sky, and remember my own commuter days, mornings when I was convinced I was the only person on the planet who could possibly be awake, only to arrive at the station to find the massed ranks of the bleary-eyed competing for space on the platform. There's no point playing for sympathy. "I was just about to get up."

"Ri-ight. You know, Rebecca, my years in court mean I always know when someone's lying. Do remember that. Anyway. Back to the matter in hand. I don't think I'll call him. Not now. I'm not sure I can respect him ever again."

I suddenly feel rather sorry for Lee. All that aftershave, all that virtuoso sex, and he's still tossed aside in the morning like yesterday's newspaper. Georgie would probably see Sam's attitude as proof that women are finally liberated, but I can't help thinking it's rather sad. "That's a shame."

"Not really. I'm sure there are plenty more where Lee came from. Which is why I'm calling. Can we put some dates in the diary, a Sunday, perhaps?"

As she launches into a breakdown of her availability — dictated by court commitments, rather than anything resembling a social life — I decide to tackle her. "I hope you don't mind me interrupting, Sam, but since we haven't been able to run through my usual detailed briefing . . . well, have you considered that perhaps *not* sleeping with Lee might have given you more of a chance to get to know him?"

I feel like a blushing vicar trying to counsel a slutty teenager. The last time I had a conversation like this was at a first meeting with a hedge fund manager whose sexual incontinence was getting in the way of finding Ms Right. He didn't take it terribly well and the last I heard he's still shagging his way round the Square Mile.

"Rebecca . . ." Just from the way she says my name, I know she's going to take no notice. "Much as I appreciate your homespun wisdom, I think that, in this day and age, romance takes second-place to realism. I couldn't spend my life with a man who doesn't measure up in *every* way, and since I doubt that you're willing to test-drive my dates in advance, I will make my own decisions in the bedroom department."

Oh, Georgie, what have you got me into? "Point taken, Sam."

"Good. Now, about that next date. I've had an idea. How about we schedule them back to back, like interviews? I would so hate to waste my precious weekends on just one man."

Tuesdays are my safety valve, and bloody hell, do I need one after my conversation with Sam.

I might have fled the countryside as fast as my legs could carry me, but I still seem to have a need for birdsong and the buzzing of dragonflies, so every Tuesday I hop on the bus towards Hampton Court Palace and get off at Bushy Park, a huge slice of wild green breathing space on the outside edge of London.

For five hours each week, from Easter till October, I ditch boasting City boys and executive matchmaking, in favour of rutting deer and pond-dipping. With a handful of other volunteers, I introduce townie kids to the wonders of nature. There's nothing unselfish about it — I have at least as much fun as they do, up to my ankles in mud or dung or both.

Today's group have been bussed in from their classroom right under the Heathrow Airport flight path,

86

and I'm assigned a dozen boys and girls who could tell a jumbo jet from an airbus blindfold, but who would struggle to tell a robin from a sparrow. After a quick safety briefing, we head out along the secret pathway only the school groups are allowed to use. The sun's on full-beam, and I'm sure I can feel the earth stirring through the thick soles of my wellies.

At first the kids are quiet, overwhelmed by the size of the park, and the lack of plane noise. "What can you hear?" I ask, as we walk along in a crocodile.

They nudge each other nervously, unsure of the answer. "Nuffink, miss, it's dead quiet," says one girl of eight or nine, dressed in loose white tunic and trousers, with a scarf covering her hair.

"What's your name?"

"Shefali, miss."

"Well, Shefali. Are you sure you can't hear anything? In fact, let's all stop for a minute. Close your eyes and listen really listen carefully. Is it *really* silent, or can you pick up any sounds from the millions of creatures who've made their home here in the park?"

They concentrate hard, even the parent who's come along to help — oh, I love it when I get a well-behaved group like this — and I do the same. The low growl of distant traffic is inescapable, you'd have to be much further into the country to avoid that, but the other sounds rise above it, as if ears can focus like eyes: the *tse-tse-tse* of a blue tit above us, the flapping of a hawk's wings, the soft crunch of moss under a walker's feet.

A tall, thin boy puts his hand up. "I can hear birds."

"What can you hear exactly?" I ask, and he mimics *see-see-see*.

"Well done, that's a blue tit, though all the tits sound the same." They giggle at the word tit. Bless. They're quite innocent, this lot, really. "But there are more sounds than that. Anyone else?" And gradually they identify five or six different calls. I've opened their ears, now I'll open their eyes. Dead things, crawly things and smelly things are all sure-fire hits with kids this age, so we start at the dead fox, a favourite spot since we noticed it when the tours began again a few weeks ago now.

"Look, but don't touch," I instruct them, as they gather round the skeleton, their mouths wide open in fascinated horror. "We don't know how he died, there are no signs of injury. Don't look sad. It's part of life of the park. See how his skull is beginning to show beneath the rotting fur? That powerful jaw that will certainly have snapped shut on his own prey often enough."

"Like what, miss?"

"Well, foxes will tuck into pretty much anything, but they like meat best, so they'll eat birds, rats or mice, a rabbit if they catch one. But they also leave the park for a nice takeaway, going through people's bin bags for bones or scraps."

Next I divide the group in two: one lot are tasked with moving a big piece of rotting wood, and examining the insect life skulking beneath. The others are on a poo trail, trying to spot as many different types of dropping as they can, so we can tell which animals have been where. I watch the children as they forget their shyness, focused on the miniaturised world under their feet, seeing it properly for the first time.

I'd never have guessed that helping out here would be so much fun — after a childhood on the receiving end of my two brothers' practical jokes involving cowpats, dead rodents and bluebottle eggs, I know exactly what kids are capable of. But the volunteering was another of my aunt's bright ideas. I spent so much time moping round the house after Marcus dumped me, sacked me, and made me homeless, that she press-ganged me into getting "some fresh air and a sense of proportion".

Of course, she was spot on. My broken heart, combined with five years dealing with egos so inflated they needed their own air traffic control system, had left me pretty jaded about human nature, and incapable of believing that fun was possible without a Gold card and a table at Umu on a Friday night. Out here, I remembered that despite my addiction to city life, sometimes it's good to get away. The park made me feel light-headed with happiness.

"Right. So who's found some good poo?" I ask, before realising that the kids aren't looking at the insects or the earth any more.

They're peering off to our right, to a clearing where two rabbits are . . .

"Miss, do rabbits always do it doggy style?"

So much for innocence.

★   ★   ★

Wednesday, and the sap is still definitely on the rise and not just in Bushy Park. The weather's even warmer than it was for the nature trail yesterday, and London's billion windows sparkle in the sunshine.

"Edward's going to know he's been set up," I tell Georgie as we walk around the corner towards the offices of Anemone International.

"Oh, Becky, so what if he does? He sounds too polite to turn me away. And what's so scary about a nice lunch anyhow?"

"Nothing. I just don't think we should pretend it isn't a put-up job as he's too smart for that. Let's explain why you're here, and offer him the option."

She shrugs her perfectly symmetrical shoulders. "All the same to me." Georgie has dressed for maximum impact today, a black ballerina wrap top emphasising her angular elegance, teamed with a black chiffon skirt which flutters as she floats along the street.

I go in first, and find Edward waiting for me in reception. He smiles nervously, and I suspect he's been gearing himself up to refuse my offer of dating help. But just as I'm preparing to admit defeat, my eyes are drawn to the tiny gap between his shoes and the hem of his trousers: odd socks. Not even one black and one brown, but one green and one sky blue. He needs help, poor guy, I'm amazed he's survived this long in the mean city.

"Now, Edward. I know you said you were going to think it over, but I've decided to strike while the iron is hot."

He looks bemused. As well he might.

90

I link arms with him, and the receptionist gawps. I need to escort him outside before the penny drops and he has a chance to run back upstairs. "You mustn't be cross with me, but I've brought someone along to join us for lunch. Do you think the restaurant will have room for a threesome?"

Edward's feet barely touch the pavement. I frog-march him towards Georgie — who smiles demurely as I introduce her, trying not to intimidate him right away — and then let him lead us to the restaurant he's chosen.

If I was expecting an expense-account-busting location, I'm disappointed. He takes us out of the City, towards Brick Lane, then down a side street, and an alleyway, towards an unmarked shopfront with the glamour of a seedy laundrette. The windows are covered with opaque film, which makes it all the more startling when we step inside and discover a dining room as flamboyant as a sultan's boudoir. It's like discovering Edward wears silk stockings beneath his Marks and Spencer no-crease pinstriped trousers. Another of London's fabulous surprises.

There are a dozen tables crammed into a space that I'd have guessed could hold no more than eight. Inlaid mahogany chairs jostle for room, occupied by men chattering away in Arabic, hunched over backgammon sets. There are a few soberly dressed city types looking incongruous against the frantic jewel-coloured room. In one corner, a fat old man is so attached to a hookah pipe that it seems to be part of his anatomy, like the caterpillar in *Alice in Wonderland*. Enormous lanterns with jade and emerald glass windows hang from the cracked ceiling, and the walls are covered with brass panels.

At the far end of the restaurant, a fairytale-prince of a waiter lolls against a counter, behind which a bearded chef is roasting lamb on a griddle.

The sights are dazzling enough. But the smells are even better . . . garlic, coriander and rosewater tickle my nose as we follow Edward to the last unoccupied table. The waiter, who has longer eyelashes than Bambi, hands us each enormous laminated menus, complete with vivid pictures of the dishes on offer.

"How did you find this place?"

"I love Lebanese food," he says, peeping over the menu. He doesn't even dare to look up at Georgie. "Not that anyone had ever heard of falafel in the village where I grew up. Maybe that's why I like it so much. I always go for the set starter: three hot or cold dishes, bread, hummus and juice. Five quid."

"Is this where you bring a girl when you want to show her a good time?" Georgie asks, twirling a strand of hair around her little finger.

"Um . . . um, no. I tend to come here alone." He disappears back behind the menu.

Georgie shoots me a conspiratorial look, and lets her hair uncoil. I know her strategies backwards: she begins with flirting and if that doesn't work . . .

"I've always had an interest in the Eastern bloc and I'm thinking of investing in the former Soviet

Republics, Edward. Kazakhstan, maybe, or Uzbekistan. Would that be wise?

. . . She asks advice. There are few things a man likes more than to be acknowledged as an expert.

"Ready?" The long-lashed waiter hovers, giving my aunt a lingering look, but Edward's eyes are firmly glued to the menu: if he has an opinion on the economic prospects of the Stans, he's not telling.

"Set menu, please. Cheese borek, fuls mesdames, halloumi cheese," Edward says. "With an orange and strawberry juice."

My aunt's face falls. "No booze?"

I groan. Edward says, "It's unlicensed. Religious reasons."

Georgie sighs. "In that case, I'm having a lamb kebab. You have to take your pleasures where you can," she says pointedly. The waiter smirks.

I order the same as Edward, and when the waiter leaves, I decide I ought to take control of the situation. If I can divert half a classful of nine-year-olds from mating rabbits, I can easily put my client at his ease.

"So, Edward . . ." I begin the sentence fully intending to quiz him about his hobbies. Then I remember he's already told me he doesn't have any. "Do you like the ballet? Only Georgia used to be a ballerina."

"Ballet's another thing we weren't really into back home," he mumbles.

"Neither were my family, to be honest," Georgie admits. "But I was a very determined eleven-year-old. I took the train to my audition, sorted out the paperwork, presented my parents with a fait accompli. And sore toes and a few homesick nights were a small price to pay for leaving behind small-town life. I grew up with countryside as far as the eye could see, but when I got to London, it was a revelation. I realised it was the only place where I didn't feel claustrophobic. I could be anything I wanted. I didn't have to explain myself to anyone."

Oh, but she's clever. For the first time, Edward really looks at her. "Yes. That's exactly how it feels."

The waiter brings our juices. "Let's toast the big, bad city," I suggest. "To London town, and all who escape to her."

We seem to bond after that: Georgie has correctly identified our common link. While I wouldn't say that it's turned Edward into a latter-day Noel Coward, he's relaxed enough to let some of that dry wit show through. And relaxed enough that when he goes to the toilet after finishing his lunch, my aunt claps her hands together in excitement.

"He's the best one in ages, Becky. Like a big northern grizzly bear, waiting to be tamed by Snow White, don't you think?"

"I think you're mixing up your fables, but I see what you're getting at."

The waiter brings us mint tea and a plate of tiny golden-brown pastries. She studies them. "Just one. Must watch my figure."

The waiter watches her figure, too, while I put one of the sticky cakes on my plate, and lick the honey off my fingers. "So what would be your strategy with Edward, then, Georgie?"

"The exterior we can sort in a jiffy, can't we? My barber friend in Chelsea will do his hair, then perhaps a light pluck of the eyebrows, and an afternoon with the personal shopper in Harvey Nicks. He'll soon be more Harrison Ford than Ford Cortina. But the main thing is getting him to believe he's attractive, and I think for that he needs quality time alone with me."

"Georgie, you wouldn't!"

"Of course I wouldn't," she says, licking the syrup off her fingers, "but just making him think I might could be enough to boost that undersized ego of his."

"So long as you know what you're doing," I say, spotting Edward emerging from the loo. "Quickly, before he gets back, what would you say I should be going for in terms of Partner Person Specification? I've got a theory, but you know how I like a second opinion."

Georgie pauses for far too long, as Edward weaves his way between the tables towards us. "I'm thinking bright, feisty old-school-trained nanny with a healthy appetite for all things sensual." She doesn't miss a beat as he sits down again. "Wouldn't you say that a healthy appetite is a sign of a person who likes to get the most out of life?"

"Err, I suppose so, yes," he says, rightly suspicious about any hidden agenda. He looks at his cheap Sekonda watch. "I ought to be heading back now, ladies."

"Oh, Edward," my aunt says, in full-on wheedling voice. "I'm only just getting to know you. And now that my niece has to leave for another appointment, I really wouldn't like to have to finish my mint tea alone. It's really rather intimidating and *masculine* in here, don't you think? I'm sure you're far too well brought up to desert a woman in her hour of need."

CHAPTER
NINE

"So how's the sex trade?"

The teasing starts before I even step over the threshold. The men in my life know my weaknesses, and are genetically programmed to exploit them. My baby brother Richie is the worst of the lot.

"The *love* business is ticking over very nicely, thank you," I tell him, as he lifts my weekend bag out of the Land Rover. And they wonder why I hate coming home.

Fatso the Incredible Jumping Dog gives me a warmer welcome, five stone of Collie launching himself into the air towards my neck, managing brief slobbery licks before gravity forces him back on to the ground. Mum appears in the doorway, covered in flour, a huge pottery bowl of dough wedged against her body. We bob above the top of the bowl to embrace.

"Good journey?" She steps back, looking me up and down as though I'm a new calf she's considering investing in. Mum's always wary of me, as she is of anything she doesn't fully understand. My brothers are as much a part of the farm as the two-hundred-year-old bricks and the battered Aga and the corrugated iron milking sheds. Whereas I think my mother's long suspected that I'm a changeling, swapped for her *real* daughter within hours of birth at Cheltenham Hospital. Not that there's any doubt when you see us side by side, as we are now. There's no escaping my mother's DNA. Cow's lick of chestnut hair? Check. Dimples in the cheeks? Check. *Generous* hourglass figure? Well, I'm still keeping that in check, but it wouldn't take many of my mother's toad-in-the-holes for me to cross the line from curvaceous to plump.

"Yep. Train was quiet. Horrible sandwich. Hey, Dad, you should approach the train caterers, see whether they'd take Double Orchard. It'd be so much nicer than that tasteless Cheddar they're using. I saved the wrapper."

"Good thinking, Rebecca." Dad wrestles off his boots before we troop into the house, the men stooping under the rain-warped doorframe. If only I could have inherited a little of my father's height. Instead, it's my brothers who got the tallness gene.

"So where's the next generation, then?"

My mother puts her finger to her lips. "Asleep, I think. Come on."

I follow her through the dark hallway and the kitchen, into the snug at the back. And there they are, sunlit like a renaissance painting of the Madonna and child. My first nephew, cuddled up next to his mum Janey, and my big brother, Robbie. All three are snoring softly.

"Awww."

My brother wakes first, rubbing his eyes, and smiling broadly when he sees it's me. Growing up, I couldn't understand why all my school friends regarded him as the best-looking boy in our village, but I see it now. It's partly the height, of course, and the dimples. If anything, my younger brother Richie is the more classically attractive, with David Beckham hair and come-to-bed eyes (though I know Richie farts monstrously in his sleep, so good luck to the poor girls he manages to tempt under his duvet). But where Robbie triumphs is the combination of farm-honed strength and gentleness, like a Young Farmers' version of that bloke who cradles the baby in the old Athena poster.

He disentangles himself carefully from his family, and creeps over, placing his muscly arm around my shoulders and squeezing hard, squashing me into his torso. He smells of the house: of wood smoke and ancient carpet and cheese, with an additional new whiff of Johnson's powder. "So what do you think of my son and heir, then, squirt?" He's trying to whisper, but Robbie's never been able to keep his voice down. Both Janey and the babe stir.

"He's gorgeous."

I'm relieved that I don't have to fib. My nephew is a beauty. With dappled red cheeks that match the faded sofa upholstery, and abundant soft hair the colour of the oak floor, he belongs here.

As I stare, his eyes pull open, slowly, and they're the blue of forget-me-nots. They lock into mine and even though I know that at fifty hours old, he can't focus on me properly, it feels like he knows me already.

Janey wakes too, and smiles shyly. Unbelievably she looks slim again already, sloughing off pregnancy as quickly and efficiently as she does everything else. Not many girls these days would relish moving in with the in-laws straight after marriage, but she and Mum are thick as thieves. I'd be envious of their relationship if this was the life I'd chosen to lead, but as it is, I'm happy that she's here.

"How are you?" I lean in to kiss her cheek, and then nuzzle the baby's head.

"Still a little bit in shock, but I'm OK. You know."

I don't, of course. Whatever I learned at college about infant cognitive development, I know nothing at all about the *world* of babies, that post-birth cocoon of chaos and love that she and my brother have been plunged into. I imagine my parents were exactly like this three decades ago, welcoming Robbie and Richie and me into their lives with that combination of common sense and instinct.

"He seems so content."

Robbie returns to the baby's side. "Oh, he's got all he needs: warmth, sleep and plenty to drink," he says, touching Janey's chest tenderly. He's rewarded with a slap.

They look so happy that I feel almost tearful, like you do when the guy gets the girl in a Hollywood movie. There's something rather wonderful about seeing my big, boisterous brother rendered soppy by seven pounds of longed-for flesh and blood.

100

"I think I'll leave you three to it," I say, before he spots my emotional state and spoils the perfect moment by winding me up for acting soppy.

It usually takes two hours back home for the claustrophobia to kick in. Today it's more like three, because the baby distracts me for a while.

After a home-cooked lunch of shepherd's pie and apple crumble, we sit round the table in the kitchen, carbs making us sleepy. Mum, Dad, Robbie, Janey, the baby, plus Richie and his latest teenage girlfriend, whose name I've already forgotten. Robbie insists on placing his son in my arms — though I notice that both Mum and Janey are on instant alert, in case he topples off my lap or suffers some other appalling accident courtesy of his clumsy auntie with her irresponsible London ways.

He feels heavy and moist in my arms. "So have you decided on the name?"

"It has to begin with R," my mother declares, even though having identical initials when we were kids caused no end of trouble with the post. More than once I opened Richie's "speciality" magazines, sent in brown paper from a shop in Amsterdam. Though if you're brought up on a farm, there's not much that surprises you, anatomically speaking.

"I want Ronaldo," Robbie says.

"Over my dead body," says Janey.

"But old-fashioned names are trendy now, aren't they, sis?" he says, as if my city-girl credentials make me the expert on all trends. "Like Henry and Harry and Freddy."

Janey nods. "But Ronaldo isn't traditional. It's a football name. And we're not having Ronald either, because of Ronald McDonald."

"Roger?" I suggest.

"Too posh. Whoever heard of a farmer called Roger?" Mum says. Posh is the ultimate insult, reserved for people like my aunt who've risen above their stations. I look at baby R: less than three days old, and already Mum has decided that he's following in his father's footsteps, his life mapped out for him . . .

"Radley's nice," says Richie's girlfriend. It's the first thing she's said all the time I've been here.

"Radley?" Dad says.

"Like the handbags," she says, then, sensing our disbelief, she returns to her crumble.

"Have you thought about doing that American thing?" I say. "Calling him Robert Junior? He could be Bob or Bobby then. Bobby's sweet."

They all stare at me, astonished I could make a sensible suggestion. Robbie nods. "Hey. That's a good plan, squirt. I like it."

There's a general murmur of assent. I decide that now is not the time to point out the further postal complications. Mum collects up the plates, and replaces the crumble dish with a huge slab of cheese. She opens the Aga to keep the last bit of crumble warm, for later: more than once, I've caught her asleep at midnight, a bowl of leftover pudding on her lap.

"This is a new variety," says Dad. "Robbie's been reading about this milk they're selling at a huge premium, taken from sleepy cows. Meant to be good for insomnia. So we've divided the cattle up, milking some of them when they've only just woken up, and we're taking it to the supermarkets as Dreamy Orchard, the bedtime snack cheese that won't give you nightmares."

"Lovely," I say, though after the lunch we've just had, I'll need no help at all getting off to sleep.

Mum drops a slab of it on my plate. "You know we've been tipped as favourites for the county show again?"

"Great." If there's one thing we Orchards are good at, it's cheese. I hope little Bobby junior is going to like the stuff, otherwise he's got a miserable childhood ahead of him. It's another black mark against my aunt: she hates it.

"And what about you, sis?" Richie says. "How are the mail-order brides?"

I take a deep breath. I should probably just accept that whatever I did for a living, he'd find something to mock, but somehow I can't help reverting to sulky middle sister mode whenever he starts. "They're fine."

His girlfriend stops mid-munch. "Mail-order brides?"

"Oh, didn't I tell you? My big sister sets up filthy rich blokes with nubile young ladies."

My mother looks at the baby and shakes her head, as if we're in danger of corrupting him by discussing such seedy matters in his presence. "Only in London," she says, as if this explains everything.

103

"It's not as bad as they're making it sound," I say. "I'm a matchmaker, really. Millions of people live in London, most of them work long hours, and they just need a bit of help to find the right person. I provide that help."

"For a massive fee," Richie chips in.

"Well, when you start giving away cheese, little brother, then you'll be able to criticise. I'm offering a service, not running a charity."

"People will pay for anything in London, Wendy," he continues. "People go and do your shopping for you. Even walk your dogs."

Wendy the girlfriend *and* Fatso gawp at me. Dad cuts his cheese into small cubes and pushes them around the plate.

"Come on. Aren't you lot ever going to get bored with this? I don't see the difference between what I do and, I don't know, Pete up the road running his bloody stud farm. I'm just giving Mother Nature a helping hand."

"I've had to accept it, though I'll never understand it, Wendy," Mum says conspiratorially. "All those pubs and bars in London, thousands of places to meet, and yet that's not good enough for Rebecca's *clients*. Too hoity-toity to do their own dirty work. I don't mind admitting that sometimes I wonder whether it's all above board, whether in fact —"

"Oh, here we go," I say. "Mum, I've shown you the bloody wedding photographs. My clients are respectable. They've been in *Hello!* magazine. I even took

104

Richie along to one of the weddings as my guest. How much more above board can it be?"

"No need to shout!" she says, holding her finger to her lips. "You'll wake the baby if you're not careful."

That's it. I stand up. "Don't worry, I'll wait till I'm a long way off before I say what I *really* think. No one will hear a thing!"

It takes me ten minutes of stomping around the meadow to calm down. It used to work when I was fifteen, and it still works today.

The tortoiseshell butterflies ignore my hissy fit, and after a while I feel a bit silly, so I inspect the grass for cowpats, and lie down amongst the daisies and dandelions, drinking in the fresh scent. I feel soothed as I close my eyes . . .

"You know Mum doesn't really mean it, don't you, squirt?"

I don't know whether I've dozed off for a few minutes or for an hour, but Robbie is now lying next to me. The sky is the colour of Bobby Junior's eyes, and the post-lunch lull has turned me mellow. "Doesn't she?"

"She'd just rather you were doing something steadier."

"Oh, I know. *All that studying, and look where you've ended up. Lodging in your aunt's loft, without a penny to your name.*"

He chuckles. "Well, she's got a point, hasn't she?"

"Oh, listen to Mr Grown-up. We can't all live our lives like we're in an episode of *The Waltons*, Robbie."

105

"The funny thing is, I don't think she'd have minded so much if it'd been one of us boys who'd gone to the city. No. Actually, she'd have been just as mad if I'd gone. Only Richie would have got away with being the prodigal son."

I stretch my arms and legs out to my side, the way we used to when we were little and made snow angels in winter. "I didn't become the prodigal daughter on purpose. But I'd never have been happy staying here."

"And are you happy now?"

I think it over. "Yeah. Course I am. I mean, there are things I'd like to change in my life, maybe, but isn't that how everyone feels?"

"I don't."

"Smug git! Anyway that's the oxytocin talking."

"What's that when it's at home?"

"It's the loved-up hormone that Mother Nature gives new parents to make up for the stinking nappies and sleepless nights."

He rolls over to face me. "I'm feeling pretty loved-up, that's true enough. A kid, eh, squirt? Doesn't seem yesterday that we were kids ourselves."

"You and Richie always used to say you'd never grow up. As if you could cheat time and stay nine years old for ever."

"Yeah, and you couldn't bloody wait, could you?"

"Anything to get away from here." I sit up and look across at the farmhouse, with its satellite barns and milking shed, and the lush folds of Gloucestershire countryside beyond: it could be an illustration from a child's story book. One field is luminous with yellow rape: another is dotted with fat ewes and their new lambs, springing up and down as though they're on invisible trampolines. "God, Robbie, I hated it so much sometimes."

"Not any more though?"

"No . . . it's gorgeous. But it still makes me feel restless. Remember when we used to get fidgety at Sunday school, and it was torture having to sit still? It's like that, for me, being here." I pick a daisy, make a tiny slit with my thumbnail, and begin to make a chain.

He laughs again. "You know what's funny? Richie and me were the ones who wanted to be kids for ever, but you're the only one who's managed it. Flitting round London like a butterfly, playing Cupid, no responsibilities, no one to answer to."

"Like Georgie."

Robbie grins. "*Exactly* like Georgie. You're going to be such a fun auntie to Bobby." He smiles at the new name, as he tries it out for size.

"It's history repeating itself, isn't it? First Georgie, now me, the irresponsible aunts seeking our fortunes in the big, bad city. But we won't end up falling out, will we, Robbie, like Mum and Georgie did?"

"Not unless you take my baby to a crack den. Anyway, I'm not jealous of you. Whereas Mum has always been jealous of Georgie."

I shift in the grass, looking for more daisies. "I don't think it's that simple. It's not like Mum would want what Georgie's got. Or hasn't got. Mum's like a pig in clover now you've provided the first grandchild."

"Do you ever want kids, squirt?"

The image of Janey, Robbie and the baby together, snoozing in the sunny snug, flashes into my mind. It makes me feel wistful. But apart from anything else, I'd have to be in love to have a child, and I have no plans to go *there* again.

And then I think of Sam Ottoway. She's been happy enough on her own for years, so this sudden craving for a husband must be related to her biological clock. Maybe I should try to be more understanding: why shouldn't she be entitled to this experience that's made my big brother glow like a bonfire? I know! What about that cheeky Adam chap I met in the pub? He reminds me of Robbie, in a way.

I pretend to focus on my daisy chain. "What do men *really* want in a woman, Robbie?"

"Ooooh . . . Let me think. Sex drive like Abi Titmuss, Jordan's boobs. And a whispery, husky voice so you can't hear her nag."

"Oh yeah. That's why you chose Janey the human foghorn."

He looks at me. "That was a serious question, was it? I'd have thought you'd be the expert on what men wanted."

"Not really. I know what my *clients* want, on paper. But say I've got three possibilities, all nice girls, ticking all the boxes, I still don't know what makes one of them right and the other two wrong. I mean, say a woman wanted to make herself more attractive. What's the key?"

Robbie puts his head on one side, the way Fatso does when he's concentrating. "Got to be partly about

108

chemistry, squirt, hasn't it? And kindness, and contentment with themselves. I mean, I like to feel needed, but you don't want there to be this big needy gap there; no emptiness, nothing unresolved. You definitely want to be icing on their cake. Not the filling."

I wink at him. "You like women who don't need filling, bruv?"

"You have a filthy mind, Rebecca Orchard. That's the city that's done that. And you'll never find a man with a mind like a sewer."

I groan. "It's not for *me*, dumbo. It's just out of interest." I coil my daisy chain around my wrist, two, three, four times.

"Oh, yeah, right. That's why you came to your big brother for advice? Out of interest?" He pushes himself up, towering over me. "Well, much as I'd like to carry on this conversation, I have a baby I haven't cuddled for at least, what, ten minutes."

"All right. See you later."

"But not before I've chased you round the milk shed." And he grabs my shoe and runs back towards the farmhouse. "If you don't come after me, this is ending up in the silage."

I jump to my feet and tear after him, my other shoe in my hand. "Come back here, Robbie! Come back, you moron! You'll never be a grown-up! Never!"

CHAPTER
TEN

Covent Garden on a Sunday afternoon is a good place to find organic raw coffee beans, or vegetarian shoes. Husbands are harder to spot. But for window-shopping all sizes, shapes and nationalities of men, it's unbeatable.

"Now I appreciate you wanted to get stuck in straight away, Sam, but I can't underestimate how important it is for me to get a full picture of what you find attractive in a partner, and what's a total no-no."

Sam pouts. "I was expecting to meet some more candidates."

Which is presumably why she's made such an effort with her appearance. She does look . . . startling would be the best word. I haven't seen her in off-duty clothes before, but I can tell that I'm going to have to broach the subject of what constitutes leisure-wear. Can't wait to see how she responds to that.

It's not that there's anything wrong with stone-washed jeans and back-combed hair *in themselves*. It's just that they're more appropriate for a retro-80s club night than a laid-back brunch in the twenty-first century. I've seen even more tragic outfits before, of course, except it's usually men who're so busy building

110

their careers that their wardrobes fail to evolve from what was fashionable when they were studying for their finals and bopping along to Take That!

"Well, you never know, we might meet some candidates today," I assure her, though the only people who'll fancy her in that get-up are short-sighted transsexuals who think they've spotted one of their own kind.

"BECCA! Cooo-eeee!"

"Please tell me that's a coincidence," Sam says, scowling at the vision in a soft-grey pantsuit who is heading in our direction.

"No. That's Helga."

She bounces towards us, past a tableful of South American women who've come to this Brazilian café for Sunday coffee and custard tarts. They gawp. So does Sam. Gawping is unavoidable when Helga is around.

"Hey, how've you been, babe?" Helga says, smothering me in her bountiful chest: she's almost six foot tall.

"I'm great. Helga, can I introduce you to Sam?"

I've already briefed Helga on what to expect. I even asked her to try to *tone it down*, which she has. A little. But the grey velour can't disguise the sheer generosity of her fantastic body, the curves that leave men speechless. She's no skinny size zero, but that never seems to matter when we go out together: my best friend is a man magnet, and that's precisely why I've asked her along. If you want to view the full spectrum of masculinity at close quarters, you need a honey-trap.

"Hey, Sam. Top fucking jeans. Love 'em! Did you get them from a vintage shop?" she asks, with genuine interest. There's no side to Helga. Her personality reflects her heritage: abundant Swedish sensuality from her mother's side, and salt-of-the-earth Scouse frankness from her Everton footballer dad. She's a one-off, which is probably just as well.

"I don't buy second-hand."

"Oh, right. So you kept them for when they were back in fashion? God, I'd love to keep all my clothes, just in case, like. You must have bloody big wardrobes."

Sam frowns, unsure whether to take this as an insult or a compliment.

"So, seen anything that takes your fancy, then, babe? Great view."

I chose this café and this table because it's like a ringside seat for the circus that is central London. Hundreds of people parade past every minute: the steps opposite are where boyfriends arrange to meet their girlfriends, or where the single and hopeful like to dawdle, pretending to text or fiddling with their iPods while they surreptitiously eye up the talent.

"They're all rather young." Sam sniffs.

"Hey, you're hardly a dinosaur yourself, are you? I like 'em young, me. There was this one bloke —"

"Actually, Sam, that's a good starting point for your Partner Person Specification," I chip in, before Helga launches into one of her mucky stories. "What would be your upper and lower limits in terms of the age of potential partners?"

112

Sam considers this carefully. "Ideally, thirty-nine-and-a-half to forty-one. I'd like him to be a shade older than me, but not too much. It may sound clinical but I want there to be a reasonable chance that his DNA hasn't deteriorated. Given that children are at the top of my to do list."

It's Helga's turn to gawp. "Fuck me, I thought I was demanding, but you're hard core, aren't you, babe? Still, good to know exactly what you want."

I ignore her. "So, no flexibility on that, Sam? You know, it's best to be as open-minded as possible. That's what I always advise my male clients."

She frowns. "Thirty-five would be the youngest I could face, up to ... well, I might go as high as forty-five, provided they've looked after themselves."

I nod. "All right. Now let's look at what I call the Marmite Factors."

"*What?*" Sam couldn't pour more contempt into a single word.

"Do you love Marmite, or hate it?"

She sighs. "I can't *bear* the stuff."

"And that's something no one could change your mind about?"

"Don't be ridiculous. Not unless my taste buds were wiped out overnight in some terrible accident."

I nod. "Well, that's the kind of thing I need to find out about your taste in men: what's non-negotiable? Tattoos? A love of country music? A season ticket for Liverpool Football Club?"

"That'd be *my* Marmite factor," Helga chips in, "me dad'd kill me if I went near a man who loved the Reds."

Sam closes her eyes, and the hard lines on her face soften: beyond all the bravado and the bullshit, she really wants this. For a control freak like her, handing over responsibility for the one thing that would make her life complete must be a last resort. "I wouldn't exactly go out of my way to find a man with tattoos, but I suppose if they were tasteful, that'd be all right. The country music would be tolerable, because I could buy him cordless headphones. As for the football, well, I work a lot at weekends so it wouldn't bother me if he went to matches while I was preparing cases."

"Is there anything you wouldn't consider, under any circumstances? Physically, mentally, professionally?"

She ponders this. On the other side of the glass, old-aged tourists walk arm-in-arm. Teenage language students with love as their common language speak ungrammatical English to each other. People stride, or saunter, or race towards their destinies. Maybe one of those blurred faces in the crowd could be Sam's perfect match. Or Helga's. Or even mine.

Stop it, you daft girl. You don't need a man. You've got enough love in your life, from Georgia, to your big soft brothers, to little baby Bobby. Your mission is to bring love to the people who're in greater need, like Dwight and Edward and Sam.

"Oh!" says Sam. "I've thought of a Marmite factor. I could never, ever go out with a Liberal Democrat."

After answering my questions on family experiences ("Growing up an Ottoway meant never, ever being prepared to lose an argument or a game of *Scrabble!*"),

114

money ("separate bank accounts, of course, I'm not justifying my spending to anyone.") and holidays ("I love hideaway beaches, but couldn't bear to be utterly cut off. No one comes between me and my Blackberry."), Sam's getting restless. So we grab takeaway iced coffees, and take to the streets.

"What do you think of blondie over there?" Helga asks, nodding towards a Scandinavian-looking man who could be her twin brother.

"I prefer my men dark and dignified," Sam says, her eyes following a tall, muscular Somali . . . followed by his equally gorgeous wife and toddler. "Oh. Ah well."

We walk down Neal Street, past smoothie bars and boutiques and a branch of Lee Laker's mobile-phone empire. I raise my eyebrows at Sam. "I hope you don't mind me asking — ignore Helga, she's a woman of the world, and the soul of discretion — but do you have any regrets about sleeping with Lee so quickly?"

Sam looks taken aback. "Shit. I don't know. Why, Rebecca, do you think I should have regrets?" Beneath her casual tone, she sounds defensive.

I stop, pretending to peer into a shoe-shop window, rather than meeting her eye. Helga takes the hint and looks away, ogling a young guy with Lennon glasses. "If you were one of my male clients, I'd warn you not to confuse lust with love, but I feel like I'm on shakier ground with you, Sam."

She laughs. "Well, I definitely wasn't under any illusions about being in love with Lee." Then the laugh stops abruptly and her face slackens, all the mirth gone in a split second. "Do you know what's worse? I don't think I was even in lust. I slept with him because he was there. Like mountaineers and summits." She attempts another laugh but it sounds hollow.

The sun's emerged from behind the fluffy clouds, and the hard light is unforgiving. Sam looks knackered and even . . . well, it seems bizarre to say this about the most assertive person I have ever met, but Sam Ottoway, QC, looks awfully vulnerable. I want to tell her what I really think: that she sleeps with men on first dates because she's lonely, because she wants to be in control. And because, deep down, she doesn't believe they'll hang around a moment longer than necessary if she doesn't — what do teenage boys say? — *put out.*

But I don't say any of that. I'm a matchmaker, not a proper psychologist. I have no more right to tell this high-achieving pillar of the legal establishment that she's insecure, than she has to tell me that I'm pathetic to be hung up about my ex.

Instead, I do what I always do in a tricky situation, and take refuge in a touch of Georgie wisdom. "My aunt would say that there's nothing wrong with a woman treating men as sex objects for a change."

Helga catches up now. "All humans are sex objects, really. Becca here seems to believe that it's all about hearts and flowers, but the truth is more basic. It's about tits and ass. Every time."

I look at Helga, then back at Sam: how come my best friend's . . . um . . . physicality seems entirely healthy, while my client's behaviour makes me nervous? Maybe it's the age difference. I still believe that Helga — the one person among my mates who has consistently refused to let me attempt to matchmake her — will grow out of treating the opposite sex like a piece of multi-purpose gym equipment. And in the meantime, at least she's having a lot more fun than she would with a medicine ball.

I tut, pretending to be annoyed. "Helg, just because I believe in love, doesn't mean I inhabit some ridiculous rose-tinted world of romance."

"I know *that*, Becca. The Pope's seen more action than you lately."

Sam gives me a quizzical look and opens her mouth to cross-examine me. That's all I need: a bloody barrister on my case. "We're not here to discuss my love life. We're here to facilitate Sam's. And as I invited you, Helga, because you're the best *facilitator* I know, can I suggest we cut the chat and get down to business?"

Helga winks. In the world she inhabits, Covent Garden is the totty equivalent of a sushi bar, with such a stream of tasty morsels going by that she doesn't quite know where to begin. "Sure, babe. At your service, Sam. Give me the nod, whoever you like, and I'll reel the fuckers in. Up to you to decide which should be dish of the day."

And as Sam begins to scan the crowds with an intensity I haven't seen since Fatso the dog mounted a raid on the Orchard summer barbecue, I wonder whether uniting the two man-hungriest women I know was the smartest move I've ever made.

CHAPTER
ELEVEN

Dwight MacKenzie stands before me a changed man. The slight stoop he used to have, that cuckolded posture no £150 an hour Pilates sessions could eliminate, has disappeared. His lack of height no longer seems a disadvantage: instead he's sturdy and grounded, like a gladiator. The biggest difference is in his face: the wariness has gone from his eyes. He looks like a man who wouldn't be able to wipe the smile off his face, even if you offered him a million pounds.

"Wow, you look well," I say, holding out my hand for his usual stiff greeting. Instead he embraces me as heartily as a footballer who's just scored a goal. This goes on rather a while, as he pats my back vigorously: over his shoulder I take in the view of the glass-and-crane London skyline, presided over by the glitzy Gherkin building, and in the distance, the timeless perfection of St Pauls' dome.

"That's what the right woman does for the right man," he says, finally letting go.

I take a seat as his gamine secretary brings in coffee exactly as I like it, my previous choices no doubt stored on a top-secret database cataloguing the beverage preferences of the entire *Sunday Times Rich List*. "So how is lucky Heather?"

He frowns at me. "This is a serious business, Rebecca. I don't want to hear you talking about her like it's some kinda joke."

"Sorry, Dwight. I'm just happy to see you so happy. It's infectious."

He considers this for a while, then nods. "Sure. Sure. You know, Heather has that very *British* sense of humour, too. Kinda dry. Sometimes it takes me a while to figure that out. The other day, we were at this whisky bar up in Marylebone —" he still pronounces every syllable, Mar-y-lee-bone, rather than the throwaway Marrlebun used by true Londoners — "and got talking to the barman, and he said something about Glasgow kisses and she said . . ."

As he repeats, word for word, a conversation that really doesn't sound at all funny second-hand, I study him more closely. He has that sparkle that makes my job worthwhile. When men fall, they fall one hundred per cent. A girl can be head-over-heels, but still fret about her dimpled knees, or convince herself that it's only a matter of time before the love of her life finds someone prettier.

Men aren't like that. Even men like Dwight — taken for a cool £20 million by his pole-dancing ex — gambol like baby fawns when Ms Right finally shows. *If* Heather is Ms Right, of course. With my client's common sense taking a vacation in Hormone County, I have to be the voice of reason . . . much as I'd like to revel in another Bride Hunter success story, my work here is not yet done.

Dwight's stopped talking and is clearly waiting for me to agree that Heather's so hilarious that she should have her own TV show. "She sounds tremendous fun, Dwight, I'm thrilled for you. Now, I take it you want to come off the books, for the moment? You know that you can give me a call any time in the next few months if ... well, if circumstances change and you'd like me to resume the search."

He laughs loudly, then reaches into his desk drawer. He pulls out two crystal flutes, and a half-bottle of champagne. "Always the realist, huh, Rebecca? But you know, that won't be necessary. I've spent too long relying on my head." He taps it, as if it's an errant child. "And, OK, maybe on my dick too." Thankfully he doesn't tap that. "But this time it's different. This time I feel it here. In my *gut*."

"Right-o," I say, feeling a slight queasiness in my own gut as he unwraps the foil from around the champagne cork.

He eases the cork from the bottle with intense concentration before it pops and the bubbly tumbles into the glasses.

"Rebecca, congratulations. You've just earned your commission ... but there's one last thing I'd like you to do for me."

I hold on to my glass before we make the toast. "What's that, Dwight?"

"I want you to help me plan the marriage proposal that every girl dreams of. The proposal no girl could ever turn down."

Six dinners, three lunches, one trip to the opera, and two weekend breaks (total estimated cost of £6,000, excluding my fee). Is that really enough time together to know you want to be with someone for life?

A middle-aged woman on the other side of the Tube carriage wipes mascara from her cheeks as she reads the last page of a novel: I don't recognise the language, something Eastern European, but the picture on the front leaves me in no doubt that it's a romance. A handsome man embraces a pretty girl, their mouths frozen a few tantalising millimetres from each other. She closes the book with such a loud sigh of satisfaction that it almost seems indecent to be nearby.

Will Dwight and Heather be a Happy Ever After — or my first serious mistake? It's all Georgie's fault. I'm sure if she hadn't put the wind up me the morning after I first met Heather, about the girl being too perfect, I'd be buying a hat for the bloody wedding instead of worrying.

In my fellow passenger's romantic world, I'm sure that the three and a half weeks my lovebirds have shared are plenty. It's not the length of time, but the quality of the time, that matters. That's why spending five tempestuous years with Marcus made us no more or less compatible than we were after five days. Or why my parents knew deep down that they'd grow old together even before my under-aged mother had taken

121

the first puff of their illicit shared cigarette round the back of the Neck of Lamb's New Years' Eve 1975 Glamourama discotheque.

The mascara lady gets off at Baker Street, her tears replaced by a rosy glow of contentment. My stop is Marylebone. This afternoon I am taking tea at the Landmark Hotel with Edward and a girl named Eleanor Bullock.

Well, of course, I won't be at the same table. I've recced the place, and there's a handy spot behind the piano and a huge parlour palm where I should be invisible to both parties. Just in case, though, I've put my hair up in a bun, am wearing a pair of huge mirrored sunglasses and a 1940s print dress from the Oxfam shop. On my aunt it would look charmingly vintage. I look like a well-preserved fifty-year-old.

I hope it'll be worth it. Eleanor Bullock is the sweetest and prettiest of three nannies I've discovered in the course of my research. The daughter of one of Georgie's friends from some art gallery or other, Eleanor is a trained Norland Nanny and as in demand, in her field, as Edward is in his. Whenever she leaves one role (perhaps when her latest charges are off to boarding school, or emigrating to Dubai or Macao or somewhere else she doesn't fancy living), mothers line up to display their offspring, their luxurious nanny flats and their villas in Portugal or the Côte d'Azur, in the hope that they might secure her services.

Currently, her "family" consists of three German boys under ten, who live with their widowed banker father in an enormous Victorian villa in Westbourne

Park. When I heard this, I was worried that it sounded rather *Sound of Music*, but then we met to discuss my mission to marry off Edward, and she explained that her employer couldn't be less Captain von Trapp if he tried. An earnest and honourable Hamburger, he's already dating the best friend that his late wife took the trouble to line up, while Eleanor is busy preparing Wolfgang, Walter and Wilhelm for life with the woman destined to become their new mummy.

"I never cross the line, Rebecca," she told me firmly. "I am enormously fond of the children, of course, but if I ever hear a nanny say she *loves them as if they were her own*, then it sets the alarm bells ringing."

Eleanor ticks all the boxes. She's very pretty, but in a non-threatening way: hazel eyes, brown hair that will bleach slightly in the sun, a trim but not skinny figure. Psychologists say that real beauty is all about symmetrical features — dull but true — and I'd say Eleanor has evenness in spades, from her sweet face, to her even-tempered nature. Within seconds of meeting her, everything felt ordered, as though the worst that the world could throw at me would be having to eat the crusts on my sandwiches (and even that would make me grow big and strong). I was slightly disappointed that she didn't wear the distinctive sandy-brown Norland uniform, but her navy dress, with matching shoes and tights, was just as composed.

Before our meeting, I hadn't been sure whether to explain the full scope of my *service*, or the circumstances which had brought me to Edward. But the practicalities of keeping both of them in the dark about my dastardly plot were beyond me, and I realised immediately that Eleanor has an admirably forthright nature. She absorbed the details of my business without a flicker of surprise, her neatly manicured hands folded in her lap. Then she nodded.

"Your work sounds fascinating. And old-fashioned in the best possible way," she said. "I don't believe in being traditional for the sake of it — I disapprove utterly of smacking, for example. But I also don't believe in throwing out the baby with the bathwater — well, I suppose that would have me removed from the Norland register, apart from anything else! Matchmaking is one of the most under-valued of personal services."

I felt myself beaming under her approving gaze. If anyone could persuade my mother that what I do is not only respectable, but even a force for good, it would be Eleanor.

Talking Edward into the date was harder, of course. His encounter with Georgie had definitely boosted his confidence, but I could see his coincidence antennae quivering when I mentioned that I happened to know this girl who was having terrible trouble meeting a *genuinely* nice bloke, among all the show-off wide boys. It was only when Perry "accidentally" overheard us, and began listing the reasons why Edward really ought to get out there and find himself a woman, that he relented, and then only to stop the lecturing.

All this subterfuge, underhand dealings and secrecy would have me running for the hills if it wasn't for one thing: I genuinely believe that finding lovely Edward his perfect partner would transform his life.

I step into the hotel, and even though I've been here before, the interior makes me catch my breath. With eight storeys of air and light, topped by a huge glass roof, it feels as though the space should be filled with something equally spectacular: dinosaur bones, perhaps, or spitfires suspended from the ceiling in a perpetual dogfight, while guests sip lapsang souchong.

A waiter checks my reservation and escorts me to my table. It feels strange to be having tea alone, but while I can blend into the background without too much trouble, my aunt cannot so there was no way she could come. Tea at the Landmark is taken in what they call the Winter Garden, though it's more like a tropical forest of enormous ferns and lush palms, with a canopy of perfect English blue sky above us, thin panes of glass shielding us from spring showers and breezes.

"Madam." The waiter is barely out of his teens, and seems to have adopted a funereal manner to compensate for his youth. He offers me the menu and I'm tempted by the champagne tea even though (or perhaps, because) my drink with Dwight has already left me pleasantly giddy. I look towards the door at the exact moment that Edward enters, and dip behind the menu, peeping over the top so only my bun and the top of my sunglasses are visible.

"The champagne tea, please. With Earl Grey. Oh, and no salmon sandwiches, just the ham and the cucumber."

I watch Edward as he disposes of his jacket, then follows a waitress to the best table in the place. He looks nervous — he's obviously taken note of Georgie's advice about his poor posture, because he's over-compensating, as rigid as a rookie soldier on the parade ground. At least he's smarter than usual, and from this distance, I think his socks match, though there's no sign that he's had that long overdue haircut. *Eleanor won't be able to see your eyes*, I want to shout, *and your lovely blue eyes are your best feature.*

He stops in his tracks, and for a horrible moment I'm convinced he's spotted me. But then I realise: he's noticed the atrium for the first time. His eyes widen, his jaw drops, and the stiffness disappears as he takes in the view. It's so sweet: Edward is still capable of being awed. I only hope his date has the same effect.

As Edward takes his seat, the waiter returns to my table with a porcelain cake stand bearing three tiers of goodies. Perfect sandwiches at the top, cut into slim dominoes. In the middle, two tiny tartlets, one with apricot slices and one with strawberries, both glistening under layers of amber glaze. And a chocolate brownie. Finally, at the bottom, a fruit scone and a plain one, still warm from the oven. The sombre waiter adds dishes of jam and clotted cream, a white china teapot and matching cup. Finally he presents a tall champagne glass with an embarrassed flourish, as though he's mortified by having to fulfil my baser needs at this time in the afternoon.

The paraphernalia of tea provide the perfect camouflage for my observations. I can stare straight at

Edward from behind my cake stand and he doesn't suspect a thing. He's currently consulting a sheet of A4 that I'm pretty sure is a print-out of my suggested topics of conversation. The history of the hotel, for example: built at the tail end of the glory days of the railway, by the same man who tried to create a British Eiffel Tower. And then left out in the cold when the station it was built to service failed to grow to the dizzy heights of St Pancras or Paddington.

Oh God. I hope he doesn't take this as a cue to bore her rigid about trains.

In the time it takes me to pour my tea — the black fragments left behind in the pewter strainer — and add a drop of milk, Eleanor has arrived. Bugger. I wouldn't make much of a spy, missing something so important. I'll never know his first reaction: was it a flicker of animal attraction or a sinking of the brow to accompany a sinking feeling inside? Right now he's waiting for her to sit down, standing awkwardly while she drapes her coat and scarf on a chair, and arranges her skirt (an old-fashioned embroidered peasant affair, worn with a white blouse) into the best position to avoid creasing before making contact with the seat.

I'll admit that you can learn a lot from body language, but right now I really wish I had supersonic hearing, because this date will succeed or fail on the small talk. I can hardly quiz Edward afterwards in the kind of minute detail I usually would, or he might smell a rat.

I sip my tea, enjoying the freedom my sunglasses give me to stare right at them. Edward points to something on the menu. Eleanor smiles. Edward points up at the glass roof, Eleanor nods enthusiastically. They order from the waitress, then Eleanor leans across the table and whispers something. Edward blushes to his roots.

"Everything satisfactory, madam?" The waiter gives me a slightly odd look, as though he's sussed out my dastardly espionage.

"Perfect, thank you." To show willing, I take a bite of a cucumber sandwich and summer explodes on my tongue. "Delicious."

I pull *Crime and Punishment* out of my handbag, and leaf through it, remembering the last time I *pretended* to read it, in All Bar One. I really do need to call that guy who chatted me up: in fact, sorting out all Sam's suitors is next on my to-do list. Georgie and I collected loads of numbers during our Richmond manhunt, and Sunday afternoon with Sam gave me a clearer idea about her taste. I don't hold out much hope of meeting all her expectations, but I've got to try. She's already sent me half a dozen angry emails asking for progress reports.

Parlour tunes trickle towards me from the piano. Now this *is* civilised. I spread a scone with dense custard-yellow cream. I take a bite, eyes closed in Cornish cholesterol heaven, before chancing a glance at my lovebirds.

To my horror, Eleanor is standing up, wrapping her plaid scarf around her neck — and around *and* around until I worry she's going to throttle herself. Whatever Edward has said or done, he's achieved the near-impossible: the unflappable Ms Bullock has

128

flipped. He walks round the table to her and attempts to help her on with her coat, but she shrugs him off, before walking to the exit. Only the too-brisk steps give away her irritation.

Edward sits down again, all postural advice forgotten, both elbows on the table (thank goodness Eleanor hasn't looked back at him as she heads out of the door), shoulders slumped. I'm longing to go over and find out what's wrong, to tell him it'll be OK, that there are plenty more fish in the sea. But of course, I can't move.

The cake stand sits in the centre of his table, its delicacies untouched. Somehow that seems the saddest thing of all.

CHAPTER
TWELVE

My phone rings within minutes of Eleanor's exit: the "Love is In the Air" melody reverberates around the Winter Garden, and I have to race for the ladies. Edward, now holding his head in his hands, doesn't even look up as I rush past.

"Oh golly, Rebecca. I am beside myself with embarrassment. I've never stormed out of anywhere in my life!"

In her panic, Eleanor's voice — already upper-class shrill — would shatter glass. What on earth could Edward have done? Confessed to a desire to be flogged while wearing a nanny's uniform? Offered her a line of cocaine?

"Take deep breaths, Eleanor, that's it. Calm down and then you can tell me all about it. I'm *sure* no one noticed anything untoward."

I sit down in one of the pink floral armchairs — thank God for posh hotel cloakrooms — as her hyperventilation subsides.

"Right. Righto, let me think. The thing is, it began so well. He's rather dapper, isn't he? I mean, needs smartening up, but boys aren't always good at being well turned out, unless they've been in the Army."

Her voice drifts off into reverie. Of course! I realise that the perfect man for Eleanor isn't a shy banker. It'd be a member of the Household Division, one of the chaps outside Buckingham Palace, in a red tunic and a bearskin hat worthy of the Hair Bear Bunch. Eleanor and her sentry could have shoe-shining competitions, and everything from the nursery to the garden shed would be shipshape at all times.

"So what went wrong, Eleanor? I feel awful for having introduced you if his behaviour was unacceptable."

"Um . . . well . . . um. It was so strange. One moment he was telling me about the history of the hotel, and the architects who transformed the old courtyard into the glazed lobby . . ."

So far, on message. "And the next?"

"I mentioned what I do for a living, and some of the families I've worked for. People like him, you know, bankers and analysts and lawyers. Before my current family there was this chap from Yorkshire, lovely man. Adorable wife and the sweetest girl and boy. Well, they were sweet when I'd finished with them. We spent a glorious summer in Grand Cayman, I mean, obviously me and the kids were in a different villa, but it was almost like a holiday . . . Anyway, I don't know what I said because Edward threw his toys out of the pram. Telling me how he thought people shouldn't have children if they weren't going to look after them. How nannies and boarding schools created monsters. He really was getting quite carried away."

"How bizarre." I remember what Edward told me about his scholarship, about the efforts his parents went to, making sure he had a good education. Maybe being sent away had more of an effect than I realised.

"I did try to calm him down — apart from anything else, he was going quite red in the face and I was concerned about his blood pressure — but my presence clearly wasn't helping. I'm an awfully patient person, Rebecca, but I don't appreciate having my profession maligned, or my *families* castigated for neglect."

"I can fully appreciate that. If I'd had any idea he'd respond like that —"

"Oh, well," she says, sounding quite chirpy again. "To be honest, I'm annoyed with myself. And devastated to have let a rather delicious-looking strawberry tart go to waste."

I take pen and paper from my handbag, and scribble a note to myself to send her a huge Pâtisserie Valerie tart the moment I get home. "I'd like to apologise on Edward's behalf, Eleanor. I'm sure he's mortified."

She sighs. "Yes, actually. I suspect he will be. I've dealt with enough temper tantrums to know that when they subside, the perpetrator doesn't know what came over them. And he seemed like such a sweet boy, really. It's just an awful shame my job was the proverbial red rag to a bull."

I check with her whether I can keep her details on file in case I find a more suitable date in future ("Oh, absolutely! Takes more than one crosspatch to put me off!"), then ring off, and sneak back to my table. When I turn to check up on Edward, his chair is empty.

I finish my scone, trying not to let my failure throw me. I'm normally such a good judge of character, but we all make mistakes, and I wasn't to know Edward's Achilles' Heel. And as I sip my tea, I silently toast Dwight and Heather: the path to love isn't always pitted with potholes.

I wake next morning feeling positive. Another day, another match to make. The view from my loft is heart-soaringly beautiful, the Thames sparkling with a thousand starbursts, and I persuade myself that each one represents a lonely heart who could be the perfect partner for Edward or Sam.

OK, that might be pushing the Pollyanna spirit a little far: it's no exaggeration to say they're the two trickiest customers I've ever taken on. Trickier even than that celebrity cosmetic dentist who, it transpired after a few disappointing dates, was looking for a woman whose jaw he could mould, *Pretty Woman*-style, into dental perfection. Actually, once I'd figured that out, it was very easy: the British reputation for bad teeth is not undeserved, and with a single crown costing more than the average secondhand car, there was no shortage of ladies willing to spend their engagement lying prone while their fiancé probed their molars with a variety of metal instruments. Mia, whose teeth had been subjected to assault by Coca Cola throughout childhood, was the lucky bride and now lives, flawlessly flossed, in Epsom.

I start my mission with Sam, catching her on the phone before she goes into court. I agree to set up a one-sided speed-dating event for Sunday, assuming I can find enough men willing to meet her. I brew myself a huge pot of morale-boosting tea before getting down to business.

"Hello, is that Christopher? Oh good. My name's Rebecca, we met the other weekend, in the Pitcher and Piano in Richmond. I was there with my aun . . . my friend Georgia. The ballerina? Yes, that's right. Anyhow, the reason I'm calling is, this might sound a bit strange, but I am looking for the perfect man, and I have a feeling you fit the bill . . ."

By noon, I've had two men put the phone down on me, but another three have responded positively to my blatant ego-stroking and agreed to meet the woman I described as "the ultimate thinking-man's crumpet, and I am sure I'm right in saying that you're a thinking man, aren't I?"

The line-up is as follows:

2p.m. Christopher (41), big in commercial property. Likes stadium rock, golf and Thai food (he'd send me to sleep within seconds, but it's a good test to see whether Sam goes for Home Counties *Homo sapiens*). House in Barnes, holiday homes in Aspen and Cannes.

3p.m. Henry (38), ecological magazine publisher. Keen on architecture, Japan and sushi (though concerns about diminishing fish stocks mean he doesn't eat it as often as he'd like). Yawn. But very good-looking. Flat in Hoxton, "retreat" in St Ives.

4p.m. Zak (40 — he claims, but I think he might have lopped off five years), high-end estate agent. Told me that everything in his apartment has been designed by Bang & Olufsen or Philippe Starck. I suspect he has no imagination. He does, however, have a Notting Hill apartment, a half-share in a yacht and an extensive buy-to-let portfolio.

I haven't organised a venue yet, but I always try to pick a talking point, if possible one that plays to the client's strengths. I look at Sam's newly made Cupid Collage: her photograph is in the centre, she's half smiling with her grey barrister's wig on, and around her are images I've picked to represent her life. A legal bag, brimming with papers. The scales of justice, held up by that woman in a toga. Board games, to represent her rampant competitive streak. And an Agent Provocateur bra and pants set in racy black mesh, because after all, underneath that barrister's cloak beats the heart of a voracious temptress. Or, if you prefer, a brazen slut.

I'm toying with the London Dungeon or the Clink Museum for the first date, somewhere that'll get them talking about the things that matter to her. I bet she's at her most magnificent in court, but the Old Bailey wouldn't be quite the right location for a first date, so I need to find a place that will arouse similar passions.

I decide to leave the final decision up to her, and prepare instead for my last call, to Adam, the man I met in the pub. I don't know why I've left him till last, except that I know I need to have perfected my patter because he's sharp, this one. I stand up to dial his number: it makes me feel more confident.

"Hello, Adam Hill speaking."

I'd forgotten his voice, but it sounds very familiar, somehow, low and calm with just the tiniest hint of Cockney that I suspect he's trying to hide. Behind him I can hear loud industrial bangs, people chatting. We never got round to discussing what he did, but that's no City trading floor.

"Hi, Adam. It's Becca here, Becca Orchard, from All Bar One? Couple of Mondays ago . . ." He says nothing and I begin to lose my confidence. "I was reading *Crime and Punishment?*"

Still nothing. I'm just about to hang up out of sheer embarrassment when I hear a click, like a door shutting. "Becca! Of course! Sorry, I was just in the shop and I couldn't hear myself think. How fantastic to hear from you."

"And there I was thinking you'd forgotten who I am," I say, then wish I hadn't. It sounds flirty.

"Now there's no way that was going to happen. I can't remember the last time I chatted up a girl in All Bar One."

"Ah. Well, about the chatting up. I take it you *are* single?"

"Yep. One hundred per cent footloose and fancy-free."

"Just wanted to check. You see, I have an idea. I didn't tell you this that night because people sometimes get the wrong idea, but when I met you I was actually working."

136

"Ri-ight. Don't tell me . . . undercover police-woman?"

"No, I'm —"

"Oh, God, you're not an escort are you? I knew there was a reason you were talking to me. Women normally don't."

"It's a good job I don't take offence easily, Adam. No, what I do is —"

"*Please* let me guess. You're a spy, aren't you? MI5, not nine to five, like on the telly. And that *Crime and Punishment* was actually a high-tech tracking device. Bloody hell. You're going to have to kill me now, aren't you, send a fatal signal down the phone to render me a gibbering idiot."

I giggle. "I don't think you need any help with that. Don't you take anything seriously?"

"Only business . . . actually, come to think of it, not even business. So, am I right? Are you the female Bond?"

"Not quite. But I was keeping tabs on someone. A client." I feel almost disappointed that I have to give the game away, I'm rather enjoying this. "Adam, I'm a matchmaker."

"Really? I don't think I've ever met one before. Is there a degree in it?"

"No. I did do psychology at university, but matchmaking is a combination of science, hard graft and instinct. And my *instinct* told me that an eligible young chap like yourself might be just perfect for my client."

It takes him a few seconds to respond. "It's that scary woman, isn't it? I wondered why you were asking me for my opinion on all those girls."

"You said she was sexy as well as scary, if you remember. And actually, she's not scary at all." I keep my fingers crossed while I say this. Sam's only scary till you get to know her. After that she's completely terrifying. "She's successful, focused and so interesting to talk to. She's a barrister, which means she can give as good as she gets in the verbal sparring stakes. And as you have the gift of the gab, I thought . . ."

"That you'd be able to flatter me into going on a date with her?" He's seen right through me but he sounds amused rather than annoyed.

"That was the general idea, yes. Look, Adam, I'm sure you have no problem meeting the opposite sex, but it's trickier for successful women. I'm just the go-between."

"Actually, I do find it tricky to meet the *right* kind of woman, but I'll gloss over that gross over-simplification, Miss Orchard."

"All the more reason for you to give Sam a chance, *Mister* Hill. What else would you be doing this Sunday afternoon?"

"Well, that'd be telling." He hesitates. "OK. I admit it. Nothing at all. Tell you what, St Valentine. How about you meet me beforehand, to give me a bit of coaching on the whole dating game? Then I'll be prepared for her. I've been so busy building up my business for the last few years that I feel completely out of touch."

I think it over. He didn't strike me as a remedial dating case, but maybe the cheesy lines he was using *do* need upgrading. And I promised Sam four dates in one, so it's a small price to pay for client satisfaction. "OK, OK. You can have twenty minutes, that's all. Now, I'd just like to take a few details. You mentioned your business. What is it you do, exactly?"

He chuckles. "Oh, Miss Orchard, don't come over all efficient on me. Isn't it better to leave a little mystery? All will be revealed, come Sunday."

I sigh, and write down *Adam Hill, entrepreneur* on my list. "All right. You'll be meeting Sam around five on Sunday afternoon, if that's convenient, at a location to be confirmed around South Bank. I'll meet you at four-forty, I'll text you the venue in advance. Is that mysterious enough for you?"

"Oh yes," he says. "Will there be a code word?"

"I don't think that'll be necessary, Mr Hill. Just keep an eye out for my message, eh?"

I felt quite fizzy after my call to Adam — even fake flirting is good for the soul, I decide — but knowing what I have to do next brings me right back down to earth.

I text Edward, telling him I need to meet him as a matter of urgency. Even his reply ("If we must.") makes him sound defeated.

On the Tube, I try to work out how to broach the subject. What business is it of an "occupational psychologist" how he performs on dates? And how on earth do I talk him into going on another date without him rumbling me?

And yet I can't give up now. Temper or no temper, Edward deserves to find love.

We meet in his office, the one with the horrible view of a loading bay. I sneaked a quick glance through the glazed doors to the other offices on my way through, and the others are airy and appealing. Yet he's the most senior person on this floor. When I mention this, he shrugs: he looks awfully depressed.

"I chose this one. Some people are so fussy about their surroundings, but it's never bothered me. Better to give the good views and the fancy desks to the people who need them."

"Ah, but shouldn't the top person have the top office to match?"

"I don't really give a toss about appearances, Rebecca. Don't tell me you hadn't worked that one out by now? You can't be much of a psychologist if you haven't." And he gives me an odd look, as though he's testing me.

"I suppose it's true that status symbols don't seem to matter to you. So, dare I ask about yesterday?"

"You probably know already."

I nod. "Eleanor did call me, yes. She was *surprised* more than anything. One minute you're having a nice time, the next . . ."

"The next I'm ranting and raving like a crazy man? Yes, she wasn't the only one who was surprised." He's blushing now.

140

"Look, Edward. It's absolutely none of my business, but it seems to me this has shaken you up a bit. If you *do* want to talk it through . . ."

He stands up, and paces up and down the spotted grey carpet: judging by the worn patch, this is something he does on a regular basis. "I made such a bloody show of myself, Rebecca. We were getting on famously and then . . ."

"She says you had a rant about people who employ nannies."

Edward frowns. "That's what you think it was about?"

"Well, yes, she said —"

He sighs. "It wasn't about *people*. It was about one person. Dacre Ingram. Eleanor's former employer."

I try to remember Eleanor's version of the conversation. "He wouldn't be the one who took her to Grand Cayman, would he?"

"Yep. And the one with the adorable wife, an eight-bedroomed house with no mortgage in Primrose Hill, a trust fund for each of his children, courtesy of his rich-as-Onassis daddy. The one who made my life a living hell from the age of eleven to eighteen."

I stare at him. "Oh."

He winces. "Yes. Oh. '*Here, Teddy. Here, poor boy! Ah, look at the pauper, everyone. Look how his head is a different shape from normal people's heads. Shall we try to kick it back into shape for him? As a favour?*' " He stops short. "Sorry. God. There I go again."

"Edward. Poor you." I wish I could reach out, touch his hand, but he seems to have retreated into himself, like a hedgehog rolled into a spiky ball.

"I'm an idiot."

"What? No, you're not."

"I am. It's ruddy stupid, isn't it? It's twenty years now and yet all it takes is one mention of his name to provoke an *Incredible Hulk*-style outburst. Because I'm jealous. Jealous of what he is, what he has. I'm a bitter failure of a man. No wonder no woman wants to stick around to bear my children."

"Do you want children, Edward?"

He stares out of the window, at the yard. The insistent beep-beep-beep of a reversing lorry drifts through the grimy window. I really do think he should move offices: it's no wonder he's so down. "You might as well ask me if I want to fly to the ruddy moon."

Oh, *Edward*. I can picture him as a daddy, even now. Melting over a newborn son or daughter, reading bedtime stories in that serious voice, making sure no one ever hurts his kids the way he was hurt himself. I long to give him a big sisterly hug, to tell him about all the seemingly hopeless cases I've married off. Instead I stand up. "Edward, listen to me. You can get help, you know. About the bullying. I mean, I know it was a while ago, but —"

He shakes his head. "No therapy. I'm with my dad on this: *therapy's for southerners*." And he manages a wry smile.

I decide to try a different tack. "Fair enough. But try thinking of it another way. If something's going wrong

142

here at work — I don't know, a company you've backed is going to the wall, or a competitor spots an opportunity you've missed — do you give up like this?"

"No, but that's my skill, isn't it? Figures I understand. Humans I don't."

"And you were born with that, were you? Along with the knowledge of how the market works, what investors are looking for?"

"No," he admits, sulkily.

I have an idea, and blurt it out before I change my mind. "Listen, Edward, I know this is going to sound a bit nuts, but I run this *sideline*. Very unofficial, more for my friends than anything else. I meet so many people in the City who haven't got time to date, that I sort of . . ." I hesitate, trying to work out what he's thinking, but his face is blank. "Well, I'm a kind of Cupid, really. Bringing people together. Georgie boosts their confidence, I fix them up! Simple."

He scowls. "So. That Eleanor. Is she one of your *lonely hearts*?"

I nod. Well, she is now. The fact that I hand-picked her for Edward is a little detail I'll gloss over. All I need to do is convince him that there's such a dearth of quality men that I can offer him my service for free. "There's nothing to be ashamed of. These days it's very acceptable. And I know you might find this hard to believe, but there is no shortage of nice girls — just as pretty as Eleanor, but maybe not all quite so . . . um . . . posh — who'd love to meet someone just like you."

"Like me? Why?"

I can't stop myself tutting. This man so desperately needs a dose of self-esteem, to replace what those posh boys knocked out of him at school. "Because you're kind, honourable, considerate, decent. And underneath that prickly, rather overgrown exterior, you've got a dry old sense of humour, too."

"Overgrown?" His hand darts to his fringe. "My hair? Or not nasal hair, surely?"

"No, silly. I'd definitely have mentioned that. No, it's only your fringe but it's nothing that a trim couldn't sort out. But anyway, what do you say? Look at it this way. If you wanted your flat decorating, you'd get in a specialist. Or if you needed your drains clearing, you'd call a plumber. What's wrong with a spot of *romantic consultancy?*"

He frowns. "I don't even know if I want a girlfriend. It seems an awful lot of trouble."

I've had enough now. I don't often lose patience, but when I do . . .

"In that case, why don't you just give up on life entirely, eh, Edward? Move a camp-bed into your office, live on Big Macs and Dunkin Donuts, and never, ever do anything for fun? Tell you what, forget the camp-bed. Why not cut out the middle-man and install a coffin? It'd save so much time later on."

Eddy the Plank looks crestfallen. Eventually he mumbles, "Doesn't sound that different to how my life is now."

There's an awkward pause before I sigh, ashamed of my behaviour. What right do I have to lecture him? It's not even as though he hired me himself. His life, his

144

choice. "Edward, I apologise, that was very unprofessional of me. So sorry. Of course, it's entirely up to you how you live your life. You run a good team, you look after your people. I'll be saying all of that in my report to Perry. I think it's time for me to stop interfering. All I ask is that you be as kind to yourself as you are to your juniors."

He stares at the bare patch in the carpet, hair drooping down across his face so I can't see his expression. "Yeah. OK. Thanks. I appreciate what you've tried to do, Rebecca. Maybe some of us are just born to be miserable bastards."

I open my mouth to argue, but then shut it again. I think I've done enough damage for one day.

CHAPTER
THIRTEEN

Somehow I doubt that the Tower of London figures in the "50 Top Locations for First Dates" chart but at least it gives Sam's potential boyfriends fair warning of the *unpredictable* times ahead.

Her choice, of course. "If we're going for something justice-related, we might as well go the whole hog, Rebecca."

I haven't been looking forward to this afternoon. I don't expect my clients to go overboard with gratitude (though naming a firstborn after me might be nice one day), but Sam's response to my line-up of dates was so muted that I felt distinctly taken for granted. I *know* I am well paid for what I do, I know this is a *service* industry, but she makes me feel like the romance equivalent of a fast-food joint. I put my heart and soul into this business, but she seems to think I'm churning out eligible partners like ten-inch pizzas, with optional toppings of kindness, generosity and red-hot libido.

Though on the plus side, Sam's independence means she hasn't needed the usual advance spoon-feeding. It seems she's quite a fan of The Virgin Queen, so has plenty of historical titbits up her sleeve, if conversation begins to flag.

I haven't needed my full disguise either. It's easy enough to hide in the crowds of tourists on this perfect sunny Sunday. The Tower is yet another of those world famous landmarks I still can't quite believe is on my doorstep. I walk up the hill, towards Tower Green, knowing there are a thousand years of murder and intrigue and betrayal and ceremony in those deep foundations: broken hearts and severed heads (the guidebook says there still are skeletons in the crypt below the chapel).

I shiver, despite the warm sunshine. *Focus on why you're here, Becca, focus!* I pinch myself, hard. I'm a bit of a sucker for atmosphere, but I mustn't lose track of the here and now, and forget to keep tabs on my client. After all, the last time I did that, my client imploded.

Poor Edward. I buggered that one up royally. I've never before left one of my *chaps* feeling worse than they did when I started my mission. There was a message from Perry on Friday, asking for a progress report on the Bride Hunt, and I haven't had the heart to call him back and confess. Apart from Edward's morale, there's the little matter of my own reputation. Not to mention my own confidence. If I don't believe I can improve people's lives, I might as well pack up and go home. Or go back to head-hunting.

That's why it's even more vital that one of Sam's dates works out. I scan the crowd for a skinny, blonde vampire.

Ah! There she is, standing at the entrance to the Bloody Tower and, actually, she's looking rather good.

At the end of our Covent Garden trip, Helga offered her some fashion advice, and now she's wearing normal, un-stonewashed jeans. Well. Normal, if £200 a time for jeans is normal. They fit her well, emphasising her long legs. On top she wears a fresh sky-blue shirt: she could be Scandinavian, with skin the colour of blanched almonds, and hair only a shade or two darker. OK, she does look fierce, too, fiercer even than the plump Yeoman who is leading the tours. But frankly, a man who is intimidated by *fierce* is never going to be the right man for Samantha Ottoway, QC.

Oh, and there's Date Number 1, Christopher, looking every inch the property developer. On paper, they're a good match . . . but even though they haven't spotted each other yet, I can tell immediately that it's not going to work. It's not Sam's ferocity that makes this all wrong. It's her spark. While her eyes dart around, taking everything in, he has a solidity about him, and not just around the belly.

During my first few months in business, when I was experimenting with my methods, I read a book called *Animal Attraction: Tips from the Natural World* and afterwards I used to imagine my clients and their dates as animals, and occasionally I do the same now to occupy myself. I've always been rather good at picking the right creature, to the amusement of Georgie and Helga. Sam is a fox, perhaps, an Arctic Fox, pale and stealthy, ready to pounce.

And Christopher is . . . Hang on. She's just recognised him from the mobile phone photo I took on the night of the man-hunt. A flicker of irritation passes across her face, and I wonder whether she'll do a bunk, letting me do the dirty work of letting him down gently. But then she shrugs to herself, a tiny movement, and approaches him. He holds his arms out wide, air kissing like a goldfish.

No, goldfish isn't right. Christopher is . . .

Christopher is a walrus. A very wealthy walrus, but even so. Maybe Georgie and I were drunker than we realised when we took his number. I watch them begin their circuit of the Tower, and wonder how long Sam will take to brush him off. He's probably a delightful man — I remember that he got all excited when he talked about raving along at a Rolling Stones concert he went to at Twickenham Stadium a year or two ago — but they're wasting each other's time.

I have higher hopes of Henry the eco-publisher. He'd be a builder ant, with his perfectly sleek skeleton and sensitive antennae, and his rather joyless determination to make the best use of available resources. He works out, too, so has perfectly proportioned muscle groups as accessories. They'd make a rather handsome couple, Sam and Henry, *if* they can find anything to talk about. The Tower is probably a good place to find out: is there a middle ground between Sam's interest in the ethics of forced confessions, and Henry's appreciation of the balance of function and design in instruments of torture?

Zak the posh estate agent wears even better clothes than Henry, and fills them better, but they're chosen by his personal shopper. He's more of a predator — a wolf in chic clothing.

Can you put a wolf and a fox together? It'll either be instant chemistry or carnage. I think of the story in the guidebook about the Royal Menagerie. It used to be near here, in a long-gone building called Lion Tower, and some sleepy keeper once let a tiger, a tigress and a lion loose in the same enclosure. It took nearly a day for the lion to give up the fight.

Sam and Christopher have disappeared, so I walk towards the Waterloo Block. While I'm here, I might as well take a peep at the Crown Jewels. I join the queue of tourists chatting in a dozen different languages, as we file past huge screens showing footage of the Queen's coronation, towards the ultimate in regal bling. I'm glad I've never sent any first dates here: some of my clients might be hovering on the fringes of the *Sunday Times* Rich List, but showing potential wives the most expensive gems in the world might set up unreasonable expectations.

I wonder where Sam's got to, whether she's going through the motions with Walrus Man. And what about Adam Hill, her final, wildcard date? What animal is he? I had to work hard to persuade her to meet him at all, as I hadn't had a chance to take a sneaky photograph of him for her approval. I can barely remember what he looks like myself, but I have a sense of him as a joker. Would that make him a hyena, maybe? Or a cheeky meerkat?

We're approaching the main attraction now, through impressive vaulted doors, into a darker chamber, all glass cabinets and discreet security guards. No. Hyenas are too snide, and meerkats are too twitchy. There was something vulnerable about Adam when he was chatting me up, something that stopped me cold-shouldering him. Perhaps he's more like a puppy . . . or one of those bouncing lambs I spotted last time I was home?

"Wow!"

Ahead of me, I watch the tourists as their faces light up, literally, as they move past the crowns and sceptres. The procession is accelerated by airport-style moving walkways, so that no one can linger too long over the plum-sized Koh-i-noor diamond, or try to plot the perfect crime . . . But the effect is rather incongruous, like a perverse version of the *Generation Game* where it doesn't matter how many of the items you remember, you're not taking *any* of them home. Still, there's no doubting the awe-inducing beauty of the jewels. My favourite is the tiny diamond-encrusted crown worn by Queen Victoria, the accompanying portrait showing it perched on top of her head, as though it had shrunk in the wash.

We file back outside into the brash daylight, and I look towards Tower Green, to see whether I can spot Sam. For some reason, Adam's animal-a-like still escapes me. That's a first. Roll on 4.40 when we meet for our "pre-date". I'll have him categorised before you can say Charles Darwin.

Christopher the Walrus was granted a half-hour audience with Ms Ottoway, before he was despatched towards Tower Hill Tube. He trotted off happily enough, according to Sam during a quick debrief round

151

the back of the Fusiliers' Museum. She pronounces the poor man as "suitable for one of the bloody secretaries. And anyway, his perfect girl would be a brood mare, some horsy girl who used to be in the Pony Club or something."

Henry gets the full fifty minutes. I follow at a discreet distance as they stare at his namesake's Tudor suit of armour in the White Tower. In fact, at one point I feel there's a serious danger of Henry the Builder Ant and Zak the Wolf running into each other, and I have to stalk Sam around the Tower, pointing at my watch behind Henry's back. Eventually she takes the hint, and as he gives her a lingering hug goodbye, she gives me the thumbs up . . .

But then she spots Zak the Wolf — drop-dead gorgeous all in black — and does a comedy double-take. I keep my fingers crossed she'll heed my warning and keep her legs crossed: if she's going to find a husband, she needs to learn not to act on lust alone. I trail around after them for the first few minutes of the date, and she keeps mumbling something to herself — I'm no lip-reader, but I could have sworn it's "*down, girl, down*" — and I wonder whether she'll be able to resist suggesting they meet again later to *get to know each other better*.

All this matchmaking is making me hungry, but I'm too nervous to eat until the dating frenzy is over. I try to distract myself by people-watching, but every one of the tourists seems to be scoffing crisps or chocolate or, in one memorable case, both. Instead, I walk down past the White Tower, to the ravens' aviaries. They're

152

certainly handsome, though their glossy black plumage and matching beaks make them seem distinctly creepy. A sign tells me that they're surprisingly loving creatures, who mate for life. They've been known to reach the ripe old age of forty-four, thanks to a diet of raw meat and blood-soaked biscuits, plus an egg once a week. Occasionally their dedicated Yeoman Warder treats them to a whole rabbit.

It's a good indicator of how hungry I am that the thought of a whole rabbit makes my stomach rumble.

"Becca?"

I turn, recognising the voice, but not sure if I'll recognise the face that goes with it. And then I do . . .

He's taller than I remembered. A real *man*, more rugby-player than footballer, though he's not at all fat or beefy. His raven-coloured hair is cut in a boyish crop, and his face is dominated by enormous brown eyes, and eyebrows that seem to be slightly raised, as if he's permanently amused. He's dressed in jeans — neither designer nor dishevelled — and a shirt the colour of my latte. He's holding two large brown paper bags, and when he steps towards me to give me a brief, polite hug, I feel heat radiating from them.

"Hello, Adam. Nice to see you again. Presents for Sam?"

He holds his finger to his lips: his hands are clean but the nails are strikingly white, as though he's been decorating.

"Let's pretend we're on a real date, shall we, Becca? It'll help me get the hang of it faster." And as he smiles, those eyebrows lift a little further.

"OK, then. Normally I'd be paid for consultancy," I say, pretending to be annoyed.

His face falls until he realises I'm joking. "Ah, but it'll all be worthwhile when I turn into the date of your dreams."

"I'm not in the market for a dream date, remember? Or a dream man." I do my best to sound suitably stern.

"Oh yes, you're accounted for, aren't you? All the best ones are."

"Well, I hope you'll find that Sam bucks that trend. She's pretty special, you know, a lot of men would be very happy to —"

He shushes me again. "What did I say about pretending, just for the next twenty minutes? Now, as your date, Becca, I'd like to show you my favourite bits of the Tower. If that's OK?" He sounds curiously formal, as though he's rehearsed this bit in advance.

"You know it well, then?" I'm surprised: whatever it is that Adam does, I don't see him as a stuffy historian.

"I only work over there . . . Monument." And he gestures to somewhere between the Thames and the Gherkin building. "It's so easy to take London for granted, isn't it? We travel all over the world, but we forget what's on the doorstep. Well, I did for ages, and now I make the effort to explore *my* city. It's such a magical place, isn't it?"

"I wouldn't have taken you for an old romantic."

He grins. "I try to keep it quiet. Not good for the reputation. Come on."

And I follow him, down towards the river.

154

"Traitor's Gate," he says, as we reach the thick portcullis leading down to the water. Even though the sun's still bright, it feels dark and desolate down here. "Where prisoners were brought, including Elizabeth the First, on the orders of her half-sister. At first she refused to come this way because she was no traitor —"

". . . but then she changed her mind when it started to rain."

He looks crestfallen. "Oh. I was quite proud of that fact."

"Sorry. Shouldn't have said anything. I've been reading my guidebook. But you should definitely mention that to Sam, I think she identifies with Elizabeth the First."

"Not a virgin, is she?"

I manage not to snigger. "Not exactly. I think she identifies with the feistiness."

He nods. "Right. Well, I've more got stories. One specially for you, with a dating connection."

Adam leads me away from Traitor's Gate, and up some steps on to the South Wall. "I can't imagine there was much matchmaking here," I say.

"Yes. A strange place for a date, I thought. Still, always make the best of things, that's my philosophy."

We reach the top of the steps and I only just resist the temptation to clap my hands together in childish delight. Below us, the river carries pleasure-boats and police launches. Tower Bridge, its metal structure as ornate as lace, is so close that I feel I could reach out and touch it and on the other bank, swanky offices glisten in the bronze afternoon light. "View's changed a bit since Elizabeth the First was here, eh?" I say.

"Yup." Adam smiles nervously.

"Are you going to tell me this story, then?"

"Oh. Yes." He closes his eyes, as though he's trying to remember something. "Right. So . . . it's the seventies. The *sixteen*-seventies. London's been through a rough few years and if you lived in the Tower, you'd have seen some nasty sights. First there was the plague. All those seventeenth-century tourists stopped coming. Fifty-eight plague victims from the Tower alone shipped off to a pest-house. The only traffic through the streets were horses and carts loaded by bodies off to be burned and buried."

I frown. "I'm not really feeling the romance just yet."

"No? After the plague, came the Great Fire. Now, I know all about the Great Fire because it started just yards from where I work. The people who lived here climbed up the White Tower, for a better view. But as the fire spread, they got a bit nervous. Because the White Tower just happened to be packed with Gunpowder."

"Golly. It never got here, though, did it?"

"No. They blew up an entire street of houses to stop it."

"So when are you going to get to the happy ending, Adam?"

He looks bashful. "Can I get my notes out, miss? I've forgotten what happens next."

"It's not an exam. Why don't you just talk about yourself?"

"Not very interesting. You're better off with the story of . . ." — he sneaks a crumpled piece of paper out of his pocket, and squints at it — "oh yes, Elizabeth Edward. That's it. Forget your life as glamorous matchmaker, Becca Orchard, and imagine yourself as the teenage daughter of the man who holds the keys to the newly made Crown Jewels. You live on the top floors of Martin Tower, over there," he points towards the far corner of the site, "and your dad earns his keep showing visitors the crown and the sceptre and the rest."

"Righto," I say, trying to enter into the spirit of things, even though I find Adam far more intriguing than some long-dead teenager.

"Now, living in a tower isn't great on the dating front. Sometimes it must seem like you're *never* going to meet a nice boy. Until this bloke called Colonel Blood turns up to see the jewels, spots you, and mentions a nephew who he thinks would like a girl like you. Pretty. Intelligent."

"Oh, stop it, Adam, and get on with the story. There's not much time before you have to leave this rehearsal and meet Sam for real."

He pulls a face. "Sorry. I should probably ditch the compliments. OK." He sneaks another look at his handwritten note. "So Colonel Blood arranges a hot date with this nephew and a few mates. Brings them along early, for a quick look at the jewels. Bad move."

"Why?"

"Well, alas, the nephew's more interested in the Crown Jewels than a wife. They thump your poor dad

157

over the head with a mallet, flatten the crown, stuff the orb down their trousers and make a run for it."

"Sacrilege!" I say, amused by the effort Adam's put into preparing for the date. Aside from the slight awkwardness, he's a born storyteller. Not what I expected at all. "What happens next?"

"Big punch-up. Shots fired. Blood and his cronies versus your dad and your big brother and a few guards. All this time you're upstairs, doing your hair or whatever. Blood and his cronies are overpowered, but only just."

"The jewels are saved! Hoorah!" I laugh. "Still not very romantic."

He frowns. "Wait for it! Sadly your dad's big reward never materialises, while Blood is such a charmer that the King ends up giving him a pension for exposing security flaws!"

"That's awful. And me? Do I live happy ever after?"

He reaches out as if he's going to take my hand, but then he seems to lose his nerve and scratches his head instead. "You, Elizabeth, end up marrying one of the tower guards who helped to apprehend Blood. So there is a silver lining."

"Nice to know it's not all tragedy. So how come you know all this?"

"Well, I researched the period when I was setting up my business, you see. But before I tell you about that —"

"Not another story, we don't have time, Adam." I look at my watch. "It's three minutes to five."

158

"OK." He tucks the note back into his pocket. "So did I do all right?"

"You did fine, Adam. Sam'll love you. Just try to relax a bit. You're not auditioning for RADA, you know."

"It's been a while since I've been on a date. Sorry."

"And *stop* apologising. Good luck!"

He grimaces. "I don't know *why* I let myself be talked into this. I feel quite worn out now, Becca, do I really need to go through it all again?"

I frown at him, as fiercely as I can muster. "Now, that won't do at all. Once more, with feeling, *Mr* Hill." And I shoo him away with my hands.

"All right. And thanks for the tips. I appreciate it." He seems to be hesitating, wanting to say something more.

"She's waiting, Adam."

"Yes. Yes." He smiles. "Off I go. Condemned man ate a hearty breakfast and all that . . . oh." He looks down at the bags he's holding. "I nearly forgot. A present." And he holds out one of the brown paper bags.

"For me? Or Sam?"

"For you. That's why I've brought two."

The bag is heavier than I expect, and feels warm to the touch. I open it up, and peek inside. My stomach registers what it is before my brain: a sweet, almost unbearably good smell of . . . "Croissant?" I pull out the light crescent of golden pastry, and reach in for the rest of the contents. "And cake?"

"A croissant in recognition of the Norman influence that led to the Tower being built in the first place. And

159

this is a Maid of Honour tart, as baked for Henry the Eighth. A closely guarded secret recipe, but we've produced our own version, with almonds and butter pastry."

It's all I can do not to bite into the cake right now. But I control myself. Just. "We?"

"They come from my shop. My business. The Pudding Lane Bakery at Monument, named after the place where the Great Fire started back in 1666."

"You're a baker?"

He shrugs. "I know it's been a bit unfashionable since the Atkins diet came along, but it's my mission to turn London back on to carbs."

I look at Adam Hill, baker and storyteller, and I feel light-headed. I haven't eaten a thing since noon. "But your immediate mission is to turn on Samantha Ottoway."

Adam gives me a quizzical look, those eyebrows higher than ever. "And I'll definitely do?"

"Oh yes, Adam. Yes, I think you'll do nicely. Now don't keep your date waiting."

It's only as he walks off towards the entrance to the White Tower, and I take a first bite of the Maid of Honour, so delicate that it seems to melt in my mouth, that I realise what it is that's made his nails so white. It isn't paint at all.

It's flour.

I stand at my post, like a dating sentry, licking almond paste off my fingers, and waiting for Date Number Four to kick off safely.

160

Here goes . . . Adam has to approach Sam, because she doesn't know what he looks like. He touches her lightly on the arm and . . .

There's something *different* about this date somehow. The moments after that first touch seem very charged. And Sam is different too: no double-take, no challenging stare, no blatant sussing out.

Bloody hell.

She's just *blushed*. And fluttered her eyelashes before — no, surely not — doing a proper, coy-as-a-bridesmaid glance away from her fourth suitor. Then, when she looks up again, she smiles sweetly and allows him to lead her off towards Traitor's Gate. I wonder if she's heard the story of Elizabeth's refusal? I hope she's gentle with him.

I don't follow them. I thought the cake and the croissant had filled me up, but I feel empty again. I walk away from the Tower, from the couples and families. As I leave I try to spot anyone else on their own but even the off-duty guardsman I see is with his family, pushing a pram and eating ice-cream. When I cross the bridge over the grassy moat, back into the real world, I don't quite know where to go.

More cake! That's what I need. I'm hungry, that's all, and that delicious tart Adam brought me has whetted my appetite. One more of those and everything will be right in the world. It shouldn't be too hard to find his shop . . . I know it's near Pudding Lane.

And anyway, it's my duty to check out my client's potential husband's business, isn't it?

161

After the crowds in the Tower, the deserted streets leading to Monument seem like they belong to a different city. Elegant stone buildings stand alongside grey concrete office blocks. Only the street names remain from the days before the Great Fire: Mincing Lane, Seething Lane, Savage Gardens. I remember Adam's story and wonder which streets were blown up to stop the flames reaching that great symbol of power and impregnability.

People will go to any lengths to protect themselves.

I wonder what Adam and Sam are talking about. Adam and Sam. *Sam and Adam*. They sound right together. Bully for them.

Stop it, Becca. This isn't like you. You believe in love, and you certainly don't resent the people who want to find it. It won't do at all.

I consult my map. Pudding Lane, *Pudding Lane*. I can't see it on the map and I stab at the index with my finger. Low blood sugar, that's why I'm so short-tempered. I've hardly eaten all day.

The street ahead of me is completely quiet, the coffee shops all have their shutters down, and it's really not looking good for finding food. I should have remembered that this part of London shuts down completely at weekends. But I suppose I might as well check out Adam's place.

Aha!

I spot it on the corner of Pudding Lane and Eastcheap. It has huge curved windows, and grey-green paintwork, with *Pudding Lane Bakery* written in modern cream lettering. At first, I can't see inside

162

because the sunshine is shining directly on to the glass, so I get closer.

My nose is almost up against the window before I can make out the interior. Wow. I didn't know what to expect — around here lots of stainless steel would go down well, I guess — but Adam's shop is like a cocoon of earthy colours and textures. Mottled walls remind me of a shimmering wheat field. Bakers' racks are made from wood stained the colour of poppy seeds. One wall is completely covered by an ancient sepia-toned world map, and straight ahead there's a high counter made from a single piece of heavily grained wood — walnut, perhaps, or something tropical — marking the divide between shop and kitchen.

"Oh!"

I see movement in the kitchen, a large man in baker's uniform sweeping the floor, and I dart back round the corner. Maybe they were open today after all? The tart and the croissant certainly tasted freshly baked.

"Can I help you?"

Shit. A door has opened next to me. A door that must lead to the back of the bakery. Standing at the entrance is the man I've just seen. Closer up, I see he's fortysomething, older than I expected. He is plump, as a baker should be, with floury cheeks and deep-set eyes.

It's the man from All Bar One . . . the one Adam claimed talked him into chatting me up. What was his name again? I hope he doesn't recognise me.

"No. No, I'm fine."

"It's just I saw you peering through the window — not many people round here at this time on a Saturday." His voice is soft, more curious than annoyed.

"I was peckish. Someone had mentioned there was a bakery round here, so I thought I'd come. On the off chance. I mean, I didn't really expect you to be open."

He grins. "We're not. Not really."

"But you . . ." And I gesture towards his white apron and hat.

"Oh God, blame the boss. *Special order*. I only agreed to do it as a favour. Very persuasive, my boss."

I nod. "Right. So I can't buy anything, then?"

The baker shakes his head. "I'm sorry, no. I only did a very small quantity and I couldn't possibly give you anything from yesterday. Quality control, you see. Adam, that's the boss. He's very hot on that."

"Ah." I feel hungrier than ever. "Never mind."

He frowns at me. "You really are ravenous, aren't you? You've got that look like my cat gets when I get home after my shift. Hang on a sec." And he disappears back through the door.

I consider doing a runner, before he can ask me more questions, but he pops out again before I've made up my mind.

"Here we are." He hands me a brown paper bag like the one Adam gave me.

"I thought I couldn't buy anything?"

He winks. "No, but there's nothing to stop me *giving* food away. Enjoy it. Last one. Free sample. Just come back during the week if you want to buy some more . . .

164

Ask for Tommy." Then he goes back into the store, leaving me alone again.

I hardly dare to peek inside the bag, trying instead to guess if it might be . . . no, it's no good. I reach inside and there it is. A final Maid of Honour.

Yes it's every bit as delicious as the first one. Adam might be a joker, but he knows his tarts.

An otter. That's what Adam is. Resourceful, playful and just the tiniest bit skittish.

I think about his date with Sam and wonder whether my client will take the initiative and invite Adam back to hers for some extra-curricular activity.

It's weird because even after that second cake — more than enough for anyone — it feels like there's a tiny part of me that's still hollow.

CHAPTER
FOURTEEN

Sam keeps me in suspense all night — the rotten thing. I spend Sunday evening watching my phone, like a teenager after a first date, and eventually I send her a one-word text:

Verdict?

My mobile vibrates back a minute later:

Jury's still out.

That is what we in the dating game call a *tease*. When she finally deigns to get in touch, at six o'clock on Monday morning, I am instantly wide awake.

"I must say, I had my doubts at first, but you're good at this, aren't you, Rebecca?" It sounds as though she's in a cab, maybe on her way to court.

"Why, thank you, Sam." I switch on my bedside lamp, and grab my notebook, always the professional. But I feel a certain *unprofessional* interest in how she got on with the candidates. Well, especially the last candidate. Adam is a nice guy: I don't want her to have treated him badly. "So?"

"I'll go through them in order of appearance, shall I? Now, Number One I assume you put in there as — well, as some of my more charming criminal clients would put it — as a ringer?"

"I'd never waste your time on purpose."

She gives a short laugh. "Oh, come on, I wasn't born yesterday. Anyway, it's fine. Christopher was obviously too stupid for me but it probably helped to soften me up so I gave the others more chance. Which was clearly your intention. Now then, Number Two, um, Henry. I rather *liked* Henry, actually. Yes. Very different perspective on the world, which was intriguing. Oh, and fit as fuck."

I decide not to write that bit down. I've never been quite sure whether my records could be seized under the Data Protection Act. "So, will you be interested in seeing him again?"

"Don't hurry me, Rebecca. Number Three was even fitter. Zak. Yes, quite a cutie. A little less interesting, perhaps, than Henry, but then again, I am never sure that *interesting* is top of my list for a partner. I find my work *interesting*. With a man, I'd prefer what you see to be what you get."

I scribble this bit down furiously. The more dates Sam goes on, the clearer an idea I'll have about her requirements. Except well, I have a horrible . . . no, I mean a *good* feeling that she might have hit the jackpot with Number Four. The sooner I match her, the sooner I can say goodbye to her. "And what about the final candidate?"

"Ah. The delightful Adam." Her voice is guarded.

"How delightful, exactly?"

"Well. He has it all, really, doesn't he?" she says and she can't help herself. She sounds all whispery and soft. "A great conversationalist. Entertaining. Good-looking, but not in an obvious way. Oh, and the cakes were a lovely touch."

A taste of almond fills my mouth. "Mmmm. So what happened?"

"Well, it was rather handy that he was my last date of the day because we were able to extend our meeting. We took a boat from Tower Pier to Waterloo. He seems to know something about pretty much everything, doesn't he? A veritable walking encyclopedia."

I'm beginning to think she's teasing me on purpose. "So . . .? I take it you want me to arrange another date with him. Unless you've already done that."

"Ah." There's a pause, and I hear her cab rumbling as it drives over cobbles.

I wait for her to tell me that it's a little late for another date, that she's had him in bed all weekend, used and abused him sexually, before tossing him out. Or maybe he's still there, tied to the bed with a collection of silk scarves, waiting for her to come home for another session wearing her sexy barrister's wig.

"Now, Rebecca. I don't quite know how to put this. It was *terribly* disappointing after all the build-up. But I don't think that it'll work between me and Mr Hill."

I sink back into my pillow. "Why not? He seems so perfect."

"There's no other way of saying this. The fact is that Adam Hill is a bit of a *fumbler*."

I drop my pen. "Really?"

"God, yes. I mean, I'd give you the gory details but really there are some things better kept a secret."

168

"Right. I suppose so but . . ." I'm still reeling. Adam? Perfect, hunky Adam a *fumbler*. How awful. I mean, I suppose it could be a compatibility failure between him and Sam, but then again Sam has no shortage of experience and if she's so adamant, then it must be true. "Is there absolutely no room for manoeuvre? I mean, perhaps it was first-night nerves."

She sighs. "You *do* want the gory details, don't you? OK, OK. I didn't shag him, but I was sure it was heading that way. He waffled on a bit, all those historical stories, but I thought we had *rapport*. So when it came to the end of the date, I made a move, to let him know it was time to go in for the kill."

"A move? What sort of a move?"

"Oh, don't worry. I didn't make a grab for his crown jewels. I simply made sure he knew it was the right time to kiss me."

"*How* exactly?"

"I kissed him first. Planted a smacker on him, as it were. But he was so *fumbly* that we'd barely made contact when he moved aside and ended up with lipstick all over his face."

The image makes me smile *and* feel outraged on Adam's behalf. "You could have tried again, surely?"

"The moment had passed. Now, Rebecca, I'm not ruling him out completely. I think what you may have there is a rough diamond. But I think he needs remedial work before I'll consider seeing him again."

"Remedial work?"

"I don't know. There must be an evening class or something, *Dating for Dummies* or some such.

Anyway, I would like to arrange to see candidates two and three again. Perhaps you'd be kind enough to set it up, Rebecca? And they'd better be romantic settings as I think it's prudent to get the snog out of the way nice and early. Like I said to you before, it really is best to know what you're getting."

"Right."

"Avoids disappointment later on. Yes, just drop me here, that's fine," she says to the taxi driver. "Better dash, now, Rebecca. They don't call this judge the Terminator for nothing. Let me know when it's all arranged."

And she hangs up, leaving me wondering what on *earth* I am going to tell Adam.

"Hello, Adam Hill speaking."

So he doesn't have my number programmed into his phone. Or he's pretending he hasn't. Oh God. I've been dreading this. I've left it twenty-four hours, in the hopes that I'd find an elegant way of saying it. No such luck.

"Hi, Adam. It's Becca. From the Tower, you know, on Sunday."

This time I recognise the background noise of a busy bakery: the clattering of industrial-sized tins and trays, footsteps on tiles, people shouting across a busy kitchen. It's so evocative I can almost smell the bread . . .

"Becca! Of course. Will you hang on a mo?"

"Sure." I want to get this over with as quickly as possible. It's not like I've never had to break bad news before: I've told clients they have BO or appalling dress

170

sense and still managed to get invites to their weddings. I don't know why this feels so much harder.

"Right. Just moved into the office, I'm with you now. So . . ." Away from the racket of the kitchen, he sounds different. The bravado is gone. Oh, holy shit, how am I going to say this?

I stare at the script I've typed into my computer. And re-edited about two hundred times. "Yes. So. The Tower. Samantha."

"Samantha." He repeats. It sounds like he's agreeing with me. But I haven't got a clue what we're agreeing about.

"She's great, isn't she?" I say, in the same voice people use when they say *she's mad, she is*, and really want to add, *but only tolerable in the smallest of doses*.

"Great. Yes. No, really, she's great." He sounds very keen. Oh, why do I do this bloody job?

"The thing is, Adam. Well, it's always awkward, rejection, isn't it?"

"Yes," he says, serious now.

"I mean, unless you're into polygamy or two-timing, there can only be one person at a time. Can't there?"

"Hmm. Yes. One person at a time." He sounds a touch baffled by this. Can't say I blame him.

"And the mysteries of attraction. Well, they're a mystery, aren't they? They make no sense *logically*. They just, sort of, *are*. I have read some very convincing theories that it's all to do with smell." Oh shit, Becca, what are you going on about? This is not in the script. Still, I've started, so I'll finish. "Yes, apparently, we instinctively know, by sniffing the other

171

person, whether their genes are complimentary to ours. They did tests. Got girls to sniff the armpits of T-shirts used by male runners. If their genes were right, great. If not, no deal. Nothing to do with all of that good sense of humour, broad shoulders stuff. Smell. Pure and simple."

There is a long pause. Finally Adam says, "Doesn't that make your job a bit random, then? Redundant, even?"

He's got a point.

"Good point! Yes! Well, there are other factors. Of course there are. I happen to believe that by identifying the most important *conscious* elements a client requires from a date, and then arranging for the conditions of a dating event to be as *conducive as possible* for attraction, then I can narrow the field. I like to use the term Romantic Conditioning. You know, like air-conditioning."

"Right," he says. "That's fascinating."

Do it, Becca. Tell him that his date thinks he needs *remedial* work — and then tell him that it reflects more badly on her than it does on him. Explain that confidence is the number one factor in successful dating, even if you have to fake it. "Samantha has decided that the person she wishes to pursue at present was actually a chap she met earlier in the afternoon. He works in property and I think they probably had the most in common of all the people she met."

"What, they *smelled* the best, did they?" His voice is muffled: if I didn't know better, I'd think he was

172

laughing. People react in the strangest ways to rejection.

"Yes. Absolutely. That's absolutely it. No more, no less."

"Well, Becca, I am thrilled. Really thrilled. I hope they sniff along together happily ever after." He sounds very sincere now.

"Let's hope so." I ought to ring off but it feels terribly brutal.

"Maybe one day I'll find someone who smells right," he says, wistfully.

"Yes . . ."

"Becca . . . you know how when you called me initially, I said I was a bit *rusty*? At the dating thing?"

"Mmmm. Though I don't think you're that rusty," I say, and then wish I hadn't. Maybe he's telling me, in a coded way, that he *knows* he's a fumbler. Maybe this has blighted his life since, I don't know, some bitchy teenage girlfriend spread rumours all round the sixth-form common room that his hands trembled or his kiss was slobbery or bite-y or too pushy or in-and-out-y like a toad on a lily pad. A toad who will never turn into a prince.

And maybe that's why a man who seems terribly sweet to me, *actually* believes he's bloody awful, why he's thrown himself into his business empire, and is single when by rights he should be fighting women off.

"That's very kind of you, Becca, but I can't help worrying . . ."

"What?"

"I know you approached me initially as a potential partner for your client, but . . . would it be ethical to take me on too?"

Oh no. I manage to cover the mouthpiece of my phone before sighing. Could I willingly set him up with girls, *knowing* he could be a let-down when it comes to the clinch? "I'm so sorry, Adam. I'd love to help you but, no, I don't think it would be *quite* ethical."

"Oh. All right then. To be totally up-front with you, Becca, I can relate to what you're saying about the smell thing. I would probably rather find my own soul-mate. But I don't have the skills. I mean, look at that night I tried to chat you up. You only took that drink from me because you felt sorry for me."

"That's not true, I took your number because I thought you'd be great for —"

"Great for Sam? There we are then. Proves my point. People don't fancy me. I missed out on that bit of my education and I need *help*. You know what women want. What works for men. Don't tell me you haven't given your male clients a few pointers about how to be the perfect date?"

"Yes, but . . ." *But I've never had to train any of them not to fumble.*

"I wouldn't ask except, well, I've got everything I want — I love my work, I love living in London — all I need is somebody to love it with me."

Bugger! I screw my useless bloody script into a big ball and aim it at the waste basket. It misses. I like Adam. And he really does deserve to get the girl. How can I refuse him the help he needs? If I train him

174

properly, Sam might even let him try again. "I *suppose* I might be able to give you a few tips."

"Great! That's great news, Becca. Honestly, I can see this being the beginning of the rest of my life. It could be just the simplest thing that's standing in my way and if anyone can work it out, it's got to be you. So when can we get together?"

"Um. I can't access my diary right now," I say, ignoring the bare expanses of *Outlook* on my computer. "I am very busy. I'll text you a few possible times, OK?"

"Whenever suits, I'll be there. Oh, and make sure you charge me the proper rate. I wouldn't want a sympathy discount. Your time is money. As a businessman I appreciate that —"

There's a huge crash on the other end of the phone, followed by a volley of swearing.

"Oh, I hope that's not what I think it is," he says.

"What do you think it is?"

"The sourdoughs. Tommy's a great baker but he's clumsy as hell. Better go. But text me those dates. The sooner the better! I don't have any more time to waste!"

He hangs up, and I put my phone down, before going to lie face down on my bed and pummelling the duvet with all the force I'd like to direct at my own head.

Great work, Becca — another mission impossible. Never mind bloody bride hunter. If I'm not careful, I'll have to change my nickname to lame-duck hunter.

CHAPTER
FIFTEEN

"But, miss, how can you be sure it isn't dinosaur poo, if you've never seen any?"

I can always rely on my junior park explorers to bring me down to earth with a bump. Three nine-year-olds are sitting on a tree stump, using sticks to prod away at a pile of firm, pellet-like stools that either came from a very large deer, or are actually the first astonishing evidence that *Tyrannosaurus rex* is alive and well and living in Middlesex.

"Love is In the Air" trills from the phone buried in my rucksack. Maybe it's because I'm so absorbed that I don't recognise the hesitant male voice when I answer on my Bluetooth headset.

"Um . . . is that Rebecca?"

I inch away from the poo detectives. "Yes, Rebecca speaking."

"It's Edward Lincoln. From Anemone International. Eddy the Pla —"

"Oh, Edward! Of course I know who you are. Sorry, I'm in the middle of Bushy Park, looking at dinosaur droppings, so I'm not really in work mode."

"Sounds a better way of spending the afternoon than investigating the investment potential of organic beet-growing in the developing world."

"Well, you're more than welcome to join us. It's a beautiful afternoon."

"Is it? I hadn't noticed."

I think about the horrible view from his office: no better than a prisoner's view on to an exercise yard. "Edward, is something the matter?"

"Yes and no. No more than usual, certainly. But then I'm beginning to realise that *usual* isn't necessarily *right* . . . The things you said to me last week, well, I can't stop thinking about them and —"

"Miss! Miss! We've found another one!" A red-haired girl in dungarees nudges me, holding a large leaf laden with furry droppings.

"Lovely, well done," I say, shooing her away. "I'll come and look in a minute. Sorry, Edward, do carry on."

"About what you said, Rebecca . . ."

"Listen, I've been thinking about it, too, and I went too far. You're a grown-up, you don't need some stranger offering you half-baked theories about what would make you happy."

"No, not that. What you said just now? About coming down to the woods and looking at poo?"

"But what about the organic beet crops?"

He laughs nervously. "About the only fringe benefit of my seniority is that I think I'm allowed to grant myself the afternoon off. Not that I ever have before.

177

But . . . heck. There's a first time for everything, I suppose."

"I'd love to lead you astray. How long will it take you?"

"If I get the fast train, and then a taxi, I could do it in about an hour."

"Brilliant. Ask for directions at the Education Centre — you'll be just in time for pond-dipping."

We've just fished out a tiny crested newt and a couple of millipedes when Edward turns up, flushed from his journey.

"We've got a spare net, Edward, so you can join in."

"Great. Is there anywhere I can put this?" He takes off his jacket. Underneath, his shirt is crumpled as ever, though I'm relieved to see that at least there are no sweat circles reaching from elbow to collarbone. I wouldn't have staked much money on Edward Lincoln having heard of deodorant.

I gesture towards the little wooden bridge that crosses the pond. "You could hang it over there, rather than put it on the wet grass. Best time to see the park, though. Rain, then sunshine, is the ideal combination for bringing all creatures great and small out of their hidey-holes."

Edward peers around him uncertainly. "I can't remember the last time I was more than ten feet from the nearest computer."

I grin at him. "But I bet you've still got your Blackberry on you?"

His hand flies to his trouser pocket.

"Go on, hand it over! Even a City hotshot can afford to spend an hour incommunicado."

Edward frowns, then reluctantly fishes the phone out and places it in his jacket. "You're a bad influence, Rebecca. What would Perry say, knowing I'm here with you, when he only hired you to *increase my efficiency?*"

I gulp. I'm pretty sure a real occupational psychologist wouldn't be dragging the top brain of Anemone away from his desk to go pond-dipping. Then again, compared to some of the weird management bonding sessions Marcus used to send us on when I worked at Benson's, this is pretty tame. Extreme Bowling, Underwater Paintballing . . . he even once tried to convince me that Topless Darts would help team dynamics. It's testament to how severely he messed with my head that I considered it.

"There's more than one way to skin a cat, Edward. You never know, maybe Perry would think it a good use of his money if you got a bit more of a life, saw life from new perspectives." I stop. "God, there I go again. Little Miss Meddler. It's a hard habit to break."

"Listen, Rebecca, about the meddling —"

"Miss Orchard, Miss Orchard, I think we've found a leech." The little redhead is tugging at my sleeve again. "Won't it suck our blood?"

"Edward, have you ever seen a leech before?"

He smiles. "What, outside of a Square Mile singles night for high-net-worth individuals?"

"Like you'd ever be seen dead on a singles night, Edward." I walk over to where the kids are huddled around a white plastic washing up bowl — all the better to see their catches in.

"You'd be surprised what I've tried, Rebecca."

"You, at a singles night?" I crouch down to where the captured creature is circling the bowl. "What's your name?"

"Saffron, miss."

"Well, Saffron. Leeches are actually very hard to find these days. What you've got there is a kind of worm and the worst thing he's going to eat is tiny insects that you and I can't even see."

Saffron looks most disappointed. "Keep collecting, though, and we'll take the best stuff back to the centre to look at close-up. And could one of you wildlife experts volunteer to show Ed here how to catch damselfly nymphs?"

Despite brilliant instruction from my junior naturalists, poor Edward fails to catch anything more interesting than some late frogspawn. The kids take pity on him and pop a ramshorn snail in his plastic sandwich box, to take back to the centre.

"So," I say, as we pack up the sieves and the nets, "what's all this about you and singles nights?"

"Once. I went once, not long after I got to London. It was one of the boys in the office who talked me into it. 'Ask the girls about themselves,' he said. 'Never fails.'"

"Well, that's not bad advice."

"Maybe not in normal circumstances. Bit different when you're fallen upon by a pack of hungry

180

she-wolves who have nothing to discuss beyond the effectiveness of different fake tans, but who are *very* keen to ask you questions. About the size of your flat, the size of your car engine and, crucially, the size of your bonus."

"Ah. Yes, I can see that normal rules of chatting up might be suspended in those circumstances." I peer over the top of my stack of sieves. "But does that mean you *did* want a girlfriend?"

"Doesn't everyone?" He glances over at the kids. "Someone you'd care about so much that you want to make babies, because you think the world would be a better place with more people like them in it."

"God, for a Northerner you're a bit of a softie on the quiet, aren't you?"

He blushes. "That's why I came, Rebecca. I'm bloody fed up with this crap life of mine. I know I'm a miserable bastard but maybe underneath all this there lurks a more cheerful me. And I wondered whether you might be able to try — on a fully paid, professional basis, of course — to help me discover it."

I stare at him. Of course, I'm thrilled on one level: my chance to redeem myself, to undo all the bad karma from Edward's encounter with the nanny. I suggested it, after all . . .

But if he's going to insist on paying me . . . well, won't I end up attracting bucketloads more bad karma by taking both Perry's money *and* Edward's for doing the same job? "Um. Well, of course, I'd be delighted. I really would. I suppose my only concern about that would be . . ." I try to come up with a delaying tactic, while I work out the logistics. I used to be good at thinking on my feet. I cast around. ". . . the current dearth of possibilities. It's the leeches, you see."

"The leeches."

"Yes. Leeches. It's sort of a . . . technical term. Jargon, you know. All jobs have jargon, and in the matchmaking industry, leeches does actually mean . . ." Come on, Becca. Think! "Well, exactly as you'd expect, it means the kind of women you met on the singles night. Blood-suckers. Gold-diggers. Awful lot of them about. More than ever."

Edward's face falls. "Really? You keep statistics or something?"

"Oh, yes. The industry is surprisingly scientific now and is all coordinated by the International Matchmaking Federation."

"The IMF?" he says, incredulous.

"Oh, yes. We all sign up to a Code of Conduct, get together for conferences and we send in all our figures every quarter. Matches made. Requests. Leeches." Now I'm in my stride it all sounds very plausible. Maybe I should set it up. Except I'd probably be thrown out at once for breaching my own Code.

He shakes his head. "I had no idea it was such big business, or so organised. Sort of takes the romance out of it. I'm definitely out of luck then?"

I feel guilty now. He sounds so defeated. "I'm not saying we definitely can't fix you up, Edward. Just give me a little time to research it."

"OK. But shouldn't I be paying you up-front for that research? I wouldn't want you to be out of pocket." He

182

fishes around in his trousers. "Hang on, I'll just get my wallet from my jack —"

And we turn, just in time to see one of the kids — prancing along the wooden bridge, modelling Edward's jacket — miss his footing and go tumbling into the algae-covered shallows of the dipping pond.

The Blackberry was a goner. But we knew that from the moment it — and the boy wearing the jacket — was pulled out of the pond, covered in bright green weeds. The water had barely reached the kid's waist, but it was deep enough to give the device an early bath. I wasn't hopeful about the prognosis for the jacket either.

As we fussed around the boy, Edward stood completely motionless.

"Edward, I'm so sorry. Is it insured? Edward?"

Still he didn't move. I mean, I know the average City boy is more attached to his Blackberry than to his firstborn, but even so . . .

I took off my cardigan and the parent helper draped it over the boy's shoulders, while Saffron and the other girls gingerly transported our catches of the day back to the education centre, trying not to splash away too much of the precious water.

"Edward?"

He was staring at the pond, but when he turned, I saw he was grinning as widely as the boy had the moment before he toppled into the water. "I tell you what, Rebecca, I reckon it's another sign. Another indicator that I'm on the right track. With you, I mean. The Blackberry is part of my enslavement to the ruddy rat-race. And someone" — Edward raised his soft eyes heavenwards, towards the sun, high in the blue sky — "or maybe some*thing* is trying to show me it's time I broke free."

I frowned. "Not sure what Perry would have to say about that."

"Bugger Perry," he said, chuckling. "This isn't about him or about Anemone International. I've spent too long being bullied by posh boys."

I handed him back his jacket. "So you definitely want to go through with it? With more dates?"

He tipped the jacket upside down, pulling out the pockets, which had become an ecosystem in their own right, thanks to the dunking. He held out his palm, to reveal a mass of writhing grey bodies. "Yep. Leeches and all. It's about time I took a risk."

Georgie hands me a mojito through the open window, before squeezing alongside me on the balcony.

"Precious niece. You are a dear creature but sometimes you're excessively dim, aren't you? The solution to the double-payment problem is so simple."

"I suppose you think I should pocket Perry's fee *and* Edward's, do you?"

She shook her head. "No. It's even simpler."

I sniffed my drink, taking in the wholesome English smell of freshly crushed mint and the slightly less wholesome top note of Cuban rum. *Perfection.* My aunt learned it from a Cuban lover. Her DCV (Dating Curriculum Vitae) would read like the League of Nations. "Do put me out of my misery."

184

"You tell Perry."

I stared at her. "Oh. Oh. Now why didn't I think of that?"

She stared back. "That's what's worrying me, you giddy girl. You're even giddier than usual these days. Has something happened?"

Automatically I think of Adam. And then try to work out why. "I suppose I've been feeling less sure of myself lately. Of my ability to engineer love, or even to spot who's right for each other."

"Why would that be, Becky?"

I haven't shared Sam's account of Adam's shortcomings with my aunt. It seems mean-spirited somehow: it's one secret you wouldn't want anyone to know. I cast around for another example. "You know how worried I am about Dwight and that girl. I don't have the foggiest idea where I can find a man who will meet Sam's ludicrous expectations. And then Edward, of course — we thought we had it sussed with the nanny, and then it all went *horribly* wrong."

She clinks glasses with me, and takes a sip of the cocktail. Below us, the sun is disappearing beyond the horizon, sweet as a ripe tangerine, and the first wave of City workers is homeward bound, the men with their sleeves rolled up beyond their elbows, sweat clinging to their backs from the heat of the Tube. "But he came back for more, Becky. Didn't he? He has faith in you. It's only you that doesn't."

"Too right, I don't. Where are we going to begin with him this time? He's a lovely chap but I misfired

185

spectacularly with my theory that he wanted to be looked after. To be bossed about."

"Hmmm." She grinds an ice cube against the bottom of the glass, releasing more mintiness. "Let's think . . . what else could be the key to Edward Lincoln, the City of London's own Little Boy Lost. If he doesn't want a substitute mummy, who else might fit the bill?"

I shrug. I'd rather indulge in a bit more agonising about my own failings as a matchmaker, but Georgie is clearly having none of it. "He wants kids, I've worked that out."

"To put things right, maybe? If his own childhood was no bed of roses, perhaps he wants to give kids the love he didn't have."

I nod. "Probably, yes. But it doesn't help me work out the kind of woman he might want." I close my eyes, picturing him. Before he left this afternoon, he pulled all the cash from his wallet — three hundred pounds in soggy twenties — and said we could have it for the centre if we could dry it out. And if we couldn't, we could send it to the Bank of England to be returned as shiny new notes. Money doesn't matter to him, so what does? Duty? Responsibility? Very worthy values, but hardly the stuff of romance . . . so what else makes Edward tick?

Kindness. Security. "Georgie, what if we got it completely the wrong way round with Eddy? What if . . ." I feel excitement bubbling inside me, increasingly certain I have got it right. "What if the last thing he wants is to be taken care of? And the thing he wants above all else is to take care of someone else?"

186

My aunt's brow furrows. "Go on."

"What if the one thing Edward wants is to be the hero he never thought he could be? The star of his own movie, the knight in shining armour. He spent his childhood as a lonely underdog, unable to stand up for himself, never mind anyone else. Couldn't love make him strong?"

Georgie smiles at me. "And *that*, precious niece, is why you must never doubt yourself. Cupid doesn't have a degree in psychology, therefore you'll always be a hell of a lot better at this game than a fat god. So, now all we need to do is find an innocent abroad for Edward to look after. Easier said than done in the mean city. When shall we start? I could do tomorrow."

"Yes, maybe." Then a horrible thought occurs to me. I reach through the window to fish my diary out of my handbag. "Let me see . . . oh shit. Tomorrow is the twenty-third. You know what's happening on the twenty-fifth, don't you?"

She shakes her head, and her crystal drop earrings ring like bells.

"The twenty-fifth is the day that Dwight flies Heather to Edinburgh for the big day. Which means I'm on the poor man's Flying Scotsman first thing tomorrow. Setting up the perfect proposal even though I've no idea yet whether they're the perfect couple." I swig my drink, wincing at the strong liquor left in the bottom of the glass.

"Only one way to find out. Do a bit of digging around while you're up there. While I go looking for the innocents abroad." She takes my glass. "In the meantime, shall I make you one for the High Road?"

I nod. This is one business trip I'd rather not contemplate stone-cold sober.

CHAPTER
SIXTEEN

All stations are romantic but Waverley in Edinburgh seems to me the most romantic station in the world. Plump cherubs keep tabs on the passengers from their frieze beneath the ironwork dome, just as they did in Victorian times. And for sheer emotional impact, what could beat that first view of the city, when you walk up the ramps on to Waverley Bridge, and find yourself in the shadow of the castle? I swear it does, actually, take your breath away.

I stop for a moment to admire it in all its brooding glory, then drag my trolley-case through the streets. I'm sure Dwight wouldn't begrudge me the cost of a cab on expenses, but I want to soak up the feel of the place again. I haven't been here since I was a student at Birmingham University, when friends of friends were putting on some experimental show at the very furthest fringe of the Festival one August.

Actually, it was the August before I met Marcus, and I think of the Edinburgh me as a total innocent, twenty-one years old yet still retaining that whiff of the country, despite my utter conviction that cities were the answer to all ills: night buses and nightclubs offering a world of opportunity.

I dump my bag at the hotel — a comfy three-star, my room kitted out with a tartan bathrobe and cellophane-wrapped shortbread fingers. Dwight and Heather will be staying in the five-star place up the road, where I don't doubt the robes are made from cashmere, the shortbread fingers freshly baked, and the tartan fittings far more subtle, or even non-existent. Five-star guests often don't care which city they've landed in.

I turn left out of the hotel and follow my nose towards Leith and the grey stone tenement block where we kipped that summer, ten to each room (the flat owner had forsaken the rowdy pleasures of the festival and used our rent to fund a month in sunnier climes). I've forgotten the details of the show — something about the war in the Balkans, I think, with a crashingly inappropriate soundtrack of Rodgers and Hammerstein show tunes — but I remember the buzz. There was a boy I rather liked playing the lead role, but although he was doggedly working his wicked way through the cast and hangers-on, I ran out of money and had to go back home before he got to me. I suppose it must have mattered terribly at the time. I remember my friend teasing me, saying she knew I fancied him, and me insisting that I was only observing him from an anthropological perspective.

I walk past the defiantly ugly John Lewis building (where I bought thermal underwear when Edinburgh nights proved so much colder than the ones in Birmingham). I pass a wine bar, and a shop selling kilts to real Scotsmen, the kind where I'm sure you need

190

your birth certificate and family tree before they'll let you wear any recognisable tartan.

The sun disappears behind a thick bank of cloud, and the city turns gratifyingly melancholy, in a way that London or Paris never could. That's when the nostalgia wave hits. Despite the need for thermals, it's what I loved about Edinburgh when I visited seven years ago: it's an uncompromising place, never afraid to wear its dark heart on its sleeve.

Finally, I reach the city's best deli, Valvona and Crolla. I knew it would be my kind of place the moment I checked the chiller and realised they stocked my father's cheese — it was early days for Double Orchard then, and only a few places stocked it outside the south-west of England. When I tried to explain my excitement to my fellow students, they seemed utterly baffled. Most of their dads did hands-off jobs; pushing around legal paperwork, or teaching quantum physics. None of them actually *made* anything. Back then, I felt ashamed of my background. Now, I feel a tingly pride when I spot the familiar bottle-green rind surrounding the creamy wheel of cheese.

I take the steps down into the conservatory-roofed café, order an Italian hot chocolate, and help myself to a pile of papers and listings magazines. Time to refamiliarise myself with the hottest tables in town. Just where would a Scotsman take a girl to ask her the most important question of their lives . . . ?

An hour later, I have my shortlist. There's The Witchery restaurant where Heather would have the best view of her old hometown, along with excellent food and wine. It's the kind of place they could return to on their anniversaries, to celebrate the birth of their first child, to mark Dwight's retirement, whichever comes sooner (sensible City boys step down early before blood pressure and expense account finish them off).

Then there's the spa in their hotel, which is offering the Diamond Couples Massage, where the lucky pair would have simultaneous back rubs, followed by some strange ritual where they coat each other in Manuka Honey and Clay, and the would-be groom then produces a diamond ring from the bottom of the clay pot and pops the question.

Then again, maybe not . . . I'm far from convinced that any woman wants her abiding memory of that moment to involve her husband coated in mud. Unless he's a tribesman or a rugby player.

There's the Observatory, but that would mean the special, private moment would be shared by scores of tourists . . . I'm beginning to wish that Dwight had gone for his original plan, and let me hire an entire pod on the London Eye, as a nod to their very first date.

My main problem is that Edinburgh is perfectly magical to a visitor, but it's hard to know how to wow a local. Dwight hasn't been much use at filling in the details of Heather's background. I suspect he does most of the talking when they're out together. She's smart, that girl, she knows that the way to a man's heart is through his ego. Oh, and below the belt, too. As far as I know, she still hasn't spent a whole night with him.

I'm normally *brilliant* at proposals. Yes, my success rate is partly due to my matchmaking, but I'm also top-notch at second-guessing what a woman really wants. Most men will never truly understand the opposite sex, but I give them the inside track. With a dash of psychology, a dollop of feminine instinct, and extensive research into the potential fiancée, I concoct a bespoke wooing methodology, culminating in the perfect proposal.

Usually I feel proud of my ability to create romance but I'm drawing a blank with Heather and Dwight. Maybe it's the melancholy weather, but today I feel more like Machiavelli than Cupid. For once, couldn't I just trust true love to find a way?

The final drops of my hot chocolate are stone cold, but I drink them anyway. *Snap out of it, Becca.* There are many, many worse ways to earn a living, head-hunting for a start.

All I need to do is to understand what makes Heather Campbell tick.

I make my way back to the hotel, and hire myself a car. What better way to discover the way to a woman's heart than to go back to her roots?

Dwight's listening skills really do leave something to be desired. The only bit of definite information I had to go on — Heather's attendance at an exclusive finishing school on the outskirts of the city — proves completely unreliable.

Because the Flower of Scotland Ladies' College doesn't exist.

193

There's nothing in the phone book, and when I call the Education Department, they tell me there's no such place. "But there is a Flower of Scotland Primary, and that's so far out you'd think it was another world," says the woman on the phone, before giving me the address.

Well, another world sounds right: didn't Heather tell me herself that she grew up around horses and dogs? Edinburgh is delightful but there's not a lot of huntin' and fishin' on The Royal Mile.

As I drive out towards the suburbs, I decide that Dwight's probably just got muddled by the Scottish school system. I should have had a cake at Valvonna's: it's early afternoon now, and my stomach's rumbling. Still, even if this does prove to be a wild goose chase, there's bound to be a nice tea shop where I'm going, perhaps attached to a castle. I might even treat myself to some shortbread.

I follow the main road for three miles, past Victorian villas, and then thirties semis, and the few tea shops are gradually replaced by pubs and pawn shops. I check my map. Definitely the right way towards the Flower of Scotland.

As I steer my car into the kind of housing estate that features in news reports about the urgent need for urban regeneration, I could be on the outskirts of any big city. Despite the map, I feel lost, dwarfed by ugly tower blocks. They've been painted pretty pastel colours, but this is no Notting Hill: the flats have a hungry appearance, as if they could bend over and swallow my little hatchback in one bite.

194

I drive past a burned-out car that looks like it's been there decades. Down another road, there's a budget supermarket, with groups of kids hanging around outside. In my day, you couldn't get away with playing truant in full view of adults . . . in my village, everyone knew you by name and would drag you back to your classroom *and* tell you dad if you were so much as a minute late for school.

No wonder I wanted to get away.

I'm beginning to think that this particular outing has been completely pointless — and with not so much as a petticoat tail in sight — when I drive down a street which is equipped with the most vicious metal speed-bumps I've ever encountered. And then I spot it. The Flower of Scotland. The most colourful building on the estate, with vibrant murals on the outside wall, a small playground paved with snakes and ladders patterns, and a sign decorated with a trail of bright blue handprints spelling out *WELCOME TO OUR SCHOOL*.

But the place is also deserted. I park the car, relieved I've hired the lowest category ("Are you sure?" the rental man asked. "This one's got no more power than a golf cart at Gleneagles.") because I can't imagine any joy rider risking their street cred by stealing it. A woman with skin the colour of milk walks towards me, her equally pale twins squirming in a wide pushchair.

"Excuse me, is the school closed down?"

She stares at me, as though she doesn't understand me. Then she shakes her head. "No. School holiday." And keeps walking.

Holiday. Bugger. My grand plan of chatting up the staff with skittish tales about my "brother's" forthcoming wedding and my role as bridesmaid, then asking if they remembered his "bride", Heather Campbell, is now defunct.

And anyway, Heather wouldn't have come here, would she? Heather, with that irresistible aura of misty marshes and lochs at dawn and the faint smoky aroma of barley and peat, as though her blood is infused with whisky. Heather, who grew up alongside ponies and hounds. I'm pretty sure the only dogs around here would be pit bulls.

"Can I help you?" The voice is bossy and unwelcoming. I turn to see a short, round middle-aged woman dressed in an overall, standing on the other side of the iron railings, hands on hips.

"Oh hi." Now what do I say? My plans to play the posh English bridesmaid feel strangely inappropriate in this environment. "I do have the right school, do I? The Flower of Scotland?"

The woman turns her head towards the sign and then back to me, as though my question is too stupid for her to waste her breath in reply. I see her point.

"Sorry, what I mean is, there isn't another school in this area with the same name? Or a similar name, maybe? A girls' school."

"No. There's not." A very tall, wrinkled man joins her now, in paint-spattered jeans and T-shirt. He stands close to the woman, snaking his thin arm around her waist. They must be caretakers. "Anyway, it's the holidays," she says. "I'd advise you not to hang around

196

school playgrounds, holidays or no." The man nods and puts his arm around his other half, as they turn to go, having presumably assessed my behaviour as barking mad, but posing no significant threat to anyone.

"It's a silly thing," I say, so desperate not to lose my one chance of finding out whether Heather was ever here, that I don't mind playing the part of a completely loopy southerner, "I know how daft this sounds, but I'm helping to organise my brother's wedding. He's marrying a girl from Edinburgh and he must have got the school wrong because this was the name he gave me and I came up here to get . . ." I hesitate, trying to come up with a credible reason, as they stare at me, ". . . to get a memento of some kind. You see, they're emigrating straight after the big day. To Argentina. Yes. He's big in beef, and I hoped maybe I could get a photo of the school or maybe record a message from the kids or anyone that knew her when she was here. Something to remind her of back home, when she's on her huge ranch among those Argentinean cows. Her name is Heather Campbell, did you know her at all?"

"Heather Campbell?" The man sounds amused. "Aye, I should say —"

But the woman interrupts him. "No, Bill. You're mistaken. I remember a Heather Daniels and a Heather James, but no Campbell. Sorry we couldn't help you."

Now she begins to shepherd her husband away: he looks back at me, shiftily. I saw his expression when I asked him about Heather. I *know* she came here. But I also know I won't get much more out of them. I decide to try my luck with one last question.

"Just before you go, I wondered . . . well, if Heather *did* happen to come here. Long ago. Well, if she did live around here" — I gaze around at the tower blocks and the unrelenting greyness — "well, Robbie, that's my brother, he wanted to bring her back to Scotland, a final whirlwind trip. Is there anywhere local you might recommend? Where would a girl who grew up here see as the ultimate dream-date destination?"

They're both staring at me and I think I've pushed my luck. But it was worth a try.

I walk away slowly, just in case, and I'm halfway back to the car, when the man calls to me. "I don't know what you're really up to, dearie, but I can't see the harm. I'd have your brother take her to Lachlan's Inn by the Loch." His wife is shaking her head, pityingly.

"Right, thank you. Lachlan's Inn by the Loch?"

"Seven or eight miles out of the city. Can't fail," the man says. "Well, it worked for us, didn't it?" And he leans down to kiss the top of his wife's head.

She shakes him away, then punches his arm affectionately. "I always knew you were nothing but a big softie. More trouble than you're worth, old man." She looks over my shoulder, as if I'm not even here any more. "What car are you driving?"

"Eh?"

"Wouldnae be an orange one, would it? Only a few of the kids seem to be taking quite an interest in your hubcaps."

My wig feels itchy, and my sunglasses make the brown décor of Lachlan's Inn by the Loch look even darker.

198

Interiors have come full circle, of course, and this well-preserved example of authentic sixties design is now the height of fashion. But when I first recced this pub, I was convinced I'd come to the wrong place. It reminded me of my granny's grimy lino-covered kitchen, the orange and ochre flooring covering a multitude of stains.

Still, you don't only come to the Inn for the decor. You come here for the view, and the food. I established that much on my first visit the night before last, and confirmed it yesterday over lunch with Dwight. I showed him the spa back in town, and the usual Edinburgh tourist haunts, but saved this place till the end. I pointed out that although the Castle and the Observatory are entrancing for a first-time visitor, they're just part of the furniture if you grew up in the city, so to make Heather's moment perfect you had to think like a local.

We took Dwight's hire car on the eight-mile journey to the Loch. The car was a flash royal blue convertible not really made for the dramatic reversals of Scottish weather, but the fates were being kind and rays of peach-coloured sunshine kept peeking out at us from behind the soft mountains, like a cheeky toddler. I had to wrap a scarf around my hair, Grace Kelly-style, and for a moment I could really imagine a life like this one for myself, sitting in the passenger seat of a sports car, Frank Sinatra providing a bittersweet soundtrack as I travelled to beautiful places in the company of a man I loved . . . after all, I had my pick of highly eligible bachelors: this could easily be within my reach. Edward would make a lovely husband. Or even Adam.

And then I shook my head, hard, cross with myself. Wasn't it enough to visit those places on my own, all expenses paid, with no ludicrous rose-tinted haze clouding my vision? Taking care of other people's dreams, nurturing them as conscientiously as Eleanor the nanny nurtures her client's children. And retaining that same healthy scepticism about the reality of my role. Always the bridesmaid? No problem. Suits me just fine.

Anyhow, once I'd dispensed with my daft daydreams, I sold the merits of Lachlan's Inn to Dwight. He loved the look of the place — turns out he's been consulting a designer in London who's suggested kitting out Dwight's entire roof terrace in Playboy-style pink vinyl. He loved Lachlan's Modern Scottish menu with its Haggis Carpaccio and its Wasabi Shortcrust Venison Pie and its Green Tea-infused Athol Brose.

And most of all he loved the view. An image straight out of a tourism brochure; dramatic hills that turned purple at sunset, framing the loch itself, changing colour before our eyes, from bright blue, to deep violet, and finally a profound, pre-historic black, so dark it could easily be home to a monster or two, along with a few thousand more undiscovered life-forms.

"You've scored the home run, yet again, Rebecca. I'd never have found this place on my own. And it's a *wee local secret*, you say?"

I winced at his Scottish accent and wished his voice wasn't quite so loud. "Yep. Though local couples have been coming here to propose for decades, back to the day when the original Lachlan still ran it. So lucky Heather will have grown up knowing that this is the most romantic place locally."

I didn't mention that anywhere would be more romantic than the tower blocks surrounding the Flower of Scotland school. Or my conviction, which grew deeper by the hour, that Georgie's initial instinct was right after all: Heather was too good to be true.

How would I prove it, anyhow? And even if that was where she started, then why should it be where she finishes? Of all people, I should identify with the need to escape your roots.

So Dwight booked the best table, and I booked the worst, the one behind the pillar, with a sliver of a view of the loch, but an excellent view of the happy couple.

My ringside seat couldn't be bettered: I saw Heather's arrival: she was dressed in a black-and-white shift dress, a homage to the sixties and Jackie O. Dwight was at her side, short but almost handsome and only the tiniest bit bouncer-like in a black tux. I watched her face as Dwight showed her the view, as if he'd pre-ordered it specially, and then I watched as the seven courses of the tasting menu were brought to them — the colours of each dish designed to match the setting of the sun, from red Scottish salmon, to the finale of darkest bitter chocolate mousse, floating in a deep green mint-and-heather-flavoured sauce.

And now it's nearly time.

Dwight excuses himself after dessert to go to the loo, and Heather checks her make-up in her broken Boots

No. 7 compact, correcting her smudged lipstick with a manicured finger. Before long she'll be checking her reflection in a limited-edition compact from Guerlain or La Prairie.

Oh yes, Miss Campbell has fallen on her feet. I just wish her imminent lifestyle upgrade didn't make me a teeny bit uncomfortable. We're all entitled to the odd stroke of luck. But I am the one who made that luck happen . . . and therefore bear a big share of responsibility for what happens next. What if she *is* a conwoman and I haven't been clever enough to realise and she's going to take Dwight to the cleaners and break his poor, hopeful heart when it's only just healed from the mauling it took from his ex-wife . . .

And then I notice Heather's feet. Above the table, she's demure and collected, but in the tiny space between tablecloth and floor, I see her feet in those immaculate kitten heels, tapping edgily against the deep pile. Tap, tap, tap, as fast as a heartbeat.

Conwomen don't spend the moments before a proposal tapping out a tattoo of nerves on a restaurant carpet.

I lean back into my seat, trying to enjoy the last mouthful of my chocolate mousse despite my own ragged nerves. The waiter takes my plate, and returns with a pot of coffee and the inevitable shortbread. I'm a novelty here: when I booked my table, the maître d' said he couldn't remember the last time a woman came here on her own.

Always the bridesmaid, and that's how I like it. But tonight it'd be nice to have some company.

202

Dwight is back at his seat, and he's seriously on edge: he keeps folding and re-folding his napkin, fiddling compulsively with his tie. But the waiters at Lachlan's Inn by the Loch have seen it all before, been responsible for more proposals than Henry the Eighth, Casanova and Interflora put together. Two of them approach Dwight and Heather with a tray of coffee and an ornate platter of ice-cold petits fours, arranged in a pyramid on a bed of ice and topped with a huge chocolate truffle.

Dwight and Heather eat a few fruit jellies, until she gestures that she's full, and at that exact moment, the waiters return with a steaming jug of what I know is whisky-and-cream, heated to just shy of boiling point. And at the appointed time, they pour the liquid on to the enormous truffle, which melts away like lava, revealing a tiny transparent case holding a diamond engagement ring that could give the Koh-i-noor a run for its money.

Dwight pushes his chair back, and is instantly on his knees in front of Heather, holding her hand. I wonder if he remembers the proposal he practised on me yesterday: *You have brought so much joy to me in the short time we've known each other that I cannot imagine being without you. And I would be the luckiest man alive if I could persuade you to spend the rest of your life with me, as my wife, when I know that joy would grow and grow. We deserve to be happy, and I would dedicate myself to making you as happy as I possibly can. What do you say?*

I didn't write the proposal. I draw the line there, though I might offer advice if a man really, really needs it. Those words have to come from the heart, after all, and though Dwight's proposal would be a difficult one for a taciturn Brit to pull off, it sounded rather moving from an effusive American ... yes, even to a hard-bitten Bride Hunter like me.

And it — or the ring — seems to be working *very* well, because Heather is jumping from her chair, putting her arms around him, and kissing him. More waiters appear, bearing champagne flutes and Cristal and the other diners burst into unsurprised but warm applause.

I join in, though it feels odd, as if I'm applauding myself for my completed mission.

I pay my bill, and slip away unnoticed. Nothing more for me to do.

In the hire car, my Bluetooth headset vibrates with an incoming call, and I answer straight away, convinced there's been some last-minute hitch. In her excitement, Heather could have choked on a jelly, necessitating the Heimlich manoeuvre. Or perhaps that weird caretaker from the Flower of Scotland has shown up at the inn in his overalls, with evidence that Heather is about to commit bigamy . . .

"What's wrong?"

A chuckle answers me and I know, immediately, who that chuckle belongs to.

"Adam?"

"Hi, Becca. Why d'you ask if something's wrong?"

204

"Oh, it's a long story . . . I've just been working, you know, aiding and abetting Cupid."

"And did your arrows hit home?"

I laugh. It's nice to have company, even if my companion is six hundred miles away. "Fingers crossed, yes. So what can I do for you? I am the fourth emergency service, you know."

"No dating emergencies to report. Or baking emergencies, for that matter. Though a whole batch of bagels were too salty this morning, too disgusting even for the homeless shelter round the corner. After all, if you're living on the streets, the last thing you need is salty bagels. Or bagels at all, because generally homeless people don't have the best teeth and bagels can be —" He pauses. "What am I banging on about now? No wonder I can't get a date."

I giggle, feeling curiously close to him as I navigate the dark roads. "No harm done, Adam. After all, you want to pay me to go on a date with you. It'd take more than a lecture about the dental problems of tramps to put me off, wouldn't it?"

He chuckles again, but he sounds more embarrassed now. "Oh yes. That's why I was ringing. You were meant to call me, with spaces in your diary. If it helps, I can do any week-night for the next month. Well, the next year, really, but I'd like it to be sooner rather than later."

"Week-nights . . . aren't good for me," I say automatically, the brush-off response I've honed so carefully.

"OK. What about Sundays? Sundays are good. I don't open on Sundays."

"I know."

"You know?"

I suddenly feel embarrassed by my secret trip to Pudding Lane Bakery. "How would you have had your date with Sam if you'd worked Sundays?"

"Right."

There's a pause. Poor bloke. I really shouldn't have reminded him about the humiliating experience with Sam. "I can do this Sunday. If it's any help."

"Yes! I mean, yes, that'll do. Doesn't give me much time to prepare the perfect date, though, does it?"

Edinburgh's sodium runways twinkle ahead of me. There. City lights always make me feel less lonely "Oh, don't fret too much, Adam. After all, this is just the dry ski-slope of the dating experience. Practise on me, and soon you'll be slaloming through the black runs like a pro."

"I suppose you're right," he says, "but I do always like to try to do my best, cub-scout style. Otherwise, why bother?"

Why bother indeed? Adam deserves a chance of happiness, every bit as much as my rich bankers and lawyers and accountants. "You're right. Pull out all the stops, Adam. Push the boat out. Give me *the* date to remember. Text me where and when. I'll be there."

CHAPTER
SEVENTEEN

Sunday. Date day.

I bet I know how poor old Adam is feeling, because I feel it every single time I organise a rendezvous for one of my clients. A cloud of butterflies fluttering around your insides. Dry mouth. A profound mental block when you try to recap your best anecdotes or carefully planned topics of conversation. The need to use the loo more often than usual.

And to compound things, it's 8a.m. at Old Street Tube, and I'm only half awake.

"It's too early for a date, isn't it?" Adam apologises before he even says good morning. "I'm so used to getting up at the crack of dawn for work that it didn't even occur to me that this is mad. And you've come all the way from Richmond."

He looks pretty good for 8a.m.: none of that bleary-eyed blokiness that often afflicts the male of the species. His hair is combed, his brown-sugar eyes are bright rather than morning-after-blood-shot, and his fruity aftershave is zingy but not overpowering.

"Calm down, Adam! I don't mind, honestly. And you get ten out of ten for appearance this morning."

Ugh. That sounded less slimy in my head than it does when I say it out loud.

"Aren't I meant to give *you* compliments? You look lovely, incidentally. That colour really suits you. The pink."

I blush. I *did* pick my favourite cashmere v-neck — just to show willing, as if I really was on a first date — but I'm not used to compliments. "Um. Thanks. Anyway, you're paying me for this, remember? You can take me anywhere you like, that's the deal."

He flinches. "Yep. Sure."

I've gone too far now. "But let's try to forget about that from now on. Treat me exactly as you would treat a date, and then . . . well, shall I give you feedback at the end?"

"Is that how you usually do it?"

"I . . ." I'm about to remind him that I don't usually provide this service at all, but that might undermine his confidence. "It's horses for courses, but that's probably the most useful approach."

He nods again. "Right. OK, well, Miss Orchard, allow me to lead the way to Phase One of our date." He draws self-conscious quotation marks in the air as he says "date". I adopt a keen-as-mustard smile, and trip alongside him, as we're absorbed into a large crowd of people: families with small children, couples with white hair and huge, empty shopping bags.

I smell our destination before I see it. I wouldn't tell Adam this, but I've already guessed where we're going . . . though at first the blossomy note in the crisp air is so subtle that I wonder whether I'm imagining it.

But the scent becomes stronger and the streets busier and then there it is. Columbia Road Flower Market.

"I hope you haven't been before," Adam says.

"No, never." I've considered it as a venue for dates before, but it feels a bit too *homespun* for my City boys, who find it hard to resist an opportunity to splash the cash on cocktails or Gordon Ramsay dinners when they want to impress a girl. Shrubs wouldn't really cut it.

Adam beams at me. "Cool!"

I smile back, pleased that he's pleased, but then remind myself I have a job to do and make a mental note for the feedback later: try if at all possible to avoid words like *cool*, in case you sound like an overexcited teenager. "Is it a favourite place of yours?"

He shakes his head. "Actually, to be completely honest," and he leans in so close that I can smell his toothpaste, "I've never been here before either."

Bless him. But I make mental note number two: always try to seem authoritative, like he was at the Tower of London. Women like a man who knows what he's talking about.

In front of us, the mass of people is so dense that we have no option but to *plunge* into the market. I thank goodness for that chill in the air, and for twenty-four-hour body-responsive deodorant technology. This is going to be one *very* hot date.

It's a jungle, but what a jungle! It's hard to imagine a much more sensual experience. We have to fight hard to keep track of each other's movements, making constant eye contact so one of us doesn't get lost in the surge.

The pushing is polite, but still intense, and I become very aware of my body and how alive I feel, especially when the crush eases momentarily and Adam and I find ourselves gasping for air, standing together in front of a display of prickly cacti or blowsy roses. I feel perspiration forming on my skin: all the better for swapping pheromones.

And then, of course, there's the perfume of the market, a fragranced landscape which my green-fingered mum would be able to identify, flower by flower. I enjoy it in a cruder way, relishing the scents of crushed grass and pepper and tea rose.

The stalls are as colourful as any catwalk show. Most of them are stocked with a pot pourri of everything seasonal, from leggy supermodel orchids to tough little heathers, but a few stalls are themed. One features flowers in every shade of blue: denim, periwinkle, sapphire . . . there are even blue-grey grasses, thrusting spikily out of their pots. Another specialises in horrible knick-knacks. I try to avert my eyes from the mating bunnies in weatherproof terracotta but wherever I look . . . well, they seem to have bred like rabbits.

And *everywhere* a certain kind of head-scarfed middle-aged woman is pushing and prodding and feeling up the plants. It's an orgy of groping. Yes, this is not a bad dating venue if you want to inspire earthy thoughts.

Not that it's affecting *me* that way, of course. I'm a professional. Mental note number three: find out what kind of woman Adam is targeting, and warn him that not all women will respond in the desired manner.

210

We finally catch our breath next to a slightly limp display of herbs. I know how they feel. One of the scarf brigade is squeezing the leaves, releasing the smells of Italian kitchens: basil, oregano, rocket.

"OK?" Adam asks. "Seen anything you like? Because if there is, I'd love to buy it for you, Becca."

"That won't be necessary, given the unusual situ —" And then I stop myself, remembering my own words about treating this as a proper date until the very end. "I'm not much of a gardener, really. I live with my aunt and she's only got the tiniest balcony."

"Ah, but even a balcony could keep you self-sufficient in tomatoes, herbs, cut flowers . . ." He looks sheepish. "That's not a very cool thing to say, is it?"

"Well, plants didn't used to be sexy, but the whole eco thing probably means green fingers are trendier than they were. So you're a gardener as well as a baker, then?"

"Blame my nan. She was well into self-sufficiency, had an allotment, and she was still digging for victory sixty years after the war finished. The only vegetables I'd eat when I was a kid were the ones Nan grew." He slaps his forehead. "Now I'm subjecting you to my boring childhood stories."

"Not at all, Adam. I *am* interested. After all, the purpose of dating is to get to know more about your potential partner, and that includes family background."

He thinks it over. "Suppose so. But I'm sure you'd be more interested to know that there's been a market on this site since the nineteenth century, but it went through a difficult period during the war when no one was allowed to grow flowers any more. And that it was only in 1962 when —"

I hold up my hand: now he's taking *authoritative* way too far. "Adam?"

"Yes?"

"You're trying too hard. And I'm starving. Can we quit the historical guided tour for a bit and get some breakfast?"

As we chomp our way through bagels, by the window in a packed café, we watch the head-scarf brigade fight over diminishing stocks of white African lilies.

"This is more civilised," I say, "but I'm not sure I'm brave enough to actually buy anything. It seems pretty cut-throat to me."

"Mmm," Adam agrees, still chewing. Finally he finishes. "How was your bagel?"

"Slightly hard work."

He inspects what's left of mine. "It's the boiling process where they've gone wrong. They might even have *steamed* it instead. Shame, because the dough's good."

"Oh, I forgot you were the bread expert. So where did you learn the secrets of the perfect bagel, then?"

He grins, with faraway eyes, as he remembers. "Poland. I was only seventeen, not sure what to do with my life, so I went travelling round the new Eastern Europe, a few years after the Wall came down. Wound up in this lady's spare room in Warsaw and persuaded her to give me her bagel recipe."

"Polish Mrs Robinson, was she?"

Adam's cheeks colour. "Mrs Liberek? Hardly. She was built like a Russian tank. But she did teach me a few things — like, did you know bagels used to be a traditional gift to pregnant women? And they're probably called bagels because they were shaped like stirrups and were given to a Polish warrior to celebrate a great cavalry victory."

"No, I didn't. You *are* a mine of trivia, aren't you? Especially when it helps you avoid giving anything away about yourself."

Adam raises his eyebrows. "I don't know what gives you that impression. I just like research. Oh, and collecting things. Facts, recipes . . ."

"Women?" I wonder if I've gone too far, but I can never resist delving into a client's psyche.

"No, not so good with women. Recipes are easier to pin down." He pushes his chair back with a squeak. "Anyhow, we can't stay here chatting all day. Things to do."

"Oh, right." I feel disappointed. Is that our date over already? I look at my watch. Bloody hell. We've been here for two *hours*. It feels like twenty minutes.

"Well, Becca, apart from anything else, we need to buy you something to grow . . . and then we're off on Phase Two?"

"Phase Two?"

He taps the side of his nose. "Oh, when I plan a date, it's like a military operation. And the first rule of battle — always maintain an element of surprise."

★　★　★

We emerge from the Tube at Piccadilly Circus. Adam is carrying a lavender bush he's bought me, each plump stalk topped with twin pink petals, long and thin like rabbit ears. Every time the plant brushes against me, the smell of the flower market is released.

We pass Eros and he says, "You know, I can see the resemblance . . . to you, I mean."

"Yeah, I've got the special hand-bag-sized fold-down bow and arrow. More portable, so I'm always ready to pierce the hearts of unsuspecting men and women."

Adam laughs. "Funny job, yours, isn't it? I mean, do you really believe you can *create* love from thin air? I'm a bit old-fashioned that way, I believe in instant attraction."

"Love at first sight, you mean?" I can't keep the cynicism out of my voice.

"What's wrong with that?"

"Oh, nothing. Don't mind me. Of course attraction plays a big part, but it's not always the most reliable indicator that a relationship will work." I hesitate. "And if I'm a bit sceptical about being bowled over, well, let's just say that I did have one of those lightning strike, bolt-from-the-blue moments with a guy once and what happened afterwards confirmed all my worst fears about love being blind."

"But that's one of the wonderful things about love," Adam says, "the fact that you can truly believe that the other person is flawless. Despite all evidence to the contrary!"

I'm about to tell him just how dangerous that is, how scientists have proved that love switches off the very

214

circuits of our brain that allow us to make objective judgements about a person . . . But maybe that's too downbeat. Instead, I say, "Yes, well, anyway. I don't think this is the kind of thing you'd normally cover on a first date, is it? So it's off limits. Now then, what's this amazing plan for Phase Two?"

"Here we are." He stops outside a doorway, one of those anonymous brown-and-black uber-tasteful Piccadilly stores. After all, it's *too vulgar, darling* to give a clue about what's sold there. "I think there are three dead cert ways to a woman's heart. The first is flowers." He waves the lavender in my direction, and that sweet fragrance wafts in my direction. "And the second . . ." He pushes open the door.

A new smell hits me the instant I step into the air-conditioned interior.

". . . is chocolate."

A suave, black-suited assistant nods in greeting, but holds back politely, giving us time to acclimatise. If Tiffany sold chocolate, this is what the shop would be like. Now the mocha colour scheme makes sense: this store takes chocolate very seriously, displaying its wares as though the raw material was platinum, not cocoa beans. There are moist cakes with discreet signs listing lemon fondant fillings or berry truffle toppings; sugared fruit jellies which sparkle like gemstones under the lights; and shelves bearing pots of thick, luscious preserves and sauces.

But the main event — oh, the main event is an L-shaped counter running the entire width of the shop. Behind the glass counter, perfect squares and circles of chocolate are stacked with mathematical precision, accompanied by handwritten name labels, as though they're guests at a society wedding.

"I tried all the chocolatiers within a mile of my office, and I decided this one couldn't fail to win a woman's heart."

"What a hardship for you." I giggle, then cover my mouth with my hand. Laughter seems disrespectful in this *shrine* to chocolate.

"Madame, monsieur. May I help you?" The assistant has a French accent as smooth as the merchandise.

"We're looking for the best chocolates in London," Adam says, and the assistant nods solemnly, before clearing his throat.

"Your journey is at an end. You have heard of ganache?"

I'm sure Adam knows what ganache is, but he says nothing. I shake my head.

The assistant glides behind his counter and I notice we're the only customers. "Ganache is a blend of cream, chocolate couverture and the essences of whichever flavour the chocolatier chooses to introduce."

"Right." I do my best to look attentive, but my eyes keep being drawn back to the chocolates themselves. Is it only forty minutes since that bagel?

"All our chocolates were developed in Paris by our founder. We refuse to use any fats other than cocoa butter, and each flavour has been sourced with ultimate care. The mint in our Zagora, *par exemple*, comes from Morocco and the flavour conjures up the drama and energy of the souk."

216

At last it looks like I might get to eat one. He uses silver tongs to pick up a single chocolate, and I take a bite. It's intensely minty but I can't quite taste Marrakesh: instead, it reminds me of Pimm's by the river. I pass the other half to Adam.

"Good?" The assistant asks. "In Morocco it is the custom to offer a mint tea to your sweetheart. It is said that the first tea is bitter like life and the second strong, like love."

Adam and I exchange glances. "You'll have to remember that, for your clients," he says to me.

The assistant raises his eyebrows and I pull a face at Adam. "People are always getting the wrong impression about what I do," I whisper, "and saying stuff like that doesn't exactly help."

He ignores me. "Do you have any more we could try, before we buy? Becca, what flavours do you like?"

I stare at the chocolate: the fancy names are all very well, but it makes it impossible to know what's in them. "Um . . . I like raspberries."

The assistant claps his hands together. "Ah, the Salvador. For this one, our founder always uses end-of-season raspberry fruit, for the best perfume." He presents a circular truffle on the tongs and I close my eyes as I bite into it.

Now that *is* chocolate heaven. The sharp, sweet flavour captures late summer at home, that perfect day when Mum would finally give me and Robbie and Richie permission to strip the raspberry canes of their ripened fruit, and we would eat so many that our bellies would hurt.

I open my eyes and Adam is looking at me, amused. "Good?"

"Good."

"I'll take two dozen," he says.

"You really don't have to, Adam." I put my hand on his arm to stop him. "Save your money for a real girlfriend."

The assistant glances up at us before returning to the serious job of cradling his precious chocolates in their discreet brown box.

"I insist, Becca," Adam says. "I know you're going above and beyond the call of duty." He hands over his credit card and I don't look at the bill. I could argue some more but then again . . . *those chocolates* . . .

"Where to now?" I ask as we emerge into the bright daylight rush of Piccadilly.

He hails a cab. "Round the back of South Bank, please, mate," he tells the driver, then turns to me. "Bet you can't guess what Phase Three involves?"

We wiggle our way through the scaffolding and builders' rubble behind the Festival Hall, and emerge by the National Film Theatre. The Thames stops me in my tracks: the sun makes the water and the buildings sparkle and everything seems right with the world.

"What's up?" Adam says.

"Oh, just the view. I love the Thames. Five years in London and I'm still a country girl who can't quite believe she's living in the big city."

He nods. "Well, I've lived here all my life and I feel like that."

218

We stand for a moment in silence, united in our passion for the place. "You know, I've never realised before, but I always seem to be drawn to the river when I'm organising a date. There's something irresistible about this spot."

I feel him very close to me now, and I can smell the lavender and even, I'm pretty sure, the dense raspberry-chocolate scent drifting up from the sealed box of chocolates. I've become very aware of the sound of his breathing, and my own, and I may be imagining it, but it feels like our hearts might be beating in sync.

If this was a *real* date, then this would be the best bit, the moment *before*. Those precious seconds become crystallised in your memory and will be replayed endlessly in the hours, days . . . maybe even the years to come. "*The second before your father kissed me for the first time, I felt like it was the only thing that mattered . . .*"

Oh God, *that* feeling. I'd forgotten how intense it is; how everything else stops, how you become a bundle of hope and nerve endings and speculation, unable to bear waiting and wondering whether he's going to kiss you and whether, when he does, that kiss can possibly live up to this glorious, painful anticipation and . . .

But . . .

Adam is a client. And, according to Sam, a fumbler.

The spell is broken in an instant. My body shifts a millimetre or two, without me even thinking about it, just in case Adam has somehow misread the situation, or forgotten that we're only on a Dry-Run Date.

219

I wonder if Sam got the wrong impression somehow? I mean, so far his dating behaviour has been good: a little rough around the edges, maybe, but with the right girl, I can imagine he'd make a good impression. Until the moment of truth, the meeting of lips, and then . . .

"Becca?"

"Eh?" I feel disorientated for a second. "Yes, yes, sorry, I was miles away."

He looks a little hurt. "So was I . . . sorry, this whole date thing has taken longer than I thought; you must be in a rush to clock off."

"Yes. I mean, no, no problem. No rush. You take as long as you like. Where were we? Phase Three, isn't it? What do you have in store for the lucky lady?"

"Right. Well, we've had flowers and chocolates and I thought that the last sure-fire way to a woman's heart was . . ." his voice sounds flat now, his heart not in it at all. Maybe he's guessed that I know about his fumbling. Maybe he realises how hopeless it all is. "Can you guess? We're very close."

I look around me. Skateboarders are racing past at the speed of sound, a man is blowing up balloon-animals, people are drinking chilled white wine in the NFT café. Ah! That must be the third element.

"Alcohol?" I feel disappointed. It seems a slightly underhand way to a woman's heart, but maybe if he gets them drunk, they won't remember his kissing technique.

"*Becca!* What do you take me for? No, the third phase is over there . . ." and he points towards the grid of trestle tables in front of the café, where dozens of people are browsing thousands of second-hand books,

220

the colourful spines bright in the afternoon sun. "The final way to a woman's heart is sweet words. Stay here."

So I wait as he heads for the book market, and has a word with one of the sellers. The man rummages around for a while, shows him various books. I watch as Adam shakes his head, puts another volume to one side as the seller continues to search. Adam really is putting his all into this: it's almost heart-breaking. There is, despite all the risk and the embarrassment involved, the tiniest part of me that understands how lovely it must be when someone is doing this for real. Even in the earliest days of my relationship with Marcus, when he was at his most persuasive, he seemed to be playing to the gallery somehow, like an actor determined to give the perfect performance.

I fell for it. No fool like a young fool, eh?

Finally, the seller produces a book which Adam approves of. He pays for it, then scribbles something in the margin. He walks back over, but he seems subdued. I smile tightly and brace myself for an embarrassing moment when he insists on reading out the poem.

"You know," he says when he finally gets to me, "I think it's better if I just give this to you. Page ninety-six. Read it on the train." He puts the book in the bag next to the chocolates. "Anyway. That's that. My dating tricks and techniques laid bare. So what's the verdict, oh wise Bride Hunter? Do I have a hope?"

"Oh, there's always hope," I say. "But I think you deserve a rest after all your hard work. Let's discuss it over a drink."

★ ★ ★

He pours me a white wine from the dinky plastic bottle and I take a sip before speaking.

"Right. On the positive side, Adam, you're not nearly as much of a basket case as you think you are. I've married off far worse cases. You're funny and thoughtful. You used your brain to plan a really original date. You're good company."

"So what's the but?" he says. "Go on, don't spare my feelings. I want to know the reason I'm single."

"OK." I attempt a reassuring smile. "Well, my overall message would be that, for a first date, you're trying a bit too hard. Of course, a woman likes to feel cosseted and desired, but if you come across as too keen, it can be off-putting. And so much pre-planning does mean a date can feel like a military operation." *Though am I really one to criticise someone for that?*

He winces. "Really? Fair enough, I suppose, though I did go out of my way to impress you because you're always setting up dates for other people. I thought I'd have to work extra hard to make an impression."

I nod sagely. "Well, that's laudable, but remember, I'm not in the market . . ."

". . . for a man, yes, I know that, Becca."

"Anyhow, your ideas are good, but I'd pick one of them, perhaps. The second problem is that you have a tendency to gabble a bit, I noticed it at the Tower of London, too."

"That's nerves. I'm always like that."

I want to pat him on the knee, but I restrain myself. "But you needn't be nervous with me. Just remember, a woman doesn't want a tour guide, she wants you. The real you, so when you're planning a date in future, try to work out an environment where you can feel at home; be natural."

"Right. Anything else?"

I look at my wine glass: somehow I've emptied it already. Today has been far more stressful than I expected, and I'm suddenly desperate to get home. "Not that I can think of. Now, is there anything you'd like to ask me, before we wrap up?"

"Um . . ." he pauses, and draws a squiggle in the foam on top of his beer. "Well, I suppose there is one thing."

"Go on. After all, if you can't ask me, who can you ask? It's my job to prepare you for a girl you actually like."

He stares at his feet. "It's the physical side. I just wondered when . . . well, in today's date, for example, when, or even if, would have been an appropriate time to, you know . . . hold hands or even kiss?"

I feel my own cheeks colour. Where has he been all these years? "Righto, well. It's so hard to tell because our situation is necessarily *sterile* and artificial, but when would you have made a move, do you think?"

"Perhaps . . . by the river, a few minutes ago?" His voice is tentative, like a pupil offering an answer to a tricky maths question.

"Hmmm," I say, not sure how to answer. "Well, that might have been appropriate. It certainly wouldn't be a bad time, but it's best to be intuitive about these things. Not to think too much. The thing is, Adam . . ." I try to work out whether there's anything I can say about the fumbling business. Could I possibly suggest he — I don't know, practises on his own hand, the way we used to when we were teenagers? Or asks an ex-girlfriend how he might improve his technique?

Oh God. I couldn't possibly say that.

"What?"

"The thing is, is to be yourself." There. The most useless bit of practical advice known to man or woman. Well done, Becca.

He stares at me, as though he wants to say something else, but then he puts down his beer. "Thank you. I appreciate it. I think I'm learning, I really am."

Poor bugger. I don't know what he's thanking me for. I'm taking his money for nothing. Still, at least I never have to do it again. "Not a problem, Adam. Anyhow, as you said, time's getting on, and I ought to head off home now. Very thoughtful of you to end the date at Waterloo, it'll take me no time at all. Oh, and don't leave it too long before acting on my advice, eh?" I consider mentioning Sam, suggesting he gives her another call. But it'd still feel like throwing him to the wolves somehow . . .

I stand up and hold out my hand to shake his. He looks a little bemused. He hands me the lavender plant, and the bag with the chocolates and the poetry book, and I consider telling him to keep them, but it seems too cruel. "Do you want to invoice me for today, or shall I settle up now?"

I wave him away. "Oh, don't worry, I'll be in touch about that. Have a nice evening, Adam, see you soon."

224

And I march off back to the station, feeling like I have failed the poor man terribly.

On the train back to Richmond, my head feels woozy from the wine. I remember the chocolates and wonder whether I should eat one, but as I reach into the bag, I touch the book. It's a volume of Tennyson poems.

What was the page number again? I open it up, and the corner of page 96 is folded over, partway through a poem called "The Princess". Adam has underlined four lines:

> Man is the hunter; woman is his game:
> The sleek and shining creatures of the chase,
> We hunt them for the beauty of their skins;
> They love us for it, and we ride them down.

Then, in the margin, he's written: *Only joking, Bride Hunter. Nowadays it's the girls who do the hunting! Take pity on the poor prey. We try our best . . .*

CHAPTER
EIGHTEEN

Monday mornings in my old job were depressing occasions. My colleagues would burst into the office, bloodshot but amplified by too much caffeine and cocaine, and limber up for the cut-throat week ahead by boasting about the excesses of their weekends. The more they drank or spent or snorted, the more successful they seemed to their peers.

Monday mornings now I'm a bride hunter are a little more civilised. I go to Maison Blanc for fresh croissants, and Tesco for fresh orange juice, while Georgie wafts around the kitchen in her dove-grey silk dressing gown, grinding the coffee beans she buys from Italy. And then we both go back to her east-facing bedroom (more of a boudoir, really, all antique furniture and white linen) to soak up the morning sun and contemplate the week ahead.

She's usually had a weekend every bit as debauched as my old head-hunter colleagues (last night she rolled home at 3a.m.), but she doesn't boast about it. She refuses to let me see her first thing, but by the time I get back from the boulangerie, she's applied a miracle-working combination of creams and masques and potions that make her look as though she's slept for twelve blameless hours.

"Now," she says, as she pulls the croissant apart, "hot news, precious niece, I think I have the perfect girl for that Eddy the Plank chap."

"Oh yes?" I try to inject some enthusiasm into my voice. I'm feeling weary today. The last week has been frenetic — Edinburgh was non-stop — but I usually find work stimulating rather than tiring. And yesterday unsettled me somehow. I don't like feeling I've failed someone.

Georgie ploughs on. "I've been asking around on your behalf. I was rather hopeful about a dancer over here from Peru. Adorable to look at, a line to *die* for. But I checked her out and off stage, apparently, she is both *coarse* and *voracious* in her appetites for men. Honestly. Never in my day . . ."

I raise my eyebrows. From what I remember of Georgie's days as a dancer, she wasn't exactly a paragon of virtue herself. "Go on. Who have you found?"

Georgie claps her hands together in excitement, nearly upending the tray on her bed. I jump out of my chair to steady it — we'd never get coffee stains out of that Bruges lace bedspread. "An adorable little thing from the Courtauld Institute, doing a dissertation in Art History. She came into the gallery on Thursday, looking for a part-time job. Beautiful. Blonde. Teeny, an absolute waif. Bound to evoke those protective instincts in Edward."

I sit back down on the bed. "There's definitely no catch?"

"No catch. Oh! I forgot the best bit. She's the ultimate in innocents abroad. She's Ukrainian, which I'll admit doesn't always spell dewy-eyed naïvety, but this is the first time she's ever lived overseas. Who better than Eddy to make her feel at home?

"Do you think she'd be interested? She might have a boyfriend already."

Georgie licks flakes of croissant off her delicate fingers. "All sorted. I've already checked. She's single, she's willing and she's free all this week!"

I climb up the spiral staircase to my office after breakfast, and sneak out the pain au chocolat I bought as a treat along with the croissants. I'm not usually one for comfort eating, but I really do feel quite out of sorts, despite Georgie's apparent breakthrough with Katerina the Ukrainian ingénue.

I log on to my email to find one from Sam:

Subject: No bloody good
Tried to call you yesterday afternoon, but your phone was switched off. I know it's a Bank Holiday weekend but a word of advice, Rebecca, it's risky to be incommunicado when you claim to be offering a personal service.

Anyhow, I was trying to call to update you on your latest failures. Neither Zak nor Henry proved up to scratch. Henry was totally preoccupied with the size of his carbon footprint when frankly it was his dimensions elsewhere which were more of an issue. And Zak's vocabulary consisted almost entirely of designer labels and computer language. By the time he'd explained TMI (Too Much Information) and ROFL (Roll On The Floor Laughing) I was in a FOAD (Fuck Off And Die) frame of mind.

I wonder whether there's been any progress with the fumbling baker? I might be prepared to give him another go, under the circumstances. Perhaps if you gave him a few pointers? I think it's the very least you can do.

Unless you can offer me an updated plan of action by close of play today, I will assume our contract is at an end. I say contract. Actually, yours isn't worth the paper it's printed on. But if I were you, I'd be less worried about my retainer and more worried about my reputation. I don't like people who waste my time and I'm not shy of spreading the word.

Sam Ottoway
Barrister-at-Law

I close the email with a sigh, wishing I'd bought two pains au chocolat. I need sugar. Plan of action? Contract? I'm more than tempted to take out a contract on her. I've had some tricky customers in my time, but no one's ever threatened to destroy my reputation, and lawyers are one of my key sources of client groups. I can't win — stay working on this impossible case, or give in and see my business trashed.

I'm too bloody soft-hearted, that's my trouble. I mean, it's all very well for Georgie to tell me I should help Sam on sisterhood grounds, but when the "sister" turns nasty because she's incapable of going on a date without dropping her knickers, then I don't really see what kind of master plan is going to work. Unless it involves a chastity belt.

No, come on, Becca. Don't let one tricky customer rattle you. Look at the positives. This Katerina girl could be about to make Edward's day. And then there's Dwight.

Dwight! I haven't heard from him since a text on Saturday morning proclaiming himself the happiest man alive. Again. A call to my latest success story should be just the job when it comes to cheering myself up.

He answers immediately. "Hey, Cupid. Hope you've been celebrating your triumph this weekend. We had an absolute *ball*. So much better than the time I proposed to my first wife. She refused to drink champagne because it wasn't on her *South Beach Diet* sheet, then got up at 6a.m. next morning for her run. 'Can't let standards slip just because we're getting married, Dwighty-Poos'." His impersonation of his ex-wife's drawl makes me smile. "I guess I shoulda called it off right then. But maybe you need to go through the bad times to be able to appreciate the good ones, huh, Rebecca?"

My mood can't help but be lifted by his boyish excitement. "That's a great philosophy, Dwight. So have you made plans yet?"

230

"Have *we* made plans! There's no time to waste, that's what we've decided. I didn't know — I guess I'd never asked — but poor Heather's folks are both dead."

"Dead? How tragic." A tiny doubt surfaces in my mind. *How convenient.* Then I push it away. She was so nervous that night at Lachlan's Inn by the Loch. I can't believe she's a con artist. "What happened?"

"Ah, she didn't go into details. I think her daddy had a heart attack and her mom died in an accident not long after. An orphan by the time she was twenty. That's why we won't waste a second. Life is precious, Rebecca, that's what my Heather has taught me. And she has a new family now."

"Yes. Yes, of course. Everyone needs someone to take care of them." *Or to support them.* "So when are you hoping to tie the knot?"

"My diary is nuts. The only space is July."

"Next month?"

"Sure. It's quiet for me then, so we're thinking a real small wedding over here, just us and a few of her friends from the country dancing, so Heather doesn't feel too bad about having no family as guests. Then I'm due to go back home for business in the Fall, so we can meet my family and have a big celebration with my folks then. And we'd love you to be guest of honour at both."

"I love a wedding, Dwight. But are you sure you want me there? I mean, not everyone likes people to know how they met."

He laughs. "No shame in getting expert help, that's what I say."

"Then it'd be my pleasure, Dwight. Although I don't know about America. Autumn's usually frantic for me and as I'm still building the business, it's not easy to take time off." I stop, remembering something. "I should imagine it'll be the same for Heather, won't it? I mean, can she just take time off work like that, without leaving people in the lurch?"

Dwight laughs. "You know, that's what she was worried about. Until I explained that as my wife, she won't *need* to work any more. She seemed real surprised, but I talked her round in the end. She's got some high-profile public relations thing to finish off for the sake of the bunny-rabbits and the puppies, so she's determined to work up till the wedding and then — well, she's so dedicated to building our home that she's leaving her job straight after."

"Yes. Of course." I feel shivery.

"First off, she'll be house-hunting. I don't think a bachelor pad is the place to begin married life."

He makes his penthouse sound like a studio flat in Peckham rather than three thousand square metres of prime riverside real estate. "No, I suppose not. And definitely not a bachelor pad with a bunny-girl themed roof terrace."

"You got it, Rebecca. Anyhow, I gotta go. But I'll call you as soon as we've fixed the date."

"Great. I'll be there."

"Oh. One last thing you could do for me. Am I right that it's traditional for newly engaged couples to put an announcement in the London *Times*?"

232

"Yes, it's normally the bride's parents, but in the circumstances . . ."

"That's exactly what I was thinking. Would you do it for me, Rebecca? Once we know the date. Charge it to my account."

"Of course." Then I have a brainwave. "And, um, well, given both your backgrounds, what about an announcement in a Scottish paper, too?"

"Sure. Hey, you're the best, Rebecca. Don't let anyone tell you any different."

I put down the phone and sigh. The best? Maybe. Or possibly the best at being devious. If Heather isn't all she seems, then an announcement in the *Scotsman* or the *Herald* could be my best chance of finding out for sure.

The first time I see Katerina Anatoly, I realise why Georgie was so bowled over.

She reminds me of the photographs of my aunt when she was young, the same Audrey Hepburn-like grace. If anything, this girl might be prettier. But while Georgie used her beauty to challenge men, daring them to approach and then playing games with their weakness, Katerina doesn't even seem to realise the power she has.

She waits outside Edward's favourite back-street Lebanese café, and fiddles with her hair. It's the colour of corn, swept up behind her head with a cheap tortoiseshell clip. Her eyes and skin are pale, and she's wearing no make-up except for an orangey lipstick which is too garish for her. But it doesn't detract from

233

her looks. If anything, it makes her seem even more vulnerable, like a child playing with her mother's make-up.

She wears a cheap fawn mac, and underneath it I can see a woollen skirt that stops mid-calf. The least flattering length possible, yet again it makes her seem quirky rather than chunky. I walk past her, into the café, and take my seat. The place is packed again and I order myself a falafel sandwich, even though I'm too edgy to eat. I *really* want this to work out for Edward.

Through the window I see him turn into the alleyway. He looks as dishevelled as usual, as he hasn't had time to go home and change after work. But that was a deliberate ploy on my part. The less time he has to worry about the date, the better — I called him this morning to arrange it, to give him no time at all to change his mind. And there's no grand plan tonight, no fancy arrangements or recommended topics of conversation (though I did send him a web-link to a site about the Ukraine, and another about the Courtauld Institute). I suggested the Lebanese because it's where he feels most comfortable. All I told him about Katerina was that she's new in London, she works in a gallery, and she'd like to meet a new friend to show her around.

I watch carefully: when I went to see him meet Eleanor at the Landmark, I missed that first crucial moment. And look what happened. He knows I'm here this time — he said he wanted me to be able to tell him where he went wrong afterwards. Nothing like optimism, eh?

234

He turns to cross over to this side of the alley and then he sees her . . .

And freezes. Stares. He looks as if he can't quite believe his eyes. Katerina hasn't seen him yet, and as he keeps staring at her, something rather magical happens to Edward Lincoln. He begins to straighten up, like one of those biology illustrations showing the ascent of man, from a hunched-up Neanderthal to besuited *Homo sapiens*. His posture, usually either sloppy or unnaturally straight, is transformed and he resumes his journey across the street.

He approaches Katerina, mouthing her name. I see her head nodding in reply and now his face changes; transformed by a grateful, disbelieving smile. As he pushes open the door to the café, heads turn and all eyes fix on Katerina, but Edward's expression says it all: *Don't you dare. She's mine.*

Bingo! The Bride Hunter strikes again!

I squirm all the way through my plate of falafel, wishing I was anywhere but here. Most of the time, my policy of observing first dates seems utterly justified, because I am on hand to offer text message advice or to debrief my client afterwards.

But right now I feel like a voyeur. Katerina is in my eyeline, so I can't see Edward's face, but I can see his body language. He leans across the table, his hands so close to hers that they're almost touching. He points out items on the menu, and when she looks baffled (a look that suits her rather well), he orders confidently for both of them. When their drinks arrive, it takes them thirty seconds to realise the waiter's there. These two are in their own bubble. An elephant could walk into the café and order a mixed kebab — I can't imagine an elephant eating hummus somehow — and they wouldn't even notice.

At first, Katerina keeps looking down, but within a few minutes she begins to meet his eye and to giggle. He's asking her about herself and her faltering one-word answers are gradually replaced by longer replies about topics that make her come to life: art, perhaps, or home. She lifts up her handbag, and fishes out a small bundle of photographs and Edward pores over them.

By the time I finish my food and manage to get the waiter's attention to pay my bill, their supper has been sitting untouched for twenty minutes. I cross the café without looking at Edward at all, and I wait until I'm two streets away before I allow myself to lean on a wall and breathe a sigh of contented relief.

Edward's pulled! Hooray for Katerina! Hooray for Georgie! Hooray for me!

I must call Georgie and give her the news. I take out my phone but then remember that she's out at some premiere. I try Helga's number, but she's on answerphone. I really want to tell someone about tonight.

But there's a text message. Probably Sam picking holes in the master plan I emailed to her last night. As well she might: the more I think about it, the more I am convinced that I can't possibly find her anyone who'll live up to her expectations. I'm not even sure that she really wants a husband at all. Though right now, anything feels possible. I am Cupid. I can change people's lives . . .

I open the text:

HOW'S BRIDE-HUNTING TONIGHT? ADAM

I know I shouldn't call him — he's a client, not a friend — but I'm high as a kite and desperate to tell someone about Edward and Katerina. He answers straight away.

"Adam! Hi! It's Becca!"

"*Hello.*" He sounds just as upbeat. "You sound full of the joys of spring."

"Oh, just another mission accomplished for London's top matchmaker."

He laughs. "Was it that fold-up handbag-sized bow and arrow again, then?"

"Something like that. It's all in the aim, you know. And the targeting." I follow my nose downhill through the deserted streets, hoping I'm heading towards the river.

"I'm sure you're right. Hang on, let me switch the telly down."

"Not out on the town putting my advice into practice then? You know you can't fail with the bride hunter behind you."

"Yeah, well . . . no use putting your techniques to work on the wrong woman, is there? So tell me about your mission accomplished."

"Oh!" I'm torn between client confidentiality and the urge to talk to someone about what's just happened. "I

237

can't tell you any personal details, but it was lovely. I've got this client, he's really shy, and hasn't much confidence around women, retreated into his shell. I was a bit stuck, to be honest."

"Uh huh. So, what did you do, O goddess of love?"

I catch a glimpse of the Thames, between two buildings. "Actually, it's a good lesson for you to learn. If at first you don't succeed . . . The first date I set up was a bit of a disaster. I thought maybe he needed someone bossy, to force him out of his shell."

"I see the logic," he says. "It must be like a puzzle, your work. Matching up round pegs or square holes."

"Something like that. Anyway, bossy was *totally* the wrong thing. So tonight we tried the opposite, a girl who really needs his help, to bring out the more masculine, protective qualities . . ."

"It's like one of those chick flicks my girlfriend used to drag me to . . ."

Girlfriend? Adam's never mentioned a girlfriend before. It throws me for a moment. "Yeah. Yeah, right. Well, tonight's premiere has a happy ending. Or a happy beginning. He was *transformed*. And so was she. I mean, it's bloody early days but sometimes you can just tell."

"Can you?" he says. "Must be feminine intuition. I never have the faintest idea when someone likes me."

"No? I'm sure your time will come. Then you'll know. Sorry, that sounded deeply patronising, didn't it?" I'm on the Embankment now: it's a chilly night for June, so not many people are out, and I feel quite

238

alone. But it's exciting, sometimes, to feel like you have London to yourself."

"Not at all. With you on my side, anything's possible. That's why I texted you, really. I wanted to set up our next appointment."

The night feels colder, suddenly. *You daft tart, Becca. Call yourself a professional?* Adam's not a friend, he's a client. "Oh. Right. Well, the thing is, Adam, I think I've taught you more or less all I know, to be honest. And I didn't envisage a long-term consultancy. You're better at it than you think, you know. You're more than capable of going it alone."

He doesn't say anything for a while. I can hear the *Friends* theme tune on his TV. "But . . . I wanted to try out what you suggested. You know, the more laid-back approach. A date where I'm letting my personality shine through."

"I still think you'd be better off doing that with a *real* girl. I mean, you just mentioned an ex-girlfriend, so you're not completely innocent of the ways of women." I'm outside the Tube station now, along with a few drunks who don't make me feel like hanging around.

"That was a hell of a long time ago, Becca. Things have changed. Texting, for example. How does that work? I *really* need your help. Just once more. Please?"

One of the drunks begins to lumber towards me, so I try to think fast. Is there any harm in giving him one last session? Can I manage to get through it without telling him about the fumbling thing?

Then I think of Edward and Katerina and how hopeless Edward's situation seemed. Is it fair to deny

Adam the chance of getting to first base? I ignore the tramp and stare fixedly at the lights reflected in the Thames. Who knows, maybe in one of those buildings, there's a woman who is just as fumbly as he is? And then there's always Sam: maybe one more dry-run with me is all it'll take to get him *up to scratch*. I could kill two birds with one stone — after all, they liked each other enough to fumble their way through a kiss, didn't they?

"Becca, are you still there?"

"All right, Adam. For a man who needs dating help, you're surprisingly persuasive. One last session. But only on condition that you ask someone else out straight away. In fact, we can do better than that. After your dummy date with me, you must *promise* to call Sam again."

"Sam? But she hated me."

"There you are again, being negative. She didn't hate you at all. She just felt you needed a little more confidence. And by the time you've practised on me, you should be bubbling with the stuff. Text me sometime and I will see what I can do. Now I have to go before I have a brief encounter with a tramp."

"Thanks, Becca. I can't thank you enough for what you're doing."

"An invitation to your wedding will be thanks enough. It's just your good fortune that I happened to be such a soft touch this evening. I don't make a habit of it, Adam."

"No. I didn't think you did. Good night. Sweet dreams."

CHAPTER
NINETEEN

"You might have made more of an effort," Sam barks at me when she meets me outside Clapham Junction station.

"Sorry." I'm not sorry at all, but I know she won't be satisfied till I apologise.

Unlike me, Sam has *definitely* made an effort. She's wearing a wrap dress with a plunging neckline and a rising hemline, plus high boots with more than a hint of bondage about them. Her hair is down, with a slight Hollywood wave, and her eyes are kohled with a thickness and precision not seen since the late 1980s. She looks like a woman who means business. Though tonight her business is pleasure.

She strides ahead of me, towards our destination: the Ball and Chain, the latest branch of a growing number of legal-themed pubs to hit London. Clapham is an obvious place to open one, the place is full of solicitors and barristers, working their way up the property ladder from one-bedders above yummy-mummy boutiques, to little terraces backing on to the railway line, before graduating to the kind of swanky townhouse that Sam owns.

About a mile from here, at the dodgier end, is the flat I planned to buy: not even a one-bedder, but a dinky studio above a dry-cleaners. I started flat-hunting when Marcus was buying his pent-house, even though my budget was a tenth of his. I convinced myself on the second viewing that the chemical smell was homely rather than unpleasant. It had the sweetest mezzanine bed above the living room, and a shower just big enough for me, though Marcus moaned that he would struggle when he stayed over. And then, of course, he persuaded me to move into the penthouse with him, to make it *our* home.

My name wasn't on the deeds, of course, but I paid my share of the bills and even contributed to the cost of the furniture he'd chosen and the improvements he was making.

"Fair's fair, Bex. I'll look after you. You know that."

What a fool I was. Now, of course, even that manky studio would be way beyond my budget. London prices have gone crazy, thanks largely to my clientele and their habit of using their bonuses to snap up flats with no more thought than I'd give to buying a new pair of shoes.

But I don't do *my* job for the money, eh? I do it for the job satisfaction.

"Now you are going to play along, aren't you?" Sam says.

"I don't know. Surely if I sit next to you looking grumpy and saying the wrong thing, it'll reflect all the better on you?"

"I need that to stand any chance, eh?" She scowls, before leading the way down stone steps into the cellar bar where we're going to be spending the next ninety minutes.

I have a feeling it's going to be the longest ninety minutes of my life.

When I wrote "speed-dating" on the master-plan that I sent to Sam two weeks ago, I didn't mean that I would come too. But she got to work on me using the same powers of persuasion that talked a jury into acquitting notorious fraudster Jack the Asset Stripper, and I found myself agreeing to join her for "moral support".

Though judging from her outfit, she's really looking for *immoral* support.

The Sloaney woman organising the event gives us each a name badge and a glass of nasty wine, and directs us to our chairs. It's *Professionals Night, 25–45*, though despite the flattering fake gaslights, it's clear that a lot of the men are lying about their age. Actually, that's not bad news for Sam, as the last thing she needs is a toyboy.

It runs the same way as every other speed-dating event I've ever attended (Helga went through a phase of dragging me along to them, when they were the new in-thing). The girls sit tight, the boys move round every three minutes, and we all have scorecards to indicate whether we want to see each person again. The trickiest bit is deciding whether to mark your cards at the end of each three-minute "date", and risk the man seeing which box you're ticking. The alternative is to leave it all till the end, and hope you can still differentiate well enough between the blur of faces so that you don't say DATE ME to the boorish banker, and RAINCHECK to the hunky human-rights campaigner.

Not that it matters to me, of course. I am only going through the motions. That's why I changed before I came out, replacing my favourite shirt and jeans with the baggy T-shirt and old cords I wear to Bushy Park. I tied my hair back and didn't bother with make-up. No man could fail to realise that I'm going along with this under sufferance. And I do happen to think my slovenly outfit and sullen manner is doing Sam and all the other hopeful, immaculately groomed women a big favour.

Sloaney directs the men to their seats. My first one is sweating — it's a warm evening outside, and his body's probably gone into shock in this air-conditioned cellar. He can't be much younger than my dad, and he has City pallor, that unmistakable lack of colour that afflicts those who've failed to make their fortunes by middle-age and are clinging on to their jobs like grim death.

"Most women make an effort for occasions like this," he says as he sits down, seemingly unaware of the dark circles of sweat soaking his shirt at the armpits and, charmingly, at his belly-button.

"I'm not most women," I say.

"Feminist, are you?"

I sigh so hard that my fringe lifts up in the air. "That's right." I peer up at the giant "three-minute" egg-timer that Sloaney has hung on the wall. Not exactly subtle, when most of the women here are Sam's

244

age and in a race against time to find someone to fertilise their own eggs.

Mr Sweaty Belly Button gives up the pretence of chatting me up, and begins eyeing up the rest of the talent. Never has three minutes seemed so long . . .

The buzzer goes off, and he stands up, ready to move across to Sam, who is next in line. She leans over to whisper in my ear. "Business tip for you: if you don't fancy anyone, why not try to pick up some new clients?"

"I don't believe in confusing business and pleasure." An image of Adam flashes through my mind. I chase it away.

Sam raises her eyebrows. "And which is this? To be successful, Rebecca, you have to be on the make twenty-four seven."

"It isn't always about the money. I made a decision early on that I would only take on clients I thought deserved to find love," I whisper back. I'm so tempted to add, "but I made a disastrous exception in your case," until I remember what she's threatened to do to my reputation, and shut my mouth.

A procession of men follows. I ask them about themselves and they tell me, at length. If they don't take the "sod off" hint that my appearance gives off, I begin to wax lyrical about my life's ambition to open a cat sanctuary, and that does the trick. Every now and then, I cast a quick glance in Sam's direction and she seems to be getting on fine. Between dates four and five she flashes me a look at her scorecard and she's ticked all but Mr Sweaty. Maybe with Sam it is quantity not quality that counts . . .

After another couple of men (one of whom simply sits down and recites a list of his cars, houses and gadgets as though I'm an inventory clerk), Sloaney announces a break, and I am first to the bar. The other daters hold back, trying to suss out whether it's too early to make a move on the people they fancy.

"You really think you're above all this, don't you, Rebecca?"

It's Sam. She's so close I can smell the booze on her breath. Uh-oh.

"God, no. Not above it. I simply don't want to go out with anyone at the moment, but if I did, well, this would be a good place to start." Only after I've answered do I think about it properly. Actually, it's the last place I'd come, but then the whole idea of dating again is such an alien concept that I can't imagine how I'd go about it.

"That's exactly the problem!" Sam says, slamming her glass down on the bar. "How can you advise other people on love when you don't want it — or maybe can't get it — yourself? Isn't it like a bloody priest giving sex education advice?"

"That's worked pretty well for the Catholic Church for the last few thousand years."

She moves even closer to me now. "Oh, you're so glib, aren't you? So pious. After all, this is only people's *lives* you're playing with, isn't it? People's hearts?"

"Sam, I'm not sure that this is the time or the place —"

246

"I thought you said it was a good place," she hisses, managing to maintain a dazzling smile for appearances. "You think you've got it all under control. Little Miss Matchmaker, with her scientifically proven psychological questions and profiling, pulling people's strings, playing God. And all the time you're sitting pretty on your own island, nice and safe. Untouchable."

I bristle. "I don't see that my private life is any of your business —"

"Private life? What private life?" She grabs one of the free glasses of wine the barman has just finished pouring, and takes a big swig. "I think it's my business when I'm paying you a fat fee to advise me on my own love life."

Her voice is getting louder so I steer her away from the bar, towards a darker corner. I'd love to walk off, but Sam's so volatile, there's no telling what she might do if I leave. I don't think her threats to destroy me are hollow. "Sam, I'm sorry if you're not happy with my service, but —"

"I've seen the way you look at me, Rebecca. Like I'm some sad, hopeless creature. You don't like me, do you?"

"I . . ." *Is it so obvious?* I thought I was good at hiding my feelings. "I respect you, Sam. I don't think it's appropriate to think of my clients as friends, anyway."

"Fucking hell! It's all about *appropriate* with you, isn't it? That's why you disapprove of me sleeping with anyone who isn't going to be my true love. Just because I'm willing to take a bit of comfort, a bit of human contact when it's offered. Because I'm not a control freak with a hundred intellectual theories on love but no intention of ever risking that whole messy business again." She hesitates then spits out her next words: "When was the last time *you* allowed anyone to get close to you? Answer me that."

"I don't . . . I mean . . . just because I want other people to fall in love doesn't mean I . . ." And then the wine and the heat and Sam's aggression suddenly seem too much, and I feel an almost overwhelming urge to cry.

But I won't cry in front of other people. I haven't done that since my last day in the office with Marcus, the day I lost everything. I swallow hard. "You seem to be getting on fine without me, Sam. I'll call you tomorrow."

And I take the steps up from the cellar slowly, because I can't see them properly through the bloody treacherous tears that are brimming in my eyes. When I get to the station I pace up and down outside before I dare go into the building, where people might see my face, which must have gone bright red from the effort of not crying.

Bloody Sam. Who does she think she is? I'm only helping her because she blackmailed me from the start with all that feminist bollocks. What makes her think she can pronounce on my life, accusing *me* of being a control freak?

I'm not a control freak, am I? Surely a control freak is someone who isn't open to anything new, who rationalises everything, who sees life as some kind of

248

battle to stay in charge of their feelings and other people's feelings, rather than let life happen to them . . .

Oh shit.

I *am* a control freak. How did that happen?

My phone rings: Withheld Number. It's probably Sam, calling to apologise, and knowing I won't answer if her number pops up.

"Hello." I put on my best strict voice which, handily, also stops me sounding on the edge of tears.

"Bex? Is that you, Bex? Sorry, do I have the right number?"

"Marcus?" *Why* did I say his name? Why didn't I just mumble, *No, wrong number?*

"It is you, Bex? Fuck me, you sound weird. You *know*, don't you?"

That voice . . . *that voice* belongs to the person who turned me into a control freak, the man who taught me to trust no one.

"Know what, Marcus? It must be something important. After all, you haven't phoned me for what, two years." Two years, four months, to be exact.

"Longer than that, Bex. I wouldn't have called at all, actually. I mean, I know it's not necessarily good etiquette to ring someone whose feelings you've hurt with news like this . . ."

Whose feelings you've hurt? Whose heart you broke? Whose job you casually removed? Whose chance of financial independence you took away on a whim? "It was a long time ago."

"Now, I'm glad you feel that way, because I was anxious you might think that I was calling out of malice."

"Why would I think that?"

"Because . . . I know this might upset you, Bex. I have wrestled with my conscience over this one."

"When did you develop one of those, Marcus?" I smile to myself — I never used to answer back. Maybe I have moved on.

"Oh, very feisty. Look. Are you sitting down? Only . . . there's no easy way to say this, but I'm afraid you're being two-timed."

"Eh?" For some utterly inexplicable reason, I think of Adam and feel *seasick*. Bizarre.

"That chap I saw you with at the gym. The one in the disastrous chain-store suit?"

A penny begins to drop. "Edward. Yes."

"Bex, I was out at the Savoy Grill last night and . . . I'm afraid he was there with a blonde. *Very* pretty young thing. And, well, I can imagine the excuses he'll use — it was my sister, my cousin, a girl from work —"

"You've used all of them in your time yourself, I guess, Marcus." I could get to enjoy Benson Baiting.

"But I'm afraid there's no question. A man knows these things. They're shagging."

The dirty rascal. I knew it was going well with Katerina but . . . "I can't believe he didn't tell me."

"Well, I'm not too surprised that he didn't, under the circumstances, but . . . hang on, Bex. There's no need to sound so pleased about it." Marcus seems put out that I haven't yet burst into tears.

250

"He's not going out with me . . . I mean, we finished a while back. It's fine. We weren't really compatible."

"Oh. Well, you don't seem terribly upset. Actually, she did look more his type, to be perfectly honest. Suggestible. Easily influenced."

"Your type, too, eh, Marcus?"

"Now, now. You make me sound like Svengali or something. Anyway, I've moved on. I like my women with more bite these days."

"That's all very interesting, but I'm afraid I need to go now, Marcus. Sorry not to give you the reaction you were hoping for, but it's kind of you to call."

"But that's not why —"

"Take care, now." I end the call and feel light-headed. That's the first time I've ever cut him off.

The train is quiet and a cleaner has taken away all the free newspapers so I have no option but to stare out of the window at dusk-darkened London, and wonder what Marcus is playing at.

I like my women with more bite these days.

Or, perhaps, women who put up more of a fight, because it makes it all the more satisfying for him when they give in. Marcus relishes a challenge.

So why get in touch again, after all this time? *I don't believe in old flames, there's usually a bloody good reason they went out.* That was the answer he used to trot out whenever I got insecure about his long, long line of ex-girlfriends. What I didn't know at the time was that he had no need to revisit his romantic past: he was too busy experimenting with his romantic future.

I examine my ghostly reflection in the train window. Marcus changed me on the inside, but did he change me on the outside, too? I look more the City girl now, of course: my hippy-chick chestnut hair tamed by five years of blow-drying, and my once wide eyes narrowed and hardened by things I'd rather not have seen.

I'm a tougher cookie than I used to be. Sam might call me a control freak but at least I can be sure of one thing: I will never let another man hurt me as long as I live. Thanks for that, Marcus Benson. You did me a real favour.

Even if you didn't do it on purpose.

CHAPTER
TWENTY

My finger stops halfway to the buzzer labelled *HILL* as I try to remember the last time I visited a bloke alone in his flat.

It must be years. Yep, not since the first time I came down to London to see Marcus. When I crossed the threshold of his rather lovely Putney maisonette, I also crossed over into the adult world — one where I learned to be cool as a cucumber when lines of coke were offered at the end of an otherwise conventional dinner party, and unfazed when people discussed the merits of different porn movies as casually as they'd compare *EastEnders* to *Coronation Street*.

Marcus introduced me to all the things that terrified my mother about the city. But he didn't corrupt me. He broke my heart instead.

Still, I'm over all that now. That phone call proved it fair and square. I used to be an amateur in the game of love: now I'm one hundred per cent professional.

I press the buzzer this time and a crackly voice says something indecipherable before the door hums and I push it open. It's an old-fashioned mansion block, and the banister curves upwards, like a finger beckoning me. The hallway smells of damp and curry, but as I puff my way past the third flight, the scent changes to something much homelier . . .

"Becca!"

Adam springs out of a doorway like a jack-in-the-box. He's wearing a blue-and-white striped apron and as I approach the doorway I realise what the smell is.

Bread.

"Is that your work uniform?" I say, pointing at his clothes.

"Oh, no, I wear a suit these days. My staff do the baking, while I do accounts and meet backers. Lucky me. But I do sometimes work from home," he says, leading me through a tiny hallway into a vast living area. At one end are huge turquoise sofas and the usual boys' toys — plasma screen, at least two different makes of games consoles, a precariously balanced pile of DVDs — and at the other . . .

"Wow. I bet even Jamie Oliver hasn't got one that swish."

Adam beams as he steps into the most space-age kitchen I've seen since the old Smash ad on TV. "Yeah, well. It's my pride and joy." He strokes the stainless steel work surface. "I managed to get the taxman to pay for part of it because I test all the recipes here so it counts as research and development. It's the kitchen equivalent of a Ferrari. Italian style, German engineering, Japanese knives . . ." he taps the side of his head, "but that's nothing without the all-important British imagination."

"I bet."

He pulls a red-and-white apron from a hook. "You said I should plan a date where I could be natural . . . well, you won't get me any more natural than I am here, up to my elbows in dough." He throws me the apron. "And I was hoping you might give me a hand."

"Well, it's the first time I've ever been paid to cook."

He pulls a face. "Oh, come on, Becca. You know why you're here, I know why you're here, but could we not just pretend that you're here to have fun?"

"Sorry." I pull the apron over my head. It rather spoils the effect of the two shirt buttons I undid on the Tube on the way over here, just to enter into the spirit of the dummy date. "Rebecca Orchard reporting for duty, chef."

"Let me see those filthy fucking hands," he says, then collapses into giggles. "It's no good, I can't do Gordon Ramsay. I don't feel comfortable swearing at a woman."

"How old-fashioned. I bet you swear at work."

"Ah, well, that's different," he says, as he pulls a handle and a floor-to-ceiling cupboard stuffed with pans and pots slides out. He selects a couple of glass mixing bowls. "That's the boys. Sign of affection among the boys, swearing."

"You're a man's man, then, are you, Adam?"

He walks to the other side of the kitchen, where a matching pull-out larder is as well stocked as Fortnum and Mason. "I suppose so. Not for want of trying, though. I do *like* women. A lot. It's the games I can't get my head round. The *Does she like me? Doesn't she like me?* stuff that mystifies me."

"Not all women are like that."

"No?" He begins taking out ingredients: different flours and nuts and dried fruit. "Well, in my *very* limited experience, I'm afraid the ones I've known are."

"Come on, Adam. You told me you went travelling. You must have had your share of girls then. You're not exactly the Elephant Man, are you?"

He shrugs off the half-compliment. "I did have a few offers. But you see . . . well, I wasn't quite single at the time."

"Really? Tell me more . . ."

He shakes his head. "Correct me if I'm wrong, Becca, but wouldn't it be better to avoid talking about ex-girlfriends on a date?"

"Ah. Yes. Now you come to mention it. Though, well, it's worth bearing in mind that by the time a bloke reaches a certain age, a woman would definitely prefer a man to have *some* relationship history than none at all."

He frowns, as though he's trying to decide whether to tell me something.

Oh God. He's not a virgin, is he?

"I'll bear that in mind," he says eventually. "But shall we get stuck in? I thought we'd try out a couple of new recipes I'm hoping to develop for the bakery. Cinnamon and cranberry muffins, and — inspired by our visit to Columbia Road Market — flowerpot bread."

Adam in the kitchen behaves like a completely different man, in command, like the captain of a stainless-steel ship. He darts about, fizzing with energy, but taking the

256

time to explain things to me. He *cares* about all aspects of the process, knows the history and origin of each ingredient, from the Madagascan vanilla pods that have been flavouring his sugar, to the unpromising lump of brown yeast that will bring our bread to life.

"So did your passion for bread start with the bagels, then?"

He shakes his head. "Nope. It was my nan, really. She had this thing about food being made with love. You know I mentioned her allotment? Well, she baked, too, and made pickles every autumn, all from the tiny dark kitchen in her council flat. She used to get complaints from the neighbours about the vinegar smell every September but she couldn't care less."

"So she taught you?"

"Kind of." He sifts the flour for the muffins, forming a pyramid shape in the bowl below. "I wasn't that interested at first, but I liked going round there, spending time with her. It was always bloody noisy at home, fighting for attention with my brothers."

I smile. "I know how that feels. I've got two."

"Yeah? I bet they spoil you."

"Not that you'd notice. Anyway. We're not here to talk about me. So you used to go to your nan's . . ."

"My mum thought my nan was so out of date, you know? I mean, this was the eighties. Ready meals, chicken Kiev, baby corn flown halfway round the world. Fancy stuff. No one wanted to know about local food or traditional dishes. But Nan ploughed on with her fresh breads and cakes and her soups and, sure

257

enough, when dinner time came, she'd generally have a full house."

"I bet."

"See this . . ." he says, taking cling-film off the top of the bowl where he's mixed the yeast with sugar and warm water. "The way it's bubbling. Smell it."

I take a sniff: "It smells sour, almost."

"Yes, that's how it should smell. Amazing stuff. In the end it was more fun helping Nan cook than just doing the washing up. 'You got to earn your dinner, Adam Hill; you don't get nothing for free in this life.' And then between the cooking, we'd talk. You know, most of the kids I used to hang around with ended up behind bars. Without Nan —" he pauses, "well, I could have so easily gone that way too."

"Oh come on, you make it sound like the Krays or something. You're a clever bloke, Adam."

"Am I? God, that's not what Anita used to say." He scowls. "I did get good marks at school, I guess, but boys' schools are funny places, aren't they? Doing well is not what it's about at all. Nothing worse than being a bloody swot."

"Did you train as a chef, then?"

He covers the yeast mix again, then opens a pack of dried cranberries. "No way. Wasn't cool, then, was it? No. I didn't know what to do. Anita —" He hesitates.

"Anita's your ex? I know we said exes are off the menu, but I don't think we're going to get very far with this story if you can't mention her name."

The glistening cranberries thud against the metal of the scales. "Yeah, all right. Anita and me got together at school. Fifth year. She was . . . well, she still is, the kind of girl who gets what she wants. And I was what she wanted, once. Not that I minded, though."

"Pretty, was she?"

"More *sexy* than pretty. Which is something no sixteen-year-old boy is going to object to, eh?"

I feel myself blushing. If the vixen of the fifth form couldn't teach poor Adam how to snog, then I guess it must be pretty hopeless. "No. So what did you do when you left school?"

"Anita got an apprenticeship at a hairdresser's, and she thought I should look for the same kind of thing. Two wages coming in meant we could save for a flat or something. My nan was *dead* against it. Nan and Anita were a bit like each other, though they'd have hated anyone to tell them so. Anyway, I went to work in a garage for a bit, it drove me mad, but then Nan had a small pools win and suggested I take off round Europe for a while. On my own."

"I bet Anita didn't like that."

He smiles ruefully. "No. You could say that. But I was faithful to her. It was before email and stuff, but I used to send her a postcard every day and after Warsaw, I had this idea of sending her back recipes from everywhere I went."

"How lovely!"

"Yeah, well, when I came back after three months, she'd lost them, except for the bagel one."

"That's rotten. So what did you do after that?"

"On my travels, I met this English guy — loaded, he was, not much older than me, buying drinks for everyone in this bar in Prague — and he worked in the City, said he'd put a word in on the trading floor. Anita was over the moon then. That's when we bought this place . . ." he waves at the room. "Right. Enough blabbing."

He finds more bowls, and divides up different ingredients. "That's the muffin ingredients ready. We're going to try them with all maple syrup in one mix, and half-and-half syrup and Demerara in the other. But now the yeast is ready, let's make the bread. We'll do the basic dough and then you can add your favourite ingredients, invent your own recipe. Just follow what I do."

I copy him as he makes a well in the centre of the flour, and pours in the bubbling yeast, along with a little more water. "Just to give it the right consistency," he explains, and then sprinkles flour on the marble work surface. "This is the fun bit."

Adam tips his ball of dough out on to the marble and begins to knead the bread. "You can't beat this for de-stressing. And then when it all puffs up . . . it always amazes me."

I watch as his knuckles dig into the dough, twisting and turning it, all in one flowing movement. While I feel all fingers and thumbs.

"Is this how you do it?"

He looks over. "Pretty much . . . I mean, it's bound to take you a little while to . . ." he waits. "Would it help if I showed you? If you don't mind."

"No, fine."

He moves across and stands right next to me, his arm brushing mine. "You want a rolling movement, it's lovely when you get the right rhythm up. You see . . ."

And I do see, as he moves the dough around, vigorously but with a certain respect. But then when I take it back again, it feels flat in my hands.

"Can I?" I nod and he moves closer, resting his hands on top of mine, gently at first, as I knead. "Try pushing down in the centre, a bit like this . . ." his palms on top of mine are stronger now, and my hands dig deep. The dough warms up and my choppy movements give way to something more fluid, so that it's hard to tell where one movement begins and another ends and then it's even harder to tell where my hands end and his begin . . .

He moves his hands away, suddenly, and steps back. I find it so shocking that I stop. "No, keep going, Becca. You're doing well, that's it."

I watch, and my hands keep moving across the dough, pummelling and stretching as his did. "It feels easier now. Um. Adam, do you think you could open a window or something? It's getting very warm in here."

"Yes! Yes, it is. Sorry. I'm used to a hot kitchen." He pulls back a metal door leading to a brick balcony, and the air rushes in, cool and welcome.

"So how long now?"

"That should do it. Now we cover the bread, and let it rise — proving, we call it — until it doubles in size. Then we'll add the ingredients we like, knead it again — the more you knead, the more flexible the gluten molecules get. It's a science as well as an art, this is."

He places the two bowls in a sunny spot on the living-room floor. "Now for the muffins."

"Golly, you're a hard taskmaster, Adam."

He looks worried. "Sorry. Let's go on to the balcony for a while to cool off. Shall I make you an espresso or something?"

"That'd be lovely."

I stand outside, looking towards the tiny gap between the other mansion blocks, and taking in the view of the City: the tall office buildings which look as if they're made entirely from glass, reflecting the blue July sky.

"Here we are." He passes me a blisteringly hot cup. "Is this a really crap idea for a date, then? I mean, roping someone in as my kitchen hand isn't very romantic."

"No, it's a *good* idea. A great chance for your date to learn a bit more about you and as for the kneading . . ." I sip the coffee and it burns my tongue. "To be honest, if you didn't know someone well, and wanted a good excuse for physical contact, then . . . I can't think of a better way to do it. The whole process is terribly *tactile*, really, isn't it?"

"Oh. Yes. I suppose it is."

"I mean, obviously with the two of us, it doesn't have that significance at all, but with someone else it could have quite an *erotic* charge. Bit like the pottery scene in *Ghost*, you know. Less phallic, of course, but . . ."

I can't believe I've just used the word *phallic* on a date, even a pretend one. Neither can Adam, evidently, as he's staring into the middle distance now, with the same slightly pained expression that my father used to

262

adopt whenever anyone kissed on TV. Never mind the fact that what we'd seen growing up on the farm left nothing to the imagination.

Adam downs his espresso in one. "I think we should work on the muffins, now, if you don't think I'm being a slave-driver."

An hour later, two dozen bread rolls are baking in their mini flowerpots: Greek Salad Version (Adam's recipe, with feta, red onion and thyme) and Sunflower Surprise (my recipe, with a melting middle of Cheddar cheese, and a topping made of sunflower and pumpkin seeds arranged in a flower pattern).

"So . . . you never explained how you went from broker to baker."

"Ah. You're not going to let it go, are you? Where had I got up to?"

I sink into the old turquoise sofa, still in my apron, now coated in flour. "You and Anita had just bought this place."

He winces slightly at the mention of her name. "Yes. It didn't look like this, of course, not then. Everything was filthy. And the stench when we took up the carpet. We gutted it and started again, really. And then . . . I dunno. The City was a mistake for me, you know. Great when you're twenty and single, but because I was with Anita, I wasn't really having much fun. And I began to feel old before my time."

"How old were you, then?"

"Twenty-six. But Anita wanted to be a young mum and I . . . I wasn't saying never, I was just saying not yet. I felt I had some living to do. At least, that was my reasoning then. Actually, I think I knew somehow she was wrong. It was what my nan was trying to tell me . . . and then when Nan died, well, I got this urge to go travelling again. I remember being at the wake, and realising I had to get away. Realising there and then, halfway through a ham sandwich with Nan's cucumber pickle."

"You ran away?"

"No. Well, not immediately. I asked Anita to come with me this time, but I guess I knew she wouldn't come."

The oven timer beeps. Adam stands up and opens the glass door just enough to look inside . . . and let a tantalising whiff of bread into the kitchen. "No, they're not quite there yet."

"So you went alone?"

"Yup. Took a sabbatical, bought a round-the-world ticket, transferred enough money into our joint account to pay the mortgage and bills. I said a break would help. Only three months, mind you."

"And did it help?"

"Yes, though not in the way I expected. I planned to get drunk on the first leg of the trip on the plane to Thailand and not get sober till I landed back at Heathrow, but it wasn't the booze that got me excited. It was the food. Everything tasted so good. I bought myself a notebook in Bangkok — I knew the mood that Anita was in she definitely wouldn't keep any postcards this time round — and made it my mission to fill it with recipes. Around the world in eighty breads."

264

"You'd decided to change careers."

"That happened later, in Sydney. I found this incredible bakery, all made on the premises, with bread that tasted nothing like anything I'd ever tasted. Sourdoughs and cholla and soda bread. So I sat by the Harbour Bridge and planned my own shop, on the back of a napkin."

"Wow. I take it Anita wasn't keen?"

He wrinkles his nose. "One way of putting it. I was so excited in Sydney, I called her and told her I was coming back, I was going to make millions with my bakery and she —"

"She what?"

"She told me I was mad. That I'd never amount to anything — well, it wasn't the first time she'd told me that — and that while I'd been away, the Atkins Diet had taken hold, carbs were the enemy, and no one would touch bread. And then when I got home three weeks later, the bank account was empty. And so was the flat. And when I say empty, I mean . . . well, everything. The lightbulbs gone. The bed. The kitchen cabinets."

"Bloody hell."

He smiles. "Yeah. I almost admire her, in a way. Anita never did anything by halves. I had to remortgage the flat to pay her share. Did the day job as normal but planned like a maniac at night and weekends. Looking for premises, visiting bakeries, doing my sums . . . and baking in my poor, stripped kitchen."

I sniff deeply. "Are they ready now, do you think? The breads."

I follow him over to the oven and peer through the glass: the golden dough is overflowing past the edges of the flowerpot rims, and when he draws out the shelf, it smells so good I could faint from hunger. Some of my sunflower seed patterns have sunk into the dough, but I spot one that's perfect. "You have that one, Adam."

"OK," he says, and lifts the best-looking of his Greek Salad rolls with an oven-gloved hand. "Well, this is yours. With butter, of course. Sourced from deepest Somerset."

"Oh, now, if you need some cheese to go with them, my dad makes the best cheese in Gloucestershire. Double Orchard. Perfect for making bread with, too, I should think. *And* he knows all his cows by name."

"Excellent! I will buy some and name a loaf in his honour. But in the meantime . . . I think these are crying out to be eaten hot."

The rolls are *delicious*. Even Adam has to admit that mine have the edge.

"I've been thinking of introducing the flowerpots for special occasions — bank holidays, Easter, or maybe just Fridays," he says. "You have to keep the customers surprised and excited. Build a buzz, so they keep coming back."

"So Atkins didn't kill off your business before you even began? Or all the people who claim to have wheat allergies?"

He pulls out the trays of muffins from the second oven, and takes one each of the ones I made and the ones he made, and cuts them down the middle. "Well

266

. . . it was a worry, but I find that most people who say they have a gluten intolerance change their minds when they walk past the shop early in the morning. I mean, is there *anything* at all to compare with the smell of fresh baking?"

I breathe deeply through my nose. "Nope. So how long have you had the shop?"

"Just over two years. Took me a year to find the premises, get it kitted out, and then we opened just before Easter. I gave free hot cross buns to every customer."

I do the calculations in my head. If he split with his girlfriend a year before finding the shop, then he's been single for three years. The perfect time to start again. "So, do I win the muffin bake-off too?"

"We'll have to do a blind tasting, to make sure you don't cheat," he says. "Close your eyes. Here's the first one . . ."

I open my mouth and take a bite of the muffin. I don't care who baked it, it's delicious. "Oh, this is good . . . none of the sogginess you get with the mass-produced ones. I feel like I can taste *every* ingredient."

"OK. Good. And what about the sweetness? Cloying? Clean? Granular?"

"Hmmm. You're getting a bit technical for me there, Adam. It just tastes sweet to me." Though to be fair *everything* tastes sweet this afternoon. My senses are revelling in delicious overload. I can't remember feeling this comfortable anywhere but Eve Terrace.

"Right. Well, try the other one, then, for comparison."

267

I bite into the second. "Oh, right, I see what you mean. This second one is more *toasty*, almost like burned sugar. Very slightly nicer, I think."

"Great. We'll make a professional taster of you yet. Would you like that? A regular invite to Pudding Lane central to give your considered opinion on our baked goods? It'd be great to see you again."

I open my eyes, and suddenly feel very shy. "Um . . . well, I'd love to, Adam . . . but I don't want to introduce any confusion. I mean, it's fun to spend time here, but we mustn't forget I'm doing it in a professional capacity."

His expression changes, and so does the mood. "Yes. Silly me. Of course." He puts his plate down without tasting the muffins. "So, never mind these. How did *I* do?"

I realise that I haven't made a single mental note on his dating performance. Which must surely be a good thing, but it leaves me rather stumped. "Very well, Adam. The baking is a great move, informal. Gives you a chance to reveal more about yourself but in a natural context."

"That's if it's actually a good idea to reveal more about myself. What if I'm revealing all the wrong things?"

"Now that is defeatist talk, and I won't hear it. You're a great catch. Lovely flat, own business, a real passion for what you do. To be honest, the only thing standing in your way is a lack of confidence. And I think . . . hazarding a cheeky guess here . . . that we might have your ex to blame for that."

268

He looks away. "She did tend to speak her mind."

"What, telling you you were going to fail at everything? That's what your enemies are for."

"Yeah, maybe."

"But forget about those times, Adam. You're ready. In fact, if I'm honest, I think you could probably teach me a thing or two about dating."

"You're meant to be the expert."

"Yeah, well. What is it they say about teaching? Those who can, do. Those who can't, teach?"

"Well, I think you're lovely, Becca."

"That's very kind of you, Adam. I think you're lovely, too. So lovely that I know it won't be long before you're snapped up."

"No, I mean it. You *are* lovely." He moves a little closer and despite the open balcony door, I feel terribly hot again. He's millimetres away from me now, so close that the scent of maple syrup on his breath makes me hungry.

But it's not hunger for bread. God, no. It's a very different craving, one that scrambles my brain with its intensity and then . . .

His lips meet mine and oh! The sweetness . . . sugar and spice and all things nice, that's what Adam Hill is made of. The kiss is soft at first, barely there, but it's not tentative at all. This is a teasing kiss, one that says *how does that feel* and I'm answering him, *so good*, pulling him to me, and I open my eyes, just for a moment, and see his, that demerara sugar brown darkened by his dilated pupils.

He kisses me harder now and I reach out to circle my arms around him, feeling the brushed cotton under my fingertips and then, through the fabric, the line of his shoulder blades.

Adam traces his finger down my cheek, so gently it almost tickles, and then he keeps going: down the side of my neck, past my collarbone, before my baker's apron stops him going any further. He moves back, his lips no longer on mine, and it feels almost painful, that sudden absence.

"We'll have to get rid of this," he whispers, pointing to the apron. His voice is hoarse and *bloody hell*, unbearably sexy, and as he pulls the apron cord over my head, I feel naked, even though I am dressed as respectably as a Sunday school teacher (except for those stray unbuttoned buttons). As he takes my apron off, the look that passes between us is an acknowledgement that this is just the beginning. A beginning that makes me feel vulnerable but so, so, so, so, so high.

His lips are reunited with mine, and his hand returns to my cheek, but moves faster now . . . neck . . . collarbone . . . the oh-so-sensitive skin where the silk of my blouse meets the very top of my chest and *bloody hell again*, how can my whole body feel so *tingly*, as though a million delicious electric shocks are passing between us, generating enough power to fire up a billion fairy lights.

How could I have forgotten how this feels? That free-falling sensation, where nothing matters but skin on skin. I haven't felt this alive since . . .

Since Marcus.

I stop, pull away. No more than a centimetre or two separates us. The tingling stops too: or rather, I make it stop, so I can think straight. It's like waking from the best possible dream, realising you've been somewhere that doesn't really exist. That can't be allowed to exist . . .

"Becca?" Adam lets his hand fall away. "Have I done something wrong? I thought — I mean, if I've moved too fast, I'm sorry. I thought it was what you wanted too."

I try to pull my own thoughts together, to explain what's just happened, and why it can never, ever happen again. I close my eyes but it's Marcus's mocking face I see, from that final day, the ice-cold afternoon when everything fell into place and then fell apart. "*Flame's gone out, Bex. No point pretending otherwise.*"

"It's not you, Adam." My voice sounds strange to me, muffled by lust and confusion. "Or rather . . . it's not your fault. I need a moment."

I shuffle past him on to the balcony, feel the cool air on my face, see the City beyond, unaltered by what's just happened. The shimmery intensity of the moment has gone now. It wasn't really there. It was an illusion.

How do I explain it to Adam? That this meant nothing to either of us? I grasp around for a logical explanation.

I know. *It's transference.* Doctors have it, don't they, their clients developing a little crush on them. And all that flattery, all that attention, well, it's natural that I might feel like I'm reciprocating . . . I take a deep breath, then turn back to face him.

"Ah, Adam. What a strange thing the human mind is. Not that what just happened wasn't very —" I grasp around for the right, safe word, "Um . . . very *nice*, but it wasn't appropriate. It's simply evidence that we were playing our roles well. Too well. It's like . . . I've got this friend who's a sports physio, you know . . . manipulating and rehabilitating athletes who've had a knock and been out of the game for a while. That's me, you see. Helping you prepare for getting back in the race . . ."

"But what if I don't want to race, because I've already found —"

I stand up, before he can embarrass us both. "And my work is done. That's what this, um, experience has just proved. You're ready. I can't tell you how satisfying that is for me. All I ask, like I said before, is that you let me know when your wedding is . . ." I become aware that the top of my bra is exposed and I do up the buttons of my blouse as far as they go. "Because with talents like yours . . . cooking talents, I mean, of course, I have no doubt *at all* that you'll be snapped up in no time at all."

"Right," he mumbles. "Thanks."

"Oh, no thanks necessary! It's been fun!" I say, bright and brisk. "I always love it when I make a difference! And don't forget you promised me you'd call Sam, didn't you? You're definitely in with a chance now."

272

I head for the door, then realise I've forgotten my handbag, and snake past his motionless body to pick it up.

"Becca?"

"Yes?"

He won't look at me. "Don't you want to know which of those muffins was yours?"

I hesitate in the hallway. "Oh, yes, of course."

I hear a rustling as he moves about the kitchen, and then joins me in the hall, with a bag. "The one that tasted of toasted sugar."

For a moment, I think I can taste him again and I feel my resolve faltering. Is this really just *transference*? "Oh."

He hands me the bag, then turns away. I open the door, raising my hand in a half-wave, but he's not looking at me. I walk briskly down the stairs, till I hear his door slam shut.

Then I stop on a half-landing and lean against the wall.

Shit. I'm sure I can still feel the imprint of his lips against mine, that feeling of spiralling out of control . . .

That's the trouble with men. You give them an inch, they take a mile.

I don't care if bloody Sam thinks I'm a control freak. At least I will never be disappointed again.

CHAPTER
TWENTY-ONE

I know I told Sam I don't mix business and pleasure, but the truth is, I don't have much of either in my life right now.

I probably should have used that speed-dating evening to recruit clients, as my current workload is light, to say the least. Dwight's nearly off the books. Sam hasn't called me since the night at the Ball and Chain. And it looks like Edward and Katerina are going steady.

Business hasn't been this slack since I first started up on my own. I'm all for a bit of work/life balance, but I can't seem to settle. I walk to Richmond Green, spend a whole morning shopping for the designer bag I'll buy with my wedding payment from Dwight, take in a matinee and afternoon tea with Georgie, meet Helga at her swanky gym . . . all the things I dreamed of doing when I was under the Benson Associates cosh. And yet whatever I do to distract myself, I can't stop thinking about . . .

"That boy. You've fallen in love with him, haven't you?"

Georgie and I are recharging after a hard afternoon watching a Tennessee Williams matinee. We've come to the Wolseley for afternoon tea and star-spotting. No celebrities so far, but the vanilla cheesecake is delicious and the restaurant itself has more than enough to look at, from its spectacular hanging lights, to the gorgeous monochrome tiles on the floor.

I stare at that floor now. "Who?"

"Oh dear God, precious niece, don't you dare try that one with me. I knew you when you used to get crushes on bloody ponies. Don't you think I can spot the signs?"

"You have a vivid imagination."

"What, and you *don't?* I bet this very minute you're imagining that boy wearing nothing but a chef's hat, a jaunty smile, and a light sugar frosting."

Well, I wasn't, but now she comes to mention it . . . "Just because you have a filthy mind, Georgie, it doesn't mean that we all spend our lives in X-rated fantasies about people we barely know . . ."

"Ah, it's so much more entertaining than fantasising about people we know well." She pushes her butter-roasted pineapple around her plate. "But I'm right, aren't I? It's the baker. You haven't been the same since you went to his flat."

I sigh. She's been going on about it for the past week and a half. "He was a client. I don't fancy clients."

"Don't or shouldn't? It was bound to happen eventually. In fact, I was banking on it happening eventually."

"It's crazy to say I could be in love with someone I've only met four times."

"Is it? Possibly. I have fallen in love with people I spotted once on the Tube, but perhaps I am exceptional. But you're definitely *in lust* with the man."

"Even if I was . . ."

"Hah! Becky's in love, Becky's in love."

"You've worn me down, Georgie. It's like Chinese water torture. In the end, it's easier to give in and say what your tormentors expect you to say." I take a sip of my drink. "But actually . . . Yes. I think I did rather fancy Adam, if I'm honest." I haven't mentioned that we kissed. I couldn't bear her knowing.

Even so, it feels *delicious* to say his name again. So illicit. My aunt claps her hands together and then waves the waiter over.

"Two more teas, please. On second thoughts, champagne, two glasses." She turns to me again. "Not every day that a niece who was showing every sign of ending her days as a spinster admits to a grand passion."

"Hang on," I say, part horrified, part delighted, "you're a spinster yourself so I don't see what's so terrible about it. And I'm not remotely in the throes of a grand passion. All I will admit to is fancying the guy."

Though, of course, that is pretty astonishing in itself. For ages after saying goodbye to him, I was in denial, sticking to my own story about transference and role-playing. It was only yesterday, three days after our clinch, that I admitted how I felt.

But I haven't once considered calling him. Honestly. Not once. Because for all the wonderful sparks and frissons I feel when I think of Adam — those hands, kneading the dough; those lips touching mine — I prefer him exactly where he is, seven miles away, so I have no possibility of acting on those feelings again. All the fun, none of the risk. It's the ultimate in safe sex.

And, of course, I haven't answered any of his calls . . .

The waiter arrives bearing two champagne flutes, leggy and elegant like my aunt. "Marvellous," she says, as we take our glasses and clink them together. "So, here's to romance. Now, what are we going to do about it?"

I let the bubbles tickle my nose before I burst Georgie's bubble. "Nothing. I like Adam in my head, not in my bed. It does me good, professionally speaking, to have a reminder of how attraction feels, but we've talked about this before. Some of us are simply happier single. You should know."

She tuts dismissively. "You're only happier single because you made such a lousy choice with your first love. Whereas I am happier single because I made a good one."

I want to probe further here, but my aunt's face shuts down. "Well, if I make such lousy choices, it's all the more reason not to trust my own judgement, isn't it?"

Georgie tuts again. "You're ridiculously stubborn, aren't you?" Then she smiles. "No doubt that you're my niece, anyhow. I shan't insult your intelligence further, but I do think you're being ridiculous. Still. Your life."

"And my business. And talking of my business, what am I going to do about the lack of clients? Any ideas?"

"You need to be out there, reminding people what you do and who you are."

"I can hardly walk around the City of London with a sandwich board reading: Need a Bride? Call 0800 BRIDE HUNTER, now, can I?"

"A little unsubtle, I agree. Have you tried a few calls around to your success stories, to see if they've got friends who need help? What about Perry? He seems to know plenty of single boys . . ."

"Yes, I suppose so. And after my success with Edward, he might be a good place to begin. Actually, it feels like Edward's my only success lately. I'm worried my luck's run out."

"What about Dwight and Heather?"

"It's probably fine but . . . remember what you said about her being too good to be true? What if she is?"

"You introduced them, that's all, Becky. Now it's up to them."

"I know but . . ." I'm not going to tell her about the weird incident at the school in Edinburgh, about the complete absence of ponies and ancestral castles in her neck of the woods. "And then there's Sam. I should never have taken her on, but I did. It makes me wonder whether I've lost my instinct."

"I talked you into working with Sam, remember. Does it make you feel better to blame me?"

I shrug. "Not much. The more I do this, the less I think I understand about people and about love. That's not the way it should work, is it?"

"That's the human animal for you, Becky. People in love aren't like, I don't know, the latest accounting

278

program, where you can grasp the basics in an afternoon. They're unpredictable. That's what makes them fun and after all —" Her phone trills in her handbag and she excuses herself to take the call. "Roger, you old cad. How the devil *are* you?"

I know she's right, but if people are so unpredictable, what on earth am I doing trying to second guess their romantic destinies? I keep thinking about what Adam said to me at the flower market. "*Do you really believe you can create love from thin air?*"

My aunt comes back to the table. "Roger's just sold a painting for half a mill. He's in the mood for a party. Fancy coming along? There might be some singles there who need your help."

"No, no. But keep an eye out for me," I say, and rummage in my handbag to give Georgie some business cards. "See you later."

"It'll be *much* later, knowing Roger. But don't be down-hearted, precious niece. You have a vocation. The sooner you're back helping the needy billionaires of the Square Mile, the sooner you'll feel better. You *know* it makes sense!"

I'm just getting off the Tube at Piccadilly — for some reason, I am craving more raspberry truffles from that incredible chocolate shop — when Edward calls.

"I need to see you. Straight away." His voice is oddly muffled.

"Of course. I'm in town already, I could be with you in twenty minutes. Is everything OK?"

"No, it's not. I'll see you in the German place, Kaffee and Kuchen, by Deutsche Bank."

He rings off without waiting for my answer. Don't say it's all gone wrong with him and Katerina? Suddenly the world of head-hunting — or, at least, of someone else paying my wages — almost seems appealing again.

When I get to the café, Edward is sitting hunched in the corner, deathly pale. It's warm outside, and oppressively hot in this place with its weird Tyrolean theme, but he seems to be shivering.

"What on earth's happened, Edward?"

He looks up, his eyes wide. "I *know*, Rebecca."

"Know what?" Oh God. Maybe Heather isn't the gold-digger at all, maybe it's Katerina. Perhaps she's heavily involved in the Ukrainian mafia, and has been trying to extort money. Or she might have been abducted . . .

"I know about your little *deal* with Perry. Your *arrangement*." His voice is scornful now and I'm sure I catch a whiff of booze on his breath. "The lies you cooked up between you to set me up with a wife."

"Ah." It must have been Perry. No one else knows. But what on earth would Perry have to gain from telling Edward? "You know, he was only trying to help you."

"And I suppose *you* were only following orders, were you?"

A frilly-aproned waitress approaches with the menu, but backs away when she sees his face.

280

"We both had your best interests at heart. I mean, I wouldn't normally consider an assignment like that, it's against my principles, and I argued that we should tell you, but then when I met you, I realised that you could be so much happier than you were."

"The ends justify the means, is that it? That's ruddy marvellous. So noble to compromise your principles for a hopeless case like me."

I close my eyes, wishing I could be anywhere else. But I have to face the music. "Edward, it's not like that. You've never been a hopeless case. You're a wonderful person, really wonderful. Kind and warm. You deserved to find someone like Katerina. You just weren't having much luck stuck in your office 24/7, were you?"

He thinks about this for a moment. "But wasn't that *my* decision? My life."

"Yes, exactly. It *was* your decision. I mean, I know I came into your life because of Perry, but you made the decision to hire me independently. Perry didn't make you come to Bushy Park. The deal was just the catalyst."

A cuckoo clock above his head hits six o'clock, and a creepily lifelike yellow bird pops out six times to chirp the hour.

"I can't agree, Rebecca. I trusted you. I believed that you saw potential in me that no one else had. I thought you were my friend. And all the time you were being paid . . ." His speech is slightly slurred: he's definitely been drinking.

I don't argue with him. Someone more confident than Teddy the Plank might shrug the whole thing off

281

as a laugh, but this is exactly what I dreaded. I try to stay calm enough to get through to him. "Edward. You have every right to feel betrayed. I don't blame you. But the most important thing to remember is that Katerina got to know you as *you*. No one was paying her. OK, so the circumstances of your very first meeting were a bit unconventional, but you charmed her. Not me. Not Perry. You made her fall in love with you."

Now when he looks at me, his eyes are steely. "Yes, well, that's easy to say. But you see, I think the plan that you and Perry hatched to make me settle down, find me a supportive little wife to keep my shirts ironed and my shoes clean, may have backfired."

"What do you mean?"

"Don't you want to know how I found out, Rebecca? Why Perry spilled the beans?"

"Well, yes, I suppose I do."

He's smiling now. "Katerina . . . let's just say that the more you get to know Katerina, the less *fragile* she seems. In fact, well, after nearly three weeks together, I can safely describe her as formidable. And my formidable girlfriend has things to say about my working hours and the workload that Anemone International has imposed on me."

"But you like your work."

"I used to like it. But that was when I didn't have anything else. Katerina thought I should go in to see Perry, ask for more support. And more money. At first I was reluctant. I've always believed in loyalty — a concept you don't seem to understand — and so I didn't want to trouble him. Then Katerina went

282

through the figures with me, and we realised I had less back-up than anyone else in the company. So much for my loyalty, eh?"

"Maybe Perry just didn't realise —"

"Oh, he realised. I took the figures in to him and he didn't seem at all surprised. I was cross, Rebecca, almost out of control, like I used to feel . . ." he realises he's been shouting, and sits back in his chair. "Anyway, it doesn't matter. What matters is that when I saw Perry's smug face, how readily he agreed to extra help, I realised it wasn't enough. I changed my plan. Told him I wanted a few months off. Katerina wants to take me to the Ukraine, we could travel for a while. Spend some of the money I've been collecting for so long."

"And?"

"He said no. I said I'd walk. I'll remember his expression as long as I live, like a fat cat after someone nicks his ruddy cream. 'But you can't leave, Eddy the Plank. You need us,' he kept saying, 'we've made you what you are today.' I half expected him to break into a chorus from that Human League song."

"I don't think Perry's much of a singer."

Edward smiles for the first time. It's weird, but something tells me he's actually enjoying this. The worm that turned . . .

"I told him where he could stick his job and that's when he said it. Shouted, in fact. 'You will be nothing out there, Plank. You'd have fuck all without me. You wouldn't have your house — you wouldn't even have that bloody girlfriend, if it wasn't for me.' And I turned to look at him and he knew he'd gone too far, then; I don't think he meant to say it. But you know Perry and his temper." He stares at me. "You know Perry very well, in fact, don't you?"

"Maybe not as well as I thought I did." I sigh. "Look, Edward. I can understand why you feel upset and angry, but can't you see that Perry was trying to help you, albeit in a slightly ham-fisted way? He's been so much happier since he found a wife — you said so yourself, when we first met — and I do genuinely think he wanted to make you happy too."

"Yes, but people must make the choice themselves."

"And would you have made the right choice? Honestly?"

"That's . . . that's not the point. You don't control other people's lives like they're marionettes, do you? It's wrong." He looks at his watch. "I'm late for Katerina. We're going to the theatre. I haven't been to the theatre in *years*."

He stands up to go.

"Edward . . . look, hate me as much as you like. But don't be too hasty, eh? However angry you feel with Perry, please don't do anything hasty."

Edward laughs, a little too heartily. "Too late! I already have. Perry's going to have to look for someone else who appreciates his unorthodox employee benefits. Because I quit. And after . . ." he checks his watch again, "one hour and twenty-two minutes of unemployment, let me tell you, it's the best thing that ever happened to me."

284

And he strides out of the restaurant, whistling. He looks back as he opens the door, just to check I'm still watching . . .

CHAPTER
TWENTY-TWO

I'm in trouble. I've never failed at anything before. At school I always managed to pass tests and exams, and if I worked hard, I sometimes even made top of the class. University was harder, but I still never fell behind. And then working for Marcus came naturally enough. My psychological skills often outsmarted the bluff and bluster of the other headhunters, and so I held my own.

So now that I am officially the worst matchmaker in the world, I don't know how to cope. Perry won't return my calls, Edward's disappeared, and Sam keeps sending me sarcastic texts asking me whether I've found Prince Charming yet.

And I keep having to tell myself that I haven't. Even though my stubborn, treacherous brain keeps telling me that I have.

Georgie thinks it's all fine. "After all, you haven't failed where Edward's concerned. If anything, you've been *too* successful."

But I've taken it to heart and I'm convinced that everything I touch is doomed. I can't sleep for worrying about Dwight or, more accurately, for worrying about Heather. So I've decided I need to see her, to make sure that Dwight isn't so blinded by love that he's about to make the second worst mistake of his life by marrying another gold-digger.

I've decided to take her by surprise by turning up at the headquarters of Action for Animal Welfare in Victoria, *just passing, you know, and wondered how the wedding plans are going.* Even if she's in the middle of essential bunny-protecting public relations missions, surely she daren't turn me away.

Maybe it's my mood, but London doesn't feel like Cupid's playground this morning. The skies are grey, and so are the buildings. I get off the bus by a boarded-up department store. There aren't many people around, just elderly women pushing tartan shopping trolleys, and chuggers in their orange fluorescent bibs, hoping to ambush passers-by with sob stories in exchange for their direct-debit details. The cynical ones target the poor, I remember reading, because the less money you have, the more likely you are to give generously.

I consult my map, to double check the HQ location again: it's such an anonymous place that I can't quite remember where it is. It feels like years since I came here to check Heather out and take a sneaky picture for Dwight's approval.

What kind of life have I made for myself? The more I think about it, the more I can see my mother's point of view: spying on women, presenting them and their vital statistics on a platter to rich men too lazy or arrogant to make the effort themselves. Oh, I have my justifications all ready: the Edwards of this world who'd need help whatever their incomes, and the Dwights who're too rich and too hurt to be able to make sensible judgements about their relationships . . .

"Excuse me, but do you care about the plight of amputees in the former Eastern Bloc?"

I'm about to collide with a fresh-faced girl in a bib. "Well, I hadn't really thought about it but . . ."

I pick up my pace but she skips ahead of me, like a netballer covering her opposite number on the other team. "Because *you* can help us supply prosthetics to the limbless in Latvia and Estonia. For a small monthly donation of —"

"No, thank you."

She gives me a long, appraising look and evidently decides that I am not gullible enough, and lets me get away. Now where was I? Yes, that's right, considering what to do with the rest of my life.

The trouble is I'm so tired. It takes almost as much emotional investment to set two people up as it does to have the relationship yourself. Which might explain why I'm so knackered: I'm on the lookout for the perfect man, I'm in the first flush of love *and* I'm planning a wedding. All three at once.

"Hello!"

I look up. Another bloody chugger.

"You look like the kind of woman who can spare a moment to hear what you can do about the plight of the Amazon rainforests," the man says, smiling cheekily.

I stop walking. "Do I? Bugger. I must have forgotten to put on my 'I don't care about anyone but myself?' T-shirt this morning."

288

The man shrugs, used to reactions like this, and worse, I suppose. They're only doing their jobs, like me, and as I stride away, I feel guilty, but not guilty enough to call him back and endure a pitch that will make me feel even worse about my carbon footprint.

Actually, it's not three affairs I'm juggling at the moment: it's four. Adam plays on my mind, like the birthday box of chocolates you know is lurking in the larder, naughty but nice. I try to ration thinking about him, because . . .

Because it would be easy to fall into the trap of not thinking about anything else.

"Did you know that by the time the average beach donkey retires, he or she will have carried the equivalent of four hundred double-decker buses of weight on their back?"

I've clearly discovered London's Chugger Alley. The only way out is to pay up. "All right, all right," I say, rummaging in my handbag for my debit card. "How much is it going to cost me to save arthritic donkeys?"

But a strange thing happens. The victorious chugger is beginning to back away, rather than closing the deal. I look up from my bag at the girl in front of me and even though she's moving quickly I see enough of the panicky face that's retreating to realise . . .

"Heather?"

She's broken into a run, and instinctively I sprint after her. She's quick on her feet, but the bright green bib means she has no hope of merging with the drab, slow-moving shoppers.

The bib turns a corner between two shops and by the time I catch up and turn into the alleyway, she's had a chance to tear off her bib and abandon it on the pavement.

But the adrenalin's kicked in now and I'm determined to catch up with her. I scan the alleyway and follow it round to the right . . .

It's a dead end. I look up, and down, feeling more like James Bond than a bride hunter. She has to be here somewhere. She can't have shimmied up the pipes so . . .

I edge past walls of ten-foot tall cardboard boxes, between the enormous industrial bins at the back of loading bays, and there, panting, is Heather. She's crouching on the dirty tarmac, her back resting against a stack of wooden pallets.

"Why . . . uh . . . did you . . . run away?" My chest is heaving: now that I've stopped I feel weak and it's all I can do not to join her on the floor.

She stares up at me, her eyes defiant. "You can think what you like," she says eventually, and her accent sounds stronger than before, "but I do love him. Whatever tales you're planning to tell on me, whatever you say, he has to know that."

And for a moment I think that she might burst into tears.

"I'm not planning to tell tales to anyone, Heather. But I do think you've got some explaining to do. I don't know about you, but I could do with a cup of tea. A cup of tea always puts things into perspective."

★ ★ ★

Heather takes me to an old-fashioned Italian café around the corner. "It's where we all go when we need cheering up after one rejection too many," she says flatly. The place itself is spotless, with floor-to-ceiling off-white tiles and a blackboard with specials chalked up in block capitals.

She orders a toasted teacake, which suddenly seems the best possible cure for a grey London morning, so I order one too.

"I do work for a charity," she says.

"Yes."

"And I do love Dwight."

"Right."

A large Italian woman brings us two pots of tea, served in retro pale green cups which would fetch at least a tenner each at one of the trendier antique markets in Notting Hill. The woman is wearing a stripy blue apron just like Adam's and I allow myself a second of thinking about him — his hands and his hair and his voice — before I return to the matter in hand.

"Are you going to tell him?"

I pour my tea: it's as dark as engine oil. Just the job. "Well, at the moment, I don't have much to tell him. Though I do know that there's no such place as the Flower of Scotland Finishing School."

"I don't know what you're talking —"

"Look, Heather, I'm not here to judge you. But I have a responsibility towards my client and that's why I was on my way to talk to you. Even before finding out that your charity work is a bit more, um, *hands on*, than we'd been led to believe."

291

Heather pours her own tea now, adding milk drop by drop, then stirs in her sugar. She's either a cooler, harder customer than I imagined, or she's buying herself thinking time. Her little pixie face looks tiny and flushed above her padded anorak, more like a kid on a sponsored hike, than a conwoman. But maybe that's the secret of her success.

"Why do you think anyone would do this job, Becca?"

I'm trying to think of my answer when the Italian lady delivers our teacakes, which smell spicy and are bigger than a DVD, dripping with butter.

"It can't be easy."

"No, it isn't easy. Even in the summer it can be bloody cold and miserable, and when it's not, it's hot and sweaty, and people are rude and call you names, and the commission's not up to much."

"I guess it might be a bit easier because you know it's in a good cause?" I say, trying to forget how rude I was earlier on.

"Oh yeah," she says, "but when my feet are killing me and some old lady's just sworn at me, somehow I don't always find it too easy to stay cheerful by thinking of the bloody donkeys. Maybe that makes me a bad person."

I smile, despite my determination to stay stern. "I found your sales pitch very moving."

She stares into her tea. "I know you're judging me, Becca. I guess you can't help yourself. I mean, I don't know anything about your background, but I'm guessing that things haven't been too tough."

I can't really argue. "You lied to me, Heather. At that very first meeting. All that guff about your idyllic childhood in the Pony Club. I went to your school. I know where you come from."

"Yeah?" She laughs, a bitter sound that echoes round the café. "Not exactly Edinburgh Castle, eh?"

"No." I think of the tower blocks and the graffiti and the kids who were keen to get hold of my hub caps. "I try not to judge people. I never lived on an estate, but I came to London to make my fortune, too, and I've had my difficult moments. But I've never misled people and that's why I can't let Dwight walk into a marriage based on lies."

She folds her arms across her chest. "You found me, Becca. Remember? I know you've already got me down as some golddigger, but don't bloody forget that I wasn't hanging around the City bars looking for rich guys. I was minding my own business, meeting my friends in the pub one night, when you decided I was the girl for Dwight."

She's right, of course. "I didn't decide anything. I'm in the business of introductions, not playing God."

"Really?" she says. "Even if you're the one who arranges every aspect of a date, every conversational topic?"

It's my turn to stare. "What did Dwight tell you?"

She shrugs. "He didn't tell me anything. He didn't have to. He's a good person, but when I first met him, the things he did felt so *fake*. Like I wasn't getting to know him at all."

"Now hang on a minute —"

"It's like that Steve Martin movie, isn't it? *Roxanne*. Do you get off on pulling people's strings?"

I take a bite of the teacake to stop myself saying something I regret. It tastes of cloves and margarine. "You're not going to distract me with your insults, Heather. I'm more interested in the lies you've been telling."

She glares at me. "All right. So I didn't go to a finishing school, but the Flower of Scotland taught me everything I know about the adult world, thank you very much. And I do work for a charity. Chugging isn't anyone's vocation but it pays the rent on my room. And I had plans to study to better myself."

"Fine, but what about the gaps? You're twenty-five years old. If you haven't been working your way up the charity pole, what have you been doing?"

She shakes her head. "You don't get it, do you? I've been clawing my way out of my old life. It isn't just a matter of going to Waverley station, booking a one-way ticket and making my bloody fortune like Dick Whittington."

I frown. "I don't think there's any point in sitting here if you're going to be sarcastic. I want answers, Heather. What about your parents?"

"You think I've lied about them dying?"

"I don't know what to think."

"Well, I haven't lied. They are dead. My father died when I was fifteen, of a heart attack, like I said. He was thirty-eight."

"Heather, I'm sorry. That's terribly young."

"Where I come from, people don't tend to get their full three score years and ten."

"And your mum?"

"Like I told Dwight, it was an accident. She fell asleep smoking. Well, asleep, drunk, whatever. After my dad died, she worked hard at staying drunk twenty-four seven. I was at school, I heard the bloody fire engines. Sometimes I wondered if she did it on purpose."

"Oh, Heather." I believe her now. The clipped, matter-of-fact voice she's using is only just holding back the hurt.

"I failed my exams, of course. Turned to drinking myself. Runs in the family, eh? I wanted to get rid of those last memories of our flat, all blackened and stinking."

"Do you have brothers or sisters?"

"An older brother. But he was in prison by then." She shrugs again. "Nothing unusual where I lived. That was the finishing school for the boys. They used to run a weekly minibus to the young offenders place from the estate for all the visitors."

"So where did you live?"

"With my aunt." She pulls a face. "Didn't really work out. And then I moved a lot. I lived with friends, with guys I met who were in love with the bottle, like me."

"And work?"

Now she looks shifty.

Oh God. What if she was a prostitute? What else does a teenager with no parents, no qualifications, and a pretty face, have to fall back on?

"You think I went on the game, huh?"

"No, that's not what I was suggesting."

"Well, even in my lowest, darkest moments I wouldn't have done that. In a way I did something worse. I took advantage of people's good natures. Scrounged from my friends. From men. It was survival but I don't feel good about it. That's why I came to London. To stand on my own two feet."

I nod, and sip my tea while I think it over. In a way, I admire her for being strong enough to make it from there, to here. But her admission makes me uncomfortable too. How do I know whether she's simply taking advantage of Dwight's good nature? It's what she's done all her life . . .

"Do you really love Dwight?"

Her face changes, takes on the kind of innocent glow that I noticed the first time I met her. "To begin with, I just thought it'd be fun. Why not enjoy nice things, with someone who wants to spend their money, but I realised pretty soon — that first date, even, once he'd stopped parroting your lines — that here was a man I understood. Who'd been through bad times, been lonely too, and had had the strength to drag himself out of that."

I think it over. There *is* a vulnerability about Dwight that most people don't see, behind the flash and the cash. And yet . . . "But you've played him well, haven't you, Heather? Refusing to sleep with him?"

She scowls. "Oh yeah. Nothing to do with the fact I wanted to turn my back on the days when men only loved me because of what I was willing to do. Nothing to do with wanting to be sure how we both felt. Just some Scottish slut manipulating the gullible American?"

"That's not what I meant."

Heather stands up now. "Look, if you're going to ruin my life . . . ruin both our lives, then there's no bloody thing I can say to change your mind, is there? You brought us together, so I guess you think you're entitled to split us up, too, huh? Your call. But I tell you what Dwight means to me. He's *family*, now. I don't think I've ever had family before, not one I can trust. And if you're going to destroy that, then at least tell me now, so I can talk to him myself."

"I don't know what I'm going to do. I need to think . . ."

She shakes her head, contempt contorting her face. "Well, while you're playing your games and doing your fucking spreadsheets or gazing into crystal balls or whatever you're going to use to make your decision, just remember that it's not a job for *us*. It's our future."

"Look, Heather, I don't have anything against you personally, I just want to do what's best —"

"Save it, Rebecca. I've got to go now. Earn my money. Arrange the fucking wedding, huh? Just in case you decide we're entitled to happiness after all." She rummages in her pocket for cash.

"I'll take care of the bill, Heather."

"Oh yeah, I forgot. You can claim it on business expenses. Nice work if you can get it . . ."

She turns towards the door, but then turns back. "And incidentally, Miss High and Mighty, Honest as the Day is Long, that first date with the 'organic

Highland raspberries' and cream. I'm no expert, coming from the concrete jungle and all, but since when can you get fresh Scottish raspberries in April?"

She waits for a second and when I feel my cheeks colour, she nods in satisfaction and marches out of the café, leaving me with a heavy teacake I'd rather not finish, and a decision I'd rather not make.

CHAPTER
TWENTY-THREE

Helga is drunk. Georgie is drunk. The remains of our picnic are spread out across a lime-green Trisha Guild rug: chicken bones, tiny pieces of potato smeared with mayonnaise, hillocks of curried rice, and plastic beakers containing dribbles of flat, sticky champagne. The orchestra is tuning up, discordant notes travelling through the warm evening air.

I've always loved the Marble Hill concerts. When I first moved here, Helga and I couldn't afford tickets for the "proper" enclosure, so we'd hover round the edges with cans of beer and sandwiches from the corner shop, enjoying the communal spirit and the opportunities for flirtation with posh boys on the next rug. Even when it rained, we veterans would unpack the waterproofs and the umbrellas, and feel the camaraderie grow even stronger.

Now we have the money for real tickets, that bit closer to the Palladian beauty of Marble Hill House, and my aunt always insists on pre-ordering a Waitrose hamper, a terribly civilised dose of al fresco living. Tonight the weather is putting smiles on everyone's faces. Bodies languorous from alcohol are already stretched out on the ground, families fitting themselves lengthwise on to their rugs, like sardines crammed into a tin.

I feel like Scrooge. The champagne has failed to mellow me, and I look at the couples and groups and envy them their easy contentment, their ability to take so much pleasure from good weather and good company.

"More wine, that's what you need, babe," Helga says, pushing herself upright to open a new bottle.

I sigh. "It's not working so far."

"Can't you just forget about work for a single evening? Might help you see things more clearly in the morning."

"Or it might just give me a hangover to go with my bad mood."

My aunt is lying stretched out, her long hair above her head, like Ophelia in the river. She opens her eyes. "I've tried telling her, Helga, but she takes no notice. I wonder if secretly she quite enjoys feeling tortured by the responsibility."

"Oh, sod off!" I snap. "For your information, I'm not sleeping, I have no appetite and I'm getting migraines. I'd have to be seriously sick to enjoy that."

Helga unscrews the cap from the wine bottle and pours me a generous beakerful. "Get this down your neck. So when's the wedding?"

"Six days, and twenty hours. And the longer I leave it, the worse it's going to be if I do tell him."

My aunt reaches out for more wine. "You could always do the full dramatic *Is there any reason why these two shouldn't get hitched*? business. I've always wanted to see one of those."

"Wonderful idea, Georgie!" I say. "Why didn't I think of that myself? Destroy Dwight's life, Heather's life, and my own reputation in one fell swoop."

Helga replaces the cap on the bottle. "All right, all right. Let's see if we can sort this out once and for all. So what makes you think you *should* tell Dwight?"

"Because . . ." I close my eyes. "Because if Heather is taking him for a ride, he has a right to know."

"And how sure are you that she *is* taking him for a ride?"

"I'm not sure. Half the time I'm convinced she's been playing this clever, clever game. Not sleeping with him. Getting his sympathy by telling him about her dead parents. All those lies about being a charity worker, about her sheltered Edinburgh upbringing."

"And the other half of the time?"

"Well, wouldn't I have done the same, in her position? Don't we all play games? Especially if we've been through what she's been through."

Georgie sits up, in one fluid, elegant movement. "The thing is, precious niece, you will never know for sure. And even if you do tell Dwight, there's a big risk he'll turn on you anyhow. If he loves her — well, he's always going to believe her word against yours."

"But at least I'll have warned him . . ."

Helga shakes her head. "And if she loves him back, then you risk destroying their relationship, to cover yourself. I'm with Georgie. I think you have to keep schtum, babe. I know you like everything to be

301

up-front, but there's so much more to lose if you tell tales. He's a fucking grown-up. You have to trust him to use his own judgement."

"He's not capable . . ." I'm about to tell them that he can't be trusted, that he married a wrong 'un before, that I am responsible for screening the women. But every time I come back to Sam's angry accusation: "Rebecca Orchard, you are a *control freak*. Worse than that, you are living through other people's dreams because you're too pathetic, too scared to pursue your own."

Don't think about Adam, it only makes things worse.

"You look miles away again, babe." Helga rests her hand gently on my arm. "You need to give yourself a sodding break. You did the job you were paid for. You found someone Dwight could fall for. The rest is up to him."

"Helga's right. You'll go mad trying to second-guess what makes a relationship work. Leave them be and enjoy the evening. Because all work and no play is making Becky an awfully dull girl."

We get home at midnight, stumbling across Richmond Bridge with the rest of the picnickers, drunk on champers and chamber music. Even I feel a little happier: if human beings can create music so uplifting, then it's not so hard to believe that Heather could be motivated by love.

I take the spiral staircase up to my room and decide to send Heather the text message she's been waiting for. My fingers are clumsy from booze so finally, I decide simplicity is best:

HEATHER. I HAVE NO PLANS TO TELL TALES. I WON'T COME TO THE WEDDING BUT GOOD LUCK TO YOU BOTH. BECCA.

There. My finger hesitates for a few seconds above the SEND button. Is this fair on Dwight?

I press SEND anyway.

There! That's that out of the way. Time to stop fretting about Dwight and Sam and Edward. We all make mistakes.

Tomorrow's another day.

I dream of brides with blank faces, and grooms wearing suits made of bank notes, and a Cupid who shoots people dead.

But if that's another sign that I've done the wrong thing, there's nothing I can do about it now. Heather's sent me a text:

THANK YOU. NOW WE CAN CONCENTRATE ON WHAT MATTERS.

Georgie suggests I go with her to Chelsea, where she's meeting a sinewy posse of ex-ballerinas who get together on the last Sunday of the month, but I still feel like the worst possible company, so I turn her down. After pacing the empty house for far too long, I get on the Tube, to ride around like I used to when I first came to London, exploring what lay behind those mystical station names: the ruthless grey of Elephant and Castle, the high society houses of Highgate, and the distinctly un-Alpine Swiss Cottage.

Only this time I have no destination in mind. Or maybe my subconscious does, because I find myself emerging at Monument. I nearly turn back, worried I might bump into Adam, until I remember he doesn't work on Sundays.

Five weeks since Sam's dating orgy at the Tower. Five weeks since the first dummy date with Adam. And a fortnight since the kiss at his flat . . .

He's tried to call a couple more times, but I haven't answered and he's left no message. It would be too easy to treat myself to the occasional phone conversation or even — worse still — to agree to advise him on his future dates, to listen and to torture myself with spinsterish secret fantasies, with endless "what if"s?

There is no "what if". He was a client. End of story.

Except, how can it be, when I've come here?

The streets are deserted and I feel gut-wrenchingly lonely. My feet carry me towards Pudding Lane Bakery. The blinds are down, the door bolted, but my mind still taunts me with memories of the little Maid of Honour cakes Adam brought to the Tower on that first date. The sweet smell of almonds, and the soft smudginess of the butter pastry on my fingers.

And then my nose twitches with an imagined scent of maple syrup and it's so powerful I feel like weeping with longing. *Could* I take the risk again? Maybe all men aren't like Marcus Benson.

My phone rings — withheld number — and I have a brief debate about whether to answer or to let it go to voicemail. I decide that any distraction would be welcome right now.

"Hello?"

There's a moment's hesitation, enough time for me to wonder — OK, to hope — that it might just, possibly, be Adam and then . . .

"Rebecca, it's Sam."

Bloody hell. I haven't heard from her for nearly three weeks now, not since the speed-dating debacle. "Sam. I suppose you've rung up to tell me there's a writ in the post, have you?"

There's another pause. "Not exactly. It's . . . awkward."

"Go on."

"Look, I was frustrated. Impatient." There's an unfamiliar tone in her voice. If I didn't know her better, I'd say it was *almost* apologetic.

"I gathered that much."

"Rebecca, it's possible that I was a little unfair to you. I've been thinking it over and I know that I'm not necessarily the easiest person to match up."

You can say that again. "If I'm honest, Sam, I wonder if you actually want to be matched up. Sometimes we don't know ourselves as well as we think."

"Maybe," she says, sounding unconvinced. "In any case, I have decided that I would like to take advantage of your service again. On reflection, I feel you're the only person who can help me."

Cold bitch. She talks about love as if it were a business arrangement. Then again, so do I.

I sigh. The thought of Sam on the books again isn't one I relish, but with precisely no other clients lined up, beggars can't be choosers. Maybe this is what I need, to distract myself from the mistakes I've made so far. "Go on, then. What is it you want?"

"Well," she takes a huge breath, "things have *developed* with one of my previous dates."

"Really?" I mentally run through the dates I've organised so far. Is it Zak or maybe even Lee Laker? But even before she speaks, I have a horrible premonition of what she's going to say.

"Yes. I should have been more open-minded, really, but it's all come right in the end. It seems you've made a breakthrough, Rebecca, because last week I had a phone call, and then a second date. Which went rather well. Well enough for me to conclude that the right man for me is actually Adam Hill."

CHAPTER
TWENTY-FOUR

I see my reflection begin to totter in the window before I realise I'm losing my balance, and I reach out to steady myself, leaving a palm-print on the glass.

". . . I shan't go into details, Rebecca, but he came, he saw and he conquered. I was so wrong about the fumbling. What a changed man. I don't know what you did to Adam Hill but it was quite a transformation . . . but now he's done the usual caveman thing. Thirty-six hours since our date and not a dicky-bird out of him."

I can't actually speak but Sam carries on regardless. "Normally I'd call and give him a piece of my mind but this one . . . well, I've learned my lesson about jumping the gun. So I thought you could call him for me. Work out what's going on. You set it up, after all. Why have a dog and bark yourself?"

I mumble something about seeing what I can do, then ring off and head straight into the nearest pub, an underground old-man's joint which stinks of sweat and beer. I work my way through four double vodkas, to try to stop myself thinking, until the landlord suggests it might be time to go home. I doze on the Tube, and struggle on the steep spiral staircase up to my loft room. I lie in my bed, the familiar taste of betrayal on my tongue, Sam's jubilant words repeating themselves in my head.

Sleep is impossible. All I can do is count the seconds till dawn. When Marcus betrayed me, I slunk away like a wounded animal. This time, it's different. This time, I will be in control.

Pudding Lane Bakery is doing a roaring trade for a Monday morning. Couriers and junior secretaries come and go, leaving the shop with arms full of brown-paper parcels. I imagine the warmth of the bread against their chests, the toasty smell tickling their noses.

I wait on the other side of the street from the bakery for the shop to empty or my courage to return. It's been twenty minutes and I still haven't moved. I need to be ready. Composed. Except I keep hearing Sam's voice.

"*All that baking means Adam's terribly good with his hands.*"

So it took him nine whole days to get over his feelings for me, and transfer them to Sam. All that flannel, all that *bollocks* about being shy and needing my help. Manipulative bastard. Wouldn't it have been easier simply to return to All Bar One with his fat baker friend and try to hook some other gullible girl with his hard-luck stories?

I'm not getting anywhere. I decide to walk once around the block and then keep walking, right through that door, into the bakery, without thinking about it any more. I take long, confident strides. Adam will get what's coming to him. Then I can move on.

Right, here we go, here we go . . . around this corner and then keep going, into the shop . . .

Ah. I seem to have walked straight past. I retrace my steps, picturing him in my mind, stoking my anger. Except the man in my head seems to have morphed into a strange combination of Adam and Marcus: Adam's face in Marcus's Armani suit. Marcus sneering, in baggy cords and crumpled shirt.

I march into the shop before I have a chance to change my mind again. It's packed with customers and staff: behind the counter, I recognise Tommy, the overweight baker who gave me free cake when I wandered in here last time. He's filling one of the open shelves with seeded knot rolls; there must be a hundred of them. The other shelves are packed with bagels and croissants and cheese cobs.

"I'm looking for Adam."

He blinks a couple of times, as if he recognises me too. "You're Becca, aren't you?"

I'm sure I never told him my name. I nod.

"Hilly?" He shouts towards the back of the shop. "Hilly, shift your arse out here, you're wanted." Then the fat guy turns back to me, staring quite blatantly. I feel like I must have spinach between my teeth, or my shirt tucked into my knickers. But I know I haven't. I took quite a lot of care this morning to make sure I looked just right.

Just right for a bearer of *good* tidings, that is.

"I've told you before about swearing in front of . . ." we hear Adam's voice before he bursts through the door, ". . . customers." He freezes when he sees me,

309

while I feel quite giddy. Could he have got taller in the two weeks since I saw him? Taller and bigger and more handsome?

Bastard.

"Hi, Adam."

"Becca," he whispers. He says my name like I'm a mythical creature, a unicorn turned up out of the blue in the heart of EC3.

They're both staring at me now, Adam and Tommy. "Have I got newsprint on my face or something? Only you're looking at me as though I've grown an extra nose."

Adam shakes his head. "God, sorry. I just wasn't really expecting to see you. Do you want to come into the office? At least then there'll only be one of us staring."

I follow him through the swing door, into a cramped office area. Piles of paper are stacked on every surface, and one wall is completely covered in postcards and pictures of people, and landscapes, and bread.

"Sit down, Becca. It's lovely to see you. Really lovely." As if to prove this, his eyes don't leave my face as he sinks into a tatty office chair.

"I'm a missionary, actually, Adam."

"Really?" He's still staring.

"Yes, an envoy. From Sam."

"Sam?"

"Don't tell me you don't remember."

"She sent you?" He doesn't even have the decency to look embarrassed.

With difficulty I control the urge to leap up and slap him. "It's really good news, Adam."

"Hmmm?"

"Yes. Absolutely." I remember the lines I practised so carefully in my loft. "Sam thinks you are the perfect man. Hunky. Successful. Good with your hands . . ."

"Eh?" He stares at me.

"What, no high-five? No whoop of joy? I mean, for a shy retiring chap like yourself, Adam, I'd have thought this would be the best news in the world."

"I don't know what you're on about, Becca. After what happened at my flat, I thought you were here to —"

"Here to what?" I feel the anger now, white heat spreading from my feet, up through my body, out of the top of my head. Or, to be more accurate, exploding out of my mouth, so loud that the customers must be hearing every bitter word. "Here to suggest a bloody threesome? To give you a certificate to congratulate you for graduating from the Rebecca Orchard Dating Academy with first class honours." I clench my fists to stop me pummelling them against his chest. "Not that you'd know anything about honour."

Adam looks utterly panicked. So he should. "I did see Sam. Just like you told me to. But it's not what you think —"

"Oh, really? I've heard that one before. You complete and utter sod. I tried to get you to call Sam because I thought you were a decent person who needed a helping hand. I thought you were better than the rest, Adam. I really did . . ." And then I feel the anger begin

311

to subside, and in its place I know tears are coming. I look at his face, those *lips*, and I imagine them kissing Sam and I feel my own lips begin to wobble. No! I cried in front of Marcus. I will never cry in front of a man again: I need to get out of here.

CRASH!

"Fucking hell! Fucking bastard brioches ..." Tommy's groans carry through the thin office wall. Adam doesn't seem to notice.

"Becca, listen to me, this is important. You've got the wrong end of the stick, because when I saw Sam again, it —"

"Shut up. I don't want to hear it, Adam. I've heard enough of your lies. You got what you wanted. Final piece of free advice, though. I'd definitely give Sam another shot. I think you have a lot in common."

"Becca, wait!"

He puts his hand on my arm and despite it all, I feel that spark again. My body has a habit of misleading me. It did with Marcus, too. Except Adam's the bigger shit: at least Marcus never pretended to be anything he's not.

"Get your hands off me before I scream the bloody place down," I hiss in his face, before heading for the door, surprised at how weak my legs feel. I don't look back and when Tommy the baker peers up at me from the floor as he picks up the bastard brioches, I ignore him too.

I run all the way to Monument station: as long as I keep running, the breeze against my face will stop me crying. Sure enough, as I stop at the barrier to swipe my Oyster card, the tears overflow down my cheeks. A few tourists shoot me odd looks, but no Londoners take any notice. Girls in tears on the Tube are ten-a-penny.

I rummage in my bag for sunglasses. They make everything around me look even gloomier but despite the general indifference I am determined no one will see my red eyes.

Not like last time.

Trina Martini wasn't her real name and they weren't her real breasts, either. But I managed to convince myself that someone so false couldn't be a real threat to my relationship with Marcus.

True, my status in the office seemed diminished after her arrival, but then again Benson's always was like a mini stock market, where each headhunter's reputation was only as good as their last hiring. Trina had been working for three weeks without a single lead, but that didn't affect her unstoppable upward mobility. Her unstoppable legs, permanently sheathed in fishnets, might have helped her ascent.

I ploughed on, trusting that my hard work would pay off. In fact, I was working longer hours than ever, because things were tricky at home. The promise of domestic bliss in Marcus's pent-house hadn't materialised. He was sulky and irritable and nothing I did placated him.

It was a bitter Friday in March: cold rain was bucketing down and the clients had knocked off early and somehow the only possible place to be was the pub.

Even though my overgrown schoolboy colleagues were never my ideal choice of companion, I was tempted to go and share a few drinks in front of the log fire in our nearest boozer.

I'd had four glasses of port, thick as cough syrup, before remembering I had a call to make to a potential candidate currently working in San Francisco. A couple of the boys needed to pick up some papers from the office so we all trooped back together, the inner glow of booze making us feel waterproof. I've never been much of a drinker, but that evening I didn't care: I wasn't looking forward to yet another weekend of surly silence from Marcus.

I had a premonition in the lift, but shrugged it off as drunken paranoia. It was only when the boys bundled out on our corridor and then froze, like kids playing grandmothers' footsteps, that I realised I'd known all along. I'd just been pretending I didn't.

They were on her work station. Or rather, she was. They didn't see us at first, because he was screwing her from behind ("What a waste, to go to all that trouble getting plastic tits and then keeping them out of sight," Georgie said, much later, when it was all a little less raw). Actually, for a good month after this, the position we found them in gave me false hope. He didn't want to look at her because she wasn't me.

Poor, deluded Becca.

We stayed frozen for a good five seconds, while Marcus's bare bottom moved backwards and forwards, in time with his grunts. Until one of the boys — Robin, I think his name was, or was it Roland? — lost his balance and toppled over into an enormous plastic plant and Marcus's arse stopped bobbing and Trina's head turned, very, very slowly, to see what the noise was.

What I remember most is the look on her face: no shame, no anxiety, just a kind of vapid triumph. *I know you think you're better than me*, it seemed to say, *but I am irresistible, even to your boyfriend.*

Marcus didn't look at me. He fixed his eyes somewhere towards the ceiling, pulled his trousers up and then zipped himself in with studied nonchalance, like a man caught weeing against a tree. The boys were backing away, towards the lift. I did nothing. I'm surprised, in retrospect, that I remembered to breathe.

Trina quickly rearranged her clothes (one of the benefits of a very short skirt is that there's less fuss if you're caught in flagrante), then headed for the ladies' loo.

"I've been meaning to talk to you," Marcus said after a while, still apparently fascinated by the grey speckled ceiling tiles.

"About?" One word was all I could trust myself to say.

"About your future. *Our* future." As he spoke, I sensed his voice and his resolve hardening. When he finally looked at me, I don't actually think he was seeing his girlfriend any more. He was seeing someone he used to know. "And your future here. You've been an asset to Benson Associates in the past, Bex, but you're no longer running with the wolves. The trick in situations like these is to know when it's time to move on. I think it's time."

I stared at him. The port kicked in, very suddenly, and I felt woozy.

"There's no need to look at me like that. I'm sure you've been expecting this."

"I —" I wanted to say that of course I hadn't, but he sounded so certain. I tried again. "Us?"

He held out his hands, palms raised, like our vet did at home when there was no more he could do for some poor cow. "Flame's gone out, Bex. No point pretending otherwise."

In the months to come, I rewrote that scene in so many different ways: begging him to reconsider, or listing the good moments we'd shared, or kissing him. Later I wished I'd slapped him or trashed the office or told him I'd been trying to think of how I could break it to him for months.

Instead I began to cry. Muffled sobs at first, seguing into choking sounds that brought the security guard up to our floor. The guard offered to fetch me a taxi but I waved him away with a snotty hand and took the Tube back to Richmond, back to Georgie.

No job. No boyfriend. Nothing to show for four years in London except a few flash suits and a lot of unpaid credit card bills for furniture I'd never see again.

The District Line train pulls into Richmond, the last stop on the line. I'm not crying any more. I take off my sunglasses but everything still looks gloomy and unreal.

As I walk out of the station, I pass Maison Blanc and the smell of bread hits me, as painful as a hard punch to the stomach. People, memories, hopes. London feels too raw. I know what I've got to do.

I'm going home.

CHAPTER
TWENTY-FIVE

My mother manages to hide her satisfaction at the return of the prodigal daughter for, oooh, at least an hour and a half. Long enough for me to unpack, visit the cows, feed treats to Fatso the Incredible Jumping Dog, and join the rest of the family in the kitchen for tea.

"I would have baked something special, of course, if you'd warned me," she says. "One of your favourites. A Victoria sponge. I tell you what, I'll make one later."

"It's OK, Mum. I'm off carbs for a while, so it'd be an awful waste." And the mere smell of baking might bring on the waterworks. It's the last thing I need right now.

I don't know what I need right now, but for once in my life I know I won't find it in London. After my moment of truth outside Richmond station, I headed straight for Eve Terrace to pack the basics in a backpack. Luckily Georgie wasn't in — I don't think I could have explained it to her, this craving for home — so I left a note, and took the first train back to Gloucestershire.

And now I'm here, there is something perversely comforting about the place I've spent most of my adult

318

life running away from. I think the reason it soothes me — despite the predatory expression on my mother's face as she waits to pounce with her questions — is because it's barely changed at all.

All right, now there's a new generation at the table. Bobby Junior sits solidly in Janey's lap, momentarily usurped from his status as centre of attention. But even that feels familiar: in all my best memories, there are *babies* of some kind or another in this kitchen: squirming puppies sired by Fatso, or biscuity kittens, or even, after occasional moments of uncharacteristic sentimentality by my mother, a sickly newborn calf.

"So, planning to stay long?" says my mother, sharpening her talons with a seemingly innocuous question that is anything but.

"Not sure." I take a mug from the centre of the table and pour out the stewed tea.

"Well, anything to rush back *for*?" she asks, displaying her technique of posing the same question in different ways until she gets an answer. She could teach Jeremy Paxman a thing or two.

"Things are pretty quiet at work."

"Ah!" she says. "Well, it's beginning to make sense."

Around the table, my other relations develop a sudden fascination for the daisy-chain pattern on the tablecloth. I'm sure Richie is actually counting the chocolate chips in his cookie.

"In what way, exactly, Mum?"

"Well, I always said that a job like that . . . not that I'd even call it a proper job, of course, would bring with it nothing but trouble and strife."

I put my cup down. "And you've concluded all that from me saying it's quiet at work."

"No, not just that. I can't remember the last time you came home out of the blue like this, looking all shell-shocked."

She's got a point. Even when Marcus dumped me and made me homeless, I went to Georgie's rather than head back to Mum. "Never?"

She folds her arms on the table. "Never. This is serious, isn't it?"

"It *might* be . . ."

I feel multiple pairs of eyes on me again. Even Bobby Junior seems intrigued — his eyes have a terribly mature intensity about them — but then he burps.

"Don't you think you'd better tell us now?" Mum asks. "Get it out of the way?"

I sigh ostentatiously, like a petulant teenager. Mum's nosiness is outrageous, but somehow I end up feeling in the wrong. "What, because you're not going to let up until I tell you?"

"Is it so wrong to want to know what's upsetting my only daughter? I know in *London* you're lucky if you recognise your next-door neighbour, but that isn't how I brought you up. And it isn't how *I* am so I am not going to apologise for taking an interest in my family's welfare!"

"Mum, I'm not saying you shouldn't care. It's just I haven't quite got it straight in my own head yet . . ." I hesitate, trying to calculate whether confessing now will save me trouble later. Ah well, in for a penny. "All

320

businesses go through their difficult phases. Don't they, Dad?"

Dad nods vigorously, pleased to have something non-contentious to contribute. "I remember when we first made the switch from milk to cheese, I mean, sometimes we didn't know whether we'd have to start burning cheese instead of logs to stay warm, it was the only thing we had. Or making new shoes for Robbie and you out of cheese rind."

My mother scowls. "Don't send your father off down Memory Lane. We'll never get him back."

"I was only agreeing," he protests.

"Well, don't." Mum turns back to me. "Carry on, Rebecca. You were about to tell us about your difficult phase. Not that it's your first difficult phase, after all."

"Thanks for that reminder, Mother. I don't have much else to say. I'm not in financial trouble, or being taken to court or anything. It's more about *expectations*. I think maybe I have been suffering from . . . delusions."

Mum grips her chair. "Proper delusions? Visions? Like your cousin Jess, at Lourdes?"

"No, no, it hasn't driven me crazy just yet. More delusions about what I can do for my clients. About how much I can influence their love lives, and whether it's for the best."

There. That's as far as I am willing to go in analysing my current predicament. I am not even *thinking* about Adam. Oh. Too late. It's harder than you'd think to keep your brain away from proscribed topics. I managed it on the train, nearly, thanks to *Heat* magazine. But even then I found it almost impossible not to compare *this* celebrity's hair, or *that* soap actor's six-pack to my memories of London's tastiest, most duplicitous baker.

Mum stares. "That it?"

I stiffen. "Why? Isn't that enough for you?"

She sniffs. "Well, I won't say I told you so. But at least you could admit that I have been right all along. If you'd listened to me, well, you'd have realised that matchmaking never had any future in it. Whatever that bloody sister of mine says. It's common sense. Not that your aunt has ever been over-endowed with that."

Robbie shifts in his seat. "Now, Mum, I'm sure that Rebecca came home for a bit of peace and quiet, not a going over. Can we talk about something else?"

I look at him in surprise: my big brother, the diplomat? That'll take a bit of getting used to. Fatherhood obviously suits him.

But my mother isn't listening. "I will have my say in my own kitchen. We've spent too long going along with what Rebecca wants, what Georgia says. After all, we're country bumpkins, what do we know? And all the time, if we'd been allowed to say our piece, we might have saved our daughter a lot of time and a lot of heartache into the bargain."

Robbie stands up and, as if my brothers are communicating by some kind of fraternal telepathy, so does Richie. They come to stand behind my chair, like bodyguards.

Robbie pats me on the shoulder. "There'll be time for Rebecca to talk later, Mum. If that's what she wants. But for now, I think we either give her some space, or she'll be back to London on the next train."

"Yeah!" says Richie.

I don't know who is more gobsmacked — me, or Mum. But I do know that my emotional fragility has reached another crisis point because my brother's show of solidarity has produced an enormous lump in my throat. I push back my own chair, touch their hands lightly to say *thank you*, and walk briskly out of the kitchen.

As I leave, I hear my mother say, "I don't know what you're all looking at. It's not like I told her what I *really* think."

I feel heavy and hot, too hot to lie in the meadow. The coolest place on Orchard Farm is the shed where we keep the Friesians so I head for there.

Even the shed isn't exactly chilly, but it's much more tolerable than outside. It's shady and steamy from cow dung. The smell's powerful at first, but not unpleasant: it reminds me of my childhood.

One of the cows turns towards me lethargically and I trace the patterns on her hide, fantastic shapes in dark brown against white. When we were little, Robbie and Richie and I used to play daft games, competing to identify what the patterns most closely resembled. Half the time the boys convinced themselves that they could see rude things: boobs and willies and . . . well, boobs and willies, mainly.

I preferred to imagine I was seeing flowers or fairies, but in truth the patterns were as random and chaotic as everything else in the countryside. That's what I hated about it. Calves got sick and died, or sometimes they survived, and there was no logic to it. Plagues of pretty butterflies would occur one year, from nowhere, but then the next it might be billions of aphids sucking the life out of Mum's kitchen garden. We were only ever moments away from falling into a cow-pat or waking in the night with a mouse running across the eiderdown. That, of course, was what my brothers loved about the place; that adventure. But to me, it was nauseating. No wonder I preferred the idea of the city, with tubes and buses around the clock and smart buildings with roofs that didn't leak in stormy weather. What I hadn't realised was that in the city, it's the people who create the chaos.

"Sis?"

"All right, Richie."

My little brother hovers at the entrance to the shed, silhouetted against the sunlight. "Mum, eh?"

I grin. "Yeah. Thanks for standing up for me."

"No problemo."

I suppress a smile. Richie speaks in what he thinks of as cool language, even though it makes him sound more like a teenager than a twenty-three-year-old. "So, how's life? How's . . ." I try to remember the name of the mousy girl he was seeing last time, ". . . Mandy?"

"Wendy."

"Wendy. Sorry."

He points his index finger towards me, with the rest of his fingers tucked into the palm. Like a gun. "Kapow. She's toast, sis."

"Oh, I'm sorry."

"Ain't into settling down. Too much lovin' to do."

I nod sagely. "Good point, Richie. She was very quiet, as well. Not really farmer's wife material. Not like Janey."

"Fuck, no," he says ruefully, then blushes so hard that I can see it in the gloom of the shed. "I mean, she's OK. But she's well bossy."

"She has to be, to stand up to Mum." I share a conspiratorial grin with my brother.

"I was well freaked to see you here, sis. You don't come home much. I wouldn't, neither, if I lived in London."

"Yes, well. London's good, but sometimes you need to get away to remember why you like it."

"Yeah?" His voice is dreamy. "I'd love it."

I stare at him, surprised. "I thought you liked being here."

"Easy, innit? But maybe one day I'll move. Maybe." He shakes his head as he says it, as though he realises that it's never going to happen. London would be one hell of a shock to his system. "So what's the deal, sis? What's this really about? Not that dude again?"

Richie was the only one of my family — apart from me — who wholeheartedly approved of Marcus and his car and his suit and his tall stories. We were both deluded, of course, but I'm convinced my brother still retains a sneaking respect for the MD of Benson Associates . . .

"No, not *that* dude."

Richie raises an eyebrow. He's always been overlooked as the baby of the family, but he's sharper than you'd think. "Some other dude, then?"

"Maybe. It's more complicated than one dude, though." It's about my own stupidity, my career crisis, the rest of my life. "Richie, if I ask you something will you promise to be honest?"

"I can be brutal, man. If that's what you really want."

"It is. Would you describe me as a control freak?"

He begins to giggle. "A control f —" He can't seem to finish the word. Before long he's doubled up, seemingly in pain, and the cows are regarding him with doleful suspicion.

"I guess that's a yes?" I say, peevishly.

"Oh sis," he says eventually. "I don't wanna hit a girl when she's down but, doh! Who else would try to toilet-train chickens?"

"I'd forgotten about that."

"Yeah? Don't make you a bad person. But the fact you're asking . . . maybe it's making you an unhappy person."

"That's a very grown-up thing to say, little bruv. Don't forget I'm meant to be the psychology expert around here."

"Not always easy to do the psychology thing on yourself, innit?"

"True. So . . . if you're the expert on me, then, what do you think I should do with my life?"

He shrugs. "What a question, sis. What a freakin' question. I dunno. We hardly know you no more. You're mysterious like Auntie Georgia. But there's gotta be a reason why you came home instead of hung out in London. I reckon if you hang around here long enough, you'll find it. That reason." And then he nods, as though he's said something very, very profound.

Who knows? Maybe he has.

CHAPTER
TWENTY-SIX

Four days, and I'm no nearer finding the meaning of life. I still feel miserable as sin. But according to my mother, I have lost "that half-dead look Londoners have". Her cooking, and a few long shifts helping on the farm, have put the colour back in my cheeks.

My old bedroom's been turned into Bobby Junior's nursery, so I'm staying in the tiny guest room, squeezed in between boxfuls of my childhood toys and teenage posters. The nursery is unrecognisable as the place where I spent my adolescence: all primrose walls and steam-train decorative borders and brand new, lead-free teddy bears.

When I haven't been sweating away in the cheese-ripening room, I've been going through the boxes, which are infuriatingly random in their contents. I have no option but to tip out a box at a time on to the bed (there's no floor space) and then pick through it, vulture-like, trying to match dice or plastic counters to board games in Sellotaped cardboard boxes, or reunite doll limbs with torsos.

Robbie comes in with a cup of tea. He and Richie are taking their self-appointed bodyguard role very seriously: whenever my mother hovers around me, they're behind her, ready to block any awkward questions.

"Oh, bloody hell, squirt. Manly! I remember him."

He sits on the very edge of the bed and picks up my most handsome doll, named for his muscly physique and perfect plastic black mop. I think he was originally bought for Robbie, but my big brother really wasn't into dolls, so I got him instead. He's currently sporting camouflage gear, but also has a wetsuit, and a naval dress uniform.

"Ah, but do you remember who he ended up with?" I wave at the orgy of figures on the bed.

He shakes his head. "I thought they swapped over all the time?"

"Robert Orchard! How could you? My dolls were never promiscuous. When I matched them up, they were together *for ever*."

I open an old school exercise book, still retaining its cardboard cover: REBECCA ORCHARD, YEAR 8, HISTORY. But inside, the pages detailing Stone Age tools have been ripped out, and the precious remaining sheets are devoted to a log of my dolls' liaisons. Manly dated Barbie but she was too much of a party girl, like a miniaturised plastic version of Georgie.

"He ended up with Peg the peg doll." I pick her up, and straighten her woollen strands of coppery hair. *Much* more like my mother, with rosy cheeks and solid legs. "He liked her because she was feminine, but also had a down-to-earth demeanour. They went on camping trips together."

329

Robbie takes Peg from me. He peers up her flowery skirt. "Consummating the relationship must have been a problem."

"Robbie!" I say, putting my hands to my ears in mock horror. "Actually, more of a problem than you'd think." I lower his trousers to reveal Manly's equally smooth groin. "No wonder he was always off on his travels, yomping and exploring. He had a lot to prove."

"Like you?"

"I have a full set of genitalia, thanks very much." I blush. "I can't believe I just said that to my own brother."

He blushes too. "I was talking about you and your travels."

"Oh, you're not going to try to counsel me as well, are you? I already had that from Richie, bless his heart. Talking about mystical forces. He'll be on about ley lines next. He's not turning into Sting, is he?"

"If he thought it'd give him a chance of tantric sex, he'd try anything." Robbie frowns. "He means well, squirt. We're worried about you. You've got to admit that it's out of character to come back home like this."

"It's just a *wobble*. I've always liked things ordered, haven't I?" I nod towards the dolls and the matchmaking record book. "I guess we all have to learn sooner or later that we can't keep everything at arm's length, however hard we try."

"It's the business?"

"Yes, mainly. I had a good run, didn't I, for the first year or two. Everyone behaved exactly as expected, I

330

pulled their strings, and bingo! People fell in love. Just like that. I felt all-powerful."

"Watch it. You're beginning to sound like a megalomaniac."

I nod. "That's exactly what I'm worried about. I really did think I had this *gift*, I was this cross between Cupid and St Valentine. One touch from my magic wand and then, poof! Hearts and flowers all the way."

"So what's happened?"

"A few people haven't behaved the way I expected. I mean, how pathetic does that sound? Some of my clients have actually dared to exercise free will and I go into the world's biggest sulk. There were always bound to be hitches, of course, but I wish they'd happened sooner, when I'd just set up the business maybe. I'd have been less devastated."

My brother picks up Tigger, and tries to fluff up his flattened orange fur. "It's a setback, that's all. You said it yourself when you arrived: all businesses have setbacks. Are you sure there isn't more to it?"

I hesitate. Dare I mention Adam? He's been in my thoughts every waking hour. Only the hard labour of shifting heavy vats of milk or feeding the cows stops the constant flow of questions: why did he behave like that? How can I have been so wrong about someone? And if I could be so wrong about him, then how on earth can I possibly take charge of other people's love lives? No wonder I messed up with Heather and Edward too.

"I'm just doubting myself, Robbie. And doubting the morality of what I've been doing, I suppose. Maybe Mum's right. Maybe I am no better than a pimp."

He shakes his head. "And maybe you're reading way too much into this. Look at all of these happy couples," he says, waving at my dolls. "Peg and Manly wouldn't be together without you. It's your vocation, but even people with a vocation doubt themselves sometimes. Give yourself a bit of time off for good behaviour, but don't leave it too long before you get back in the saddle, eh?"

"Maybe you're right, but —"

"REBECCA! REBECCA!" Janey's voice — the farmhouse's own public address system — rumbles through the thick walls. "VISITOR!"

"Expecting someone?" Robbie asks.

"No. No one knows I'm here," I say. Except . . . I know it can't possibly be, but the only person I can imagine with the initiative and the incentive and the knowledge to track me down to the wilds of the Cotswolds is . . .

"Sam?"

My stomach drops, like a lift in a skyscraper. Of course, I never believed it could be Adam, not really, but even so, I feel terribly disappointed. Not to mention intimidated. It's a Thursday: I can't imagine Sam taking a day off work unless she is really gunning for me.

She's in the entrance hall, and it feels like she's *glowing* with rage. Janey has withdrawn discreetly, but my little brother is standing in the kitchen doorway, transfixed.

"Rebecca. Quite the moonlight flit, eh?"

I've never really understood the expression "looking daggers" before. Now I do. I have palpitations. "Would you like to . . . come to the living room? Sit down?"

"I've been sitting down for the last three hours, in the car. I'd rather stretch my legs."

I look down at her spiky stilettos — they're not exactly prime rambling footwear. In fact, she's dressed to kill.

Not, I hope, literally.

"OK, fine. Would you like to borrow some wellies?"

She stares at me. "I haven't worn wellies since prep school, and I don't intend to start now."

I nod, then gesture towards the front door. Still, Richie stands stock-still, a hungry look on his face. She is quite something, I'll admit.

Once outside I try to calculate the least boggy route underfoot. Down past the milking shed, maybe, then through the yard, to the edge of the meadow. The cows should be out, chomping their way through grass and wildflowers. Surely it's almost impossible to stay enraged with cows around, isn't it?

I trudge, and she totters, until we reach two grey plastic stacking chairs that Dad nicked from the village hall decades ago. He comes here to smoke and to think, and though the chairs aren't all that sympathetic to the surroundings, the view is something else. Up here, you could believe you were in paradise.

"Do sit down," I say and she looks dubious. But I take the grubbier of the two chairs, and she joins me. The chair legs sink a little into the mud. "It's a good spot for privacy. Not much of that on the farm. Or in the countryside at all. Funny, you'd think that with all this space, you'd feel more alone than in the city, but it's the opposite —"

"I'm sure your theories on the rural-urban divide are quite fascinating, Rebecca, but if I want that, I'll watch *Countryfile* with John Craven. I haven't driven one hundred and twenty miles for a debate."

God, she's rude. "Why are you here, then, Sam?"

She tuts so loudly that the cows are momentarily distracted from their meal. "I'm here because I do not appreciate being abandoned in my hour of need."

"Hour of need? It's not like I'm an ambulance driver, or a lifeboat man."

"I trusted you with my heart," she says, striking a pose like a tragic opera diva. "I told you how I felt about Adam. I waited. I heard nothing. I called your mobile, nothing. Emailed you. Nothing. I am not used to waiting, Rebecca."

I'm about to make some sarcastic remark back, but then I look at her face. Behind the thick make-up (who wears Juicy Tube to the country?) and the terrifying heels, I have to admit that Sam Ottoway is just as vulnerable as Edward. Or even me.

I remember what she said to me the first time we met, that drunken night when she cried into her wine and told me I had to beware of ending up like her. And the awful truth is that I am well on the way. With one crucial difference.

At least Sam is willing to risk falling in love.

"You know, Sam, you're right. I have failed you. I deserve your anger, and more besides. I took you on as a client and the very least I owed you was my respect. I am sorry."

She seems dumbfounded by this, and looks away, towards the horizon. It's as if she hasn't noticed the view until now. "Wow," she says.

"Yes. It is kind of special, isn't it?"

"Why, Rebecca?" she asks, still not looking at me.

"Why didn't I call? It's . . . complicated." I am not about to tell her what happened with Adam, or I'll look even more unprofessional. "Because I've still got a lot to learn about people, I suppose."

There's a long, ominous pause before Sam nods. "Right . . . you know, I almost wish you hadn't apologised. I spent the whole journey planning my vicious rant, my threats to sue you under three different pieces of legislation. My promise to ruin you. And you've taken the wind right out of my sails."

"Sorry."

"Ah, whatever. You're obviously going through some kind of existential crisis."

"Existential? That makes it sound much more interesting than it is. Really, I've just lost my bottle."

She takes a tissue out of her handbag and begins to wipe mud off her heel. I consider telling her that it's a pointless exercise, unless she's planning to levitate back to her car, but she speaks first. "I lost mine, once. I lost a case. One where I genuinely believed my client was innocent . . . I mean, I don't defend anyone I *know* to be guilty, but I'm realistic. This woman, though. She was accused of killing her father, you know. For the inheritance."

"How horrible."

"I think she did kill him. The father was awful, a cruel bully, and he pushed my client too far, and she snapped. Just once. It was a burst of anger, not calculated premeditation. I really did believe I could persuade the jury it was manslaughter, but they were having none of it. She got life. And I was convinced it was down to me."

"What did you do?"

"I went to pieces, ran away. No one ever found out, so it was a bit of a hollow gesture, but that Friday night, on the Tube, I went past my stop, got off at Victoria and took the train to Brighton. Bought a bottle of vodka. Walked on the beach until I dropped. Next day I found a B&B — a rough one, I mean, I could have afforded the Grand, but the rough one fitted my mood. Drank more vodka, slept, and then something woke me up on the Monday morning. So early. My body put me back on that train to London, and I went into work in my old suit, my hair unwashed with one of those mini-packs of soap. No one realised. But it made me stronger. I knew I couldn't quit."

"When was this?"

"Ten years ago. I was your age. Don't they have a name for it now? The quarter-life crisis? I read it in *Metro*. Hah. If I'd known it was my quarter-life crisis, maybe I'd have changed direction. Too late now, though, eh?"

"But it's not too late, Sam. I mean, you came to me, didn't you? That has to be a sign that you weren't prepared to accept the status quo."

"Maybe." She looks at me, shyly. "Adam said no, didn't he?"

I shrug. It's not as though I actually gave him the chance to say anything. "Like I said, it's complicated, but I don't think Adam is quite the man he seems. I'd forget him, Sam." Easier said than done, of course. I suddenly have the strangest sensation, as though I can smell the bread, feel the warmth of the ovens. Must be Mum's scones baking. It's nearly tea-time.

"It wasn't really on, was it, asking you to do that?"

I think it over. "I could have said no."

"No, you couldn't. I can be very difficult to turn down. Unless you're a man, of course." She laughs, hoarsely. "And what about you, Bride Hunter? Are you really jacking it in?"

"I . . . I don't know. I can't help feeling that this should be a labour of love, not a business."

"Your decision, of course," she says, "but don't forget you're offering something people need. There are worse ways to earn a living."

We sit in silence for a while. The cows continue to chew, the trees rustle and the green fields manage to be both still and completely alive.

"There's something else . . ." Sam begins, then stops abruptly.

"What?"

Her eyes narrow. "I . . . no, it's not going to change anything. I ought to be going," Sam says, pushing herself up from the plastic chair.

"All right, but you'll have to stay for tea. My mother will never forgive me if you leave without sampling her scones."

There is a surreal quality to tea this afternoon. Baby Bobby cries when he sees Sam, and has to be laid down in his cot early. Richie can't take his eyes off her. My mother, perhaps sensing someone with a will to match her own, lays off her usual pointed questions about decadent London life, and acts instead as though the queen has dropped by.

"You know, I have *never* been on a farm before," Sam says, more like the queen every second. "Not a real, working one. It's terribly reassuring to know places like this still exist. Like the farm set I used to have when I was a girl."

"Show you round, if you like, innit?" my little brother says. We all stare at him. Robbie winks at me.

"Well, I ought to be heading back to town," Sam peers at the kitchen clock, "but I have got time for a whistle-stop tour. If it's not too much trouble."

Richie doesn't need asking twice. I just hope he's noticed her ludicrous shoes and doesn't take her into the barn. I try to catch his eyes as he leaves the kitchen, but he looks rather glazed.

I think he *has* noticed her shoes.

Later . . . a good hour later, in fact, when we've all assumed that rude City girl Sam has left without saying goodbye, I take Fatso for a run around the field. He races ahead of me, yapping excitedly, and I'm surprised

338

to see a zippy purple convertible that could only belong to Sam, still parked outside the farmhouse.

She couldn't . . .

Fatso keeps yapping, fuller-throated now, running then looking back to check I'm still behind him. He trots past the creamery, and the milking shed, but when I veer off towards the yard and the meadow beyond, he barks his disagreement.

Eventually, I follow him towards the ugly barn where Dad stores all his old equipment. There's *nothing* for a visitor to see in there. The door is slightly ajar and even before the dog gets there, I have the most awful sense of déjà vu. But Fatso isn't stopping, so I run after him, determined I should get to the barn before he does, except he has four legs and I only have two and . . .

I am neck and neck with him, my feet moving so fast that when I finally reach the door I can't quite stop in the mud and I try so hard not to look, but somehow, as I collide with the metal, grasping the bolt to steady myself, my head turns and . . .

A pair of mud-coated red stilettos, still attached to a pair of perfect legs, are thankfully all that's visible, projecting above the piles of boxes and old suitcases and tractor parts. The ankles stick up like doll legs, frozen in mid-air, as Fatso barks for dear life, and I make a grab for his collar, nearly strangling him in the process, but managing to yank him out of the barn and slamming the door behind me. I just hope my little brother knows he's playing with fire . . .

CHAPTER
TWENTY-SEVEN

Cheese-making gear is the least sexy attire in the world. The combination of white over-trousers, white wellies, white coat, and a spectacularly unflattering white cap with netting at the back to catch my hair makes me look like Alf Roberts. I'm just getting stuck in when —

"REBECCA! VISITOR!" comes the Janey foghorn.

Another one? I've only just recovered from the shock of seeing Sam yesterday. She really got me thinking: should I give the bride-hunting another go? And if not, what *am* I going to do? I'm as fond of cows as the next girl, but life on the farm is not for me.

"REBECCA!"

Sod's law must surely dictate that this is Adam . . . Apart from the outfit, I also smell, well, cheesy. And though the light aroma of ammonia is oddly appealing in a Ploughman's lunch, it's not so good on a prospective lover.

Prospective lover? But this is a man who has played with my affections, and Sam's affections, while all the time pretending to be a man with dating special needs, to gain my sympathy. I'd have to be some kind of masochist to want to go anywhere near him.

340

Still, as I peel off the over-trousers and trudge towards the house, I can't help but fantasise that he's been relentlessly scouring the web for dairy producers by the name of Orchard, tracking me down to come to beg my forgiveness, to rescue me from cheese hell. It must be all those dog-eared 1960s romances of Mum's that I've been working my way through. Life's not like that any more.

I stop by Dad's Land Rover and check myself out in the enormous wing mirror. I tear off the loathsome cap, to reveal hair that hasn't seen serum for five frizzy days. I'm just wondering whether I can get away with sneaking round the back, through the bathroom window, to repair my appearance, when the foghorn sounds again. "REBECCA! HURRY UP!"

Too late now, I guess.

I come in through the back door, pulling off my white coat, and running my fingers through the tangles in my hair.

"Oh dear God, what *have* you done to yourself, precious niece?"

"Georgie!" Of course, it had to be Georgie, didn't it? She's the only person who knows where I am. "Hey, listen, I'm sorry I did a bunk."

"*C'est rien.*" She dismisses my apology with a flick of the hand. "But a minor breakdown really is no excuse for letting yourself *go*. You look frightful."

"Apparently it's a quarter-life crisis," I say.

"More like a sartorial crisis. Only a size zero can get away with all white. And it's a wonder that the state of your skin hasn't turned the milk sour." She steps closer and sniffs. "Actually, it has, hasn't it?"

"That is ruddy typical." My mother stands behind Georgie, hands on hips. "Come in here like you own the place, then do your best to make my poor daughter feel even worse. And whose fault is it, eh? Who has she been living with for the last two years? Fat lot of adult guidance you're giving her, eh?"

"Mum. I'm twenty-seven. I don't think Georgie can be expected to act *in loco parentis* any more."

Mum looks at me closely, as though it's escaped her notice that I am now eleven years past the age of consent. Georgie adopts a smug expression: in fact, I have the distinct impression that she's fighting the urge to stick her tongue out at her older sister and chant, "nur-nur-nur-nur-nur".

"What exactly are you doing here, Georgie?" I ask.

She holds up a vanity case. "You left without your products."

Part of me wants to grab the case off her and scoot to the bathroom this instant, but it would feel terribly disloyal to my mother. "It's a long way to come with hair serum. I mean, there are branches of Boots the chemist in Gloucestershire."

"All right, I will admit it, Becky. I was worried. With good reason, judging from your appearance. The longer you stay here, the harder it'll be to come back, you know."

"She was like this when she was little," my mother says. "Backhanded compliments. It wasn't the ballet that made her bitchy, she was born that way. Always thought she was too good for the likes of us."

"Rubbish, Gloria. I just wanted to get away from my jealous older sister. Just because I was the one who could get any boy I wanted."

"Funny how I'm the one who ended up happily married, then, isn't it?"

I hold up my hands like a traffic cop. "Ladies, please. Can we try to *elevate* the discussion a little? Georgie, it's very kind of you to come all this way, but I am fine, honestly."

"Good. There's room in the car if you want to get going now. I can wait while you pack. And have a quick shower," she adds pointedly.

"I . . ." The thought of returning to London makes me feel dizzy, even though I know I'm going to have to face it sooner or later. "I appreciate it, and I will be back soon, Georgie, but I don't think I'm quite ready today."

Now it's my mother's chance to look smug. Georgie sighs. "I didn't want to have to do this here, Becky, but actually there is another reason for my flying visit." She reaches into her croissant bag, and pulls out an envelope, marked *Scottish Prison Service* on the back. On the front is my name and address. "I opened it. I'm sorry but I thought it might be important."

"Oh, Rebecca," my mother says, snatching the envelope from me. "You haven't gone and got involved with a prisoner, have you? You read about vulnerable women getting married to jailbirds."

I snatch it back. "Don't be ridiculous, Mum." I pull out two sheets of thin paper: the handwriting is large and looped, with thick strokes. "*Dear Miss Orchard, You don't know me but I am the brother of Heather Campbell.*" Uh-oh.

"Who's Heather Campbell?"

Georgie and I exchange glances. "She's one of my brides." I let that sink in while I read the rest of the letter. "*I found your address via a friend of a friend of a friend on the* Herald . . ." Oh God. The wedding announcement. "*I hadn't heard from Heather for six years, since I went inside for the seventh time.*" I skip through a list of his convictions, each one accompanied by an explanation of how he was fitted up or made a scapegoat for something he had a minor role in. "*Then one of the family spotted the notice in the paper. Seems my wee sister has fallen on her feet.*"

I shake my head, not daring to read on. "I suppose he wants money, does he, Georgie?"

"He doesn't say so." She takes the letter. "He reckons he wants her address to 'send her a wedding gift', but I don't know. It seems there's no love lost between them."

I slump into one of the wooden chairs. "This is all my fault. If I hadn't been so bloody suspicious, I'd never have put that ad in the paper and no one would ever have seen it."

"True," my aunt says, "but then again, you were right to be suspicious, weren't you? Heather wasn't exactly what she seemed."

344

My mother shakes her head. "Don't mind me. It's only my kitchen after all. I don't have any right to know what's going on."

"Sorry, Mum. Heather's a nice girl who had a difficult childhood. She's engaged to one of my rich blokes and the wedding is — oh shit, it's tomorrow, isn't it, Georgie? What if this guy breaks out of jail or something?"

"You watch too many movies, precious niece," she says, but her voice is less flippant.

"Tea?" My mother switches the kettle on.

"I suppose it's too early for something stronger? Yes, thought so," my aunt answers her own question. "Do you have any espresso, Gloria?"

Mum gawps back, as though Georgie has casually requested ketamine. Actually, ketamine is probably easier to source than espresso around here — just ask the vet. "No. I don't. You can have instant or tea."

"Instant then," Georgie says, and makes a gagging gesture behind my mother's back. They really are as bad as each other. "Look, Becky, I brought the letter just so you know, but I honestly don't think you should do anything about it. Unless you want to warn Heather?"

I think it over. It's the worst thing you can do, worry a bride just days before her big day, isn't it? And anyway, hasn't she had enough bad luck in life? Like Georgie says, the chances of the long-lost brother turning up as the uninvited guest are considerably reduced by the fact that he's behind bars. "No. What

345

could she do about it anyhow? Let's just hope for the best."

"Good girl." Georgie winces as my mother opens up the biscuit tin. "Not for me, Gloria. Second on the lips, and all that." She glances quickly at my mother's hips.

"Funny that," Mum says as she takes out two cookies, "After you pass forty, I always think that the odd extra pound is worth a million skin creams. It avoids that awful *haggard* look around the face."

Ouch. I'd never describe my aunt as haggard, but now Mum mentions it, perhaps there is something the tiniest bit pinched about her. No. NO. I will not let myself get caught up in this pathetic feud.

"Georgie. I've just realised, you haven't met your great-nephew, have you? You can't leave without meeting Bobby Junior, future star of the UK's most pre-eminent cheese dynasty."

After Georgie goes, having made appropriate but unconvincing cooing noises over the baby, I return to my room, and the dolls.

I can't focus. I wish I could kid myself that I'm worried about Heather, but I'm far more selfish than that. I'm worried about me. Georgie's presence in the kitchen was as incongruous as Victoria Beckham turning up in the yard, and it's made me more confused than ever. I feel that familiar longing for the city, for the life and the possibility and the anonymity.

But that desire is weakened by my complete confusion about my future. Just a few hours ago, I was nearly convinced that matchmaking was my vocation, that my recent problems are nothing more than plain bad luck, and that my role ends, like a forties Hollywood movie director's, once the bedroom door closes. Now, after reading that letter . . . well, if an escaped prisoner turns up at Heather's wedding then I have no one to blame but myself. Maybe I should simply accept that cheese-making, not bride-hunting, is in my blood, find myself a jolly young farmer and make hay while the sun shines.

July's arrived — and with it, even hotter weather. Heather's wedding should have happened yesterday and I begged Dad to buy the *News of the World* just in case it had made the headlines.

But there's nothing in the paper except Posh, Becks, Angelina and Brad. I can relax — at least until tomorrow's newspapers come out. I lie in the meadow, eyes closed, the sun on my face, and I listen to the sounds of the summer: the crickets, so close that I can't *quite* doze off in case one hops into my ear . . . the birdsong that my dad would be able to identify, note by note . . .

Oh, and the frightful KLAK-er-KLAK-er-KLAK-er-KLAK of helicopter rotor blades cutting through the clear sky as another of the Cotswold brigade comes in to land at their country residence. Our part of Gloucestershire never used to be posh but land shortages mean we're attracting the attention of the jet set. Mum and Dad are approached more or less every fortnight by property agents acting for supermodels or no-longer-quite-so-Young British Artists, looking for their own taste of Arcadia: pretty farmhouses, a cow or two, located in a newly desirable postcode that ensures no interruption to Ocado deliveries or supplies of Class A drugs (most will find their regular dealer has already set up a rural subsidiary).

It's progress, I suppose. But it spoils my mood, another sign of the city encroaching on the country, of the decision I have to make between the two.

It would be easy to settle back in here. My mother keeps hinting that my father's not getting any younger. Robbie makes pointed remarks about the need for someone to do more Public Relations to increase the market share of Double Orchard, a job that would suit me rather better than milkmaid. Even Dad has mentioned the possibility of an extension to the back of the farmhouse, and I'd have to be unversed in family subtext not to realise that this extension could house me, and my dolls, and my cashmere jumpers and my strappy sandals.

And there's the problem. By London standards, I'd never be described as high-maintenance, but here, they all think I'm Imelda Marcos. Janey lives in jeans and trainers — even when I babysat Bobby Junior so that they could all go out to the pub, she simply swapped her fleece for a black T-shirt and oldest trainers for a slightly newer pair. Janey is the only woman I've ever met who wears her *own* hand-me-downs: her wardrobe isn't colour-coded, but dirty-coded, with different grades of heavy wear. She has never heard of yummy mummies.

I'm a City girl, I always was. An accident of genetics, like Georgie. I know she'd take me back in her loft like a shot, and try to rehabilitate me, just as she did last time.

The trouble is, although I didn't realise it then, a broken heart and a broken career are relatively easy to mend, first time round. This time it's much harder. Not that I want to mend my heart — I intend to be a hardbitten career woman from now on. But what career? I've messed up two of them already. I keep running through the possibilities: maybe I could go back to psychology, but I'd struggle to get a place on an MA course. Or maybe something back in recruitment, something less cut-throat than City head-hunting. But I only went into that business for one reason.

It always seems to come back to Marcus, even now.

"REBECCA! VISITOR! AGAIN!"

Janey's voice drifts across the valley, and I shiver slightly, despite the heat. My adolescent fantasies about Adam coming along to the creamery to whisk me away, in true *Officer and a Gentleman* style, are now eclipsed by the more realistic fear my visitor might be Heather's escaped criminal brother. If he can track me down to Richmond, it couldn't be hard to track me down here too.

Whoever it is, at least I'm not in cheese-pressing uniform — and I do look better for my break in the countryside. I've got used to going without the tinted moisturiser that brightened up my cadaverous skin tone in London. In fact, of all the "emergency products" that Georgie brought me on her mercy mission, I've only used the hair serum and a quick flick of mascara. I look, you know, all right. I wouldn't be embarrassed to meet Adam again looking like this.

I glance through the alleyway towards the front of the house: the yard and the drive are both empty. Then I peep through the back door . . .

Shit, shit, shit. I immediately dart backwards, flattening my body against the outside wall, like an undercover cop.

I edge along the wall towards the kitchen window and try to see inside without being seen. He looks so at home, and Janey is already fussing around him, charmed into making coffee. He's dressed in dark linen trousers and an ecru short-sleeved linen shirt, a poster boy for a smart-casual lifestyle. He instinctively seeks out the sunlight and positions himself in movie-star poses, all the better to show off his toned upper arms or make his cheekbones look sharper.

"Bex!"

Bugger.

His eyes are pretty bloody sharp, too. I wave at him through the window, and skulk back round the back door. "Marcus. You are the very last person on earth I was expecting." As I speak, I realise that's only half true: somehow, in the back of my mind, I'm always expecting him to crop up, like the proverbial bad penny.

"Not the last person on earth you'd want to see, though, I hope?" He smiles that eternally charming smile and I stare at the floor. When he takes a step forward, I take one back and he decides against a handshake or embrace.

Janey gives me a funny look. "Must nip down the shops," she says, and I feel the tiniest frisson of envy, even though I know the shops she means are a rough and muddy six-mile drive away, and sell nothing more exciting than bumper packs of detergent and nappies.

I wait for her to leave — it takes her ages, gathering up Bobby Junior and all his paraphernalia — before I look at Marcus again. "And the reason you're here is what, exactly?"

"I'm in the area to do a little . . . direct head-hunting."

"Not like you to get your hands dirty."

"No, well, this is quite a personal quest." He spreads his fingers, as though he's warming them up for something. "Bex, I want you to come back to Benson Associates."

My jaw drops before I regain enough control to close it again. "You're offering *me* a job? After all you said? All you did?"

He nods and shakes his head at the same time, a strange gesture that makes him look like a puppet. "Well. Yes."

"You're not serious? First, you screwed another woman. Well, probably more than one, but we'll gloss over that for now. Then you sacked me because I wasn't . . . *running with the wolves* any more. Then you refused to repay me any of the money I'd invested in our home because, what was it you said to me . . ." I dredge my memory for those hurtful, horrible things he told me, quite calmly, on the day when I turned up at our flat to pick up my things, "Ah, yes, that's it. I had no more right to a share than the cleaner. Or less right, because at least the cleaner had some talents whereas I had none." To my surprise, I find the words have lost their capacity to hurt. "Oh, and, you thought that, frankly, I'd be better off getting a one-way ticket back to Bumpkinshire where I belonged?"

"Did I say all that?" he says, quietly, leaning against Mum's Aga.

"Er. Yes. You did. Funnily enough, those phrases have stuck in my mind."

"I must have been . . . under pressure." He grimaces.

"So was I, with no job, no man and no home. But let's move on. What the hell makes you think that you can persuade me back from Bumpkinshire now?"

"What would it take, Bex?"

I shake my head. "Oh, very good. You haven't forgotten the old techniques, have you? Draw the candidate out, however hostile he is to begin with. Work hard to tune into his psyche and use questions to assess his expectations and his critical finance and benefits thresholds."

Marcus can't stop himself smiling in satisfaction. "You remember? Ah, but I'm a good teacher, aren't I?"

"Teacher? More like some sodding Svengali."

He manages, with difficulty, to remove the smile from his face. "All right. I've changed, though, Bex. I am a more humble man. I am able to admit that I made mistakes."

"Yeah, right. What kind of mistakes?"

"Um . . ." his eyes dart about, looking for the right answer. "For a start, I was wrong about your

352

capabilities. I underestimated your influence on the team. After you left, well, it had a very destructive effect, put it that way. I lost most of my boys within six months. And let's face it, they were never what you'd call *loyal* before. After you went —"

"After you sacked me, you mean."

He sighs. "Well, I didn't think you'd want to come back after —"

"After finding you giving Trina some hands-on guidance . . ."

"With you gone, the atmosphere changed. You were good for the team, Bex. You made people feel better about themselves. Kept the boys under control."

"You make me sound like the office version of Barbara Woodhouse. If you're trying to butter me up, it's not working."

"Thanks for the feedback. Let me try again. You were much more than a calming influence. You were also bloody good at the job *and* you had integrity. Set an example, which helped to curb people's worst excesses."

I sniff. "I don't think I ever curbed your worst excesses, did I?"

He thinks it over, fiddling with the fringe on Mum's best tablecloth. "Only in retrospect. Once I realised what I'd done."

"At what point did you realise what you'd done, then? When you were in bed with Trina, perhaps? Who was, hang on, let me remember your exact words, *leggier than a dozen supermodels, with the sex drive of a French legionnaire posted to an Essex nightclub?*"

"Ah. Well, I always did have a tendency to exaggerate. But since you ask, I did realise pretty soon that Trina was something of a one-trick pony."

"I bet I can guess what her trick was."

He ignores me. "I also realised that, after what I'd said, you weren't likely to take too kindly to any attempts to win you over again."

"You're right," I say, knowing that for months afterwards, my ego was so shattered that it would have taken little more than a text message to tempt me back to him, "but surely if someone means so much to you, you'll risk it all . . . humiliation, a hard kick to the groin, whatever, if there's the tiniest chance that you can be with the person you love."

"I was in a strange place within myself at the time, Bex. Not entirely human, looking back at it, very detached from my emotions and certainly not willing to admit I needed someone. And, you forget how much someone meant, don't you?"

"Eventually," I concede.

"And then I saw you at the gym. With Mr Marks and Spencer Easy-Care suit. It all came flooding back."

"Yes," I say, remembering the weirdness of the encounter, and feeling a burst of affection for sweet, kind-hearted Eddy the Plank.

"Look, Bex. I know it's probably fruitless, all this, but I want you back so badly."

"Back at Benson's?"

"Ye-es." He hesitates and a remarkable thing happens: he blushes. I have never ever seen him blush. "Look, cards on the table, not *just* back at Benson's.

But even with my inflated ego, I know that having you back as my girlfriend isn't going to happen. And the way I've been feeling ever since that chance meeting, even having you in the office would be almost enough."

"That's what that phone call was about, too?"

He nods. Even though Georgie used to insist that you could always tell when Marcus was lying because his lips moved, I do believe he's actually being honest today. "I went to Georgie's house, but she slammed the door in my face, so I sat outside the house, waiting for you. And waiting."

"How long for?"

"Three days, two nights."

I feel a rather ignoble sense of triumph. "Golly."

"And then I realised you weren't there any more, I tried your mobile, but it was switched off and I didn't think a voicemail message would begin to cover it. So I thought I'd fly over here. On the off chance."

"Fly?"

"Oh, I own a third share of a helicopter. Increasingly indispensable for the serious business traveller."

So it was Marcus and his third share of a rotor blade that had interrupted my afternoon snooze. "Right."

He looks at me steadily, a look that once upon a time would have caused internal earthquakes throughout my body.

I don't feel so much as a tremor.

"Bex. I haven't apologised properly for what I did. It was atrocious. Cruel. Despotic."

I nod. No wonder I fell for him when I was young and foolish. He does have a great vocabulary.

"I'm here to grovel and to plead. I'll also do my best to meet any reasonable request you might have regarding salary package, benefits and so on. Bloody hell, I'll even try to meet unreasonable requests."

I know I must be dreaming now. That's it. I've fallen asleep in the meadow, there is no helicopter, no blushing Marcus, no contrition. Marcus Benson never begs. This is one of those dreams I used to get all the time after the break-up, the ones which took wish fulfilment to new levels, only for the awakening to crush me utterly.

"Bex?"

"Sorry. Miles away."

An irritated look clouds his face, then disappears almost instantly. "Name your price, Bex. Name it."

"Righto," I say, deciding that if this is a dream, perhaps I am dreaming for a reason. Maybe this is part of a *Joseph and the Amazing Technicolor Dreamcoat*-style parable dream. The Rebecca Orchard Book of Revelation. "Well, obviously I'd like a joining bonus, enough to put down a significant deposit on a flat equivalent to the one I was planning to buy until you talked me out of it."

"Obviously," he says, as though I'm asking him to pay my bus fare.

"Though, actually, now I come to think of it, studio flats are terribly tricky to sell so perhaps something more like ten per cent of the cost of a one-bedroom place."

He raises his eyebrows. "I admire your bottle. Go on, then."

356

"Oh. Great." I wonder how long it'll take before I wake up. I decide to sit down at the table, and he sits at the opposite end, as though we're in a boardroom rather than Mum's kitchen. "A clothes allowance would be necessary, as I'll have to update my wardrobe, to reflect my move back into the corporate world."

"I can arrange for an account to be opened at the store of your choice," he says, with a wave of the hand. "One phone call."

"Good, good. Basic salary, well, shall we say *double* what I was on before, to reflect the entrepreneurial skills I've picked up running my own business?"

"Of course." His quick smile convinces me I've underplayed this part of the deal.

"And a fifty-per-cent bonus. Guaranteed bonus."

He nods. "Yep."

No strange furry monsters have appeared in the kitchen yet. The flagstoned floor seems in no imminent danger of collapsing, and I don't feel like I'm about to wake up with a big, woozy thump. How bizarre.

What would stop him in his tracks? Ah! "I also require every Tuesday afternoon off for voluntary work."

He blinks, hard. "*Voluntary* work? And the point is?"

"The point is, I'll be giving something back to the community, Marcus. And you'll be getting a lovely warm glow from knowing you made it happen. Corporate social responsibility is all the rage these days."

"Hmm. I think I prefer my warm glows to be more hands-on. Does it have to be every week? Charity begins in the office, as far as I'm concerned."

"OK. How about every *other* Tuesday afternoon?"

"Done," he groans. "I think I have been."

I rack my brains for the one thing I could ask for that would break the deal and, presumably, break the spell too. *Salary, bonus, clothes, time off* . . . transport? The mood he's in, I reckon my newfound fairy godfather would agree to a Porsche. But they're so *tricky* to park in the City.

Then I work it out. The *ultimate* test. "And finally, Marcus, I should like first call on your third of the helicopter. Only for essential trips, of course. You know the sort of thing, networking opportunities at Ascot, Henley Regatta."

He winces a little but it seems even this isn't enough to push him over the edge. "You've changed, Bex. You're steely." Then he shrugs. "But you know, I like steely in a woman, especially one who's going to be working for me. And that's definitely it?"

I nod. "Yes. That'll do for now."

He stands up now, and moves towards me. "Shake on it?"

I find myself giggling nervously. OK, so this is how the dream ends; when he holds out that hand and I go to take it and the hand dissolves into nothingness, and either the Devil appears to celebrate his pact, or I wake to find Fatso licking my hand and barking for dog treats.

I will wake up, won't I?

"You're on, Marcus. Or Lucifer, or Fatso, or whoever you are," I say and I am sure he nearly withdraws his hand but it's too late as I reach out to shake it and I wait for the inevitable weird rushing noise and . . .

And he's still here. And his hand feels warm and dry and soft and indisputably *Marcus*-like, not horny like a devil's or furry like a dog's.

"So. When can you start?"

"What?" This is real? Oh shit. *What have I done?*

"I mean, if you *like*," he says, and at this point if he had a moustache, he'd be twiddling it, *Magnificent Men in Their Flying Machines* style. "I could wait for you to pack up and you can have your first ride in the helicopter this very afternoon."

"No, no, I don't think so."

"I'm perfectly safe," he says, sounding a little hurt.

"It . . . it's not that, it's just, I can't really up sticks without saying goodbye to the family properly."

"No, I suppose not. Not knowing *your* mother." He winks at me, and I don't wink back. This isn't happening. I can't have agreed to go back to work for the only person in this world I hate.

And yet . . . wasn't this exactly what I was looking for? A way of escaping the rural idyll, returning to London, my *true* first love. Even affording the kind of flat that would have been for ever out of my reach. Maybe Marcus really has changed. And even if I did go off the whole head-hunting industry for a while, it has to be easier than anything involving weddings and dummy dates and human hearts . . .

"Bex? Bex, you're not having second thoughts, are you? Not after we've shaken on it?"

What other options do I have? Cheese-making, or a life of luxury? The last few days I've been imagining devious, cruel Adam Hill playing Richard Gere to my Debra Winger. Yet it's Marcus who has come to my rescue. Better the devil you know, eh?

Best of all, in this new life, it's not Marcus who's in charge. It's me. And the hardbitten career woman I must become finds that ... well, pretty much irresistible.

"No ... no, I'm still rather overwhelmed, that's all. I'll tell them tonight and then I promise I'll call you tomorrow, Marcus. With dates, times, all that. I mean, it's going to take a little getting used to ..."

CHAPTER
TWENTY-EIGHT

"It's remarkable how little time it's taken me to get used to being back!"

Helga and Georgie stare glumly back at me.

"Fucking great," Helga says.

"No it bloody isn't," says Georgie. "It's a disaster."

"Thanks for the support, auntie. I suppose you'd rather I'd stayed in Gloucestershire, would you?"

Georgie wipes the condensation from the outside of her wine glass, thinking it over. It's a sultry evening in the sultriest August on record. The Tube is almost unbearable, and if you work in the City you probably need two changes of clothes in your briefcase — one to change into after the sweaty morning commute and another for the evening. Nights like this are crying out for icy lager and white wine by the Thames, nights when you almost expect to see steam rising from the river, nights when it feels as though London is populated entirely by over-heated twentysomethings trying to pull.

We arranged to meet outside the bar and restaurant complex by Putney Bridge, because Helga has a new job at a gym nearby. It's the first time I've gone out since I came back five weeks ago. Returning to the nine-to-five (or, the eight till eight working day everyone follows at Benson's) has tired me out, but I'm also lying low. I've cut my hair, changed my mobile number, and always carry an *OK!* magazine as a shield (*Heat* isn't quite big enough) in case I spot someone I don't want to see: Sam or Heather or Edward or Perry or . . .

Or Adam.

". . . and so, on balance, I think you should have stayed in Gloucestershire, yes, because you might have come to your senses without the intervention of Mr Slimeball. Becky, are you listening?"

"Sorry, Georgie. I'm tired, that's all."

"Well, I just think it's lovely to have you back." Helga pats me on the hand. "Oh, I'd kill for them nails. Lovely! You're really going for the City girl look, aren't you?"

"Yup." I can afford it this time round: twice-weekly manicure (Rouge Noir varnish is high-maintenance but gives off the right, slightly predatory, image); weekly eyebrow threading; a complete new wardrobe, courtesy of the account Marcus has opened for me at Selfridges; and couture shoes on order from Georgina Goodman in Green Park.

And then the clincher: an enormous cheque in my bank account that will, at last, allow me to step up on to the property ladder, skipping the bottom rung. Now, that has to be worth twelve-hour days, doesn't it!

"I want the name of the girl doing your eyebrows, they are *fab*. And how's the flat-hunting going?"

I pull the file marked Property Acquisition out of my enormous briefcase, and list the possibilities so far: an upper maisonette in Barnes, a tiny but perfect mansion flat in Fulham, and a couple of new-builds very close to where we're standing. Marcus is trying to steer me towards the new-builds. "Take it from a property tycoon, Bex, wet rooms and underground parking are the way forward," he told me when he came with me on my first viewings.

"But I don't have a car, Marcus."

He shook his head patiently. "Yes, but this is just the beginning. You'll be renting this one out before you can say *desirable riverside pied-à-terre*. Parking will net you an extra three hundred a month."

I haven't mentioned to anyone else the *real* reason I think he wants me to move here . . . the fact that the flats I've looked at are so close to his place that he could, literally, keep an eye on me from his roof terrace.

Not a chance.

Helga flicks through the particulars. "Fulham. Gotta be Fulham. Think of the totty. Dim *and* rich, what a stellar combination."

"I am not in the market for any totty, as you know."

She raises her eyebrows. "Doh! I'm talking about me, not you. What's the use of having a filthy rich mate if you don't use their place as a launch pad for pulling?"

"I'll add that to my *must-have* list, then, Helg: array of good bars in spitting distance. What do you think, Georgie?"

"Well, it seems what *I* think isn't given any credence by you, is it?"

Helga glances at Georgie, then at me, then begins to back away. "Time for a top-up, I think, girls. Same again?"

Georgie doesn't even acknowledge the question and when Helga is out of earshot, she says, "I think we should go somewhere quieter."

We move away from the packs of shirt-sleeved office workers, closer to the benches along the river bank. "Look, Georgie, before you start, I know you don't approve, but I am in control now. And I didn't exactly have that many options —"

She holds up her hand and silences me. Marcus called *me* steely but really it fits my aunt so much better: light, strong, ageless. "Precious niece, I don't want you to justify yourself to me. I'd never try to tell you how to live your life: people spent decades doing that to me and it never made the slightest difference."

"What, then?"

"I want to tell you something about me, about the way my life has gone. Yes, of course, there is a moral to the story, but I hope it doesn't dominate. My life, Becky, is defined by one thing. What do you think that is?"

My immediate, instinctive answer surprises me. *Sadness*. It seems so ridiculous. Georgie is the most effervescent person I know. I must be projecting my own low mood on to her. "Um . . . ballet?"

She sighs. "I do hope not. Defined by something I was, fleetingly, competent at. No, my life is defined by love."

I stare at her.

364

"Yes. Love and Gregor Jung, that's what you'd find on my tombstone."

I keep staring. I've never heard this name before, but I can guess who he is. "Our house in Eve Terrace . . . was that his?"

She nods. "Yes. Well, he had lots of houses but he bought that one for me, actually. Gregor Jung was what people used to call an impresario. Of the best kind. He had money and he used it to fund the arts. If he made a profit, marvellous. But if not, there was always more money. No one liked to ask where it came from."

"You met him through the ballet?"

She nods. "Indirectly. At a party. I nearly didn't go; one became rather weary of parties after the thousandth. Perhaps he might have found someone else that night . . . Actually, I am being silly. I believe we would have found one another if we'd lived on different continents."

"Blimey." I'm not used to my aunt's romantic side.

"It was immediate. He was older, of course, and married. I did feel guilty, but . . . well, it felt like normal morality was too parochial to apply to us. A proper bolt of lightning. So much so that within six months we were living together."

"You lived with him?"

Two drunken girls totter past, spilling the last of their drinks on the paving stones.

"Yes. No one else in the family knows this, Becky — can you imagine what your mother would say? But it's important that you know. We moved to West Berlin together, just before the Wall came down. Gregor had

365

contacts there, business he could do. We managed to travel all over: Russia, Poland, but our favourite was Berlin, where no one judged us. Such a vibrant place, grand love affairs, hearts broken, families divided. We felt right at home. The four best years of my life."

"And after four years?"

"He died," she says, in a small voice. "I wasn't surprised. Not that he was ill, or anything like that, but I always knew somehow that no one would be allowed to stay as happy as we were."

"How did he die?"

She waves her hand to dismiss the question. "In his sleep. One morning, I woke up. He didn't. I had to tell his wife." She grips the railing. "And I brought him home, made all the arrangements. I was twenty-five."

She stares up at the sky, which is turning pink.

"I'm sorry, Georgie."

"Ah. It was years ago, after all. Though the house reminds me of him, every day. He made sure it was left to me. I suppose I could have sold it, but I like to remember him." She picks up her glass, sips the last of her wine. "And that, Becky, brings me to the moral of my story. My life is defined by Gregor Jung. You might say that's a waste. I say it's a blessing. He was worthy of that centre-stage role. I've never fallen in love again because I can't imagine anyone better."

"Never?"

"Never." She sounds resolute. "I've had boyfriends, of course, but nothing like what we had. And that is my point. Becky, the reason I feared you going back to work with Marcus was not that you'd also end up back

366

in his bed. I hoped you'd have more sense than to do that. No, it's because the more time you spend with that *rat*, the harder it will be for you to believe there are good men out there. And the less likely it is that you'll let yourself try again."

"But I did try again and look where it —" I stop. I never did tell her what happened with Adam, but I think she guessed some of it.

"I've told you about Gregor because he was worthy of defining my life. Can you honestly say Marcus is worthy of defining yours?"

"He won't. I am in control this time."

"Is that why you crawl in late every night, exhausted and — well, defeated, is how it looks to me, I worry that you're sacrificing so much more than you can possibly imagine."

"*Defeated?* I thought I was looking every inch the top head-hunter."

She shakes her head. "Not to me. But then I'm probably out of touch with what a top head-hunter should look like. I'd rather see you happy, that's all. Just promise me you'll think it over."

"Hey! You two! What's this about, playing hide-and-seek? Anyone'd think you don't want this fine wine I have spent my hard-earned dosh on!" Helga skips towards us, clutching a bottle of white. "Come on, cheer up, nobody died, eh?"

Georgie and I stare back at her, momentarily speechless. Helga pulls a face. "Done it again, haven't I? Put my fucking enormous foot in it."

I shake my head, feeling a giggle growing from inside my tummy, along with a wave of intense affection. "Oh, Helg," I say, "you are the best mate a girl could have. The very, very best." I put one arm around her, and reach out to put the other round Georgie's tiny waist. "And you are the best aunt. I don't know where I'd be without you."

"What the fuck brought that on, babe?"

"Nothing in particular," I say, winking across at Georgie. "It's just that sometimes you have to remind yourself how lucky you are to be surrounded by the people you care about . . ."

CHAPTER
TWENTY-NINE

Marcus is trying. In every sense of the word.

It's an old joke, but a good one. He *is* driving me crazy. In meetings he treats my every word as gospel. If I ask who's getting the coffees in, he reappears a few minutes later with a tray full from Costa (with a choice of iced coffee or skimmed-milk latte for me). It's unnerving.

This morning he's definitely up to something. Laughing so heartily that I get to see every single one of his perfect white fillings. Pacing the office. At least I only have a few more hours before lunchtime, when I can leave under my "voluntary work" clause.

My special treatment doesn't exactly endear me to my colleagues, but then again are these people ever going to be my friends? There's no one left from last time I worked for Benson's, but this lot are indistinguishable from the previous lot: ex-public schoolboys with braying voices competing for business with comprehensive school duckers-and-divers. Plus a couple of women my age who wear five-inch stilettos to work.

Together my colleagues achieve the impossible on a daily basis: they make Marcus seem like a fully rounded human being.

"Can I have a word, Bex? That is, if you're not too busy?"

"Sure." I follow him into his office: maybe I'm about to find out what he's up to.

He sits down in the "soft-seating" area. Thankfully, the irresistible rise of Benson Associates means Marcus moved to swankier premises this year, so there's no daily reminder of sexy Trina's gala performance at her work station.

I take the red leather sofa, which faces the full-height plate-glass window. This must be how it feels to be a goldfish. I have a terrible urge to wave at the fraught-looking man in the office opposite ours, or pull a silly face.

"I can't tell you what a difference it's making having you back, Bex."

"Um. Actually, you already have, Marcus. On a daily basis. Which is very flattering, I must admit, but it's also a little embarrassing, I'm running out of things to say."

He smiles tolerantly. "Always one for hiding your light under a bushel, eh? OK, then, how about actions speaking louder than words? I've got a big opportunity coming up, a two-year exclusive executive search contract for one of Europe's largest banks. We're the favourites, but you can't be too careful, so I was hoping you'd come to back me up at the presentation, be my number two. You're the next most experienced, after all."

"Sounds good. When's the pitch?"

"Just over two weeks. There is a catch. Well, I say a catch. A catch that involves a night in one of the world's most wonderful hotels. And the pitch meeting itself will only be an hour or so, with plenty of time for shopping or exploring."

"Where?"

"Paris. I have First Class Eurostar tickets on standby. And there's availability at the Georges Cinq. And don't worry, they're holding *two* rooms."

The very fact that he makes that point confirms what's on his mind. I guess it's to be expected. Then again, the Georges Cinq hotel . . . I sent one of my clients there to propose and even a man used to every possible luxury was bowled over by the exquisite rooms, the Spa, the Ice Bar, oh, and the breakfast, the . . .

I could lead him on. Accept the invitation, travel to Paris and then refuse to go through with it at the very last moment.

No. I might be a control freak, but I'm not a game-player. If I do this, it brings me down to his level. Or Adam Hill's.

"Marcus, listen, I'd love to do the presentation, you know that. But that's not what this is about, is it?"

He raises an eyebrow. "Isn't it?"

I take a deep breath. "I'm not going to sleep with you. Not in Paris. Not ever."

He still looks amused. "Not ever is an awfully long time, Bex."

I stare at him. "Not even you would be vain enough, *stupid* enough to employ me as some kind of extended foreplay, would you?"

Marcus stands up and walks behind his desk, as if he needs to protect himself somehow. "You've got a short memory. *I* haven't forgotten what we had together."

"You *wrecked* what we had together, Marcus. And then you tried to wreck me, just for the fun of it. Guess what? I survived and now you want to try again. Never could resist a challenge, could you?"

He flinches, turns away from me. Surely I can't have hit a nerve?

"You really have changed, Bex. You were always sparky but you were never hard."

"I had to become hard, remember?"

The silence between us grows, until it feels quite suffocating. The sofa leather squeaks as I push myself up. "I need to get going to the park, now, Marcus."

"Yes, yes, of course, can't keep the junior explorers waiting, can we?" he says, tetchily.

"So good to have a boss who takes the welfare of the next generation seriously," I say, as I leave the office. Somehow, silencing Marcus hasn't been quite as satisfying as I'd hoped . . .

I take the District Line which crawls West until the train stops suddenly between Hammersmith and Ravenscourt Park. No explanation. I stare out of the window, thinking about what Georgie said last night. I was moved by her story, but despite Gregor's death, my aunt was lucky to have what little time she shared with her soul-mate.

She was wrong about me. I don't want to have those feelings again: love and fear are too similar, thank you very much. I am not going there again. Not with Marcus, not with Adam . . .

Bread. I can smell bread. This *keeps* on happening to me, whenever I think of that lecherous *bastard*, I get this whiff of baking and I'm convinced I'm going crazy.

I hear a crunch and look up to see a large woman in a lilac nurse's uniform tucking into a baguette. The train jerks and moves off again. I peer around the carriage for something to distract me from this nagging feeling deep in my belly. I've made my decision and no real or imaginary smells are going to throw me off course.

That's that, Becca. That's that.

I pick up a discarded *Daily Mail*, and flick through it, straight to the *Femail* section in the middle, where today's Focus is Fall Fashion. Marvellous Macs for Autumn Showers, one headline shouts, and another features a line-up of winsome children and is headed Back to School in Style for your Little Star Pupils.

Nearly September already. The wedding season is over, I guess. No more matches to be made. At least head-hunting is a year-round thing.

I turn the page and . . . no! It can't be!

I snap the newspaper shut again and realise I'm shaking. What the hell are Dwight and Heather doing in the centre pages of the *Daily Mail?*

Surely they can't be divorcing already. Or maybe their wedding was hijacked by the long-lost brother? Worse still, perhaps the journalists have found out about me and my list of failures.

I open the paper again, wincing. This time I look first for the headline, scanning the top of the page . . .

MR AND MRS MILLIONAIRE: LOVE AND MONEY BUT NO HOME SWEET HOME

I read the headline several times before looking back at the photograph and realising what I hadn't spotted earlier: it's a *wedding* photo. I scan the feature, looking for bad news: *newlyweds Dwight and Heather MacKenzie have it all* . . . I read on as the piece details their *intimate, private wedding to be followed by a full family affair with Dwight's family in America* . . .

I get to the end of the article, which explains that they've sold Dwight's penthouse to a Russian cash buyer . . . blah, blah . . . but now can't find their dream family home for love *or* money . . . blah blah . . . symptom of the state of the housing market, of the influx of buyers at City bonus time . . .

They're married — and happy. I study the wedding photo, and the two of them are beaming. It's catching. I can't help smiling, too. How could I have doubted Heather or, in fact, myself? I had my moments of bride-hunting brilliance.

The train pulls into Richmond and I consider taking the newspaper with me, as a souvenir. But why dwell on the past? The Bride Hunter is dead. Long live Rebecca Orchard, Corporate Recruitment Consultant and Independent Woman of Means . . .

I lied to Marcus about this afternoon. In the school summer holidays, the nature walks don't run at all, but I don't feel guilty for taking a stroll on my own. If I had my way, all head-hunters would be forced to spend an afternoon a week somewhere that reminds them that life isn't all about golden handcuffs.

Today the Park looks parched but beautiful, and the sky is heavy with overdue rain. *Life* is everywhere — from the gaudy parakeets sheltering in the shade of old English trees, to the skittish fawns being guarded by the elders of the deer herd.

I drop in at the education centre for a tea and a catch-up, before heading towards the ponds, my favourite part of the park. Dogs and ducks, what more could you want on a ridiculously close summer's afternoon? Even watching their endless chase makes me feel exhausted . . .

The sky is darkening by the second and I'm excited by the prospect of a fantastic storm, even though it occurs to me that all the trees might make this a slightly risky place to be when lightning strikes.

"Rebecca!"

At first I convince myself I've imagined it — that it's the parakeets squawking or the trees rustling, or something — but then I hear it again.

"Rebecca!" I don't think trees can rustle quite so precisely. I turn, wondering whether Marcus has been spying on me and is about to withdraw my volunteering privileges.

"Edward!"

Eddy the Plank stands before me, as ludicrously dishevelled as the very first time I saw him. But he looks so relaxed . . . he's even got a suntan.

"Bloody hell, you're a hard woman to find, Rebecca."

"Am I? I don't think many people bother to look." I hear a rumble of thunder from the Hampton Court direction. "Um, Edward, I don't know why you're here, but I have a funny feeling the heavens are about to open, so do you think we should take cover?"

Just call me Michael Fish because a split second later, the rain starts to fall in huge splodges, and we run, unsure of where we're running to.

"I seem to remember," I shout, as we head for trees, "that you're supposed to get close to the ground, but not close to the trunk."

"I never was in the Scouts," Edward shouts back, "so I'll have to take your word for it."

We stop to catch our breath right at the edge of a circle of branches projecting from a giant oak. I prevaricate over whether to sit down on the damp ground in my Nicole Farhi suit, and before I know it, Edward has whipped off his fleece — fleece? — and laid it out on the grass.

"Walter Raleigh eat your heart out."

"Well, you wouldn't want to ruin your fancy skirt."

Lightning cracks across the sky, and I count to eight before the thunder sounds. "I think you're meant to count to four seconds for every mile, so it must be two miles away. We could run for it."

"Or we could sit it out. You're not trying to do a runner are you, Rebecca?"

"No. But before you castigate me, I've given it all up, Edward. The bride hunting. Too much room for error. So, if you've come to tell me what a terrible human being I am, it's too late. I am free."

"But . . ." he stares at me, bewildered, "No. No, I came to *apologise*. It was out of order to deceive me initially, of course, but I did go a bit over the top afterwards. Katerina and I have discussed it in detail and I decided I wanted to say sorry. But I couldn't find you. Tried your phone, but it was dead. My emails kept pinging back and —"

"You and Katerina? You're still together?"

He beams. "Yes. Oh yes. We've just got back from visiting her parents, and then exploring the Baltic. Six weeks with nothing to do but sunbathe and drink Pilsner."

"Wow. Congratulations. On the relationship. Not the Pilsner drinking, obviously."

"Yes, well, I'd never have done it without you. That's no bullshit, Rebecca. You are a life-changer."

"Um, that's lovely, Edward. I'm thrilled, really I am. Though I'm not at all convinced I change people's lives in the right way. You left your job, didn't you? How are you going to support yourself?"

Even if he wasn't soaked to the skin, with hair plastered against his face and rain running down his cheeks, Edward would look sheepish. As it is, he looks utterly shame-faced. "The thing is, I . . . realised I'd been a bit *hasty* in slagging Perry off."

"You've gone back?"

"I've gone back. With a huge pay-rise, it turns out, and a new deputy. Didn't even have to ask. I'd never have got that without you, Rebecca. Love life *and* career sorted. Are you sure you want to give that up? You really are ruddy good at it."

I feel a glow, but I know not to be fooled by it. For every moment like this, there were weeks of worry and stress. There are good reasons why I went back to work at Benson's.

"I decided to quit while I'm ahead, Edward. I mean, I really do appreciate the trouble you've gone to, to track me down. And I am *so* happy that you're happy with Katerina. But I've moved on now. Truth is, I don't think I know any more about love than the next person."

"Right," he says. "Right, well, I suppose you know what you're doing . . ."

"Yes," I say, more confidently than I feel. "I do."

Edward and I sit next to each other on the wet grass and the lightning arrives overhead and we watch it, warily but with a certain fascination. I don't know for how long, but by the time we find ourselves a taxi back to Richmond (and fight each other for the privilege of paying the fare), it's past four o'clock.

"Bye, Edward. Good luck."

"I won't need it, Rebecca. I've had my stroke of luck. Now it's down to hard work, eh?"

The streets are shiny with rain, and full of people who're almost as drenched as me. But there's a mood of relief, too, as though we're not suburban Londoners but drought-stricken villagers whose raindance has paid off at last.

I turn towards the Vineyard area, feeling relieved to be home and oddly exhausted. I've only worked a half-day but even walking up the path seems like climbing Everest. As I grope around in my handbag for my keys, I spot a huge box tucked into the covered porch by the front door. I lean down to see what it could be, but before I open it, I can smell what's inside.

Bread.

I unlock the door and then carry the box through to the kitchen. I lift off the tea towels and peer inside: croissants; muffins; Maid of Honour cakes; bagels; flowerpot bread . . .

How does he know where I live? And why *now*?

There is an envelope with my name written on it tucked between the muffins, and my fingers hesitate above it. I close my eyes and focus hard on Paris and property particulars and my six-figure salary. Better the devil you know . . .

I take the box and wrap it in a bin-bag. I can't let it go to waste. No, I'll take it to work with me. But whatever happens, I have no intention of eating a single crumb. Because I have this irrational conviction that even one taste of Adam's bread will wreck my resolve.

Which is presumably why he sent the bread in the first place. That man could teach Marcus a thing or two about manipulation.

CHAPTER
THIRTY

My life is so busy that I am thinking of hiring one of those personal lifestyle managers. Well, I would if I ever had time to call and actually employ one.

Yes, I have joined the ranks of the cash-rich, time-poor, and my to-do list would make Superwoman feel faint. Buy a flat, lose five pounds, stay coiffed and fuzz-free, pick up the dry-cleaning, prepare the perfect pitch for the Paris trip tonight, act professional . . .

I've just checked in for an emergency pre-Paris eyebrow wax — well, the French expect a certain level of grooming — when my phone rings. I ditched the "Love is In the Air" ring-tone for "Money Money Money".

"Rebecca? It's Sam Ottoway."

"Oh. Hi." A picture pops into my mind of a pair of stiletto-clad feet suspended in mid-air. "Last time I saw you, you were exploring our barn."

"Hmmm. Yes. So I was."

Another thought occurs to me. "How did you get my new number?"

"Um. Shall we say . . . family connections?"

Bloody hell! So she's still seeing my baby brother. I just hope my mum never gets to hear about it. "Sam, I hope you won't take this the wrong way, but when I promised to find you a husband, the last person I was thinking of was little Richie. He's sort of . . . notorious for being flighty and I don't think he's at all a good prospect if —"

She laughs down the phone at me, a carefree sound quite unlike her previous cynical cackle. "Oh, Rebecca. You've no worries on that score. Richard is an absolute delight, but too much of him would be like gorging on champagne truffles. We're both absolutely clear about that."

"Oh. Pleased to hear it. Owww . . ."

The waxing lady has got tired of waiting for my call to end, so has gone ahead and ripped half the hairs off my right eyebrow.

"Rebecca? You OK?"

"Yes. Just being depilated."

"Oh. Right. Well. I'll get to the point. I think I owe you another apology."

"You don't need to apologise for cradle-snatching. He is an adult. Well, chronologically, if not mentally."

"No, that's not it. I want to apologise for setting you an impossible task. Look, this might be easier face to face."

"I don't have a moment to call my own at present, Sam. I'm heading off to Paris in" — I check my new silver Gucci watch — "two hours."

"From Waterloo? I'll meet you there, before your train. Please. It's important."

The beauty therapist hovers menacingly with her wooden spatula and I shift the phone to my right ear so she can wax my left side.

"I can't see that there's anything more to say."

"Rebecca, believe me. There is."

"Bloody hell, you don't give up, do you? Ouch!" I give the waxing woman a dirty look: she has a certain maniacal expression that isn't reassuring.

"No, I don't. That's why I'm fucking brilliant in court."

"Ten minutes. That's all I can give you, Sam. I'll see you at a quarter to six in, let me think, All Bar One. I hope it's worth it."

I switch my phone off, and the beauty therapist holds up a mirror. *Shit.* I thought an eyebrow wax was meant to work like a minifacelift? Instead, my face looks empty, and permanently surprised.

"I do your legs?" the woman says, hopefully. "And your bikini? Yes? Special price?"

"No thanks." It's not as though I ever let anyone close enough to see . . .

I pull my brand-new Louis Vuitton trolley-dolly case behind me as I walk out of Waterloo Station, towards the bar, and the Eye. The crowds are business-like tonight, a back-to-school feeling pervading everything.

I allow myself a few seconds' self-indulgence as I remember Dwight and Heather's first meeting just along here, the two of them in their matching green outfits. And despite everything, they lived happily ever after . . .

What could be so important that hotshot Sam "two-hundred-pounds-an-hour" Ottoway would leave work early to meet me? Maybe she lied about Richie. Maybe they'll both be waiting, flashing his 'n' hers engagement rings. Stranger things have happened.

I walk into All Bar One, and, too late, remember the last time I was here. The night of Sam's first date, and my first meeting with . . .

No, I won't think about him. I am a strong, decisive career woman. I do not entertain self-defeating thoughts. I look for Sam: she's by the bar, tapping her fingers impatiently, but stops as soon as she sees me.

"What can I get you?"

A nice fizzy mineral water would be a good idea before the train journey, perhaps. "A vodka and tonic please."

The girl behind the bar pours my drink and adds a wedge of lime. Sam looks at me nervously. "Shall we sit down?"

"I don't have long before my train leaves."

She nods, but leads me to a table anyway. "I've got this feeling you'll want to be sitting down to hear this. I . . . I'm not in the habit of apologising to anyone, Rebecca, but if anyone deserves one, you do."

"Right."

"You're entitled to be very, very angry with me. But please hear me out. First of all, since my . . . friendship with your brother, I've realised something important. I don't actually *want* a husband. Not right now, anyway. Doesn't mean I never will, but at this stage in my life, I have so much else going on that, frankly, a spouse would get in the way."

"Well, I'm glad you've worked that out, Sam but I don't think you need to apologise."

She sighs. "But don't you realise what this means, Rebecca? It means you didn't fail with me, because you could never win."

"Ah. I suppose you're right. It's a bit academic now, because I'm through with bride-hunting. But at least my success rate is back at one hundred per cent." I swig my vodka and tonic. "I have to go now, Sam."

"No, hang on. There's something else," she says, and her voice is less strident. "I've been a selfish bitch, Rebecca. You see, before I realised I didn't want a husband, I was rather . . . unbalanced. And I lied to you about something important."

"Right." I'm not sure I want to hear anything important. I'm a forward-looking executive head-hunter. Regrets are for wimps. I stand up. "All in the past, whatever it is."

She reaches out to grab my hand. "It's Adam."

I sit down again.

"I was . . . sore. I'm not good at rejection. My counsellor —"

"You're seeing a *counsellor*?"

Sam blushes, then holds a finger to her lips. "Don't you dare tell a soul. It wouldn't go down well in Chambers. Anyway, my counsellor says that's why I jump into bed with people so quickly, so I can do the rejecting before anyone else gets the chance."

384

I don't want to think about her in bed with Adam. "Good luck with the counselling, Sam, but I'm not going to miss my train to hear about your therapy."

"No! Listen to me. I didn't sleep with him, Rebecca. I didn't even kiss him, not properly. Oh, I tried to, at the Tower. I thought he backed away because he was clumsy. He let me think that, because he's a gentleman: so much nicer than me knowing that he didn't fancy me, plain and simple. So when he rang me up, desperate to meet again, I was convinced it was all go."

"And it wasn't?" I can't manage to say any more, as my brain attempts to process this information.

"Quite the contrary." Sam fiddles with her glass. "He wanted to meet me to talk about *you*. I was the only person he knew who knew you too, you see, but I was absolutely furious. I didn't actually believe him. Refused to believe him."

I close my mouth, which has been hanging open as I attempt to rewrite history in my head: the pained conversations with Adam, Sam's phone call, that final showdown at the bakery . . . "So you sent me to go after him, *knowing* he wasn't interested?"

She grimaces. "It's probably the worst thing I've ever done. No excuses. But my counsellor says that confessing is the beginning of the healing process."

I feel sick and dizzy as the past weeks unravel and I try to make sense of them anew. "But why tell me all this *now*, Sam? Why not just leave me be?"

"Well, for one, I can't believe you're ditching the bride-hunting and I couldn't bear it if it was because of me. Anyone with a loud tie and a louder voice can be a bloody head-hunter, Rebecca. It takes a special kind of person to do what you did, and do it well."

I stand up: my legs feel unsteady. "Too bloody late, Sam. I've changed my number, I've cut all the ties. Including with you."

She stands up too, pulls a note out of her pocket. "Rebecca. I know I'm out of order, but can't you give it one last try? With the matchmaking? I've got the perfect client for you, a friend. Much nicer than me. Attractive *and* ready for a proper relationship. He's even got a list of requirements. Take one look, and then tell me honestly whether you don't prefer bride-hunting to head-hunting?"

Sam thrusts the note towards me and before I can give it back, she legs it, out of the bar. I sink back into the chair, feeling utterly drained. I know I'll have to run for the bloody train now, but I need a moment to get things straight. I close my eyes, try to focus on my breathing. *Calm, Becca, Calm.*

And now I can smell bread again. I'm in a bloody bar, I should be smelling beer and Bacardi Breezers.

I put the note down on the table, glance at it. It does look just like a shopping list . . . Bloody City wankers, who think they can have anything they like, who think money can buy them the perfect woman.

Requirements for the only girl for me:
1 x good heart (preferably marinated in old-fashioned common sense, with a generous measure of wit)
1 x sharp brain

1 pint milk of human kindness (long-life variety, never goes sour)

I pick up the note. It's less a shopping list, more a recipe.

1 x spectacular figure
1 x face of an angel
2 x strong forearms, for kneading

I read and reread. I've had more specific requests before, that's for sure, but this is different. I turn over.

Allow to steam through July and August. Hope things have settled down by September. Allow feelings to double in size. In the right conditions, can last a lifetime.

I shiver. It can't be . . . can it?

I have to be on a train to Paris, not wasting my time working out some stupid riddle. I am a hardbitten career woman. But I can't seem to move from the spot.

"I suppose you can't think of anyone who meets my requirements."

The voice is behind me. *Right* behind me. And the voice belongs to . . .

"Adam?" I turn and there he is. Not that I can see much of him, because he's holding the most enormous bunch of pale pink dahlias.

"No one at all on your list who might be suitable? And you call yourself a bride hunter?"

"No, I don't. Not any more."

"Well, now, that's a bloody waste." He puts the flowers down on the table. He looks shy and anxious and . . . well, absolutely *gorgeous*.

I open my mouth to speak. Nothing comes out.

"Sam's told you the truth?"

I nod.

"A bit late in the day," he says, shaking his head. "But I'm hoping it's going to be better late than never."

"Late." I repeat, looking up at the clock on the wall. "Late. I'm going to be late."

"One minute to explain, Becca. You didn't let me get a word in last time, remember?"

"Yes."

"I know I should never have agreed to go on that date with Sam. And I must have confused the hell out of you by asking for those dummy dates. But I was desperate. Would you ever have agreed to see me again otherwise?"

"Probably not."

"I hoped that if we spent time together you might begin to feel what I was feeling. And then at the flat, I thought I'd hit the jackpot —" he hesitates. "Sorry, I didn't mean to sound like a wide boy, I just felt so good and then you broke off and you wouldn't answer my calls. I didn't imagine it, did I, Rebecca? You felt it too?"

How do I answer him? Tell him about Marcus and my muddled thinking, as tangled as the cord on an iPod's headphones. "I suppose I didn't trust my own instincts."

388

"But you felt it too?"

I nod. "At the time I did, yes, but . . . look, I really do have to get going."

"Oh. OK." His face falls. "Can I carry your bag?"

"Don't worry, it's got wheels —" but he's already picked it up and is striding towards the door. I take the flowers, my arms barely reaching around them. Outside, the sun is setting and the Eye has turned the colour of a huge apricot. I feel this urge to run on to the grass, lie down (never mind the designer skirt) and stay here until the sunshine's been replaced by a thousand lights dancing on the water. How could the Seine possibly look as gorgeous as the Thames? Bugger Paris . . .

"It never fails, does it?" Adam whispers.

"It never fails."

We keep walking, but more slowly. My legs feel too wobbly to go faster.

"Did you ever get the bread, by the way? And the cakes?"

I look down. "I did but . . . I gave it all away."

"Why?"

"Because . . ." Because I was convinced that just one taste would be too much, would transport me back to the Tower of London, Columbia Road Market, the afternoon at Adam's flat, that last time in the office at Pudding Lane Bakery. "Because I'm off carbs."

"Really?" He looks at me curiously and I look back, fully intending to try to freeze him out with a cool glare. But something odd happens. Everything behind him blurs, the Thames and the people and the world melting away until all there is, is him and me and . . .

Bloody double vodkas. I knew I should have had mineral water. "Yep. No bread. No potatoes"

"Your aunt didn't mention that."

"Georgie?"

"I'd decided to leave you be, Becca. After the Pudding Lane incident. God knows I wanted to get in touch, I tried to call you and then call Sam, but she wasn't answering and in the end . . . well, sometimes even a bloke as thick-skinned as me takes the hint. Then I got this visitor in the bakery. A flowing vision in beige silk."

I smile. "Georgie! She never said."

"The bread was her idea. When I didn't hear anything after that, I put it down to experience. Well, it wasn't quite that easy, you know, but there was no point if you didn't feel it too." He stops. "But then Sam called, told me she'd lied to you but was going to come clean. I knew I had to give it one last try."

"Right." I look down, around, anywhere but at him. I gaze up at the Eye . . . and it's the weirdest thing. I'm sure I can see two green figures together in one of the pods. Just like Heather and Dwight on the day they first met. And, next to them, there's a man with an overgrown fringe and glasses sparkling in the sunlight, his arm round the tiny waist of a young woman. And then a willowy figure with hair that's glowing like copper, just like my aunt's . . . but they can't be here. Can they?

I shut my eyes. First I'm imagining wafts of baking bread, now I'm having visions. *Get a grip, Becca.*

"Look, say the word and I'll walk away, Becca. I would have done already, except in the bar, you mentioned instincts. Aren't you the one who believes in head over heart?"

"And you're the big softie, the old romantic, the believer in love at first sight."

Adam blushes. "I didn't believe in love at first sight until recently, Becca."

He's blushing more deeply now, his cheeks as pink as they were when we were baking muffins and flowerpot bread in his flat.

"How recently?" It must be my imagination because although the sun has almost set now, I feel warmer and warmer.

Adam takes a single step towards me. "Very recently. In fact, it happened right near here. An ordinary bar on an ordinary night. Such an ordinary night that I nearly didn't bother to go for a drink at all. One of those nights that marks the teeniest episode in that chapter of London history called, I don't know, hopeless cases and unrequited crushes."

He laughs at himself and it occurs to me that this is a sound I can never imagine Marcus making. And I realise what a prize idiot I've been to assume every man is like my ex.

"Actually, Adam," I say, wondering whether this will change everything or change nothing, but knowing everything's changed for me, "is it possible that it could go in the chapter called *better late than never?*"

As he moves towards me, I can smell maple syrup and baking bread and I feel that wonderful, unbearable hunger. And I know that this kiss will prove that however two people meet, whether it's eyes across a crowded pub, or painstaking matchmaking, what really matters is chemistry, chemistry, *chemistry*.

And just a pinch of perfect timing.

I Never Fancied Him Anyway

Claudia Carroll

Cassandra never set out to become a famous psychic, with her very own magazine column and a glamorous TV slot. Let's face it, it's not exactly the usual career choice a girl might make. But whether she likes it or not, and most of the time she doesn't, ever since Cassandra was a little girl she's been able to see into the future.

While she can make predictions with 100% accuracy for everyone around her, there's a bit of a twist. Cassandra's incredible psychic gift seems to float right out the window whenever there's a decent single man around whom she actually fancies . . . and what if the same man just happens to be her hot new TV producer boss?

But even being able to tell the future can't protect Cassandra from what destiny has in store . . .

ISBN 978-0-7531-8094-5 (hb)
ISBN 978-0-7531-8095-2 (pb)

The Love Academy

Belinda Jones

Do you have enough romance in your life?

Journalist Kirsty Bailey would have to answer no. She has the essential starter kit — a boyfriend — but somehow Joe seems to have skipped the romance.

But then just as she's on the verge of settling for a swoon-free existence, Kirsty's magazine sends her to Venice to attend the much gossiped-about Love Academy . . . Her undercover mission? To prove her editor's theory that this "school for singles" is nothing more than an escort agency with an Italian accent and fancy chandeliers.

But what if her editor is wrong? Will Kirsty be able to resist the kind of moonlit temptations she's been dreaming of for years?

If you think Casanova was a bad boy, just wait until you see what Cupid has in store for Kirsty . . .

ISBN 978-0-7531-7972-7 (hb)
ISBN 978-0-7531-7973-4 (pb)